SHERLOCK HOLMES
and
THE MAD DOCTOR

ed. by Michael Halm, BSI
as told by Dr. John H. Watson

© 2015 Hierogamous Enterprises
michaelhalm.tripod.com

Sherlock Holmes and the Mad Doctor – 2

Introduction

To the editor of the *Norbury Chronicle*,

I must correct some minor errors in your proposed article on myself and our mutual friend Sherlock Holmes. As many Irregulars before you have deduced from the clues I left scattered in what you Baker Street Irregulars so quaintly call the Canon, we were indeed time travelers. As you aptly pointed out, the most obvious one was that what has become the most famous address of all time, 221B, did not exist before Upper Baker St. and Baker St. were merged and renumbered in 1930.[1] If I hadn't let "slip" the most well known address of all time, just because it didn't yet exist, how would it have become the most well known?

I also purposely gave the obvious clue in "The Five Orange Pips", that Mary could visit her mother, who in "The Sign of the Four" I had written had died before 1879. I indeed was able to take Miss Morstan back to get her parents' blessing while they were both alive, that is, long before we had yet met.

It was also a clue that I wrote I knew nothing of Holmes's archenemy Moriarty in "The Adventure of the Empty Room", but that I did in "The Adventure of the Copper Beeches" three years earlier. As for my much discussed war wound, I was shot while bending over to tend to a wounded soldier, whom I didn't know was Holmes in disguise, when I was wounded in both my shoulder and leg by a single bullet. In this alternative timeline, Holmes told me later, if he hadn't intervened, I would have taken it between the eyes! Then too there was what the ufologists would call "missing time" in the Jabez Wilson case, to say nothing of the whole "missing year", November, 1895, to October, 1896.

Holmes had made use of H. G. Well's time machine when Herbert challenged him to solve the greatest unsolved mysteries of the Twentieth Century,[2] before Moriarty had stolen it.[3] This however was sans yours truly, and for much of our acquaintance quite hush-hush.

When I first moved into "221B", in 1881, Holmes was using "the needle" or the mere mention of the codeword "cocaine" to summon time traveling clients when he became bored, not to actually inject himself with drugs. After our final confrontation with Moriarty in 2368,[4] Holmes had, as was often the case, became bored again.

After the police destroyed his own time machine that he had built from Moriarty's plans, nicknamed the Needle's Eye,[5] he became bored again, but this time not for long. We soon discovered that the equilateral triangular-shaped hole left by his prototype was actually a small window into the space-time continuum, a portal. Together we concluded that the mysterious "K2L2" was our Client still, still trying to teach us not to lean on our own understanding.[6]

When Holmes had first looked into the mystery of the strange hole that appeared on one side of the wall and not on the other side, he found that if he concentrated on a particular time and place, he could often see and hear past and even future events through it. He quite soon discovered however that if he got too close, he also could change those observed events. Sometimes his apparently disembodied eye became visible to those on the other side. Sometimes his voice could be heard as a whisper or frighteningly amplified as if through a megaphone. Sometimes his magnifying lens even focused and amplified the parlor's back-light into a dangerous heat ray. Holmes soon became the legendary Eye of Providence.

To prehistory he was the sun god, the all-seeing eye that never closes. To the ancient Egyptians he was the Eye of Ra or Horus. To the Hebrews he was Aleph, the Beginning. To the Freemasons he was the Great Architect of the Universe. The Hindus identified the Eye with the third Eye of Shiva and the Buddhists with Buddha's third eye. The Greeks and Turks called it Nazar. A student of Leonardo finally painted the Eye of Providence in 1525 including the sometimes discernible surrounding triangle. The Eye's contribution throughout the formative history of the United States was remembered in that country's seal since 1783. The original "private eye" Alan Pinkerton took it as his detective agency's symbol in 1850.

The Twentieth Century detective Jack Barrister however fittingly named this most fantastic of Holmes's personae the "Detective Eye" in 1939, although the warning "the Eye!" had been used by the underworld much earlier. As John said of Jesus, I can assuredly say of the Detective Eye adventures,[7] "If they should be written every one, I suppose that even the world itself could not contain the books that should be written."[8]

Holmes became rather addicted to peering for hours at a time at the scenes visible through the portal, so much so that he rigged a projector and microphone contraption to project sounds and pictures from the Eyehole onto the parlor's opposite wall. I confess that I too became interested in watching and sometimes assisting in the adventures of clumsy Inspector Clouseau,[9] gormless Gadget[10], weariless Willoughby,[11] and secret agents Maxwell Smart[12] and Mandy Stevenson[13] and the archeologist Henry Jones, Jr.[14]. I naturally was more concerned about saving their lives, while Holmes enjoyed being the hidden "Wizard of Odds", secretly advancing their incredible, illustrious careers as he had the Lestrades.[15] It became a comic routine sometimes, with Holmes asking from his bedroom, "What's on?" and me answering to the call, "Watson?" instead.

From 1896 221-B, we also thwarted evil and saved lives in all six world wars as the legendary British operatives "Altamont" and "Nimrod".[16] Following the infamous "John Clay" lead us to follow his notorious sons, particularly the time traveling Scott. His sons Lawrence and Alexander, were confusingly fond of impersonating each other. Introducing David to Annie however proved the most successful of our interventions.[17] Many others whose adventures we followed became more than mere heroes, veritable superheroes with alien or futuristic technology, like Clive Arno and his children, Carl and Carla[18], Kristin Wells[19], Robby[20] and Suzie[21] Reed, Nylor Truggs[22], Chris King and Vicki Grant[23], etc.[24]

In 1986 we were however able reunite an e-ternity of such virtual timelines by getting Laurie Lemmon to wear Carla Arno's Supergirl costume rather than a mermaid costume for Halloween[25] and patched innumerable rips in the fabric of time by preventing Michael Jon Carter's slip of the tongue.[26] Holmes would eventually see beyond all these heroes and villains, superheroes and supervillains, to Moriarty's successor, the elusive and mysterious "Time Master", but I'll save that for another time.[27]

Holmes was far more adept at accessing and amending his virtual file memory implant than I.[28] My own case files however have proved quite a handy, since I expanded my avocation of writing into ghostwriting for films, radio, television and video games. Nevertheless I will attempt to share with your readers a fuller version of some of our more interesting adventures. Sorry about the Britishisms and anachronisms, but since your readers are all or at least mostly Mensans, I believe they will follow my drift and continue to debate the "spoilers".

Ever your colleague in Holmesian Studies,
John H. Watson, M. D.

SHERLOCK HOLMES AND THE MAD DOCTOR

I will choose to start my first such story rather arbitrarily on that late summer morning, when I heard Holmes break away from his "observations" with a disturbing gasp. I put down the morning paper to see him now staring at the old familiar VR with the color slowly coming back into his face. He let "Chinese" Gordon swing back into place and explained that he was merely confirming that he was indeed back in Victorian times witnessing after a harrowing adventure in James VII's reign[29]. When he did not choose to elaborate, I silently returned to leisurely finishing Mrs. Hudson's hardy breakfast, while Holmes ignore both it and me to turn to his neglected mail.

"Eureka!" he finally said, breaking the welcome silence.

"Good Lord! Not another rogue Celestial Intervention Agent, I hope?"[30]

"No. This is even better. This is a request for assistance from Scotland Yard via CountessGallowglass in 2012."[31]

"Lestrade or Gregson?"

"Neither, March."

"Not, Simon? I say, I thought we saved him from Dr. Phoenix in 1973."[32]

"We did, indeed, but I was referring not to Simon but to Col. Perceval March of Scotland Yard. I am not surprised that you have never heard of him. Most in the Yard have not. His Department D-3 was, to say the least, obscure."

Holmes handed me the letter which I noted was postmarked not in the past or present but sixty years hence, specifically September 18, 1956. As he took the time to nibble at his now cold eggs and muffin, he told me how he had originally become acquainted with the colonel.

"It began, as I recall, earlier this year when you were away from Baker St. for some time while your oldest, James,[33] was home for the hols from boarding school. I was thinking of my own lonely days back in the Himalayas, trying to make contact with my old teacher, the high lama of Shang-ri.[34] I unexpectedly found myself rather looking at a yeti footprint, not at all where I'd seen them before in the snow, but in March's office at the Yard. I was impressed by his rather quick identification of it as a fake. All I had to do in helping him solve the associated murder at the Himalayan Mountaineers Club was to gently direct him to the last vital clue. In later cases he further gained my respect by his dogged thoroughness and attention to detail, just as rare then as it ever was at the Yard.

"It was however his own clever idea to persuade the club's prospective lady mountaineer, Mary Gray, to pose as the bait in his trap.[35] I suspected that he had not been quite so observant before acquiring his trademark eye patch. I soon found myself peeking in on him since from time to time ..."

"Ha, that's good one, 'from time to time '."

"Ah, yes, quite, as I was saying, I had returned again and again to watch Col. March since then, because of his department's intriguing 'impossible' crimes. He learnt that most of what is thought impossible can be explained, while I learnt that there remains some residue that can never be. I had not however been able to focus in on him since Martha Pollard's alleged suicide.[36] The countess now informs us that this is because his timeline is dangerously close to sliding into the fifth dimension."[37]

We took turns watching as the unconventional detective in tweed and left eye patch[38] paced his office. His own chronicler Sgt. Carter Dickson entered and said, "Something is bothering you, colonel. What is it?"

A bit apologetically, Col. March sighed and answered, "It's this case, the disappearance of Dr. Henry William Marco. I have gained something of a reputation in my time here as the brilliant, if eccentric, head of the Department of Queer Complaints, as you've called it. What I have never told anyone however is that I still have only a fuzzy memory of the queerest, my life before I found myself alone and half-blinded in Southern France. I was misidentified as the missing Perceval March then and have played that role ever since, but I now think I may very well be this missing doctor."

"Ah, so that is why you seem to find so many mysteries on your so-called vacations there. You were trying to solve the mystery of yourself."

March only nodded, his secret revealed, and pointed to the open case file with the photographs the doctor's wife, Jane, had provided. Moving and refocusing the scene in my mind's eye, as Holmes had taught me, I read that Marco had been born on November 23, 1887 in East Dulwich, the youngest of nine children, studied medicine at London University like his oldest brother George. Unlike his bachelor brother he finally married in 1930 and had one child, a daughter, Jane Sarah, born on his birthday. Dr. Marco's colleagues, Drs. Laskey and Giles confirmed that he had been behaving strangely and passing on his patients to them. I also saw that except for the lack of the eye patch they could have very well been brothers. Both were about the same age, mid sixties; same height, five foot eleven.

"There is certainly a strong resemblance." Dickson commented delicately, even though he had noticed the resemblance instantly.

Following an awkward pause, Dickson continued, "That's not always a clue, is it? The Snowman bore little resemblance to his brother, did he?"

"Nor to a Snowman for that matter, as I recall," responded the now smiling March.

"There's more to it than the physical resemblance." March continued, putting on his grim, professional face. "My so-called brilliance has been, more often than not, based not on my detection skills, but rather flashes of insight and leaps of faith, an inner voice that directs me. Sometimes I have even experienced insights into the past or future which I can only label as postcognition or precognition, but cannot explain, but I can't even do that in this case."

Holmes and I shared knowing smiles. I could easily see how addictive this eavesdropping on and covertly re-directing other detectives had become for my friend.

"Here are some other photographs I have called you in to look at. I need other, fresh eyes on this problem. Do you see any resemblance here?"

Dickson warily studied the new photos as Holmes and I looked on.

"There is some resemblance here too, I'll admit. They're not you in disguise?"

"No, certainly not. This older photo is from 1903 of an amateur detective from Sussex named Diogenes Mycroft[39] and the newer one is from 1940 of a Chinese-American detective James Lee Wong.[40] This is not just a case of having a look-a-like, a double, or two or three doubles. What troubles me is that I cannot shake the strangest feeling that I actually worked on these cases of killer bees, chemical spies, and artifact thieves that Mycroft and Wong did. I remember them as if from half-forgotten dreams."

Holmes nonchalantly paused puffing his pipe and took up his glass to meticulously, yet quickly, examine the files spread out on March's desk. Amazingly to me, he was able to focus his attention and even pause and reverse the time flow of the timeline he was observing. He had humbled however in the years I had known him however and admitted coming to the conclusion that our Client still had hole control. We could only see and hear what He allowed us us to, like He had allowed Paul to evangelize Europe and blocked him from converting Asia too soon.

"This cold case has been haunting me for three years now," I heard the colonel continue, "ever since Jane Marco reported her husband missing — missing in time. As she explained to Ames, her husband had built himself a contraption he claimed was a time machine with the grandiose plan to take the new miracles drugs, like penicillin, into the past and so save untold generations of lives. She had become concerned that he was becoming obsessed with this fantastic idea to the point of totally neglecting his present patients and even other activities such as going to the theater they once enjoyed together."[41]

"I can sympathize with her there." I commented in a whispered aside to Holmes.

"Before you trusted me enough to allow me to share your adventures in subjective metatime, my patients and family life suffered sorely, I am sorry to confess."

March continued, "The Chief sent the case to me, not because he ever believed her story."

"He never does." Dickson agreed.

"It's because he doubts her sanity. He believes that she killed her husband either intentionally or unintentionally and expects me to determine which."

"But you don't think so, do you, sir?"

"No, Dickson, I do not. I do not believe Dr. Marco is even dead. God knows we've see some strange cases before, but before I retire I have to close this last one. If this doctor really did have a machine that could travel through time, he could just as well have gone to Sussex in 1903 or America in 1940 or Korea in 1950, anywhere — or rather anywhen. I believe this is a decidedly queer missing person case. With no corpus delicti proving either murder or accidental homicide would be difficult."

"Sounds like a challenge from the Yard to me, Watson. Let us see for ourselves. The game's ..." Holmes said handing the glass back to me.

" ... Afoot!" I finished.

"Let us concentrate together on Dr. Marco's basement workshop when he disappeared."

When I looked all I saw was a bright flash of light that made focusing on Dr. Marco and his machine nearly impossible. It was all a blur and then suddenly he and it were gone. I saw no debris as would be expected with an explosion. It had looked more like a superimposed explosion and implosion[42], like when lightning splits the air and then collapses thunderously back on itself. If I'd blinked I would have not even seen that much.

I concluded, "It looks to me as if the machine did malfunction, that the wife did vaporize her husband, albeit unintentionally."

"No, Dr. Watson, once again you look, but you do not observe. Try again. Close your eyes and remember what you saw, not what you thought you saw. Can you do that? Good, you saw not one, but several Marco-like figures moving in from all different directions and out again all at once? Marco's machine then did not simply propel him backward or forward in time to disappear from the present, but allowed him to travel sideward in time as well. He is, as the philosophers have called it, 'sliding'.[43] That is why our friend, whom I will continue to call Col. March until I learn otherwise, quite justifiably suspects he may be this Dr. Marco and not merely the doctor's double.

"The key to solving his most intriguing last case seems to be finding each of the branching points where these many converging alternative timelines have split from our home timeline and repair them."

Seeing the confusion on my face, Holmes illustrated what he meant by holding up two fingers on his right hand in a V for Victoria. He then moved his other hand in a similar though inverted V to form a four-fingered loop.

"Marco's malfunctioning machine has apparently created innumerable splits or Y-forks in the timeline, some desirable, some indifferent, and some undesirable! As Berkeley's Laws say, 'Most problems have either many answers or no answer, few a single answer.' and 'An answer may be wrong, right, both, or neither; most are both.' We will more likely find Psi-forks or threeks with three possibilities or more."

"Fourks spelled with a U?"

"I trust not, my trusted comrade. Our Most Illustrious Client will guide us to the timelines that need to be closed. That we will create new ones that will have to be closed I do not doubt. Although it sounds a daunting challenge, I have learnt from having observed other chrononauts far more experienced than ourselves that such complexity is quite normal. With an amateur like Marco trying to change the past, even with the best of intentions, however we may even find ourselves dealing with a time knot."[44]

"A whatnot?" I asked.

"A time knot, a complex tangle of these time loops almost impossible to untangle."

"I hope not!"

"Nearly all time travelers protect themselves from creating paradoxes, or bilking, by applying the Krasnikov paradox exclusion principle to their advantage.[45] If we are able to observe without being observe, the past remains unchanged. Even if we do something that can be observed it may be ignored, misinterpreted or otherwise providentially result in not changing the past that is meant to be. We must take care however that in using the Eye to close all the timelines created by Marco with time loops that do not return Dr. Marco to his wife and so clear her of suspicion of his murder, nor do we want to leave March trapped in such a time loop without beginning or end."[46]

"Like Melchizedek?"[47]

"Or worse, 'As a dream whe0n one awaketh'", a "branch ... that beareth not fruit".[48]

Holmes had apparently taken a keener interest in the Bible since our adventures in Biblical times via the Needle. I silently thanked our Client. We had both heard in March's quavering voice the great gumption that it took to not just file this amongst mundane cases or leave it to his successor. It would, I thought, be like my having to face Holmes's own return from the dead in 1893 and all our adventures since as mere self-delusion.[49] It would then be Dr. John H. Watson who would have been the lost and mad doctor, not my colleague Dr. Henry W. Marco.

We began our impossible mission by following an arbitrary one of Marco's innumerable time trails to March's past, our future, 1910 London. We found a dazed Marco on the appropriately named Great Wild Street in the middle of the night.

"He has a wound to the head." I said, "He may have fallen, but considering the time and place it is likely he was mugged."

"I concur." Holmes responded, always music to my ears.

"I do not think it is life threatening, though he will suffer from confusion and possibly amnesia."

"Timelag may also be a factor," Holmes said, throwing a zinger at my confident diagnosis, "a common symptom in time travelers. It can be quite disorienting, especially for novices."

We searched the area and did not observe any fleeing assailant in the area, so both we concluded that he had suffered the concussion prior to his arrival, during the initial time machine malfunction. Holmes carefully used diffuse light and whispers to guide Marco to the Strand and then to Whitehall and the Yard. When he got there he still did not remembered who he was, but did remember vaguely that he was a doctor. He was given the name "Terrence Drury" after Inspector Terrence and the Drury Theatre tickets found in his otherwise empty pockets. We scanned through his career over twenty years as he worked his way all the way to an inspector himself, albeit with a little guidance from time to time along the way from the Eye.

Then came the time when the discovery of John Stanner's bones in Clomelly, Devonshire, lead to what looked like this timeline's crisis point, what Holmes called the Jonbar hinge.[50] Marco had been misidentified by lonely Sarah Ashley-Norton with her husband missing since 1910 and so a cold case murder suspect.

"Aha," Holmes finally said, having focused in on John Stanner,[51] "I found from police reports that Stanner had died of food poisoning two years earlier.[52] By tracing back all the foods Stanner had eaten in his final days to their origins, I proved to my own satisfaction, if not that of the Yard, that it was accidental rather than intentional. I was then easily able to trace the trail of Stanner's skeleton forward and confirmed that it had been sold as an anatomical model, but mistakenly delivered to Dr. Ashley-Norton, rather than to a Dr. Ashley Norton.

"He buried the skeleton, I suspect, because it reminded him of his accidental killing of his mistress Cora Crippen and he mistakenly believed that he had been or would soon be either blackmailed or arrested. In any event he almost certainly fled the country under an assumed name."[53]

None of our efforts to redirect Inspector Gordon Lestrade however proved successful in the solving the Crippen case. He had the poor, but not so innocent, husband Dr. Hawley Harvey Crippen arrested and executed.[54] I however happened to notice, what providentially no one else had, that the theater tickets were anachronistically dated 1953. That would have caused a dreaded time paradox. A heat ray from the Eye took care of that.

"Just as I expected", Holmes said, after watching the Ashley-Nortons for some time. "Marco's machine protectively extracted him from his timeline in 1953. It is similar to the case of Gart Williams who died in 1960, but who autochronoported to 1888. He happily and rather uneventfully lived out the rest of his life until he died again in 1918, and was reborn as 'James Firman Daly' to die a third time in 1978."[55]

"So he was born twice in 1918, once as Williams and once as Daly, lived 42 plus 20 plus 60, 122 years althogether?"

"Yes, he did. In this case however Marco's time machine is doing it quite unnaturally, creating this tangle of time loops to save his life with many, many more deaths than three."

"Correct. A chronoport may get himself or herself out of a life-threatening situation once, but usually by re-materializing to a relatively safer time and place. It is nearly impossible however to determine when a time traveler finally dies", he explained, "because of the Shelborne effect built into all the best time machines.[56] The body and soul of a time traveler may become separated and the body appear dead, during this out-of-body experience, but when these time travelers 'die', temporarily unable to return to their original bodies, they become Human beings again.[57] This is because the soul is naturally attracted to a body; it cannot grow without one, even if it must 'borrow' one. Sometimes the time traveler's soul connects with an ancestor's,[58] sometimes with a stranger's or even his or her younger self.[59] Sometimes the interaction is very temporarily, but can benefit both souls, especially at a timefork. Sometimes a new host body is conceived by an altering of the timeline that results in a similar, though not identical, time clone."[60]

There was also, I thought, guiding and misguiding spirits present with every newly incarnated soul, the conventional right-shoulder "good spirit" and sinister "evil spirit". Our mission was surely to encourage the good and discourage evil. As always that can oft times not be easy. I always tried to keep in mind my, and this time Dr. Marco's, Hippocratic Oath, "Above all, do no harm."

The forty years that "Drury" spent as a detective however seemed to have overwritten Marco's own memories as merely a doctor as we followed up on the Mycroft and Wong timelines. The obvious clue of Marco's choice of name, "Diogenes Mycroft", lead us to focus in on September 1893, the month and year when I had revealed to the world Holmes's older brother's name and club.[61] Observing the next ten blissfully uneventful years of his sedentary rural life in Sussex, prompted Holmes to plan his retirement there also tending bees.

For the Wong timeline fork we had to backtrack all the way to 1863, when we found that Marco had accidentally caused his father, John Edward Marco, Jr. to not marry his mother Sarah, but instead nut merchant Li Wong. That union resulted in a Chinese-American half brother. Marco himself closed the time loop in which he prevented her from marrying either, the one in which she prematurely became Mother Sara of Calcutta, causing himself to have never been born.[62] Both the "Mycroft" and Wong timelines were close enough to our home timeline that we were both confident that our Client would want us to leave them as is.[63]

Some subjective days later, as I was trying to relax after we had with not a little welly, what you Yanks call oomph, successfully averted the Anglo-American War.[64] Holmes was yet again looking through the Eyehole, when he suddenly remarked, "It's just as I expected, Watson. Marco did not have any more success at promoting futuristic medicine in the past than other time travelers,[65] because of the Zeitgeist's well-documented resistance to new ideas.[66] He has however caused some rather major kerfuffles, disturbances, in the timeflow."

After passing me the *Encyclopedia Britannica* opened to "Egypt", Holmes instructed me to focus on the Thirteenth Dynasty. As I looked through the Eyehole myself I observed that the still amnesic Dr. Marco had retained enough medical knowledge to gain a reputation as a healer over the reigns of several pharaohs, even to having acquired the nickname of Imhotep, the legendary Father of Medicine from the Third Dynasty. When however he could not prevent Princess Ankh-es-en-Amen from dying in 1780 BC, this "Imhotep" mistakenly attempted to revive her by stealing the sacred Scroll of Thoth. In punishment he had been buried alive.

His time machine's life preserver program however had difficulty in this very unusual situation. It stuttered, chronoporting the living-dead Marco over again and again. So strong was his fatal attraction to the princess, he was in every new time obsessed with seeking host bodies for her restless soul from other beautiful women throughout history. With a persistent reincarnation delusion,[67] he attempted to force Ankh-es-en-Amen into a still-living woman and allowing the princess's will to dominate.

"The technical term for that", Holmes explained, "is dybbukism[68] or what could be translated as body trespassing. It is not exactly mindswapping, where two minds and two bodies are involved, but more like battle of two wills in one body, something like hypnotically-induced multiple personality disorder. It is understandable that the mad Dr. Marco would mistakenly believe he could force this to happen."

Because of my pre-Y5K[4] memory implant I thankfully could understand Holmes much more easily than I had without it. Even after researching it though, I still did not understand MPD very well. I doubt if anyone does who has not experienced it first hand.

To better share our observations, Holmes rigged up some retractable lenses and a megaphone that projected the sights and sounds from the Eyehole to reflect off the mirror of our sideboard like a window into the past and future, yet could be hidden at a moment's notice. When we concentrated together we very often zeroed in on a specific scene, though Holmes, as usual, observed far better than I what it was that we saw and heard.

When some time later we were again focusing on Egypt, we saw many foreigners emigrating to Egypt during a famine, and heard the pharaoh's officials singing the praises of Sarai, the most beautiful of all. This soon reached the ears of "Imhotep" in the body of the chief adviser to Pharaoh Wahankh Intef II, who persuaded the "god-king" to take for himself the Hebrew beauty, whom he planned to take for himself later. The pharaoh rewarded her co-operative brother with slaves and livestock. Abram however had been too fearful of the pharaoh and not as trusting in our Client as he might have been. He kept to himself that she was both his half-sister and his wife. The Eye however acted as an "evil eye" against the royal household, preventing him from getting too close to her. The pharaoh recognized the Eye of Ra in this, abandoned the advise of "Imhotep", confronted Abram, returned Sarai to him and sent them on their way richer and wiser.[69]

In an alternative timeline, since all thing are possible for Him, our Client had permitted His will to work through Sarai's plan, through Abram's alternative wife, Hagar, through Abraham's son Ishmael rather than through Isaac. It prove both different and yet simultaneously similar. The Ishmaelites replaced the Israelites as God's Chosen People. Mohammed took the place of the prophet John and Mohammed's daughter Fatima that of Mary. Islam rather than Christianity flourished after the fall of the Roman empire throughout Europe. The schism between the followers of her sons al-Hasan and al-Husayn, the Shiites and the caliphs, paralleled that between the Western and Eastern Christians.

Because of the great wealth Abraham received from the pharaoh, despite his deception, he was able to organize a small army to rescue his nephew Lot when Lot's family was captured by the alliance of the Four Kings. He was tempted to credit his victory to that rather than to our Client from Whom ultimately all his blessings, including Sarai herself, had come. He was reminded by Melchizedek to thank God, forcing him to realize that neither Lot nor his steward Eliezar were suitable to pass on his true wealth, his faith in the Most High.[70]

After our Client's Covenant with the re-named Abraham, his faith wavered again. The Eye again had to save Sarah, whose new name meant "princess". "Imhotep" now as adviser to Abimelech, king of the Philistines, tried to acquire Sarah's body again for his princess. This time the Eye appeared to the king before he had gotten close to her as if in a dream, or rather a nightmare, with the message, "You are to die, because of the woman you have taken, for she is a married woman."[71]

Through these experiences Abraham's faith grew, as ours does as well, slowly and in spurts. "Imhotep", seeking immortality, not death, also learnt from this experience to seek only as yet unmarried women as hosts.

Abraham's son, Isaac, was warned by our Client not to go on to Egypt, but surprisingly to stay in Gerar, where Abimelech had coveted his mother Sarah. He too succumbed to the same temptation that his father had, lying about his beautiful cousin Rachel. The Eye this time was allowed to guide Abimelech to take a dekko, or look, out of the tent just in time to see Isaac and Rachel in a more intimate than cousinly embrace. Remembering the death threat against adultery, he confronted Isaac as he had his father. Protected from "Imhotep" by the king and blessed by our Client, he learnt to trust as we indeed we all do. With new adviser Ahuzzath, Abimelech made a peace treaty with Isaac, who had grown more powerful than the king himself.[72]

Had Isaac not heeded the advice and gone to Egypt prematurely, Esau would have married an Egyptian rather than Judith the Hittite and not become the ancestor to the Edomites. Isaiah's curse on the Edomites would have fallen upon Egypt instead, drying up the Nile. Egyptian history ended in the Sixth Century B. C. There was no Ptolemaic or Caliphate Empire. Viewing such allohistories certainly made one appreciate the one true Way, certainly at least a partial reason of our Client in gifting us with the portal.

Abraham's grandson Jacob's Rachel was saved as well quite unexpectedly, because her sister Leah had not been able to attract a suitor. This happened because Leah's eyes had been weakened by an accidental flash from the Eye as a child, causing her to became near-sighted. As the nearest cousin on her mother's side, "Imhotep" had stubbornly refused to accept her father Laban's offer to take both sisters, just as Holmes had predicted such an obsessive-compulsive would. Because we pointed Jacob however in the opposite direction, he submitted to the proposal and agreed to marry both sisters to get Rachel. There were still the full twelve tribes of Israel and so twelve apostles[73] for all twelve eternal gates of the New Jerusalem.[74]

In the alternative timelines in which Jacob had married the more desirable Leah, rather than Rachel, Joseph was not born to Rachel and so did not save Egypt or the Israelites from the famine. In one all save Judah perished, but there was no Moses, no Torah, no Israel, only the tribe of Judah surviving only to be enslaved by the Canaanites.

In the timeline in which "Imhotep" married Leah and Jacob married only Rachel, Joseph was not sold into slavery,[75] since his brothers were now his cousins. He did not have the sons Ephraim and Manasseh by Asenath. Again there was no Moses, no Torah, no Israel, only the tribe of Benjamin, which like Judah, was enslaved by the Canaanites.

When his nine half-brothers sought to kill Rachel's son Joseph, the Eye redirected a caravan to pass the dry cistern so that he would eventually marry Asenath, daughter of Potiphera, in Egypt and so save her from a "Imhotep" clone.[76]. Tamar of Chezib was similarly saved from the evil brothers Er and Onan by the Eye, to bear by Judah a son, Zerah.[77] He separated from the Israelites[78] to become an ancestor of Tros, founder of Troy. The Eye also saved the legendary beauty Helen of Troy from another pharaoh, "Baneure Menenptah", while in Egypt in 1203 BC.[79]

In 1089 BC, another "Imhotep" clone was in Egypt again, but with the Greek name "Kharis" ironically meaning "undeserved kindness". He again tried to make himself and the Princess Ankh-es-en-Amen's look-alike Princess Ananka immortal. This time by stealing the sacred tana leaves, rather than the Scroll of Thoth entombed with "Imhotep". He was again punished, as he had been almost seven hundred years before, this time by being kept zombified by the secret Guardians of Karnak cult with three leaves per month.

"Kharis" was not revived completely until Karnak was threatened by the expedition of Claude-Étienne Savary in 1785. He was revived again by guardian Yosef Bey in 1895, escaping with his princess's newest host Amina Mansori.[80] The evil and unfaithful servant Andoheb however coveted both Princess Ananka and the position of authority of his master, the cult's high priest.

"You are very beautiful ... so beautiful," We heard him say, gazing upon her preserved body after he had become high priest. "I'm going to make you immortal. Like Kharis, you will live forever. What I can do for you I can do for myself. Neither time nor death can touch us. You and I together for eternity here in the Temple of Karnak. You shall be my high priestess."

He disobeyed the warning of his predecessor not to brew more than nine tana leaves at a time, he turned poor "Kharis" into, as the high priest described him, "a soulless demon with the desire to kill and kill." More accurately, I'd call him an addict overdosing on a dangerous combination of alkaloids. Having seen more than my share of addicts, I would be very hesitant to demonize them or underestimate the endurance of the Human soul, however lost she may seem.

Andoheb sought to direct this demon of death at the archeologists Steve Banning, Jr. and Babe Jenson and their patrons, Timothy and his daughter Marta Sullivan, better known as "The Great Solvani and Marta". He ended, not at all unexpectedly, by being killed himself by Jenson. The Sullivans named their youngest son, their "babe", Steven after Steve Banning, Jr.

In an alternative timeline in which the "immortal" Andoheb was killed thirty years before however, he survived long enough to pass his medallion and so the cult leadership on to Mehemet Bey. Bey followed the body of Princess Anaka to America and revived "Kharis" just as Andoheb had, to avenge Steve Banning, Sr., his son, John, his partner "Babe" Hanson and the new expedition leader, Joseph Whemple, Bey was killed himself by the not quite so mind-numbed "Kharis". The Eye made sure that John Bennet, also in the expedition, not only survived, but saved his beloved Isobel as well.[81] They named their sons Joseph and Steve Bennet, who also became Egyptologists. Their uncle, Steve, Jr., did not.

We traced "Kharis" and his companion's flight through swampy refuges all across the Eastern United States, discouraging the Karnak cultists one by one along the way, until the last and most foolhardy one, Ragheb, finally caught up with the two.

"It seems we are the Hounds of the Karnak cult, eh, Holmes?" I commented watching our quarry tromp through yet another swamp.

"Yes, indeed. The trail does harken back to the Moors, does it not?"

Then he shocked me out of my melancholy thoughts by suddenly bursting out with "My God! You've hit upon the vital clue once again, my dear man! I have not been able to see forest for the trees!"

"What do you mean?" I asked, still completely missing his point.

"I had been trying to find some method in this mummy madness by looking at the details of where and when they moved from one location to another, from one state to another. I had not noticed the obvious, that Marco spent more time hiding out in the swamps along the East and Southeast Coasts of the United States than he had traveling between them or out of them. He has been avoiding areas that were dry except when absolutely necessary."

It was this seemingly irrelevant comment of mine that gave Holmes the clue to how to finally free both Marco and Amina. As the Eye he started the fire that finally destroyed the last of the cursed tana leaves and burned their undead bodies to dust.[82]

The Eye had also saved Simon Thassi by directing him to the holy sword[83] from the martyrdom of his brothers and so saved many princesses throughout Judea, the Roman Empire and Europe through the centuries.[84] We encouraged the discouraged Helena and discouraged the plot against her after "Imhotep" caused Constantinus to divorce her in 305. As a result of her faith in our Client however her son Constantine also converted.

In one timeline that we had to loop however her prayers converted him to Judaism rather than Christianity and the Jews for Jesus Movement began growing sixteen centuries earlier that it ought to have, encouraged by Jewish persecutions of the Messianics through the centuries.[85] In others Constantine misinterpreted his vision as a UFO or a vision of Mithra.[86] As Mithraism inevitably secularized, the cult of the Son grew.[87] In yet another he converted to Christianity yet was still defeated by Maxentius, so Christians remained but a small minority in Persian-besieged Jewish Rome in 999[88] and the Dark Ages lasted far longer than a thousand years. "A horrible ending's better than endless horrors." as they say.[89] These less traveled paths, viewed through the Eye of Providence, do help give one perspective. We truly do live in the best of all possible worlds.

The Eye saved both Cartena and her daughter Clotilda from the timeline in which their brother-in-law and uncle Godegisil, killed his brother King Chilperic, tied a stone around Cartena's neck and threw her into a well. The Eye helped Princess Chrona get refuge with another uncle in Geneva, where she founded the church of Saint-Victor and became a bride of Christ. We also encouraged Clovis, king of the Franks, to secretly sent his friend Aurelian to Lyons, rather like Eliezar had been sent to fetch Rebekah for Isaac after the death of his mother Sarah.[90] Disguised as a beggar he presented Clotilda with a gold ring and she found refuge in Paris.

In this timeline "Aredius" was chief advisor to Godegisil, not to be confused with St. Aredius, former chancellor to Theudebert. This "Aredius" persuaded Godegisil to take back his permission to marry Clotilda from Clovis, so "Imhotep" could have her as host for his princess. In 496 Clotilda prayed for her husband Clovis and Clovis and so all the Franks finally acquired the Faith after a Constantine-like victory.[91]

The Eye also saved Bathildis from the timeline with "Erchinoald", the mayor of the palace of Neustria. When yet a young girl, a relative of Ricberht, the last pagan king of East Anglia, she had been kidnapped and sold into slavery. We helped her evade "Erchinoald" and distracted him long enough that she was able to became a trusted member of King Clovis II's court and they eventually married in 649.[92]

Our Client in His infinite wisdom did not however let us save all those threatened by "Imhotep" clones. We could not save Bilichild, the wife of her cousin Childeric of Austrasia. We had to let her husband and her eldest son, the five-year-old Dagobert, be attacked and killed by a band of Neustrians lead by "Bodilo". That was because in the timeline in which Dagobert lived to succeed his father he lead a genocide against the Neustrians, like Jehu had against the house of Ahaz and Jezebel. We were however able to save young Prince Daniel by helping him find sanctuary in a monastery, like Jehu who was rescued from the evil Jezebel.[93] He returned forty years thence to lead the Franks as king under the name Chilperic II.[94]

When we saved Rotrude de Bourgogne to marry Charles Martel, the Muslims still conquered Constantinople in 718. Nestorianism spread to Asia and defeated Islam in 731.[95] We were greatly helped during the Middle Ages by the first superhero group, the Holy Helpers, lead by our Client's mother, particularly George, patron of England, Christopher the Strong, angelologist Denis of Paris, Leonard of Noblac, patron of prisoners, and Margaret the Invulnerable.[96]

We eventually limited the "Imhotep" clones to just the baronesses of Ixworth for his princess's body donors.[97] We were able to thwart his revisionist history by truncating the line of ever-more beautiful baronesses. There were however consequences. Our rescue of Lady Catherine from "Algernon Simeon" in 1887 undid the battle of Gilbraltar,[98] the theft of van Gogh's self-portrait[99] and the birth of Marco's infamous alter ego, "Agnes Simeon Tewksbury", alias "Mother Muffin", the assassin matriarch.[100]

In this same timeline Moriarty stole the crown jewels,[101] but working with Baker Street Irregular Archibald Francis Wiggins we saved the queen.[102] We also aided Lestrade against a Fenian plot[103] and prevented the assassination of Grand Duke Alexei.[104]

Our shadowing of Col. Oliver Pendleton-Smythe led to the discovery of no less than three secret societies[105], the murderer of Julian Trevor and the rescuing of Lady Dorothy Broxton[106] and Teddy, the son of my war buddy Maj. Adolphus Venables.[107] It surprisingly also prompted a temporary alliance between Holmes and Moriarty to solve the murders of Lord Walbine and several other Amateur Mendicants.[108]

We saved Holmes's distant cousin Lt. Richard Hornblower and steward Jack Luhulu on the *Sophy Anderson*[109] and investigated her namesake reported sunk twenty years before. The Grice-Patersons, then owners of Uffa Island, were suspected of wrecking her. Beatrice and Henry were however involved in an even more peculiar case of a murder at an archeological dig,[110] while Alexander and Donald reported sighting the legendary Black Pig and were accused of stealing the MacGlevin Buckle.[111]

Investigating the original *Sophy Anderson* led us to Sir William Carey and the theft of the Bagdah Emerald by yet another ancient Egyptian cult, the Sons of the Pharaohs cult,[112] the murderer of Prof. Edford[113] and the cover-up by Joseph Nully and Michael Lofthouse.[114] To close this time loop we trivialized the cult into the fraternal organization the Sons of the Desert[115] with the help of Lord Paddington, Arthur Stanley Jefferson.[116]

Having inadvertently led Holmes and myself into a trap set by Moriarty, we were rescued by my Mary[117] without any assistance from the Eye. God bless her! It was however Moriarty's little joke to get Dr. Paradene to name his alleged hyperdimensional material and Baron Maupertuis his criminal organization[118] after the torture chamber of the Paradol Club in another timeline.[119]

In 1831 we saved Prime Minister Wellington from assassination[120] and another Lady Catherine Blount from "Robert Wellesby" alias "John Gray".[121] Saving her mother Henrietta from "Richard Vernon" in 1764 involved recruiting young Leopald and Johannes Mozart as Irregulars. That in turn led to stopping a murder and royal scandal in 1820[122], saving Princess Victoria in 1827[123] and in 1791 saving Franz Süssmayr[124] from the robot time travelers Cessares and 9-Eyes from 1992.[125]

We also saved Lady Alexandra for Percy Armand Blakeney[126] and Lady Jane from "Robert Warre" in 1730. We saved Lady Mary from "Thomas 'Peeping Tom' Davis" in the first re-enactment of the ride of Lady Godiva in 1677.[127] and the original Lady Godiva from Imhotep in the 11th Century.

In 1626 we saved Lady Sydney from "Richard Mostyn", thus rendering descendants Hugh Mostyn[128] and Edward Halliday-Mostyn[129] contafactual. Saving yet another Lady Catherine from "Richard Cotton" in 1509 did the same for Cotton the Pirate[130], Victorian black widow Mary Ann Cotton[131], G-man Jerry Cotton[132], Larry and Kirsty Cotton and so the hellish Cenobites[133] and Cotton the space colonist.[134]

Because we prevented Lady Johan from marrying "Robert Fitton", there were no Ezra and Lucy or Arthur and Jenny Fitton.[135] Rather Lady Johan Grosvenor married Robert Piper and they all became Pipers. Similarly Lady Joan did not marry "Ralph Eton" and so could not be an ancestor to singer Ruth Eton Hopkins.[136] Another Lady Joan did not marry "Robert de Pulford" and so was not an ancestor to gunman Jack.[137]

We could not however prevent Lady Catherine from marrying "Robert Norris", but we did repeatedly prevent him from summoning Princess Ankh-es-en-Amen. The most famous of their offspring in this timeline was the legendary Carlos "Chuck" Norris[138], able to do more than six impossible things before brekkie, breakfast, without thinking.[139] Less fantastic nearby timelines had secret agent Waldo Norris[140] and Fr. Brian Norris.[141] Without Richie Norris the invading Martians could not be defeated in 1962.

Without Grandma Florence, Billy Glenn, or Sue Ann Norris they couldn't even attack Earth.[142] The timeline with "Switchblade" Killingsworth, alias "Chuck Norris", was only very loosely connected to the others.[143]

Before saving Lady Eleanor from "Robert Egerton" in 1794, Holmes and I became involved with time traveler Nicholas Segalla's investigation into the disappearance of Prince Louis Charles[144] and Napoleon's defeat by Lafayette[145] and his loss of Louisiana to Britain.[146] With no French Revolution, the French Empire grew, especially after the 1850 French W. Australian gold rush.[147] The French claimed Palestine in 1917[148] and all of New Zealand by 1930.[149] Finally in 1938 we watched as Hitler lead his AmerInd-Negro army against the French Empire.[150]

To protect Lady Christine from "Roger Myddeton" in 1649, we had to first save Hans and Greta Strauss and other pairs of children at fifty year intervals over several centuries.[151] In 1529 we saved Lady Maud from "Thomas Poole", so that Riley Poole was not born to discover the Templar treasure[152] or Derek Poole to become a bomber[153] or Frank Poole to become an astronaut.[154] Before closing that timeline however we had to help Hecate Poole against Dorian Grey, "Victor Frankenstein", witches and vampires[155] and Socrates and Iphigenia Poole against the John Bly gang.[156] In the John Poole timeline we even helped a Robert and Thorpe Holmes against giant robots.[157] Fortunately we'd had, uh, would have, quite a bit of experience dealing with them before in other futures.[158]

With all that we finally curtailed the "Imhotep" clones to harassing the Grosvenors, the marquesses of Westminster and barons of Ebury. Alas, we necessarily had to allow the baronies of Assheton and Barrington to go extinct in 1765 and 1832 respectively.[159]

With all the "Imhotep" clones vanquished, "Imhotep's" still restless soul was forcibly returned to his original mummified body by Ralph Norton in 1922, regrettably at the cost of Norton's sanity. Holmes however rather enjoyed this too much, I thought, suggesting the assumed name of "Ardath Bey", without "Imhotep" ever recognizing it as an anagram of "Death by Ra". I have to admit that I too felt very relieved that we had taken a part in saving as much as we had, though we had no idea how much more would be required of us.

After ten years "Ardeth Bey" finally found another suitable host body for Ankh-es-en-Amen's own lost soul in Helen Grosvenor, granddaughter of Algenon and Catherine, and niece of Amina Mansori. As the Eye Holmes simulated a death ray which is taken as an "act of goddess" and so enabling to her to marry Frank Whemple, son of Joseph Whemple. They named their firstborn daughter after her aunt Amina and their second after her grandmother Catherine. As we had learnt in 1944, that reducing a body to ashes is was the surest way to end "Imhotep's" undeath. We used this knowledge to good effect in dealing with many other undead mummies between 1037 BC and AD 4067. Even that however was not always permanent.[160]

Soon after this mummy madness Holmes discovered that Dr. Marco had also earned himself a reputation in Fifteenth Century England.

"He has been living not so much as a physician, but rather as a magician by the use of the same power of hypnotic suggestion he had used as 'Imhotep'. By 1486, he however coveted the position of the Grand Master of the Brotherhood of Magicians and used his knowledge of the Scroll of Thoth to put Rodrick Craven into a death-like suspended animation. He had by this time acquired the uncomplimentary name of Scarabus 'the Beetle', because of this occult knowledge and a substantial fortune acquired after successful dealings with barons Beverly[161] and Dowson[162] as the new Grand Master."

By 1504 however we watched as he plotted against his rival's son, Erasmus. The younger Craven had dropped out of the Brotherhood at his father's "death", but "Scarabus" sensed and plotted against the power still active in Craven Manor. We watched as he gloated over the death of Erasmus's wife, Lenore.

"Ah, that must be the deviation in the timeline, Watson." Holmes, said, abruptly snuffing out and p utting down his pipe.

"What? That 'Scarabus' killed his patient as he had tried to do with all those other women as 'Imhotep'?"

"No, that he did not. To save lives was the motive when Marco started this ill-fated venture with little or no success. Without his futuristic medical skills, which would have been called magic then,[163] Mrs. Craven would have very likely died. Missing his own nagging wife however and unable to resist Lenore's enthusiastic gratitude, he undoubtedly assisted her in faking her own death.

That was indeed what we found had happened. "Scarabus" had gained a female companion and she shared his fortune and power, a match made in hell.

"That was the elusive deviation, that she did live, not that she did not. We must follow the trail uptime to see how this unnatural relationship developed before deciding if the Eye must intervene yet again."

Several years passed in subjective minutes as we watched that doomed relationship deteriorate. Finally another magician, one Adolphus Bedlo, became too nosy, too greedy for power as well, and made the mistake of disturbing the reclusive Beetle of Dartmoor. Focusing in on Scarabus castle, we quietly observed without being observed in real time.

"Watson, wake up!", Holmes whispered, tapping me on my good shoulder with his finger. "You did NOT see 'Scarabus' turn Bedlo into a raven."

"But I did, Holmes! He turned him from a little predatory man into a little predatory bird and then I saw him fly out the window."

"No, my friend, he did nothing of the kind."

His calm and confident words made me feel calm and confident, though still confused. Then I remembered how resistant Holmes had proved himself against the spell of Irene Onslow in the Finger Murders case, when I had not.[164]

"It must have been hypnosis," I suggested, resignedly.

"Quite right, old fellow. This 'Scarabus' has a very strong will, which is understandable considering he has had to endure both the strong-willed Mrs. Marco and Mrs. Craven. I nearly succumbed to the illusion myself. As I rejected that impossibility, what remained was him leaving in the normal way through the front door. I could do nothing to stop him as the Eye without very likely making Bedlo's delusions worse."

"Do we have to go back to prevent 'Scarabus's' saving of Lenore Craven's life now, er, then?" I asked Holmes, as the Eye followed Bedlo's footprint trail on the ground outside, and not through the air.

"We will not, you will be happy to learn, doctor, need to participate in her death. It seems best that we let her live out the lie a bit longer and see what develops. Her fraud and desertion may well have untoward consequences yet, even if she abandons 'Scarabus' as she did Craven. For the time being we will continue to observe."

My "And as the yogi Berra said, 'You can observe a lot just by watching.'", only brought a begrudging half-smile to Holmes' face.

We did both watch and observe as Bedlo returned with Lenore's husband and daughter and his own son. When it looked as if Bedlo was losing the battle of wits against "Scarabus" once again, Holmes finally decided it was time to stop observing and take action. He interposed a second lens between himself and the portal that intensified our gaslight and quickly removed it. It zapped Bedlo with a flash of light so close that it sent him running. To me it had looked as if "Scarabus" had, like Elijah called down "fire from heaven" as he had obviously conjured the storm.

When the real battle, that between "Scarabus" and Craven, took place their special effects were remarkable. Much of it I did recognize as illusion and pyrotechnics, but some of it seemed truly magical. It was however a little assist from the Eye that cause the castle to start to crumble and put an end to this battle of wits.[165]

"This timeline seems to be stabilizing," Holmes chortled. "None of the historically significant people 'Scarabus' has touched so far, including the seemingly insignificant Lenore Craven, have triggered any lasting divergence in the time flow that I have been able to trace. Rexford and Estelle seem to have been destined for each other with or without 'Scarabus' or Lenore, based on the very dull genealogy of their children, Erasmus and Lenore Bedlo."

It wasn't until all, including the revived and restored Grand Master Rodrick, were celebrating the wedding of Rexford and Estelle that we finally saw Adolphus suddenly and unexpectedly freed of his raven delusion. He stopped flapping his arms and tested his rediscovered hands.

"God bless you, Erasmus!" he shouted, dancing toward Craven's larder. "You are most kind."

"But I didn't do it!" Craven protested.

"Me either," Rodrick added.

"Thank God!" Adolphus raising a toast.

Upon overhearing this exchange, Holmes let out with a satisfied "Aha!"

"What do you mean 'Aha!' If the Cravens didn't disenchant Bedlo, who did?"

Holmes explained that as Erasmus and "Scarabus" were so equally matched, it had taken the combined effects of our wills to tip the balance. It had something to do with what he called the Psi Power Laws by Mentor of Arisia,[166] which I did not quite follow. Bedlo's post-hypnotic suggestion that he was a bird and not Human ended, as I understood it, because the link between "Scarabus's" mind and his subject's had been broken and broken so suddenly, Holmes concluded, that it could only mean that he had died and been chronoported again.

"I made certain that the damage to Scarabus castle did not extend to injuring either 'Scarabus' or Lenore, just to frightening them a little." he continued.

"Could Lenore have killed him?"

"I am afraid it may be worse than that," he said as he invited me to examine the two dead bodies amidst the castle ruins through the Eyehole.

They were tangled in a mutual death grip strangle hold. They had apparently died simultaneously with each other's hands around their throats. Had he been younger and not just defeated by Erasmus, "Scarabus" might have survived. Holmes did not, of course, admit it but by the way he glanced over at Irene's photo, I knew he had once again underestimated a woman.[167]

"Lenore, it seems was as strong-willed as 'Scarabus' and strongly mind-linked even in their final struggle, just as I and Moriarty were in ours. When they killed each other, the Shelborne effect took her along with him."

"It may not have been such a good idea to let her continue to live after all then. Now we have twice as many time-altering time hoppers to deal with! If this goes on there will be no end of them."

"I sincerely hope you are wrong with your diagnosis this time, good doctor. I was rather looking forward to a successful conclusion to this missing person case."

"So was I, Holmes. So was I."

I was thinking that I was looking forward to a swift end to this quest, but then I probed deeper. Deep down I felt that I was actually looking forward to this quest becoming even more challenging than it had been so far, just as I suspected Holmes was.

"At least for the time being," I said with an encouraging grin, "It is two time-altering time travelers against two others!"

This time the time trail was not a doddle, not so easy to follow, even though we now had a double worldline. We felt we had to search through all the Bedlo descendants since Marco as "Scarabus" had inadvertently and indirectly begot them by bringing together Rexford and Estelle. A few tended to the what Holmes called the ultradimensional anachronic probability state[168], but what I simply thought of as directed toward goodness, like our making André Mondreau[169] or Kentaro Moto[170] look good. A few were borderline.[171] Many others tended toward the infradimensional or evil[172], however Erasmus throwback Jason Winter's *Time Express*[173] providentially helped greatly by facilitating many corrective time loops.

We followed the double time trail to when they were found in the bodies a couple who seemed to have survived a near-fatal car crash in 1963. Marco recovered enough memories to be able to assume the identity of the late Prof. Marcus Montserrat. Lenore however was traumatized not only by the accident, by by finding herself trapped in the crippled body of a woman twenty years older that she had been.

We observed things go smoothly, suspiciously smoothly, for three years. Lenore recovered both physically and mentally with doctoring of "Dr. Montserrat". He finally had to try something new however, because Lenore's hypnotic therapy was destabilizing. She was no Stepford wife.[174] In response he built a thought transferal device so that she not remember she was not the sweet, lovable Estelle, but Estelle's evil stepmother. It worked. It worked too well.

They tried the device out on the free-spirited twenty-something owner of the "Glory Hole" antique shop, Mike Roscoe. While "Montserrat" still had his original desire to use his invention for good and, even if it could not heal, at least would give the crippled and elderly a virtual vacation from their suffering. Both of them become rather addicted to this new kind of string-less puppetry. Lenore however enjoyed living through her avatar rather too much after having been temporarily paralyzed after the accident. She reveled in the novelty and freedom of the East London and then turned to the addictive thrill of committing crimes anonymously. As both Holmes and I expected, this inevitably lead to attempting the "perfect" crime, destroying them both, a perfect example of the Sully Syndrome.[175]

Eventually she became paranoid as well as obsessive-compulsive, coming to suspect that her husband had been using the device on her as well as on Roscoe, that he had been controlling her for years. He hadn't, though he subconsciously had encouraged her identification with Estelle rather than Lenore. She remembered more and more confusingly who she had been and also who she was vicariously. Eventually Lenore's and Roscoe's identities merged permanently and she became him/her and he her/him.

We watched this scenario play out until the very end, as we had on Inspector March at the beginning, as Inspector Matalon stopped puffing on his pipe. It was then a year since "Dr. Montserrat" had given the evidence against his wife and her alleged lover that had led to their convictions. I read in the open file what had attracted Holmes's attention, how during the trial she had referred to herself as "Lenore" and as "Estelle" and as "Mike". S/he claimed s/he had used a "that infernal machine of his" in revenge after "Montserrat" had used it on her/him.

Seeing by his condescending smirk what Matalon, unlike Col. March, thought of such 'impossibilites', I blurted out, "Absurd!"

"Quite so!", he agreed out loud, mistaking my overheard outburst for his own thought and utterly mistaking my meaning. "Absurd is just what the judge thought of her story and that's what it was. It's unthinkable that such a device could be possible. Roscoe was been rightly executed and Estelle Montserrat mercifully institutionalized. Case closed!"[176] Lenore did not however improve when Roscoe was executed. In fact her "multiple personality disorder" got worse. As our Client undoubtedly foresaw, this sharing in the torments of the damned before death was just what she needed to see the error of her ways and avoid the eternal punishment afterward.

On some of the stronger time trails, Marco's desire to use therapeutic hypnosis endured and combined with his detective experiences. One lead us back to 1867, when the Eye'd saved the life of one of Holmes's time clone's mother in London.[177] Yes, in case your readers are curious, and they being Baker Street Irregulars undoubtedly are, it took us quite a while to reduce the number of Holmes's mothers, or my wives for that matter, down to just one.

As I was saying, without any help from the Eye at all and virtually no use of hypnotism either, Marco, known simply as "Le Mesmerist", solved the otherwise unsolved Baruch Koweski murder case in Alsatia. Matthais's own guilty conscience got the better of him. We happily watched as he repented to our Client's Blessed Mother and was forgiven by his victim before he died. We followed "Le Mesmerist" through many other such cases throughout Europe, and his son Dolomar in India.[178]

His American cousin, also a Marco time clone, calling himself "Swami Talpur", was not so talented or justice-loving. We found him at the Lost Caverns ski resort where he had followed his former lawyer, Amos Strickland. Holmes, of course, did not believe the rumors that Strickland was there to write his memoirs, but he knew many would. Having encountered many blackmailers, I too well knew that keeping business records greatly reduced a blackmailer's life expectancy.[179]

"Talpur" became Inspector Wellman's prime suspect when Strickland was murdered, primarily from his having acquired the nickname "King of Killers" before his acquittal for his association with a series of mysterious gangland killings. Other very suspicious residents however were also all other clients that Strickland had also defended and cleared on murder charges, Angela Gordon, Mrs. Gerald Hargreave, T. Hanley Brooks, Lawrence Crandall, Mrs. Grimsby, Madame Switzer and Mike Relia. If Talpur was the king of killers, he had many courtiers. Even the recently fired bellhop, Freddie Phillips, became a suspect when the numpty foolishly blamed and threatened Strickland.

The resort was literally full of suspects. Two of them, Relia and Gregory Millford, Strickland's secretary, however very soon turned up dead along with him and then turned up missing altogether. Temporarily Angela Gordon, the black sheep of the Gotham City Gordons, became the prime suspect, when she attempted to poison Phillips, but the Eye was able to stop her, saving them both.

When "Talpur" tried using his usually very persuasive technique on Phillips. Like Gordon, he did not succeed, but without any help from the Eye.

"Perhaps you should choose the manner of your death," he suggested to Phillips, as he had with the rival gangsters. "How would you like to die?"

"Old age."

After several similarly abortive attempts, but having noticed that the corpses kept disappearing after being found by Phillips, "Talpur" tried to cover himself.

"You didn't see me. You didn't see me. You didn't see me. I wasn't here.", he said as he left Phillips alone.

When the house detective Edwards came in, he asked Phillips, "Ready to go?"

Phillips answered, the swami's efforts finally working without any reinforcement from the Eye, with comic effect, "I didn't see him."

"You didn't see who?"

"The man who wasn't there."

Edwards, remembering Relia and Millford who weren't where Phillips said they were, had to ask, "You didn't see who?"

Phillips answer, "The man who wasn't here." wasn't much help.

"What man?", however Edwards continued.

Also remembering the other men who weren't there, Phillips tried to remember what he couldn't, saying "All I did was open up the door, see if the coast was clear, my mind went blank."

This Edwards dismissed with, "Your mind's been a blank all your life."

Inspector Wellman, who did need a little help from the Detective Eye, sorted through the many remaining suspects and managed to capture Strickland's actual murderer was the blackmailing hotel manager. It was obvious after Holmes explained it.

"Melton repeatedly accused Phillips of being the killer to divert suspicion away from himself, even though Edwards, who knew him best, had vouched for him. Melton continued to do so even after Phillips kept incriminating himself by pointing out murder victims and murder weapons. The stocky silhouette in the cave only matched Melton's. As the hotel manager, he was also the only one who had access to all the rooms to both kill and hide all the bodies."[180]

"Talpur", having sufficiently failed to mindcontrol the simple-minded Phillips and no longer blackmailed by either Strickland or Melton, decided to give up on even stage hypnosis. He replaced Melton as manager at Lost Caverns.

Rather often, or rather more often than I had expected at any rate, when we were focusing on Marco time trails, we also encountered Bedlo descendants. It always was rather startling to to me, no matter how many times I experienced it.

"Dr. Lorenz bears a striking resemblance to …"

"Our old friend Alphonsus, yes. It is strikingly obvious, is it not, Watson? He certainly has the characteristic physiognomy, the raspy, tenor voice, bulgy eyes, tichy stature. It is not however the coincidence it seems. Nothing is as it seems.[181] I have often noticed that the stronger currents of the time stream tend to force weaker worldlines together when they do not diverge too widely.

"'The thing that hath been, it is that which shall be; and that which is done is that which shall be done: and there is no new thing under the sun.'[182] The descendants of Roxford and Estelle Bedlo would tend to pick spouses like their parents and so their physical and psychological characteristics would tend to reoccur rather frequently. That is the real basis for the false notions of avatars and reincarnation, time echoes. I wrote a monograph on the subject, next year I believe it was, uh, will be. The Society of Psychic Research rejected it!"

I almost suggested that Holmes send it to my literary agent Doyle, thinking "Doyle would believe anything, but then fortunately gave that idea a second thought. From the concentration on his face, Holmes was likely re-writing the monograp or would that be pre-writing? One's tanses get rather tengled when time traveling.

We confirmed from observing Jinxville's grand poobah that Dr. Arthur Lorencz not only was descended from the Bedlos on his mother's side, but that a man fitting Marco's description was a murder suspect. The former owner of the Old Colonial Inn, "Prof. Nathaniel Billings", had been accused of making the new owner, Winnie Slade, an accomplice to murder. There was however no evidence for "Lorry" to prove this allegations one way or the other.

Rather like his Bedlo ancestor used magic tricks, Lorencz superstitiously used a pocket Siamese kitten, as a living divining rod to detect crime and corruption, failing to detect it in himself however. Bill Leyden, Winnie's ex-husband, showed up not to renegotiate the large settlement but to reclaim his wife. He claimed also to have discovered five bodies in the wine cellar, but the sheriff was not convinced.

Holmes kept repeating the rumor so unconvincingly in Lorencz's ear that he finally changed his mind, as hoped, and went to investigate the rumors. Our own and his further investigations were more than somewhat hampered however by old lady Amelia Jones's chickens, handyman Ebenezer, J. Gilbert Brampton, obviously not who he says he is, and the mad Dr. Lorencz himself.

He also, like a true Bedlo, tried to cover-up his cover-up of "Billings's" "martyrized" supersoldiers. Fortunately upon closer examination I found "Billings" had only put his volunteers into a kind of suspended animation with his newest device, like he had done as "Scarabus" to Grand Master Craven. Gentle Eyebeams were able to thaw them, as the bobbies from the neighboring town caught the maddest madman, Silvio the Human Bomb.[183]

Revived traveling salesman Steven Rogers went on to volunteer again for the government's similar FLAG serum project.[184] Maximilian Rosenbloom teamed up with barmy William Barron and Samuel

Horwitz.[185] Percival Popp became "Super-Cop", teaming up with Jim "Spectre" Corrigan in Cliffland, N. J.[186] Merton McSnurtle became "Terrific Whatzit" in Zooville.[187] Jacob Gilbert Brampton got a job at Pearson Military School.[188] Bill and Winnie Leyden did indeed reconcile, agreed on having children, and added the reward money for the capture of Silvio to her inheritance. They named their sons Arthur, after Dr. Lorencz, and Fred, after Winnifred, and their daughter Amelia, after old Lady Jones. Arthur eventually took over the Inn and Fred was the one who became a doctor.

The meandering trail of our mad doctor lead through an interesting, though a dangerous 1845, involving a Capt. Edgar Allen and the Georgia-Florida war[189]. To close the time loop we had to go back to 1814 to stop Georgia's secession in 1807[190] and then back even further to 1765 to save what would become the United States by saving Holmes's American cousin several times removed, Ambrose Altamont.[191] We spent a bleak December night at an intersection of knotted timelines listening to eerie tales with Edgar's civilian time clone and friends.

An actor fan of Poe named Vincent Leonard, Jr., movingly read some of his stories. He was obviously a Craven, with his tall, slender physique and distinctive low-pitched voice.[192] An old war veteran André Duvalier, perhaps not co-incidentally, was also a throwback, a Roxford. He told in his slow drawl of how he'd met Helene, a beautiful, mysterious damsel in distress in 1806. She believed she was possessed by the long-dead Baroness Ilse von Leppe. André eventually learnt however that 'tweren't a ghost that was behind all the strange goings-on, but the village witch Katrina, who bore a grudge against the baron. What Katrina did not know however was that her son, Eric, whom we knew to be Marco, and whom she thought had been killed by the baron, had actually killed the baron and taken his place out of his shame all these years. When she realized this after she drowned "the baron", she out of greater shame called down lightning upon herself without any help from the Eye. With a subtle, somewhat maniacal, laugh André told and re-told how after he had seemed to save Helene she too was gone, vanished like a mist,[193] a mere projection of the poor, mad, dying "Eric".

Poe himself told of his own eerie visions of an Arthur Doyle and Ehrich Weiss and a killer gorilla in New York, haunting daymares that had inspired his pioneer detective story, "Murders in the Rue Morgue", four years before.[194] The widow Mary Norrich shared about her first sea voyage on her husband Roger's ship, the *Vestris*, over twenty years before. The ship's doctor, Dr. Pierre, died unexpected, but then even more unexpectedly spookily appeared and disappeared. Mrs. Norrich tried to warn the captain and his crew but to no avail. They all dismissed her fantastic tale as hysteria just as the apostles did Mary Magdalene's. The ghostly doctor did however manage to rematerialized enough to leave a mysterious chalk message that did save the ship and all others aboard,[195] and so too Capt. and Mary Norrich's unborn children, Pierre and Roberta.

Even more eerily a hundred years later the scenario was repeated again on another ship named *Vestris*, but the warning of cargo imbalance in the face of the oncoming hurricane off the Virginia capes was not heeded and the ship was lost with all two hundred aboard. It made the name *Vestris* famous, being the first major ship disaster reported on radio and the Pulitzer Prize winning photo of the capsizing.[196] It had been the last vessel to sight the *Cyclops* before it vanished in 1918.

We found "Dr. Pierre" under several other names on several other doomed ships large and small. Holmes nicknamed him "the Wandering Frenchman". He was, for example, on the *Gen. Slocum* in 1904 when nearly 1100 people, mostly German immigrants, died within sight of New York City, the largest lost of lives in New York until 2001.[197]

Such tragedies as these once grieved this doctor's heart sorely, but in our visiting innumerable disasters, we have many times seen time travelers like the ubiquitous Fishers[198] or time police, like Louise Baltimore, find crew and passengers who choose to live and rebuild the future rather than die in the past.[199] The scout for a great many of these rescue missions, Peter Guzli, nicknamed "Tourist Guy", has been a great help in our quest and was often photographed by Marco clones.[200] This was especially helpful in those disasters erased from the memories of witnesses neuralized by MIBs.[201]

The huge gigantism epidemic timeline, for example, that multi-megayear series of disasters caused by Szalinski radiation poisoning in plants, animals[202] and people,[203] was finally closed. No, this was not directly by an act of God or indirectly by the Eye, but by the giantkillers of G-Force, namely: Tadihisa "Kino" Kinoshita, Také Fukuda, Marina Melter and Burton Helzer.[204] The gestalt and golem timelines were similar, but different, timelines that the Eye was able to stop and the even all three G-Forces were not, by stopping "Nathaire" at the crucial Jonbar hinge in 1231.[205] The madness of creating giants by making gestalt monsters from many smaller living, dead or undead things was a bit too much for them.

Some however chose to stay, like crash survivor Ginger Maguire in 1944 who became known as "Sky Girl", to change their present.[206] Sam Posner stayed in 1989[207] and David Dunn stayed in 1975 as "No Ordinary Man".[208]

Although I knew Holmes's bias against the supernatural, in this case I was convinced by his identification of the *Vestris* incident as one of Marco's benign attempts to do some honest doctoring in this timeline, cut short by his malfunctioning machine. Poe concluded the storytelling with a very bad, impromptu poem, but excused himself with "Rhymes fly when you're having rum."[209]

Usually however it was more difficult. Through the sole survivor of the Lost Colony not killed by monsters and zombies[210] or abducted by aliens from tau Ceti II,[211] Carolina Dare, we found "Guyasuta", aka Stands-up-to-the-cross, chief of the Senecas, called "Tall Warrior" by George Washington.[212] Before the American Civil War we found "Tishomingo", a Choctaw friend of the non-secessionist Dabneys,[213] whose grandmother'd been saved in the Great New Madrid earthquake in 1811 by Zoey Smith from 2007.[214]

After the American Civil War we found yet another among the Pawnees, a non-American Indian,[215] "Ali Khan Singh", son of the first maharajah of Rampur, Faizullah Khan, was traveling back to India with his three sons, Chandra, Gupta and Sarrakan and his daughter, Veda. His great nephew Muhammed Yusef Ali Khan Bahadur having just died, he thought his sons may have a chance at the disputed succession.[216] Holmes cleverly instructed secret agent James West and the Singhs in the art of baritsu with each side thinking that they were learning it from the other.[217] They failed in their bid for the kingdom, but Veda did marry an Englishman serving in India and became Marco's second-great grandmother. We later, or was it earlier?, in any case encountered another Indian time clone in Singh's descendants, Jenan Singh, still trying unsuccessfully to claim the title of maharajah of Rampur. He was connected with the Norma Graves suicide case in 1922, but we helped clear him[218] and he married Doris Burnham.

He seemed to give up all claims when Rampur lost its independence in 1930. Unfortunately his ex-daughter-in-law, Dr. Sarina Kaur, did not. In fact although she could not pursue any claims of her own, she had far greater ambitions for her son, born in 1970. As co-founder of the Chrysalis Project, she with slightly mad Drs. G. Heisen and Patel augmented several select children, including Noonien Singh as supersoldiers,[219] like "Prof. Billings" had tried to do, though involuntarily. Noonien Singh assumed the title of Khan and his followers temporarily controlled a quarter of Earth, but were force to flee to space in the first sleeper ship, the *Botany Bay*, to eventually settle on Khan's world in the Mira system.[220] I had to stand by and watch as his wife Marla McGivers Singh and their son died in 2265, because when I hadn't, the son revived the Khan dynasty as the tyrannical Genghis Khan Singh, eventually controlling not just a quarter of a planet, but a quarter of the galaxy! Noonien tragically died more bitter and hateful than ever at 315.[221] His cryogenic sleep seemed to have aggravated his monomania.

It was an anachronistic death ray report from the Galactic Council,[222] with which we had had many dealings, that led us to investigate "John Mayer" born in 1803. All seemed to rather go well until 1890 when retired professor "Mayer" let himself be manipulated by a woman once again. He built an anachronistic nuclear-powered laser for a former student, Isabel Reed, at his retreat in Gutenberg. Once again his intentions had been good, just as they had been in building the time machine originally, to save lives this time by destroying a threatening asteroid. As we seemed to prove over and over again in this and countless other cases, the road to hell is paved with such good intentions.[223] A passing alien happened to decide without authorization of the Galactic Council that this space gun posed too great a threat to the galaxy and took it upon itself to destroy it.

The non-corporeal attempted this by possessing "Mayer's" assistant Thomas and when that proved insufficient Marco himself. Dr. Paul Rosten meanwhile complicated the situation by attempting to court "Mayer's" niece Laura. He and Thomas managed to rig the ray gun to explode, killing themselves and all who knew its secret.

Holmes attempted to close the time loop as the disembodied Eye, explaining the situation to the alien in the name of the Galactic Council, so that it released his host "Mayer". Thomas however reacted negatively to being dispossessed and we could not prevent him from killing either Isabel or Laura.[224] The explosion did indeed destroy the death ray, even to providentially and retroactively bent this timeline pastward. Holmes was therefore able to warn Paul about Thomas's possession soon enough to save not only Isabel but Laura as well. With the death ray destroyed, the alien destroyed the asteroid itself.

Paul and Laura were therefore able to marry along with Thomas and Isabel in a double wedding in 1936. Their children Thomas and Isabel Rosten and Paul and Laura Thomas eventually married. Their grandchildren Thomas and Laura Rosten and Paul and Isabel Thomas also married, both naming their oldest son after great granduncle "John Mayer". In an alternative timeline Thomas Reed and Isabel married and Paul Mayer and Laura Rosten married. Their children, Paul and Laura Reed and Thomas and Isabel Mayer married, and again named their oldest son after "John Mayer". John Reed, Sr. became a Chicago detective.[225]

As a side effect Marco's new time trajectory now veered off in the direction of xenometallurgy, not definitely good or evil, but possibly either. The amnesiac Marco was found by Mother Rukh in Hungary, giving him the name of her son, Janos, lost in the Great War. This "Janos Rukh" earned a doctorate in astrophysics, which her biological son would never have been able to do, eventually organizing an expedition to Nigeria. There however he became exposed to the element he called Radium X, but which because of its mutagenic effects and greenish glow I suspect was more likely kryptonite.[226]

With my knowledge of futuristic medicine I surreptitiously assisted Dr. Felix Benet in saving "Rukh's" life, but unknown to either of us, because of his multiple exposures to it, he had built up an immunity, but acquired fatal, contagious dosage, a "death touch". Even worse his madness returned triggered by his mis-perceived betrayal of his wife Diane with Ronald Drake, reminding him subconsciously of his wives Jane and Lenore. We were aided in triggering a timely time leap by his foster mother Rukh. I had accidentally blinded her with the Eye, like Leah, while attempting to stop Marco before developing the chronoscope that lead to his ill-fated expedition. By the gracious intervention of our Client she did not hold my error against her "son" and he temporarily overcame his madness to cure her blindness. I reckoned it as miraculously as Tobit's cure.[227]

"Mother, can you see, can you see?", he asked.

"Yes, I can see...", his foster mother answered, "more clearly than ever and what I see frightens me."

What she saw was that not only his body had been affected by exposure to the meteor's radiation, the "cure" had affected his mind. He had become blinded by intellectual hubris, a temptation to which my friend Holmes was prone to as well.

Feeling yet again betrayed by his wife, and forgetting that he had let Diane think him dead to protect her, he now sought to kill her and all the rest of the cursed expedition. When Ronald Drake and Diane

Rukh were married at the Church of Six Saints, its six statues came to symbolize those he thought of as his six enemies. [228] He monomaniacally did <u>not</u> kill a seventh person <u>not</u> on his list, the innocent Prof. Meikeljohn, but only knocked him out to gain entrance to the objects of his vengeance.

"He broke the first law of science," Mother Rukh said, as she mercifully destroyed Benet's "medicine" sending her "son" to yet another death. "There are some secrets we are not meant to probe."[229] She said this, of course, having been clued in by Holmes that he shan't stay dead and that we were working on repairing what he'd broken.

Dr. Benet's discoveries in optography[230] apparently were also one of those secrets, not meant to be known, at least not yet. In his shock at identifying "Dr. Rukh" as the killer, he dropped the evidence and then killed by him.[231]

A nearby branch timeline lead to an alternative "Janos Rukh", whom I and Dr. Benet actually did manage to cure without the maddening side effect and who did re-marry Diane. He did however change his name to "Karl Mandel", since "Janos Rukh" had been declared dead and to discourage ex-husband Drake from tracing them, though he did remain a globetrotting astrophysicist. He contributed his greatest discovery to the field however, when he accidentally detected strange radio waves from a Mexican volcano in 1971. Diane had by then died, but with their daughter, Corinne, and her fiancee Mark Wilhelm we watched as they found a "primordial plasma" that fed on blood enriched with fear-induced hormones such as adrenaline.

With psychologist Helga's assistance they built a chamber of horrors to collect this needed "fearjuice". The bloodthirsty lava creature however eventually extruded a feeding tentacle to acquire food for itself, so "Mandel" decided to end the experiment by cutting off its heat source and shutting down the computer interface.

As Holmes and I observed Mark and Corinne near the volcano, all four of us saw Roland now apparently completely mad, ranting about diamonds. I'd noticed the lobotomy scar on his forehead when we'd first seen him and suspected that something like this would be the result.

"That's what the creature promised if we fed it, diamonds, the location of all the diamonds in the world." Corinne explained.

"What shall it profit a man ..."[232] I commented.

"Indeed." Holmes replied. "We must not faff. We cannot waste a moment."

We re-focused our mind's eyes back on "Mandel" and found him trying to reprogram the computer. He explained, as Mark took over for him, that Helga had kept the experiment going, getting Roland to kill the rest of the staff for the rock creature with promise of diamonds. When she belatedly realized the creature was a harbinger of an infestation from the underworld and tried to shut down the computer again, Roland fed her to the creature.

As I whistled a happy tune taught me by Anna Leonowens during a similar situation[233] to encourage Corinne not to be afraid, the other men, guided by Holmes, managed to reprogram the computer in record time . The would-be invader cooled back into a living lava, then cooled further into obsidian dormancy. The exertion however had been too much for "Mandel" and his machine chronoported him out of Corinne's arms, out of his body and out of our reach once again.[234]

Mark and Corinne Wilhelm named their children Karl and Diane after the names she knew her parents by, while in the alternative timeline in which Roland and Helga Mandel survived to marry, they named theirs Wilhelm, Mark and Corinne. Karl Wilhelm married Corinne Mandel, while her time clone Diane Wilhelm married Wilhelm Mandel, so their children in the two equally viable timelines were respectively, Mark Mandel and Karla Wilhelm. We were pleasantly surprized when they converged with their courtship and marriage and the birth of Wilhelm Mandel, who also became a xenogeologist.

Holmes and I encountered a similar Obsidian invasion after the bengilbertite meteor shower near San Angelo, California, in 1957. With a well-aimed Eyebeam Holmes set off the unexploded dynamite that burst the dam that released the flood that stopped the rocks that threatened the town[235] that St. Juniper Serra built. I managed to save little Ginny Simpson from death by petrification like her mother by using the Slade vita-ray. Geologist Dave Miller named the strange and deadly new mineral after his colleague Ben Gilbert who discovered and died from it. After adopting Ginny, he and his wife, Cathy, honored him further by naming their sons, Ben and Gilbert, after him also. Ginny's side effect super powers would come in handy for Dr. Wilhelm Mandel when rare rain in the desert re-activated the remnants and threatened San Angelo yet again.[236]

The Marco suspect we found in 1939 turned out not to be either a Marco relative or a time clone, but the escaped murderer Jonathan Brewster. Plastic surgeon and Adolphus throwback Dr. Herman Einstein, seemed to have retained an ancestral memory, since he had transformed Thomas into a "Scarabus" look-alike. Holmes was able to assist the police in apprehending him and his mostly harmless, yet criminally insane aunts, Abby and Martha,[237] just in time to prevent Mr. Witherspoon from being added to their list of victims, unknowingly beating Thomas's kill count.[238] After this trauma Thomas's brother Mortimer and his new wife Elaine sold the family home and moved away, changed their surname to Cook, and raised several children, including a son named Theodore.

Holmes immediately detected the hand of our mad doctor again when Theodore was dubbed "The Atomic Sailor" by the tabloids in 1968. Our mad doctor was then still using the name "Montserrat" after re-locating from England. His repressed memories had prompted him to return to experiments with radiation, this time for the U. S. Navy, with volunteers again like he had as "Prof. Billings". Fortunately I was able to cure Theodore "Cookie" Cook with vita-rays from my little black bag of tricks.[239]

"Montserrat" tried a different sort of experiment on Theodore's cousin Clement,[240] cybernetic puppetry,[241] an "improvement" on his "thought transferal device". His old rival Dr. Browning from London had found him just as we had however, reviving the nearly forgotten "Scarabus"-Craven feud.[242]

Back in 1947 we visited the New York morgue where a man answering our mad doctor's description had been brought in by plain clothes bobby "Pat" Patterson. From the evidence of the violent attack on the morgue attendant, Holmes suspected this missing man was not our missing man Marco himself, but rather his evil look-alike Jonathan Brewster, now nicknamed "Gruesome", the real "King of Killers" that "Tulpur" had been misidentified with. Soon afterward banks begin to be robbed using a sleeping gas. Holmes connected the two, concluding that Brewster was not actually dead as first reported, but only temporarily paralyzed, and that he was the one behind the robberies, though not the futuristic weapon.

Following that trail lead us to discovering that Dr. Lee Thal's gas was actually stolen from another missing man, Prof. A. Tomic, by the professor's colleague Dr. Irma Learned. When the piano player "Melody" Fiske shot a cop and was in turn shot by the trigger-happy Det. Richard Tracy, Holmes tried to suggest that a body be substituted to draw out Brewster. The ever-impulsive Tracy however resisted Holmes's suggestion and insisted on taking Brewster's place himself. Holmes and I meanwhile discovered the kidnapped Tomic and destroyed the rest of Tomic's gas. Tracy's deception however triggered Brewster to kill both Learned and Thal and he seems in turn to be killed by Tracy.[243] When we let it play out other ways round, with Brewster killing Tracy, or alternatively with them killing each other, alas Chief Brandon resigned a year early, Patterson was promoted to police chief and "Fearless" Fosdick,[244] rather than Sam Catchem, tried to replace the irreplaceable Tracy. Dyne O'Matick thus did not invent the Space Coupe in 1962, and so no Moon Valley People were found in 1969 by Neil Armstrong or "Buzz" Aldrin, Jr.

To confuse our quest further we found two more Marco clones in the Tyrolean Alps, his "half-brothers" or "hyphenated halflings" as Holmes called them. The malfunctioning time machine this time had evidently split Marco's personality into the proverbial good twin and bad twin, Anton and Baron Gregor de Bergman.

Gregor had been torturing and killing women in the secret room of the family estate. Holmes explained to me that to rejoin the two personality fragments back into one Marco, we had to wait until both of them had been freed from a particular timeline and then close both time loops. It literally was "murder" for me to watch as the baron killed his brother, his good half, and then took his place pretending to be good without trying to intervene. I had to watch further as Gregor killed Thea Hassel's father and framed her lover Albert. By way of soothing my discomfort and perhaps his own as well, Holmes graciously allowed me the honor of releasing Anton's dog with a well-placed Eye-beam and end the madness, or so we thought.[245]

Marco's personality remained fragmented even after both Anton and Gregor had died, and the fragments careened off in two completely different directions through metatime. Holmes designated the good personality fragment as "Henry W." or "Henry" and the evil one as "H. William" or "William",[246] so that we now had Henry the Good, William the Bad, Jonathan the Ugly and the original, just plain weird Marco.[247] Much of our quest would now involve determining which was which and dealing with each appropriately.

Holmes was well aware of the problems of having such an evil twin, a fact my secretive friend had revealed to me only a short time before. His own twin half-brother, Sherlock Rutherford Holmes, not only frequently impersonated my dearest friend, William Sherlock Holmes, but was a dhampir, a half-vampire.[248] He was eventually able to control his condition well enough to start his own rival detective agency.[249] It was Rutherford however who during his manic vampiric episodes begot several children by Irene Norton neé Adler. John Hamish Adler,[250] aka "Auguste Lupa", "Julius Adler", and "Cesar Mycroft" became better known as "Nero Wolfe",[251] after contracting lycanthropy. Others were Scott Adler[252] aka "Marko Vilšič?" Other half-siblings were: Damian Adler[253], Johanna Adler,[254] Neige Adler[255] and Mycroft Adler.[256] By Vassiliev she had a daughter, Nina Vassilievna.[257]

She also had several children perhaps by her husband Godfrey "Jeffrey" Norton, but perhaps not, Christine[258], Ralph[259], Irene[260] and Emily[261]. We did not investigate too closely. We did manage to stop the conception of Hamish John Adler in an alternative timeline, but awkwardly lycanthrope John Hamish Adler nevertheless had a dhampir son, Spenser Holmes.[262] He also adopted a lycanthrope daughter, Carla Luvchen Wolfe. Scott, who because of his compulsive sexual addiction, Holmes deemed also likely a dhampir, begot at least four sons by four different women, including Archie Goodwin, "Wolfe's" biographer, by Leslie Goodwin; Frank Cannon[263] by Erica Canon née Russell; Jason Lochivar McCabe[264] by Emily McCabe née Russell and Michael Wiseman Knight[265] by Michele Wiseman. Damian and Yolanda Chin Adler had a daughter, ironically named Estelle.[253]

By a wife with the maiden name Falkland, Rutherford begot a son he named Sherlock Rutherford Holmes, who had sons Junior [266] and Richard, and a daughter Shirley.[267] She married a Mr. Robinson and had a son Dan. Junior had sons, Mycroft and Richard, and daughter Shelley. By Vivian S. La Graine he also begot two daughters, Minerva Holmes and Alice "Boomer" La Graine.[268] By a Miss Moth he begot Abraham Moth.[269] By Emilie Charlotte "Lily" Le Breton Langtry he begot a daughter Jeanne-Marie.[270]

We found no evidence that "Henry" was either a vampire or a dhampir, thank God!, though he, like "William", had many time clones. Holmes and Musgrave had first met a truly evil "William" time clone while students at Cambridge using the name "Ch'ing Chung-Fu".[271] It wasn't until the Boxer Rebellion that Shan Ming-Fu became obsessed with a vendetta against Holmes's uncle and later especially his nephew, Denis Nayland Smith, who battled him as "Fu Manchu", "the Devil Doctor"[272] many times.

Shan's son, Shan Shilin Li, however, with a little help from the Eye, escaped the influence of his father, anglicized his name to "Charlie Chan", moved to Hawaii[273] and providentially became the father of a whole clan of crime fighters. Our Client did yet again delight us by turning evil to the good. We helped Chan quite few times as well as his sons, Lee[274], Charlie, Jr.[275], Jimmy, Tommy[276] and Barry[277] and his grandchildren, Anne, Henry, Nancy, Suzie, Alan,[278] and Lee, Jr.[279] as well as the adopted Chan, "Jackie".[280]

We encountered great grandfather Shan many more times under many aliases, particularly after he also found the life-prolonging royal jelly elixir as Holmes had. He masterminded countless evil schemes under the aliases "Dr. Lo-Fan"[281], "Hanoi Shan"[282], "Mr. King"[283], "Dr. Sun Ah Poy"[284], and "Dr. Natas,[285] from the Arretian for Satan. Arretian is the language of Arret in a fast-flowing, backcurrent of time, the so-called Counter-clock timeline.[286] It has been use by Rock Men of Mongo,[287] Giovanni and Zatanna Zatara,[288] the Iarcho[289], and satanists[290].

As with other such subuniverses, like Narnia, time flows vary widely.[291] In the Arretians' ancient future they will have/once had explored and colonized a contracting galaxy, but their empire was finally destroyed with their home planet half a million of their years in their past. Since the interdimensional time ratio is -3000:1 that synchronizes with our year 2430. The Arretian language survived throughout the isolated colony worlds and by our year 2271 they had, or will have, or whatever the tense is, finally became or will become a spacefaring civilization again for the first or second time.

One group of wayward colonists crossed an interdimensional bridge and settled on Scalos. They soon found however they had retained their speedster metabolism[292], and even worse that all their males had been rendered sterile. They were dying rather than growing younger and doing so very fast. They solved the sterility problem by literally introducing new blood, so that Queen Deela became the Eve of Scalos, "Mother of the Living".[293] They soon also found that the blood of the newest starship captain they'd kidnapped had also supplied them with the adrenaline needed to slow them to our continuum's normal time flow.[294] By 2268 three survivors in soul-spheres were discovered buried deep beneath Arret, the loyalists Sargon and Thalassa and the revolutionary Henoch, but all three soon were dead,[295] undeniably and reliably dead.[296]

Ah, yes, I was on the subject of the "William" clone, Shan Ming-Fu, wasn't I? He had another son Shang Chi[297] and a daughter by Princess Sonia Omanoff, Fah Lo Suee, who also had a fondness for using aliases, "Madame Ingomar", "Queen Mamaloi", "Ling Moy"[298]. As "Lin Tang", she had at least one daughter, Dwan Ming aka "Myra Reldon", by none other than Holmes's archenemy Prof. James Moriarty[299], two sons by two fathers, Robert Greville by Shan Greville[300] and John "Hannibal" Smith by her father's archenemy Sir Denis Neyland Smith[301] and a granddaughter, Leiko Smith.[302]

We found both "Henry" and "William" manifested in "Dr. Henry Jekyll" as he was known in this particular timeline. He had turned his medical experiments away from biology to vitology, the science of artificial life. This was not, as Stevenson misinterpreted it, to separate the good and evil in Everyman, but rather to reunite one poor fractured soul. We had investigated this multiple personality, Henry/William, for G. Jeffery Utterson back in 1883 without learning much at all about the case.[303] Now we observed half-brother "William" murdering Sir Danver Carew after hitting the Palmer girl.[304] We traced the timeline back further and discovered that it was 1874 when "William" had first burst out, triggered when "Henry" caught his wife Kitty cheating with gambler Paul Allen. "William" periodically and unpredictably continued to kill thereafter.[305]

Tracing back even further we learnt that "Henry" and Kitty had become the guardians of his patient Mrs. Edwards's fatherless daughter Vicky in 1871. Her father had disappeared ten years earlier at the outbreak of the American Civil War. As Mrs. Edwards's health finally failed she trustingly turned to her friend and doctor, neither of them suspecting "what evil lurks in the hearts of men".[306]

When Vicky's father, Louis Burton "Slim" Edwards, Jr. along with his partner, Harry Tubman

"Tubby" Phillips, an ancestor of Freddy Phillips, finally returned from America, we assisted in their investigation of Dr. Stephen J. Poole's murder in Hyde Park. Edwards's involvement in what was called in the papers the Hyde Park Killer case prompted "William" to call himself "Edward Hyde". Phillips not unexpectedly had gotten them both removed from the case. Mostly we just tried to prevent the two of them from suspecting each other. Edwards often disappeared, secretly checking up on his now grown daughter, which made Phillips suspicious. The accident-prone Phillips's accidents were almost beyond the Eye's power to circumvent.

Phillips accidentally drank concoction, apparently similar to metamorphine[307], which temporarily manifested his latent rodenthropy.[308] Later he also was accidentally injected with another formula that turned him into a beastly High Park Killer look-alike, spreading a contagious infection by bite, like rabies though much faster-acting, confusing the Yard even more than usual. Bruce Adams saved Vicky and freed Henry/William to separate again.[309] Meanwhile having reconciled with her long-lost father, Vicky and Bruce named their children Louise and Burton.

One of Jekyll's potions became contaminated with werewoman virus[310] however, splitting his personality ever further, metamorphing "Hyde" into "Rowena" and "Henry" into "Heidi", so that there were now four personality fragments.[311] "Henry" and "Rowena" co-operated with each other, but were no match for the other two, even when they worked against each other.[166] "Hyde" lusted for both his half-sister "Heidi" and his sister-in-law Sara Crawford. We managed to protect Miss Crawford, but he also threatened Lucy Harris,[312] cousins Millicent Carewe[313] and Muriel Carew and murdered both Ivy Pearson and Muriel's father.[314] Yet another "fiancée", Fanny Osborne, killed Dr. Lanyon, Rev. Donald Regan and Mrs. Osborne,[315] after which "Hyde" killed her and managed to frame her for all of his and "Heidi's" killings.

The time knot got more complicated when "William" as both "Hyde" and "Heidi" went in league with Moriarty against "William" as Shan Ming-Fu.[316] Incredibly it got even more complex as "Hyde's" and "Heidi's" and "Henry's" and "Rowena's" children and grandchildren continued to rediscover the family's secret recipe.

Sarah Lanyon's son Edward by "Hyde" was raised by Dr. John Utterson,[317] while his half-sister "Edwina" killed totties Betsy, Susan, Yvonne, and Prof. Robinson.[318] Dr. Marlow had an evil half-brother "Edward Blake",[319] as well as a half-sister also named "Edwina" and so was both uncle and aunt to Ellen Farrell, the love child of Dido Utterson.[320] By Howard Spencer, this "Edwina" gave birth to Howard Spenser, Jr., father of Richard Jacks and his half-sister "Helen Hyde".[321]

Benjamin Grimm[322], and especially the Banner boys[323] and their cousin Jennifer Walters[324] bimorphed into violent subhuman beasts, worse than even their grandfather, the Hyde Park Killer, or the Banner boys' father. I diagnosed this as the result of exposure to phazite that causes incredible, fantastic metamorphoses.[325] Janet Smith, although not inheriting the affliction, was viciously told she had by George Hastings, who was trying to cover his own murders. We were gratuitously allowed by our Client to influence Dr. Lomas to counter the heterosuggestion. She eventually married her savior and they had a son Robert, who also became a doctor.[326]

In a particularly refreshing timeline, for me more so than for Holmes, in which Benjamin Grimm was permanently freed from "The Thing", he and Alicia Reiss Masters were married and had children, Reed Richards "Rich", Susan and John, who became an actor.[327] Then, that is in this same timeline, Robert and Betsy Banner's child, Robert Thaddeus "Thad", and David's wife Caroline both survived. David and Caroline had a son, David Benton "Ben" Banner. Jennifer married Mark Mason after his first wife, Louise died, and they had triplets, that they named for her cousins, Roberta, David and Bruce. David, Jr., became known as "Section" in 2025.[328]

Teddy Hyde merely morphed into a party animal[329], while Daniel Jekyll became a sex and drug addict.[330] Worst of all however was Norman Hyde who morphed into politician "Brent Jekyll".[331]

We could only agonizingly observe Inspector Willowby's seemingly futile, but ultimately successful, apprehension of Vampira Hyde[332], ending her many exploits in Prof. Grossenfibber's time machine.[333] Sister Jacqueline Hyde also had access to a time machine, a chronoskimmer, stolen by the Viper gang, which she used to steal from the Polos in 1271 and from "Beethoven", in 1808 as his "Immortal Beloved". To find Vampira however we had help the Acme Detective Agents track down the rest of gang.[334]

They found Sir Vile in 1446 BC when he stole *the Book of the Dead*, encountered Christopher Peeper and Joy[335] and prevented the Exodus[336] and again in 1505 BC when he stole the "Mona Lisa" and providentially broke "Leonard's" jester machine.

They found Ivan in 50 BC when he stole the whole Roman forum and Baron Grinnit in 1002 when he stole Leif Eriksson's ship and prevented him from bringing Christianity to either Greenland or Vinland[337] and in 1805 when he stole Lewis and Clark's journals. They found Medeva in 1015 Japan where she stole Murasaki Shikibu's *The Tale of Genji*. Gen. Mayhem they found in 1086 when he stole the *Domesday Book* and apprehended him in 1776 when he stole a draft of "the Declaration of Independence."

We watched as Buggs Zapper stole Mansa Musa of Mali's salt during his pilgrimage in 1324 and they confiscated Zapper's anachronistic scales. In 1519 they stopped him from stealing Montezuma's headdress. They also stopped Jane Reaction from stealing Patchacuti Yupanqui's quipu in 1460 and again in 1599 from stealing a manuscript from Shakespeare, while he was distracted by the Carrionites invasion.[338] Dr. Belljar in 1493 stole Columbus' charts, while the captain was distracted by Herbie "Fat Fury" Popnecker.[339] Dee Cryption in 1879 stole Edison's first lightbulb, but left behind an anachronistic force field generator, allowing Edison to reverse engineer the time machine used by Robert "Qwerty" Stevens in the future.[340] Voyager Phineas Bogg and Jeremy Jones helped Edison re-invent lightbulb.[341]

After helping round up all of her gang we finally found their leader Carmen Sandiego herself in 1492 trying to steal Columbus's ships. In the timeline where she succeeded, Magellan discovered the New World, Texas remained independent and President of Texas L. B. Johnson was assassinated in 1963.[342] Columbus however was encouraged by Isabella's bravery broach[343], though Sandiego did manage to steal his fourth ship[344] and was finally found with her stolen chronoskimmer hiding in *Vostok I* in 1961.

What we didn't know in 1808 however was that the author of the mysterious "Immortal Beloved" letter was not actually Ludwig von Beethoven, but rather the long-lived Akharin, who had also been known as "Methuselah", "Solomon", "Alexander", "Lazarus", "Merlin", "Leonardo", and "Brahms", among other historical personages.[345]

Because of the portal opened by Vampira, "Beethoven" was nearly driven mad by telepathic time travelers.[346] Akharin, of course, survived as he had many times before, but in an alternative timeline his "Tenth Symphony" reunited Germany in ten years.[347] Time travelers Sherman "Pet Boy" Peabody and his foster father from 1962 visited twice.[348] William Preston and Theodore Logan from 1989[349] and Oliver Gates from 1999 went even further and fetched him.[350]

Akharin's *History* revealed in 2270 that he'd not only experienced, but shaped history. He was Daedalos, "the Craftsman", inventing the saw, axe, plumb-line, drill, glue, and isinglass[351], who built the Labyrinth to house the bull-headed Minotaur and invented the glider to survive the fall of Minoan Empire in 1629 BC,[352] used again in 2010 by Pete and Myka escape Warehouse 2.[353] He helped steal Pandora's box that turned Medusa's hair to snakes[354], but she refused to let anyone sacrifice their life for hers.[355] His son Ikaros also opened the infamous box at "Daedalos's" re-marriage[356], disobeying his father.[357]

He was the Two-thousand-year-old Man[358] described by "Qoheleth", the former Prince Solomon. Originally a pauper called "Jedediah"[359], he took the place of the prince on the condition that he commission the building of the Temple and so indirectly was responsible for Hiram Abiff founding the Masons. When Sadler the time traveling assassin killed Hiram,[360] Akharin raises him from the dead by the Name[361] written on Enoch's Gold Plate, made and hidden back when he was "Methuselah".

They ironically helped the destroy it in 586 BC.[364] The Eye however helped the scribes Joshua, Ezra, Deuel and Paltiel escape with the sacred scrolls.[363] He added some slight modifications to Hiram's design however by adding the narrow way between the Righteousness Gate pillars, the so-called Paradise Bridge gap between the courtyard stones and the Voice of the Prince of the World trumpet.[364] He taught Shazam how to turn the powers of Hercules, Achilles, Zeus, Atlas and Mercury to the good via Wisdom.[365]

As "Alexander" Akharin did not really need the cell activator that Atlan gave him[366] to save him from being "killed" by the savage Vandar Adg's time-bomb[367] or Thaddeus Tugwell's help to "save" him from "Mean" Morgan.[368] Holmes and I did however make sure that the Green Lantern from 1947 undid Per Degaton's undoing of Alexander's victory at Arbela.[369] The Eye also stopped him from attacking queen Candice of Nubia[370] or being defeated by Queen Sisygambis of Persia.[371] We also prevented him from "dying" in 334 BC[372] or not "dying" until 280 BC[373], but exactly as prophesied by our Client's spokesperson Daniel thirty-nine weeks of years before.[374]

At just over three thousand years old Akharin finally did die. By then he was providentially calling himself "Lazarus" a variant of Eleazar meaning "Whom God saves". Like Abraham, he had lied and called Martha and Mary his sisters when actually they were his granddaughters, though no one in Bethany except him remembered that. Jesus however knew and used the name in a parable to contrast the poverty of this life with the glory of the life to come. Akharin remembered the pauper-turned-prince "Jedediah", recognized the no-longer mysterious Name on the Golden Plate of Enoch and became a disciple and friend of the Savior.[375] When Jesus raised him from the dead,[376] he was given a new life, another couple millennia in which to gain the Wisdom the real Solomon had asked for. "Lazarus" then become a name associated with resurrection.[377] He became the first bishop of Marseilles, leading to much confusion within and outside of the Priory of Sion. Time traveler Dan Brown aka Jean XXVIII, nautonnier of the Priory of Sion, tried to replace Mary Magdalene as the Beloved Disciple, and thus the first Christian priestess twenty centuries ahead of time[378], and the mother of Jesus Secundus.[379] This other Jesus and his wife, using the names "Narcissus" and "Pallas", lived in Rome under Claudius and their sons served as procurators of Judea.[380]

After four centuries Akharin gained a reputation as the demonspawn "Myrddin",[381] mentoring young "Wart"[382] and with Solomon's ring helping the demonized Etrigan re-incarnate as "Jason Blood".[383] He learnt much about the future from visiting time travelers Tony Newman and Doug Phillips from 1964[384] and from visiting it himself when summoned to 1955 by Lana Lang.[385]

In the steampunk timeline triggered by the Voracian C20 plot[386], Akharin again as "Merlin" revived the former "Wart", King Arthur, from suspended animation in 1892 to fight time-traveling Morlocks.[387] In 1976 he helped Arthur's successor Brian "Capt. Britain" Braddock,[388] Arthur having finally died.[389] He went a bit mad during the battle of Arfderydd in 573[390] from being both fetched with and without Princess Genevieve and/or Duke Leland of Tunstall to 2002 by Jimmy Noseleather's time machine.[391]

Akharin assumed the identity of Leonardo da Vinci, when the young painter was accused of the capital crime of sodomy in 1484 and assumed his role of nautonier of the Priory of Sion. Leonardo, who was actually what would later be called genderfluid, became "Lisa di Firenze", the model for the most famous painting ever by "Leonardo".

Holmes and I watched helplessly as Mr. Peabody accidentally destroyed the original canvas "Mona Lisa", so that "Leonardo"[392] was forced to paint another, much better version, the one with the legendary Mona Lisa smile, on wood. That Sir Vile of the Viper gang stole the painting we already knew, but after the Acme Agents restored it, the robot Bender Rodríguez from 3007 re-stole it.[393]

"Leonardo" was then forced by "Capt. Tancredi", actually one of the fragmented time clones of Scaroth the Last Jagaroth from 40,000,000 B. C., to paint six copies. They were however secretly identified from the original by Dr. John Smith", of which only one of the copies survived the fire in 1979.[394]

Rodenthrope Geronimo Stilton from 2010 searched for the painting as "Stiltoneaux" in 1517, but found it was not stolen after all.[395] In 1894 Moriarty had yet another copy made, but was foiled in making the switch.[396] Peter Vernet painted still another copy when the original was stolen in 1911, when Ryder was poisoned.[397]

On the *Titanic* in 1912 we watched helplessly again as Prof. Van Dusen[398] remained behind so others might be saved. Arsène Lupin[399], Lecoq[400], C. Auguste Dupin[401], Luther Trant[402], Holmes's cousin A. J. Raffles[403] and Holmes himself, found many copies throughout the ship[404], including six by Yves Chaudron.[405] Phineas Bogg and Jeffrey from 1982 saved both original "Mona Lisa" and Olivia Dunn.[406]

Benjamin Smyth[407], Irene Norton, Holly Storm-Fleming, blackmailed Elisabeth Von Stern, and Col. Moriarty escaped the sinking ship. Ed Strickley did not, but was garrotted,[408] while Van Dusen's chronicler Jacques Futrelle died saving Holmes's life.[409] Simon Morley from 1970 survived, but he could not save Archibald "Agent Z" Butt, who would have prevented the Great War.[410]

Even after five tries Holmes and I could not prevent the ship from sinking.[411] We were however able to prevent the angel Balthazar from preventing it.[412] When he had, the stock market did not crash in 1929,[413] Astor financed Tesla, so that Tesla could invent the laser deathray,[414] Tesla and Edison shared the Nobel prize in physics in 1915 and prevented the sinking of the *Lusitania*.[413] Tesla lit New York City in 1916. In 1920 veep Cox died in the crash of *Airship One*, witnessed from the *Titanic*. In 1921 Tesla Broadcasting Corp. was founded. By 1935 Tesla Dynamics invented the chronoscope. In 1945 they hired ex-convict Alan Turing.[415] Having time travel soon after ward Tesla recruited Richard I in 1192, Natalie Walker in 2012, and Redjac-possessed Robbie Mueller in 2014.[416]

We helped these Chrononauts find and destroy Earth-threatening futuretech at Chernoble in 1986,[417] They also destroyed Thorian A-bomb in 1898[418], H. G. Well's A-bomb in 1914[419], Hitler's in both 1939[420] and 1944[421], Japan's in 1945[422], Korean's in 1954[423], the plutonium bomb in 1957[424], the G-bomb in 1962[425], the N-bomb in 1979[426], Sadam Housan's in 1990, Crughons'[427] and Vandar Adg's time-bombs throughout time.[356]

If Butt had prevented the first world war there could logically not be any other world wars[16] until the First-and-Last World War, which would have come much sooner than it should have, with the prophesied thousandth generation of the Covenant with Abraham.[428] This in turn implied much shorter, unnatural generations as with manimals[429] or underpeople.[430]

All the time travelers escaped the *Titanic*, including Randall, Fidget, Strutter, Og, Wally, Vermin, Kevin,[431] Jack, Annie[432], Isabel Soto who dealt with a cursed mummy,[433] Tony Newman and Doug Phillips.[343] 1114-yr-old Amanda Darieux sank with the ship, but being an undead vampire could not die again.[435] Helen Magnus[436] was saved by "the Unsinkable" Molly Brown.[437]

When "Leonardo" timetraveled himself with the Martian Exigius-12½ to 1966, his "Mona Lisa" seemed accidentally destroyed again by the Martian's adopted nephew Timothy O'Hara, cousin of the Banner boys. This copy was however replaced by the Martian's copy.[438] This copy of a copy however would become the one destroyed in the fire in 1978, the original having been rescued again by Phineas Bogg and Jeffrey just as they did in 1911 and it was returned by one of Bender's timeclones.[393]

"Leonardo" also timetraveled with Gallifreyan "Dr. John Smith" to both 2 BC and 1961.[439] He was visited by many times by timetravelers, Jason and Gareth from 1968[440], 9-Eyes the robot from 1992[123], Amelia the robot from 1996[441], Providence Traveler from 2003[442], the barmy Time Warp Trio, Joe, Sam and Jack from 2004[443] and Mario Ravelli from 2523.[444] He therefore soon improved upon them all to build a hand-held space-time machine, the first omni. Akharin had not only shaped history, but also re-shaped it and left his mark on it.[445]

With his omni "Leonardo" recovered the second canvas "Mona Lisa" in 1533, which had been stolen by gypsies after Mister Peabody had destroyed the first the one. In doing so he also reunited Danielle and Prince Henry.[446] He helped build Machu Piccu in 1090,[447] met Sir Wilhelm "the Robin Hood of Wursthurg" and Helena in 968[448], and reached the moon in 1483[449]. He visited and then undid a future in which his own premature futuretech[450] was misused by Nicoli Machivelli,[451] leading to the Spanish Rebellion's Reign of Terror and reanimation.[452] He also suppressed the introduction of computers that would have been opposed by the Inquisition.[453] After his "death" the Vatican however did unwisely try to use his timemachine to prevent the Reformation and promote the Stuart dynasty.[454] The Stuarts had to flee to New Britain however when France conquered England in 1745[455], and by 1831 abolitionists were still fighting slavery in Camelot.[456] The timemachine was eventually stolen by Capt. William Blood[457], of no known relation to Jason Blood.[383]

It was, in fact, used and misused, many times once it fell out of Akharin's possession. The vampire Livia Quintus Lucellus used it to travel back to the reign of Caligula to find Jergan.[458] Françoise Suchet used it to go back to avenge Henri Foucault who'd cursed her with vampirism.[459] Lucy Rossano used it to bring Galen from the Ninth Century[460] and Diana Dearborn to bring Sir Gawain from the original Camelot to 2010.[461]

Akharin's next notable secret identity was "Nicolaus de Thuronia", the name he used to finally get a University education, after which he Latinized the name "Nicholas Koppernik" to "Nicholas Copernicus". As such he was again visited by a robot from 1996, this one named Spark.[125] In 1443 he was persecuted by our Client's archenemy, the actual saboteur of Marco's time machine and the thief of Akharin's.

We had come to know our adversary[462] quite well in fact under many disguises. We knew him in Mesopotamia as Akem-Manā, the "creator" of unreality, the Father of Lies[463] and as Azza(z(el)).[464] We knew him in Greece as Apophis and in Egypt as both Apep[465] and Set.[466] We fought him in the Great Galactic War of 1,200,000 BC, when he set, no pun intended, Garbesh against the Cyén empire. We aided Andrea "Isis" Thomas against him in 1977,[467] Henry "the Hammer" Jones, Sr., in 3000[468] and on Aitheran in the Cigar galaxy in 4012.[469]

As Belial we saw him dance before "Solomon".[470] Only after many such confrontations did we come to understand our enemy as As(h)teroth, able to manifest as either the evil, ugly Asteroth[471], or *en femme* as the seemingly beautiful, seemingly good Ashteroth.[472] He became so well-known to us we began calling him simply Ol' Nick.[473]

We were not successful in saving Tom Walker in 1727,[474] but did help Daniel Webster beat Ol' Nick in 1849.[475] Nevertheless our Adversary was able to spread hatred from the War between the States and successfully possessing Hitler in 1920. Without any help from the Eye s/he was however exorcised from Giovanni Luciani, the father of the future John Paul I, in 1930 and Dag Hammarskjöld resisted him/her in 1961.[476] We helped thwart and his/her Antichrist many, many times[477] and Satanists even oftener.

In Hungary, for example, between the first and second world wars, the Maro's trail lead to a Satanic cult in the old Marmorosch Fortress, where our suspect had served during the war and ten thousand had died. "Hjalmar Poelzig", trying to distinguish himself from his more famous cousin, the architect Hans Poelzig, had rebuilt it in his own unique Bauhaus/Art Deco style into his "House of Destiny". We helped Peter Alison save his new bride Joan from the proverbial "fate worse than death", when she was threatened not only by "Poelzig", but by the mad Dr. Vitus Werdegast, who claimed to have endured fifteen years in prison. Although "Poelzig" lovingly preserved the bodies of the Werdegast's ex-wife Karen and his own stepdaughter, after he had unintentionally killed them when he was "not himself".

He pretended to intend to reanimate them with unexpected visitor Joan Alison's life force to lure Werdegast and "Baron Latos" and other vampires. His incantations were a clue missed by them and by me, but obvious to Holmes.

"Kah-vay kah-nee-oom." was actually "Cave Canium", Latin for "Beware of the Dog." he explained. "In vee-toh ver-ih-tass." was "In Vito Veritas." or "In wine there is truth." and "Koom grah-noh sah-liss." was "Cum grano salis", "with a grain of salt". They were similar to the mumble-jumble and hocus-pocus that "Scarabus" and the Cravens spouted to mask their legerdemain.

"Poelzig", who had now died more times than he could remember, calmly asked Werdegast, "Are we not both the living dead? And now you come to me, playing at being an avenging angel, childishly thirsting for my blood. We understand each other too well. We know too much of life. We shall play a little game, Vitus. A game of death, if you like..." They played a life-and-death chess game like Antonius Block did with Ol' Nick himself.[478]

Holmes and I knew even before "Poelzig's" reference to bloodthirst what kind of living dead Dr. Werdegast was, a vampire. We had investigated his claim of being a prisoner and found that he had indeed become one in Omsk, but died there shortly thereafter. Since then he had been pursued for most of those years by vampire-hunting catwoman, Catherine van Helsig.[479] That naturally implied that "Poelzig" in this timeline was the vampire's unnatural enemy, another kind of undead, a lycanthrope fighting a war far older war than the so-called Great War.[480] The sudden sight of his archenemy, "Cat", unnerved Werdegast enough to lose the chess game, yet he still ungentlemanly attempted to flay "Poelzig", knowing that that would not kill him. An Eyebeam was able to trigger the unexploded explosives in the old fortress, setting these prisoners free from each other, at least temporarily, if not from Ol' Nick.[481] "Cat", having used up her nine lives "gave up the ghost" and was freed as well. Peter and Joan Alison, who had survived the bus crash caused by Werdegast when he attacked their driver, also escaped "Poelzig's" madhouse with the Eye's help and finally reached Budapest. They named their daughter Catherine.

Oh, I didn't finish with the story of Akharin yet, did I? His unfinished *History* of the Trojan War, the War of the Roses, the rise and fall of the Roman empire and his time in Denmark in the Twelfth Century inspired plays ghostwritten for William Shakespeare. He also wrote about his time in Scotland in the Ninth Century BC, when King Bladud died attempting to fly with artificial wings like he had as "Daedalus".[482] Shakespeare had Mister Peabody from the Twentieth Century ghostwrite comedies for him, though he edited them extensively.[392, 359] Since Akharin was also later also "Francis Bacon", he did at least write some of Shakespeare's plays,[483] including the "lost" ones, *Vertigen and Rowena*, *Henry II*[484] and *King Arthur*[485] which Sherman "Pet Boy" Peabody returned and so "brought home the Bacon."

"Pseudo-Shakespeare" also encountered "Dr. John Smith" again, whom he'd kept missing as "Leonardo", now with new companion Martha of Freedonia,[486] and helped them defeat the evil Carronites.[487] He met this timetraveler yet again while a spy in Venice.[488] He was also visited by the short, but super, Mario "Jumpman" Mario, when he returned the pen and ink stolen by King Bowser Koopa[489] and visited Oliver Cates in 2001.[490]

By the time he assumed the identity of army deserter René Descartes in 1620, and because of his practice with mathematics as "Copernicus", Akharin was able to express in rigorous mathematics what he had known intuitively of geometry back as "Leonardo".

By the time he was known as "Isaac Newton", he was able to stretch his mathematics even further. Mario returned, without ever suspecting they had met before, this time to return a stolen apple.[489] "Newton" re-invented calculus that Archimedes had tried to teach him, but we did manage to close the timeline in which he discovered philosopher's mercury,[491] provoking the fall of the London asteroid.[492]

Akharin returned to his love for music as "Christoph Willibald von Gluck" and "William Schwenck Gilbert" and even found love and married Lucy Agnes Turner in 1911. Tragically however he too quickly lost her to death as he had so many other wives and lovers, yet again without siring any children. It was no wonder that the alternative timeline in which he instead married Johanna "Anne"

Sullivan[493], and in which they had a beloved daughter Rayna and a grandson Gilbert Kapec, remained for him but a fondly remembered dream. Their mime operettas, "The Lass That Loved a Sailor",[494] "The Slave of Duty"[495] and "The Town of Titip"[496] were unpopular with both critics and theatergoers alike however and so quickly forgotten, except by their fans, the Grateful Deaf.

By the 1960s Akharin was using the cover name "Derek Flint" and his vast experience and acquired abilities as an agent of Zonal Organization World Intelligence Espionage (ZOWIE). By the time he was trying to enjoy a well-deserved retirement to work on his Mayan cookbook and revised Kama Sutra, he was recruited by Mandated Actions for Covert Enforcement (MACE) to save the world yet again, this time from Galaxy's Proj. Damocles.[497] He came out of retirement to continue to fight Nazis, Commies and cyborgs.[498] He worked with Capt. Action, Honey West[499], Jethro "Green Lama" DuMont and Terry "Black Bat" Quinn[500] and at over five millennia rescued a kidnapped oilman.[501]

In the 1980s he worked undercover as "Wilson Evergreen" at the ironically named Da Vinci base in Antarctica and later for the infamous Khan Noonien Singh.[221] In 2051 as multimillionaire "Micah Brach", he backed Zephrem Cockrane's research into warp drive for the crew of the *Millennium*.[502] "Brach" had to disappear in 2070 however when we were unable to stop three attempts on his life and his survival was drawing undue suspicion.

He eventually fled his beloved Earth and assumed the identity of master painter "Sten of Marcus II", before homesickness forced him to return. There he worked with Richard Daystrom as "William Abramson" and shared the Nobel with him in 2237.[503] He helped save Boaco VI in 2266.[504] In seeking solitude to work on a secret project, he bought Holberg 917G, but in 2269 lost his near-perfect fembot that he'd named Rayna Kopek. Just as we had observed with Noonien Soong's Data's Lal on the starship *Enterprise*[505] and D'joan's robots on Fomalhaut III,[506] having the capacity to love, even for an AI, means being mortal. With his wounded heart finally broken, Akharin learnt he too was finally dying from Antaeus[507] Syndrome, terminal homesickness.

Ah yes, when was I? Sorry about that. I sometimes get sidetracked like I did with "The Country of the Saints", but that was way back when I was padding my first novel, a temptation of many novice authors. As I was saying, the anachronistic sousaphone stolen by Vampira from James Welsh Pepper in 1893 was returned and that Gordian time knot was undone.

Then in 1483 we managed to prevent "Mord the Merciless" fka "Mord the Hairless", no relation to Ming[508], but an obvious "William" time clone, from killing George the Duke of Clarence, a Craven relative, only to have the duke accidentally drowned in a vat of wine.[509] Neither could we prevent Richard, the so-called Black Duke of Gloucester, an ancestor of Holmes however from acquiring a sinister reputation, even by using the mind-swapping Kru-El ray.[239] After the disappearance of his nephews, Edward and Richard, he was the victim of cruel rumors by his in-laws.[510] The boys had actually been kidnapped to 1805 by Capt. Blood and freed by Nicholas McIver from 1939 with Akharin's, that is "Leonardo's", time machine.[457] See, the tales of Marco and Akharin finally tie together again. The princes were re-kidnapped out of space-time altogether by Octan, re-rescued by "Dr. John Smith" and finally adopted by Ernest Fleetward in 2004.[511] They found and married princesses Elizabeth and Joanna[512] and named their sons after their rescuers, John and Ernest.

After the death of his wife Helen in a freak auto accident, "Henry" as "Dr. Julian Blair" made the mistake of building another thought transferal device, this time to contact the dead at their country retreat on the Kennebec River, Maine. When he could not contact Helen through her cremains, he had brain-damaged Karl collect corpses to boost the reception.[513] We tried dissuading him through his daughter, Anne, his research assistant, Richard Sayles, and his colleagues, Drs. Van Den and Sanders, but to no avail. He unexpectedly did connect however with his mirror counterpart "William" across the interdimensional barrier though through Blanche Walters, rather like Saul did though the witch of Endor[514], causing Anne's "freak accident". The Eye managed to cause the building to collapse about him just in time to prevent a major zombi infestation,[515] reminiscent of that avoided at Marmorosch.[481] Richard and Anne had sons Augie,[516] Darrius[517] and Matt.[518]

Reborn as "James Rankin" in 1809, we followed Marco's relatively uneventful life until 1880, when his repressed memories as both doctor and murderer combined as an obsession with proving the innocence of "the Haymarket Strangler". When he began remembering being hung twenty years before however, his personalities that had seemed to be integrating began to fragment again.[519] "The Strangler" proved not to be "William", but Rankin's brother "Henry" infected by Redjac, the energy-based phobovore or fearfeeder that possessed men and killed women for several centuries on several planets.[520] It killed, but only as an instinctual predator. We managed to help my future literary agent Arthur Doyle save Elizabeth Cochrane, better known by her byline, "Nellie Bly", from it. Our centuries-long alliance with the Catlanders against the truly diabolical, gynocidal Klopts from Arachosia was a much more difficult and much more glorious victory for womankind, indeed all humankind.[521] But I digress yet again. To tell that story would sidetrack me into the Virdra War[522] and the Time War timelines, best saved for another time.[523]

"I believe I have found another timeprint of our lost doctor." I commented looking over the obscure medical journal I had been reading.

His curiosity aroused, Holmes put down his violin and asked, "Pray tell, what has he been up to now?"

"Not now, but in 1915 he will be up to something. In the *Proceedings of the Robinson Foundation* from that year a doctor fitting Dr. Marco's profile was dismissed for unauthorized experimentation."

"That does sound like our wayward doctor."

"Ah, but there's more. I have found no other references to him again until 1940 when a Dr. McNaulty of that institution proposed that he be readmitted, but I find no mention in any subsequent *Proceedings* that he never was if fact reinstated."

We discovered that "Dr. Bernard Adrian" had been working on a cure for the polio that took his own daughter, Frances, in 1930 Red Creek polio epidemic. His research had come to the notice of the Foundation, but he was unable to save the life of the circus's mortally wounded animal trainer. Taking a sample of the needed spinal fluid "fearjuice" and subconsciously remembering his bestial Hyde Park Killer past, "Adrian" killed and skinned the escaped gorilla that he found and subdued in his laboratory, attracted as it had been by its hated keeper's scent. "Adrian" used the shocking the Ape costume to trigger the adrenalin rush needed for his polio cure.

As Holmes pointed out to me the footprints at the scene, unnoticed by me or by Sheriff Halliday, proved it was Mrs. Brill who killed her abusive husband and then returned to her mother downriver and not "Adrian" as "the Mud Creek Ape".

Although he was not able to pass on his formula before passing on himself, mistakenly stabbed by George Tomlin, he did have the satisfaction of seeing that the Clifford girl, also named Frances, had been cured and able to free herself from her co-dependent boyfriend Danny Foster.[524] She did however find herself in two other failed marriages before finally finding, as they say, marital bliss,[525] naming her sons Bernard and Adrian and her daughter Adrianne. Neither McNaulty nor Holliday, of course, ever did find the doctor's notes, even with Old Jane Pritchard's help. The Eye made sure of that.

Pianist "John Ellman" was falsely accused of one of his look-alike Brewster's murders. Holmes and I helped uncover the evidence to prove him innocent, but that proved too little too late. Our whispered hints fell on the governor's deaf ears. As "Ellman" was about to be executed however Marco's thoughts turned upward, recognizing our Client. His last words were "<u>He</u>'ll believe me." It was not scriff [56] however that revived him this time, but a similarly well-meaning, but not perfectly sane, Dr. Evan Beaumont. He and the DA Werner had pondered what had happened during the time that "Ellman" had been dead, echoing Holmes's and my own thoughts.

"What happened during that transition? What effect did the experience of death have on his subconscious mind. Can he remember?", I asked, rather rhetorically, of Holmes, repeating Dr. Beaumont's words.

Holmes answered, "Well, it's rather a large order, doctor, and I'm afraid a bit beyond the province of law and beyond the province of science too, but it's a challenge, and somewhere, I think, we'll find the key to all this." and Werner and Beaumont echoed them as their own. Holmes later found that this Jonbar hinge had triggered a very persistent harmonic in the time waves that lead Marco's poor soul being replanted again and again and again before it ever was summoned back into "Ellman's" body. Marco's mind was greatly affected, though he would only vaguely remember his experiences.[526]

The epicenter of the harmonic, Holmes found, manifested in space-time in the eruption of the Mt. Tambora supervolcano in 1815, the largest eruption on Earth since Rabaul in East New Britain in 540. If the harmonic had not been triggered, Napoleon would have won at Waterloo[527] and the French Revolution would not have happened until led by Hitler's AmerInd-Negro army in 1938[528] with Emperor Napoleon VI fleeing to New France[529] and Andrew Jackson losing the Battle of New Orleans.[530] It was in rectifying this timeline that Holmes and I again found succor from our Client's blessed mother.[531]

The aftermath of this supereruption also caused the next year to be called "The Year without a Summer", when the very air was filled with darkness, not only natural darkness, but supernatural darkness. Mary and Percy Shelly unexpectedly spent their vacation in Villa Diodati by Lake Geneva bored and indoors, thinking dark thoughts. The stories she[532] and their friend Dr. Polidori[533] told slid down from five to four dimensions when Joe, Sam and Jack from 2006 activated Jodie's *Book* from 2105,[534] a prime example of both the timetraveler's axioms "Your mind makes it real."[535] and "To unfoul a foul-up varies inversely to how long it took to foul up."[536]

Retroactively therefore Marco as "Victor von Frankenstein" succeeded in his experiments with transplantation and reanimation in 1790 in Indolstadt, rather than fail like his grandfather Richard had twenty years before.[537] He was able to successfully transplant a brain into an oversized mosaic body and stimulate it into artificial life, naming his creation Adam Frankenstein.

Just three years later the murder of Irena triggered the centuries-long feud between the undying Adam and undead vampires,[538] somewhat overshadowing his feud against the Frankenstein family. Victor found and revived Adam again, but was hindered rather than helped by the greedy hypnotist Zotán in Karlstaad, Switzerland.[539] Adam temporarily retreated to the Arctic.

We did manage to help Paul Kempe, the mentor of "Victor", try to save his fiancée Elizabeth, who "happened" to be a Lenore throwback, from Adam's revenge and get "Victor" caught, convicted and executed.[540] Cautiously continuing to observe however, we proved once again "Things are not as they seemed."[541] "Victor" was reanimated yet again by another re-animator, Dr. Hertz. When Marco, in the body of Victor's assistant Hans, killed Christina's father defending her honor, he was unjustly guillotined and she even more tragically committed suicide. "Victor" however transplanted "Hans's" brain into Christina's body. The internal conflict within the transgendered Hans/Christina naturally expressed itself externally as revenge against the one who caused him (or rather them) to suffer in this most unnatural state.[542] Mercifully Hans/Christian died shortly thereafter and Marco and Christina were able to move on. Most mosaics are not so fortunate, but rather cursed with unnaturally long lives.

"Victor" escaped yet again and then with good, albeit misplaced, intentions transplanted his dying colleague Frederic Brandt's brain into Prof. Richter's body, not knowing that he, that is Marco, was also "Dr. Brandt", just as he had been "Hans", ironically "martyrizing? himself again in the name of Science.[543] The repressed memories of that experience as both victim and torturer drove our mad Dr. Marco ever deeper into madness.

"Victor" however escaped execution this time and even managed to blackmail asylum director Adolf

Klauss, so that he could continue his diabolical experiments, this time as "Dr. Carl Victor". With fellow inmate Simon Helder's help, they made yet another mosaic with the brain of Prof. Durendel.[544]

"Victor" relocated to Carlsbruck as "Dr. Victor Stein", however was blackmailed himself by Dr. Hans Kleve. Working together they transplanted hunchback Karl's brain into a more normal body, but almost immediately the body began to reject Karl's brain and vice versa. Before the authorities arrived, Kleve managed to save the brain of "Victor" yet again in a cloned body he called "Dr. Franck".[545]

With the publication of Frankenstein, Adam exited from the so-called Mountains of Madness in Australia after traversing the length of the Inner World.[546] We managed to keep "Victor" from recovering The Secret of Life and Death.[547] We also with even greater difficulty prevented Adam from getting involved with Queen Leonore the Gargoyle's war against the demon Naberius.[548]

In 1849 James Polk encountered one of the mosaics, of which by now there are several wandering the Earth.[549] After arranging the death of his nephew Wilhelm aka William in a hunting "accident" in 1857, "Victor" assumed the identity of his estranged, female impersonating grand nephew as the fifth baron.[550] With the help of medical student Wilhelm Kessman from the University of Vienna, they make yet another mosaic that Holmes nicknamed Wilhelm for the two Wilhelms.[551]

We'd been consulted about the murder of William's son, the grand nephew of "Victor", Wilhelm or William III, in 1888 by Henry Clerval. We'd traveled with him to Switzerland, but in the end there was nothing we could do to prevent Clerval also from being killed or Justine Moritz from being lynched or from Victor, whom we did not then know to be Marco, from marrying the great grandneice of the first wife of "Victor" and her namesake Elizabeth Lavenza.[552]

Alphonse traveled to America and married the daughter of Margaret Saville, Felicia, by "Victor" in New York. "Victor" also traveled to America to visit Maria, his daughter by Constance Bundy, but had a close encounter with both Adam and abolitionists.[553] We had our own harrowing encounter there with time travelers Wesley McCulloch and Troy Harmon from 1983,[554] whose meddling gave birth to Nova Africa in the American Southwest.[555] Even after that was corrected "Victor" and Marie were still forced to flee back to Germany.[553] Adam however caught up with them and buried his "brother" Wilhelm.[556] Holmes, as the Eye, was able to help a third "brother" escape to England and was adopted by Lady Munster as "her man", a unique status symbol.[557] "Herman" became more or less integrated into Shroudshire society, married Lilith Copplepot, and emigrated with her and their two adopted children to the United States.[558]

"Victor" now as "Dr. Gustav Niemann" escaped from the asylum where he had been for fifteen years to encounter Bruno Lampini's traveling circus with gypsy dancing girl Ilonka and "Dracula". Lampini's vampire's skeleton was not actually that of the infamous Vlad Tepes himself, but one of his many victims, Thomas Caine alias "Baron Latos Margulak". Caine was revived and killed the local burgomaster Carl Hussmann, but Holmes vanquished it, at least temporarily, with a dose of the Eyebeam.[559] As Superboy pointed out against another so-called "Son of Dracula", it's not the weapon used that's important it's the faith behind it.[560] Holmes did manage however to thwart the mad doctor from transplanting the brain of Frederick Ullman into Adam's body. Neither did he cure lycanthrope Lawrence Talbot, marked with the pentagram, the mark of Cain[561], by transplanting his into Strauss's. Alas I could not save Daniel or poor Ilonka. Despite everything the Eye could do to thwart him, Dr. Awooo the time lobo manages to "save" Talbot from the silver bullet.[562]

Alphonse's son, Heinrich, or as he preferred the Anglicized "Henry", discovered The Secret of Life and Death and could not resist perpetuating the family tradition, or rather the family curse. He made a mosaic with the questionable help of Ygor "Fritz" Zeleska in Goldstadt, one animated with Marco's poor soul.[563] Later he was blackmailed by his old professor Septimus Pretorius into the not entirely successful creation of the "Eve" mosaic. She, even with a completely blank-slate synthetic brain, instinctively screamed upon seeing the Marco mosaic. Overwhelmed by rejection after having made and losing his one friend, the blind hermit, after centuries of failures as Imhotep, Marco tries to kill himself, Eve and Pretorius. He does not entirely succeed. He does however mercifully let Henry and Elizabeth escape with the words, "You live; we belong dead.", so we knew that some of the original altuistic Dr. Marco still lived.[564] Moira, a daughter of "Victor Frankenstein", tried to improve upon Henry's "Eve" with a mosaic she called "Thea" ("Goddess"), but with equally, if not more, disastrous results.[565]

Meanwhile back in the States the other daughter of "Victor", Victoria Maria, transplanted a brain to turn Hank Tracy, a member of the James gang, into an "Igor", but he proved not to be even as subservient a servant as Ygor. He killed her brother Rudolf, but was in turn killed by Juanita Lopez with Jesse's gun.[566] Maria managed to escape back to Italy with her unborn child by Jesse James.

Maria, accompanied by her fiancée Eric Mann and their mutual friend Krista whom she met shipboard, joined "Victor" at Castle di Squilibrati. The other guests included a Neanderthal throwback called "Ook" from his habitual Dutch phrase "Ik ook", meaning "Me too.", another Igor, a voyeuristic, necrophiliac dwarf named Genz, uncle of the brilliant yet mad Dr. Migelito Loveless,[567] aka "Mr. Big".[12] Their newest mosaic, Goliath, escaped and killed "Ook", fighting over Krista.[568]

Eric not unexpectedly did not marry Maria after all that chaos, but rather Krista, so Maria raised her son by herself, giving him the name Irving Frankenstein.[569] "Victor" continued to experiment in Italy, but his newest attempt proved to be an even more sex-addicted monster than Goliath that sought to mate with his assistants Alice and Janet and Maud.[570]

There was, of course, much, much more to the story that Doyle maddeningly edited and re-titled "The Final Problem" than Holmes told me or my readers ever knew. Let me at least tie it here into the Frankensteins by referring back to one of Holmes's earliest cases at the University, the Tullyfare Abbey Mystery. Prof. Moriarty was attempting to marry, for ulterior motives naturally, the sister of one of his students, Jack Phillimore. When that did not go well he tried playing into the family superstition that Col. James would die at fifty, like his father and grandfather had. George Stoker dared "Shear Luck" Holmes look into the mysterious happenings, when Holmes pooh-poohed the proposition that ghosts were responsible. Before he could do much investigating however, the colonel suddenly and inexplicably vanished after joining the rest of the party on a walk and then returning to the abbey for an umbrella.[571]

When we heard about the very similar circumstances in the disappearance of James Phillimore we were both more than usually curious. My own curiosity at least increased when we found out that James's wife was indeed the same Alice Phillimore, the daughter of Col. James. She had married a Harvey Maynard, but took back her maiden name after their traumatic divorce. Her second husband had unexpectedly taken it as his own as well, something only usually heard of in title inheritance cases. His past was very much a mystery, and even more so with his sudden disappearance. Escaped convict and blackmailer Maynard was recaptured at the Twin Lambs Hotel,[572] with no apparent connection to the disappearance.

It did of course become a more common scenario after the publication of "The Problem of the Thor Bridge" in 1922, as did sadly suicides on a bridge. In the Cabpleasure case, for example, Holmes did not reveal his solution to Lestrade, so intent was he on the missing Cowles-Derningham diamonds. He mistakenly even suspected George Cabpleasure of being Gloria Cabpleasure. As it turned out henpecked George did not steal the diamonds; he owned them. He had not disappeared; he had become "milkman Alf Peters".[573]

We found a "Jimmy" Phillimore dead in London 2009, who had been going back to get his mother's umbrella, was poisoned by serial killer Jeff Hope.[574] Financial adviser Arthur James Phillimore went back for his umbrella as well and was later found dead in 2013. Mystery writer Sebastian McCabe and journalist Lynda Teal Cody investigated.[575] With Charles Hoy Fort we could well have asked, "Is someone collecting Phillimores?"

Yet another complication was finding the body of Jack and Alice's brother, Montague, hung in apparent suicide. The suicide theory rather unraveled however upon the disappearance of his valet Jarvis. "Jarvis" turned out actually be Terence Middleton and yet again there was no connection with brother-in-law James's disappearance or the apparently cursed umbrella.[576]

Holmes did however recognize the meddling of shapeshifter "Samuel Gossage" despite his/her changed appearance when s/he attempted to distract us with the alleged murder of his/her mother. S/he was the same being he had previously encountered as "Señor Mercado-Mendez" and "Herr Doktor Bechstein", recognizable by his/her alienness.[577] S/he had been trying to confuse things by making connections of Phillimore's disappearance with the Yellow Tophat Mysteries. He had asked a cabbie to take him to an address where he did not live, while leaving a mysterious suitcase behind in the cab that contained only bricks and newspapers.[578] We later learnt that the alien had already been discovered at Phillimore's disguised as an armchair as Raffles and his companion Bunny attempted to burgle the place, but s/he eluded them.[579]

We encountered another James Phillimore performing the same disappearing act. Having worked himself up to headwaiter, he had attracted the unwanted attentions of Cora Page. As it turned out however it was all a ploy on Miss Page's part to get James's friend Charles Nelson to "pop the question".[580] Charles did not mind losing James as a friend at all and let Cora name their sons James and Phil to remember how they'd met.

This "Phillimore" began own fantastic story by telling me that his name was actually Prof. J. Adrian Fillmore from Parker College back in 1999. He had apparently quantum leaped a hundred years to Greenwich 1899 into the body of his great grandfather James Phillimore.[581] The James Phillimore Society, devoted to science fictional and magical things Sherlockian, also took the name. The alternative timeline with a J. Adrian Fillmore Society that studied, if you can you believe it,[582] Sherlock Holmes as merely a fictional character.

When he tried to open what appeared to be a used back-up umbrella he'd bought, he found himself transported to a beach in Cornwall. When he comes out of the courtroom where he had defended himself against the charge of piracy, he meets John Wellington Wells[583], ancestor of "Superwoman" Kristin Wells, who tells him the true nature of the "umbrella". It sends him to London where he meets a Mr. Pickwick, who in turn sends him to 221B. There he found not Holmes and I, but Holmes's other older brother, Sherrinford. He had not therefore apparently visited the time tine in which Sherringford tended the family's Yorkshire homestead, got involved in the insectoid invasion or died in the San Francisco earthquake,[584] or the one in which he was accused of murder.[585]

Isadora Persano[586] told Fillmore that the "umbrella" was invented by Moriarty, a compact version of the much bulkier Needle's Eye and obviously controlled by Ol' Nick, rather than our Client. Fleeing back to Baker Street, he was betrayed and handed back to Persano by the new landlady, Mrs. Raddle. He escaped Persano's sword by using the "umbrella" again, but found himself in a worse fix in Vlad Tepes's castle. He used the "umbrella" again more skillfully now and found himself at Reichenbach Falls in 1891, where he intervened in the duel, but lost the umbrella in the falls. Back in London Mycroft suggested that Moriarty may have used it to survive Reichenbach.

Continuing his search for Moriarty and the "umbrella" Fillmore was attacked by a purple troll[548] on Madagascar, but was saved by the timely arrival of a Frankenstein mosaic. Together they traveled to Chinese Turkestan, defeated Al-Maghrabi and gained possession of Ala ad-Din's lamp.[587] Fillmore ordered the jinn of the lamp to send him to "whatever place Moriarty is" and so found himself in two-dimensional Flatland.[588] He was rescued from a Flatland mental institution by Holmes, who had also fell into the umbrella's interdimensional vortex. Together they infiltrated Moriarty's fortress, but got captured by him. A providentially articulate Frankenstein mosaic arrived, having gained possession of the Lamp, just in the nick of time, and in the ensuing battle Moriarty dies. Fillmore used his brolly to return himself, Holmes, the Frankenstein mosaic and Moriarty's body to our four-dimensional world.[589]

That was however not the end of Moriarty, for Alphonse Frankenstein found Fillmore's companions, transplanted Moriarty's brain into the brain-damaged mosaic's body, and nursed the dazed Holmes.[590] While we visited a demonstration of Edison's Kinetoscope at Edisonia Amusement Hall in New York 1906, Holmes recognized James Fillmore alias Phillimore, as the man photographed vanishing into thin air.[591] Further investigation confirmed our suspicion of Ol' Nick's involvement via Ambrose Bierce and Edward Alexander "Aleister" Crowley.[592]

In 1910 we found one of the mosaics, likely Adam himself, had joined Lord Greystoke, Arthur Conan Doyle and Nikola Tesla against Edison's evil experiments in vitology.[593] In 1912 "Hjalmar Poelzig" managed to revive the Eve mosaic.[594]

In 1919 I used the Kru-El ray [239] to swap Holmes into Wolf Frankenstein's body to try and stop the madness. He was quite good at playing the part for Elsa and Peter, especially with coaching from Wolf back in 1896. We uncovered the important role that cosmic rays played in the survival of the mosaics. Inspector Krogh was however difficult even for both Holmes and Wolf acting together. The Inspector had a grudge against the monster for the loss of his right arm, even though he would have lost it in the war in the alternative timeline anyway long before he ever had made general. Wolf's wife Elsa and son Peter were put in grave danger by both the mob of villagers and the evil plotting of Ygor Zeleska, but when I explained it all to Wolf he was willing take the risk with us to help end his family's curse. He already knew that nothing is terrifying if it is understood.

The "murdering ghost", Henry Frankenstein's mosaic turned green from the sulfur fumes, had been enough to frighten to death on sight the jurors that had judged Ygor guilty of graverobbing. The music that Ygor played not only provided an alibi for Ygor, but soothed the unhappy creature. When Krogh accused "Wolf" of knowing who had killed the butler Benson, he was quite right. The wound on the side of the body immediately proved to Holmes, Wolf and I that Ygor had killed him with scalpel, something the man-made man's big hands could not do. This time the butler didn't commit murder, though from the food scraps nearby, the mosaic had nearly, but not quite, frightened the butler to death over his chicken leg.

Actually it was Wolf himself who shot Ygor through the Eyehole to save both Holmes and his own body. We all knew that the mosaic was only trying to protect his new friend, Peter, after the loss of his only other friend Ygor, the only other one not frightened at the sight of him like his bride Eve had been. After I swapped Holmes and Wolf back into their respective bodies, Wolf "saved" his son by pushing the mosaic to his apparent death. The Frankensteins, Krogh and the rest of the villagers, of course, celebrated the end of the "Frankenstein monsters" prematurely.[595] The Frankensteins did not change their names to Smith. Krogh however did get a new and improved arm and even married the now unemployed maid Amelia. They observed the second half of the local custom, "In a house full of dread, lay the beds head-to-head, but in a home where joy may abide, lay the beds side-by-side."

In 1920 we found Adam Frankenstein in a California asylum, driven mad by the five dybbuks invading the other five body parts making up his mosaic body. Each donor tried to regain control of the whole body from his brain.[596] It was a case of polydybbukism. It was no wonder that he had been driven mad. By careful application and re-application of the Stanz ray,[239] I was able to surgically extract the dybbuks one by one. With each extraction however the Adam personality become more and more dominant again.

We found that the even uglier mosaic was lured by the even eviler Ygor to Vasaria, seeking out Ludwig Frankenstein, after he seems to be revived by being struck by lightning. This Ygor hated own body and wanted his brain transplanted into the mosaic's body. Ludwig hoped to replace what he considered a defective brain with a normal, or even superior, one from Dr. Kettering, to try to restore the good name of Frankenstein. The green mosaic tried to befriend the girl Cloestine Hussman as he had tried to befriend the blind, old hermit and the boy Peter. Demoted and imbittered Dr. Theodore Bohmer switched the brains so that Ygor got a body, but took Marco's brain and Ygor's heart in exchange. Ygor didn't like that his new body was blind and blamed and killed Ludwig in the burning castle. Through all this madness however Dr. Kettering did get to keep his brain in his own head and Elsa and Erik escaped.[597]

We caught up with Bohmer, as a Nazi scientist, using the code name "Reinsendorf", in Japan during World War II. The end of the war by Pepper Flynt "Little Boy" Busbee[15] also put an end to Bohmer's experimentation, but the interaction of the radiation caused Ygor's heart to mutate into a tuly giant clone. Drs. James Bowen and Sueko Togami working at the Hiroshima International Institute of Radiotherapeutics naturally gave the fast-growing, nearly indestructible mutant the infamous name Frankenstein. This seemed to be part of the gigantism timeline, that I believe I've already said was closed by the G-Force. Before that happened however the Ygor clone battled the burrowing dracoid daikaiju called Baragon, responsible for the mysterious disasters blamed on it.[598]

Before this timeline was closed, the Ygor clone continued to grow and grow, finally splitting like "Henry" and "William" into two hundred-foot giants, the evil Gaira and less-evil, but equally destructive, Sanda. Akemi and Dr. Paul Stewart saved Sanda from the joint Japanese-American army, but Akemi in turn was saved from a dangerous fall by Sanda. With a broken leg Sanda pursued Gaira to Tokyo until both were finally stopped by an Eye-triggered volcanic eruption.[599] In an alternative timeline in which they did not re-mutate and split, Ygor fought other giants.[600] In yet another alternative timeline in which the giant Ygor lost, Baragon later battled Gamera[601] and joined the other daikaiju against Ghidora.[602] In still another they continued to split and grow and grow and split like the horrible, unstoppable Battle Creek Monster.[603] I used all our Allen and Minyan rays[239] on those timelines.

Dr. Adam Steele's android "Frank Saunders" acquired the nickname "Frankenstein" when damaged by invading Martian Princess Marcuzan and her mad doctor Nadir. Steele and "Saunders" work together to rescue Karen Grant and other women, and with some help from the Eye, were successful.[604] Go Go was sent as a scout to Earth, but got adopted by "Aunt Wendy", was renamed George and fell in love with her nephew's girlfriend Connie.[605]

Nevertheless another attempt was led by Dop a couple of years later, but it was not successful either. It started well with his crew quickly abducting co-ed artist Pat Delany, stewardess Donna Lindberg, exotic dancer "Bubbles" Cash and homecoming queen Brenda Knowlan, without our being able to stop them. Capt. Dop however, pressured to outdo their selections, impersonated a reporter to get into the lecture "Sex and Outer Space: A News Conference On Extra-Terrestrial Reproduction" by Dr. Marjorie Bolen. I was able to use the Rachel ray[239] to induce Dop to eat the forbidden Earth food so that his metabolism adopted to it, making him in effect an Earthling and so unable to return to Mars.[605]

There were several mosaics which we could not positively identify, for example, the one who adopted "Bulldog Denny" Dunsan in 1930[606] or the one sighted by Jack P. Pierce at a celebrity baseball game in 1940. Since Dennis Dunsan joined with Black Owl, Green Lama, Yank and Doodle against a mosaic in 1942, it likely was not his foster father.[607] Another mosaic aided the Creature Commandos in killing Hitler and saving Matthew Shrieve in 1945, but got imprisoned for the next 65 years.[608] We stopped "Victor" as "Gen. Victor Hammer" and his "son" Franz von Hammer's horrid experiments for the Nazis in a secret Arctic lab[609] and helped Sgt. Novikov find and destroy another secret lab in Serbia.[610]

Elsa gladly changed her name to Ernst when she married, but was still sought out by those seeking the "secret" of Frankenstein. After a mosaic was unintentionally revived by graverobbers who expose him to moonlight, lycanthrope Lawrence Stewart Talbot found the Ygor mosaic, now no longer blind, trying to talk but unable to make any sound. Inspector Owens from Cardiff suspected Talbot of faking his death four years before to escape murder charges in Wales. Dr. Frank Mannering on the other hand tried to help him find a cure for his lycanthropy, though he considered him criminally insane, rather than supernaturally cursed.

Maleva tried to explain to Elsa, "Insane? He is not insane. He simply wants to die. That is all he asks of the doctor."

"Are you asking Doctor Frank to kill a man?"

"It would not be murder." she continued, "It would be an act of grace to deliver this unfortunate soul from the curse of such suffering!"[611]

Lawrence Talbot, whose "cure" proved only temporary, finally tracked Lajos Zaleska and Ygor Frankenstein to McDougal's House of Horror's in Florida. Although he rather easily convinced Wilbur Grey of his weird tale, he had great trouble convincing his co-worker, the much more skeptical Chick Young. They discover Lajos, going by the name "Dr. Lahos", with the assistance of Dr. Sandra Mornay, is planning to replace Ygor's brain with Grey's more docile gray matter.[612] Dr. Ahooo arrived in time to save James Karl McDougal from contracting a case of lycanthropy and with Lajos's spell broken Dr. Mornay and Prof. Stevens could marry and retreat into academia, naming their sons after Lawrence and Wilbur and their daughter after Joan Raymond, who became a traveling companion to Dr. Ahooo the timelobo. We were all, unknown to them or us, aided by the invisible man Geoffrey Radcliffe, apparently a stowaway with them.[613] This prompted Holmes and I to re-examine Radcliffe's subtle intervention, especially with other Erasmus throwbacks.[172]

Wolf's son, Paul Frederick Frankenstein, also tried to distance himself from the name Frankenstein, pronouncing it Fronken-Scheen, and the family curse, but is lured into making his own mosaic by Frau Blücher. Igor, the grandson of Ygor Zeleska, finds Marco's brain, left behind by Bohmer and Paul transplants it into seven-and-a-half-foot "gorilla" Peter Boyle. Along the way he meets and marries Inga, while this new mosaic, called "Junior", finally finds a willing bride in Elizabeth.[614] They did however later consult divorce lawyers Alanna Wolff and Jeff Byrd.[615]

Sheila Frankenstein gladly changed her name to von Helsing when she married, but also succumbed to "Baron Latos Margulak" impersonating her ancestor Dr. Victor Frankenstein. The deserted island she and her husband were lead to experiment on, Dödens Ö or "Death Island", proved not so deserted. It had indeed been avoided by outsiders, because it was uncharted, but it was uncharted because of the centuries-old sailor's yarns of half-alien jungle girls that turn hapless sailors into zombies. Capt. Clay Jayson had escaped zombification for seventeen years, because of the intimidating power of his eyepatch[38], not unlike his namesake Jason and Ulysses who escaped similar sirens.[616]

It became even less deserted when Dr. Paul Hadley and his fellow castaways, Curtis, Dino, Mark and Melvin the dog arrived. Their leaking rubber raft barely made it to land, but the technology left behind by the aliens generated a telepathic-like jamming signal to block revealing the location of either the alien's homeworld or the island. Only via the 'golden thread', the ectoplasmic link between their preserved bodies and their thought-activated alien technology were they able to generate maddening holograms, most memorably Dino's "weirdest thing I've ever seen", the transformation of one woman into another and a mirror into a snake.

"Latos's" devilish trident had transformed some of the islanders into vampires, but the mindless zombi sailors attacked them. When Dr. Hadley and Capt. Jayson finally disable the jammer, with a little help by the Eye, all the zombies and vampires and satanic and ghostly illusions vanished. The sailors and the jungle girls returned to normal. These men and women did rather better than Pitcairn's inhabitants, the ratio being more equal, so that they renamed the island Födelse Ö, "Birth Island", soon populated by many Shirleys, Clays, Curtises, Dinos, Marks, Melvins and Pauls in the Jayson, van Helsing and Hadley families.[617]

In 1967 Boris von Frankenstein, the 11th baron, hosted an extraordinary party on another island, Île du Mal in the Caribbean, upon his retirement as chairman of the WWOM or World Wide Organization of Monsters. It was catered by Mafia Machiavelli and Yetch with the Skeleton Quartet for entertainment. He'd invited Marco's "half-brothers", a male and female mosaic, an invisible man, a lycanthrope, an undead mummy, an ichthrope, and a hunchback. It, the giant pink ape, however crashed the party, literally crashed it, but it was Boris's anti-matter bomb that finished the destruction of the island. Of the Humans present only Boris's nephew, Felix Flanken and his beloved Francesca escaping.[618]

At Dr. Duryea's Creature Emporium in Venice, California, we finally encountered Adam Frankenstein again. He had been revived by Groton under the influence of vampire Zandor Vorkov, self-proclaimed "count of Darkness, lord of Corpathia". Groton himself was nearly as evil, a drug-addicted, axe-wielding, homicidal maniac, who collected the heads of young girls. Both were mindcontrolled by "Dr. Acula", Vlad Tepes himself, who in turn was controlled by Ol' Nick. We tried with some success to assist Judith Fontaine, looking for her sister, Jodie, one of their victims, while simultaneously saving Mike Howard, Samantha and her boyfriend Strange, from the Blood Freaks biker gang lead by rapist Rico and the very strange dwarf Grazbo.[619] Samantha Strange named her children Judith, Jodie, Mike and Howard and they became a very Strange family.[620]

Since 1942 Dr. Freida Frankenstein had been secretly collecting the cell-restoring blood of the legendary Mexican superhero, Samson "Santo" de la Llata. By 1971 however she, Dr. Yanco and her henchmen needed a less dodgy supply and so kidnapped de la Llata's girlfriend Norma to get to him. Santo had to fight both Ursus, her mosaic,[621] and Dr. Krallman's Monstruo.[622] Santos also encountered Nathanael Frankenstein several times[623] as well as Irving Frankenstein, Freida's father.[624]

Dr. Tania Frankenstein, back in our Victorian era, transplanted her lover Dr. Charles Marshall's brain into poor, burked Stephen. Not even the usually stoic Holmes could watch as the villagers dealt with them.[625] In Serbia we found Katrin Frankenstein and her "brother" "Victor" the fifth baron and their assistant Otto. Their branch of the family predictably self-destructed, transplanting stable boy Nicholas's brain into shepherd Sasha and trying to make a female companion, and their daughter Monica and son Erik experiment with vivisection.[626] The timeline collapsed upon itself, accelerating in the direction of the submetaphysical[627] forming a disconnected time loop, a personal hell.[628] Allowing Marco to impersonate his grand nephew really was easily the lesser of two evils.

"Victor", having been tortured and disfigured by the Nazis, returned to try to finish the work started by his grandfather. He had had his brain transplanted many times in his two hundred years, but now hoped that adding an atomic reactor would be the key to unlocking the secret of life. He permitted Douglas Row to film his documentary because he needed new body parts. We were unable to prevent him, either by subtle or overt means, from using body parts from members of the crew and his mind-controlled butler Shuter as an "assistant" to build himself a younger body, just like the mosaic body he'd had forty years before.[537]

Back in 1770s we had been able to thwart Richard von Frankenstein, the father of "Victor", even while simultaneously having to deal with vampire Countess Dolingen Grotz.[629] The countess had called together and nearly united the scattered vampire nobility, the Karnsteins, Princess Asa Vajda, Counts Yorga, von Krolock, and St.-Germain[630], Countess Elizabeth Bathory, Don Sebastien de Villanueva, and last and certainly not least, Count Vlad Tepes. Although he continues to intrude in the story of the Frankensteins, I will leave our vampire hunting adventures for another time and return to Dr. Marco and the Frankensteins.

In 1978 a Frankenstein mosaic is encountered by some young mutants, but it turns out to be merely a tulpa subcreated by a new mutant Andrew Forbes. Assisting the boy's father, Bruce, we were able to rechannel his power and imagination.[631] Twelve-year-old Earl Williams also found a mosaic, "the true Frankenstein" from a defunct sideshow, revived it and encountered a lycanthrope and vampires.[632]

We pursued the trail though the Eighties. In 1980 we had to help a weakened Kal-El against the combined assault of both Vlad Tepes and a Frankenstein mosaic,[633] not likely "Mosaico" put together by Otto Frankenstein, named for Katrin's assistant.[634]

The next year the not-so-young Dr. Paul Frederick Frankenstein returned to experiment with reanimation in France by attempting to bring Albert Camus and Sir Philip Vian back from the dead.[635] The Drs. Tom Halman, Philip Spires and Paul Vaughn were killed by the man they revived in Texas in 1982[636], whom we helped Norris[138] defeat.

In 1987, the hundredth anniversary of Abraham van Helsing's encounter with Vlad Tepes[637], Sean received van Helsing's journal from his mother and with his friends, Patrick, Horace and Rudy, founded the Monster Squad. Exploring the infamous house on Shadowbrook Road, they encountered the one they called "Scary German Guy", but whom we knew as Marco. With him he fought Vlad Tepes, and the ichthrope, 2000-year-old undead mummy and a lycanthrope that Tepes had summoned using a portal-opening amulet.[638]

The vigilante group, "the Mystery Men", helped Capt. Amazing stop "Casanova Frankenstein" from using his psychofrakulator.[639] He may or may not have been related to his namesake, the sex-crazed Italian mosaic.[569] He seem not to be, but we didn't investigate further.

Following the trail into the Nineties, we found Mark Chrisman inheriting a mosaic from Prof. Lippzieg. He and his friend Jay Butterman turned him into the proverbial football hero, "Frank N. Stein".[640] Frederick "Riot" Frankenstein however mass produced mosaic clones.[641] Sir John Talbot revived from a coma-like state to fight Lejos Zeleska and another Frankenstein mosaic.[642] The werechipmunk brothers Alvin, Simon and Theodore Seville encountered "Victor" and his newest mosaic at Frankenstein Castle, Majestic Movie Studios, whom they name "Frankie". "Victor" was able to morph Alvin into a monster chipmunk, but only temporarily. He had to disguise himself as the Majestic moscot, "Sammy Squirrel", to escape.[643] Lawrence Stewart Talbot encountered a Frankenstein mosaic, an ichthrope, and vampire yet again.[644]

We aided CIB agent Earl Jazine against the mad Dr. Hobbes on Horse Island.[645] and Arnold van Helsing[646], but couldn't prevent Igor from substituting a lesbian's brain for Helena Frankenstein's in a self-destructive, anachronistic timeline with automobiles and cellphones.[647] We also aided Carson O'Connor and Michael Sloane in New Orleans in thwarting "Dr. Victor Helios" and his newest mosaic "Deucalion".[648]

Well-meaning, but mad scientists Oscar Omar "El Ángel" Puentes y Molgado, Moroe Lazaroff and Ulor Foranti revived a mosaic, but it battles their nearly as indestructible ichthrope mosaic rather than terrorists as intended.[649] The cove was actually called Blood Cove not because of the tragedy there, but after Capt. William Blood.[457]

We found "Victor Franks" himself still experimenting now with nanotech resulted in Bryce Daniels killing Dr. Hank Clerval, his assistants Elizabeth Weatherly and Rebekkah Clarke and himself.[650] By the early Twenty-first Century mosaics had become so iconic we found one promoting life assurance policies for zombies and mummies[651] for Wesley Stiller[652] and another, or perhaps the same one, attended a most unusual dinner[653] with the ghost of Rodney Dangerfield, who spoofed him in the movies[654], roasting Ol' Nick, along with Carrie White[655], Lisa Vampirelli, Bernie Drac and the invisible Jerzey Samuals.[656]

Vincent Frankenstein killed hunchback Ivan when threatening his mosaic. After his wife Lenore died in childbirth, he was in turn killed by their maid Betty, who blamed him.[657] Their son, the orphaned Basil, became a Nazi and was killed by his and colleague Kitagowa's mosaic in 1942.[658]

His son Ludwig was able to create a Norrin Radd doppleganger, but was killed by his assistant Borgo.[659] His daughter Victoria Frankenstein alias "Victoria Fronken-Schteen" was kidnapped by Dr. Kraft, who thought she would interfere with his mass produicing "Frankenclones", but she was freed by Peter Parker[660], or possibly his doppleganger Clive Arno.[18] Her sister Veronica, with the help of Eric Prawn, was able to give a mute mosaic the power of speech.[661] She was able to shed her maiden name by marrying Eric. Unsure of Victoria's hero, they named their sons both Clive and Peter and their daughter Victoria.

Intrepid reporter Burton Lapp rather foolishly became a monster hunter without benefit of Monster Insurance.[651] He encountered male and female mosaics, a Dracula mindclone Bumblesnore[662], lycanthrope Tim Rassmussen, Jr.[663], witch Lisa Pechmiller and the invisible Count Creepy.[664] Fortunately he had the Eye watching out for him.

A mosaic befriended fatherless Brandon Bailey,[665] likely the same one who had befriended Denny Dunsan seventy years before.[606], possibly even Adam Frankenstein himself, finally freed after fifty-five years[608] allegedly by Jonathan Vaenkenhein.[666]

We found "Victor" attempting to create another Eve mosaic with his new assistant Ingrid, but although this one turned out better exteriorly, she seemed to be Lesbian like he thought his Helena had.[667] Holmes considered it quite possible that this "Eve" may actually have been the first actual case of a "man's brain in a woman's body", a victim of the "green-eyed monster that eats little boys", like the infamous Glen(da) Blaskó case.[668]

A mosaic, likely one of the ubiquitous Frankenclones, took part in the wrestling "fight of the living dead" held in a cursed graveyard against another witch, lady vampire, zombi and werewolf.[669] An undying mosaic joined forces with an undead vampire, mummy and zombie against the Seven Ninjas[670], after we had been able to help the ninjas fight and survive both vampires led by Seth and his minions[671] and hordes of zombies.[672] The ninjas lost.

Holmes, of course, clung to the alternative theories of these undead, rather than accept the supernatural. To him there were merely mental and/or physical aberrations, perhaps drug-induced, by unfortunate, sick individuals. I took a more holistic approach, seeing them as curable, possibly in both mind and body.

Adam seemed to actually take on the supernatural when we saw him confront the demon Naberius tempting Dr. Terra to create a zombi army[673], much as Hitler had tried to do. Meanwhile "Victor" tries to extend the life of his newest assistant Carter, but only gives him more opportunity for killing. Prof. Naihla Khalil's revived pharaoh across campus does the same, until they finally battle each other.[674]

By 2020 Adam Frankenstein allied with Dr. Reed Crawley's Monster Force (lycanthrope Luke Talbot, Tripp "Martial Artist" Hansen, Lance "Powerhouse Marksman" McGruder, and Shelly "Psychic" Frank). They fought against a blue-haired, yellow-skinned Dracula clone, leading lycanthrope "Niles Lupon", an ichthrope, and "Imhotep" and Eve Frankenstein. "Imhotep", whom we had reduced to dust in 1944, were able to partially revive that dust into a dustdevil. Eve just wanted to be left alone. Hansen, McGruder and Frank used EMACS, Crawley's Energized Monster Armed Containment Suit and although Hansen and McGruder both admired, Frank she was intent on revenge.[675] Once that had proved fruitless, the shyer McGruder won her hand. They named their sons Reed, Tripp and Luke.

It was not until 2031 when Dr. Joe Buchanan "accidentally", with a little help from the Eye, was able to travel back and rescue his ancestor, Adam Buchanan that the whole convoluted Frankenstein time knot was thankfully, finally undone.[676]

Only remnants of the horror that was Frankenstein remained, like "the Groovie Goolies" band, that included the mosaic-like drummer/xylophonist Franklin "Frankie" Frankenstein, lyre-guitarist Wolfgang "Wolfie" Wolfman and albino organist Tom "Drac" Dracula. Other residents of Horrible Hall included the witch/cook Hagatha and her nephew Haunteroy, the skeleton Boneaport, Batso and Ratso, "The Mummies and the Puppies", "The Spirits of '76", "The Rolling Headstones" and "The Bare Bones Band". The Goolies song, "Chick-a-Boom (Don't Ya Jes' Love It)", later became a hit for Richard

"Daddy Dewdrop" Monda.[677]

Nearly all of Ol' Nick's plots for evil came to naught. All of the descendants of Richard Frankenstein had very different lives, if any at all. His daughter Caroline Frankenstein married Alfonse Beaufort and so the barony never was created. Madeline von Harben married Guilliam Delacroix, Magnus James married Freida Caligari, Josef Schoenbein married Irene Mengel and Frederick Drury married Alice von Juntz.

With the mummy madness and the Frankenstein freakiness finished, we finally could follow the fainter time trails. We aided "Dr. Maximilian Meissen" and Sir Ronald Burton, alias Richard Beckett, captives of the sadistic, eyepatch-wearing former ivory poucher Count Karl von Bruno. He was also holding Count Steiken, Count Ernst von Melcher and his latest wife, Countess Elga, prisoners at Schwartzeschloss. The Eye helped them as much as we could against the crocodiles, big cats, Gargon the hunchback and burial alive. We gave Burton clues to his friends' deaths without having to help him too much, though we did have to prevent him from escaping too soon without "Meissen" or the countess. We did not reveal to anyone, what we alone saw, that "Meissen" had only appeared to poison Count Steiken after he'd eavesdrops on Burton and the countess. We did not really need to save Gargon from the crocodile pit since they knew him as their feeder, but I did use a dose of vita-ray[239] that was able to regrow his tongue and straighten his back.[678]

We found "Matthias Morteval", whom Holmes quickly identified as Marco's half-brother "Henry" in the 19th century, having lived the life of a pianist. This Morteval family however also seemed under a curse like the Frankensteins or the Talbots, this time that of "brain shrinkage". I had initially categorized this as on a par with the uselessly vague diagnosis of "brain cloud",[679] but soon found it common in fibromyalgia and Adrenal Fatigue Syndrome and associated with such life-threatening conditions as hypertension, diabetes, obesity and tobacco addition,[680] all of which Mycroft shows.

He made a promise to his father, "If God will give me strength in the twilight of my life, I promise you that I will find that weed and tear it from our soil with all its evil seed once and for all."

He tried to warn his nephews Ivar and Morgenstern, niece Julissa and her boyfriend, but the mysterious deaths at Morteval Manor were from toys designed by his evil twin Henry, Marco's half-brother "William", to fit their crimes, a toy cannon, an axe-wielding knight-robot, a dancing sheik. Once again the Eye started a house fire and freed "Matthias". "William's" evil spirit's last words were "The whole house will go with me."[681]

We next found Marco experimenting with cryogenics in 1939 as "Dr. Henryk Savaard". When he was interrupted by authorities sent by his student volunteer's girlfriend, Betty Crawford, he cannot revive Bob Roberts before it is too late. He unjustly, rather than she, was convicted of Robert's murder.

Before his execution the priest commented, "It seems strange to see you in such good spirits, doctor."

"Strange that I should have no fear of dying? Well, I have lived so long questioning the unknown that this plunge into its depths is only the last and perhaps the greatest of my experiments." he responded.

"Ha, 'I have lived so long'! There seems to be no end of this doctor's lives, does there, Holmes?" was my own response.

"Indeed", was all my observant friend said as the conversation continued, and as I observed him.

"Have you no faith?"

"As a scientist, I'm afraid I'm a professional skeptic who doubts everything -- even the 'certainties'."

"But do you not recognize the Great Truths?"

"I never found one that would bear analysis."

"Can't you conceive of a Truth too great for the Human mind to analyze?"

Then "Savaard" turned a bit more philosophical, answering, "Tonight, no, but tomorrow I may know better!"

Holmes was slowly being forced to to consider the Great Truths of life, death, heaven, hell and eternity, rather than "the game" of detection. I knew that like Marco however he could not keep his mind from trying futilely to analyze the Mystery.

"Savaard" was hung, but as he had been so many times before was revived again this time by his assistant Dr. Lang. Reviving with a broken neck and a thirst for vengeance however, he then rigged his home as a death trap. He electrocuted Judge Bowman, poisoned jury foreman Kearney and threatened both the DA Drake and the coroner. We tried to plant the idea that vengeance is our Client's alone and seemed to meet with some success. When he discovered that his daughter Jane and her boyfriend, Shane "Scoop" Foley also were trapped in his booby-trapped home, he had a change of heart and allowed himself to die so that Jane can be revived by his own machine.[682] Realizing this they named their son, Henryk "Hank" Foley after him.

In 1905 "Gabriel Hornel" killed his wife Agnes and walled her up in wall, but a hole made wailing sound that haunted him for 40 years, rather like the almost trivial case of Reggie Taunton.[683] "Hormel" also killed an actress, the namesake of the latterday Dorothy Carter,[684] and driven by overwhelming guilt eventually burned down the house, trying to commit suicide, but of course, was instead reborn.[685]

We helped Fedor escape from "Ivanoff", his abusive foster father, only to have him found by club-footed Vladimar Ivan Tsarakov, who also was suffering from the Frankenstein curse. He quickly turned from manipulating puppets to manipulating Fedor.

"I will create my own being: that boy!", he said megalomaniacally. "That boy will be my counterpart, he shall be what I should have been. I will mold him. I will pour into him my genius, my soul. In him all my dreams, all my ambitions will be fulfilled - the greatest dancer of all time !"

Of course, that was madness, Tsarakov abuses the boy by smothering him, getting him leads in ballets and procuring for him many young women lovers. Even Holmes tried to help me fight ballet director Sergei Bankieff's cocaine addiction, but to no avail. To manioulate him, Tsarakov became his new faithful supplier, blackmailing him into firing his "son" Fedor's lastest beloved, Nana Carlova and getting her together with Count Robert Renaud. We could only watch helplessly as Bankieff, mad with withdrawal, murdered the older Tsarakov on stage with an ax.[686] Neither could we prevent the inevitable break-up of Nana and Fedor, as he took on more and more of the character flaws of Tsarakov and she returned to the count.

In 1904 we helped Peter Banning and other Lost Boys, and John, Wendy, and Michael Darling fight "Capt. James Matthew".[687] We had not been able to turn him from piracy after serving under Capt. "Black John" Sazarac.[688]

There must have been some residual "Imhotep" in Northwoodsman "Jules Borney" since he was compelled to fight stock market speculator Harvey Judson for heiress Mary Willard. She had kidnapped Judson to teach him a lesson and protect her shareholders. But "Borney" lost without any help from the Eye. While escaping to the nearest train station, Willard and Judson were in an automobile crash that nearly, but this time thanks to the Eye, did not kill them. Once they finally reached the station, they were told that the government had seized their property. It is only when they learnt the value of life and each other that Mary and Harvey discover that they don't care dash about the dosh any more, but do care very much about each other.[689] Their son Willard became a woodsman himself.

Marco just as daft as "Buck Tavish", when he carried off the hysterical Mrs. Michael O'Doone when her husband went missing. Margaret recovered enough to escape from his cabin, but lost contact with her daughter Marge for many years until David Raine found and befriended her. We then helped guide him to Michael O'Doone, now living a good, but lonely, existence as "Rolland" and finally reuniting all three of the O'Doones.[690]

In the 16th Century we found Marco as "Dakar", high priest of a Temple of Kama-Sita when treasure hunter Tavanier stole the large blue diamond from the Golconda mines by the Kistna River. He swore vengeance and put a curse upon the jewel, before he himself was tortured and killed for failing to guard it. Like "Imhotep" his monomania kept him focused on the diamond as his was re-born again and again. The stone was sold to a French merchant in 1642, who in turn sold it to King Louis XIV for a handsome profit, only to be mauled to death by a pack of wild dogs.

Both King Louis XIV and Marie Antoinette lost their heads, supposedly because of the curse, and the diamond was "lost" during the French Revolution, possibly "found" by Holmes's ancestor Percy Blakeney.[691] It was cut down into several smaller stones and the 46-carat stone that became known as the Hope diamond. Holmes strongly suspected that it was cut down to more easily pay off George IV's enormous debts. The largest piece, the 45-carat, walnut-sized stone, became known as the Hope diamond when Henry Thomas Hope acquired it in 1839. Owners committed suicide, were murdered, and left penniless through bad investments. Those who came in contact with the diamond suffered failed marriages, dead children, drug addiction, and insanity.[692]

It was said, and not without credible evidence to support it, that only a person with a pure heart could escape a doomed fate — in this case a "pure heart" meaning someone who did not try to sell it but instead generously gave it away,[693] particularly if they gave it back to a "Dakar".[694]

In the Twentieth Century Sidney Atherton, a gentleman jewel thief tried to steal it. Using his skill as a hypnotist, and impersonating Asian crime-lord Nang Fu, he tried to mindcontrol collector James Macon's secretary Mary Hilton. He was opposed by criminologist John Gregge and Kama-Sita devotee "Dakar". They in turn were opposed by the real Nang Fu's gang and kidnapped by Atherton.[695] We helped them escape the both Nang Fus and our "Dakar".

We found Marco again in 1907, a gentleman of temperate habits, a good husband, a very affectionate father, and popular with all who knew him. Like Neville St. Clair[696] however he had lived a long, happy-go-lucky second life as a "sweep" until his retirementat the ripe age of 77, when he passed on the business and his theme song to his multitalented grandson Bert.[697] But we also found him being shot as a counterfeiter by his partner-in-crime Benjamin Kubelsky in 1947. He must have retained some memory of his countless past lives, because his last words were "Why must I always die in the end?"[698]

As "Gravelle" Holmes believed him dead yet again in a tragic, but accidental, opera house fire in 1923. I Norburied[699] him however and he determined that it had been no accident. "Graville" remained an amnesiac "John Doe" for thirteen years at Rockland State Sanitarium until he saw his former wife on a front page, that we pointed out to him as the voices in his head, a story about her current appearance at the new opera house. After many unsuccessful attempts over the years, this as we'd hoped finally, triggering the return of his memory. Not quite as we'd hoped however he knocked out a guard at the sanitarium during a storm and escaped. Disguised in a Mephisto costume, he seriously intended to seek revenge for the failed attempt on his life by his wife Lilli Rochelle and her lover Enrico Borelli.

Despite the death threat "You will die tonight." on a floral greeting card, it was rather an inside joke when we heard stage manager Arnold reject the idea of cancelling Oscar Levant's "Carnival" with "This opera is going on tonight even if Frankenstein walks in."

After "Grevelle" revealed himself to his wife and both she and Borelli were found stabbed to death, both Sgt. Kelly and Inspector Regan immediately suspected "Gravelle". Charlie Chan does not.

"Case still wide open like swinging gate." Chan tried to explain.

"What d'ya mean?"

"Gravelle not murderer."

"It was obvious." Holmes said.

"It wasn't obvious to me." I responded.

"The first time I saw Anita Borelli, I was sure she was guilty. She had the proverbial 'looks that could kill'[700] whenever she saw his husband or her rival. I just had to subtly direct Chan to the evidence so it would be obvious to him as well."

"It didn't help that Sgt. Kelly kept insulting him, did it?"

"No, but it is somewhat understandable since it was his previous encounter with Chan that got him demoted to sergeant."

"Those fans of Lilli's, Phil and Kitty, were a bit distracting too, weren't they."

"The stoical Chan never let any of them get to him though. He never does.[701] He learnt that undoubtedly from having to deal with his infamous father."

We found Marco in 1919 leading the populist movement in the tiny Central European kingdom of Alaine, supporting Grand Duke Sarzeau. Many of the people were demanding a new dynasty. Aging King Phillipe IV was considering introducing a new, more democratic constitution, because of a lack of a male heir. His sons and their sons had all died either in the Great War or the Flu Pandemic that followed. The only possibility remaining was that Douglas, the grandson by his daughter, Princess Marguerite, kidnapped as a child, had survived. Backtracking twenty years we found that American adventurer "Bill Brooks" was actually the long-lost heir and, with very little help from the Eye, apart from luring him out of New York to Alaine via Mexico, he was able to win the right to the throne and the hand of countess Felice of Montenac.[702] King Douglas and Queen Felice's oldest son survived to become King Guilliam of Alaine.

Marco was to a lesser extent involved in opposing the American John Maude's impersonation of a long-lost prince on the Mediterreanian island nation of Mervo in 1912. This was a publicity stunt by Benjamin Scobell for his casino. The "prince" however doublecrossed Scobell and the remnant royalists by closing the casino, trying to win over Scobell's disapproving stepdaughter, Betty Keith. The president put down the incipient rebellion, reopened the casino and John and Betty escape back to America to raise their children, Keith, Elsa and Marvin, named for Betty's sister and brother-in-law Marvin Rossiter.[703]

We encountered Marco as a prince himself, Prince Kapolski, in 1902. He was a guest at the wedding of Prince Ugo Ravorelli and Dorothy Garrison along with lesser nobles Count Sallonica and Duke Laselli. It was disrupted by the appearance of her childhood sweetheart Philip Quentin, who accused Prince Ugo of being an impostor a murderer under another name in Brazil. After rejecting a duel challenge and being branded a coward, Quentin boldly kidnapped Garrison and then risked his life to save her from being "rescued" by Prince Ugo's henchman Courant. She finally believed him and rejected the "prince" as "the king of evil-doers".[704] They named their son Garrison "Garry".

We encountered Marco as a Khan again, this time "Ahmed Khan", playing a minor role in the tragic case of John and Ameera Holden and their son Tota.[705] Another time we found him as a wealthy Anglo-Indian, a nabob, not a Khan, getting involved in another romance, that of Cyrus Flint and Lola Dainty.[706]

Somewhat earlier in America's Wild West we found Marco as "Al Meggs" being led astray by a woman yet again, the notorious "Hellion". She was said to be the daughter of an Indian chief,[707] Willowbud, a survivor of the battle of Little Big Horn,[708] later known as "Squaw Mary".[709] Her gang was thwarted by William Lester's ranch hand Ted Gardy, who loved the farmer's daughter, Aline.[710] They had a son Lester. As "Diego" Marco became involved with Duncan MacKail's courtship of Chaddie Green,[711] who called their son "Chad" from his grandmother's maiden name Chadwick.

As another backwoodsman, like the Scottish "Tavish", Marco, now the French "Baptiste", encountered Margo, "a girl gone wild", somewhere between the wildness of Margaret O'Doone and Willowbud the "Hellion".[712] As "Raoul Maris" he was also slightly involved in Lola's kinswoman, Ninon Le Compte, who had inherited Hudson Bay property from her uncle. Fortunately her would-be-suitor, Frederick Van Court, III, continued to pursue her there. Lawatha the Indian guide killed Lazar the caretaker to protect Miss Le Compte, but alas died doing so. Upon finally getting her back to civilization again, she finally relented and married Van Court.[713] Their first son, of course, was named Frederick Van Court, IV, but the next was named Raoul.

In 1924 Marco as "Antonio 'Tony' Garcia" was bullied and even knocked out by troublemaker Daniel McLeod. In retaliation he accused McLeod of stealing from the company safe, so that McLeod was shadowed by the inept detective Sherlock Jones. McLeod also quickly lost his next job as phys ed instructor at his girlfriend Helen Havens's college. He got his next job from a fight promotor as "Dynamite Dan" when he knocked out an opponent with one punch. The climax of his fighting career was when he defeated gangster-backed "Brute" Lacy and saved Havens from "Garcia". "Garcia", not such a bad guy as he pretended to be, returned the missing money, reconciled with McLeod and ended up with Betty "Tootles" Brockton, the "ugly" woman, the munter, no one else wanted.[714]

We found a Marco clone "Nei Hamid", among the kidnappers of Thomas Gordon near Morocco in 1908. Although the alcoholism that his brother Barry had inherited from their father, Col. Fairfax Gordon, had caused him to lose his girlfriend Muriel Beekman to Tom, we encouraged her to she reveal to him that she had always loved Barry better. This spurred Barry to rescue Tom, with some welcome help from Naomi, a kinswoman of "Hamid", and the Eye.[715] Muriel kept Barry sober, even after the death of their first son, Nathaniel, named for her father. Tom eventually married Naomi and they had a daughter Ruth.

We also surprisingly found Marco in the most illustrious ancestor of the henchman "Nei Hamid", no less than "Imam Mowaffak", teacher of famous astronomer-poet Omar Khayyam,[716] one of the greatest of the wise men of Khorassan.[717] Although some of Marco's lives turned toward evil, more seemed to be turning toward good, and those which were tending toward evil seemed to bear no fruit, proving "A good tree cannot bring forth evil fruit, neither can a corrupt tree bring forth good fruit."[718]

As "Hugo" in the South Seas Marco got involved in a love triangle involving Rod McLean, Tony Heritage and his wife Joie, the daughter of Capt. Jean Malet, who disappoved of her marriage. He gave Heritage the job of helping Rod establish a new trading post on another island. McLean held a grudge against Heritage who he had saved from some natives, but who had stole money from him and escaped to France. So much so that when Heritage got the natives squiffy and they burned the chapel, it was only the minister and the Eye that stopped McLean from killing him. Heritage stole McLean's boat to escape, but McLean went after him and the minister after them both.[719] Like the Gordons however the Heritages bore good fruit. The wives did not give up hope and were able to bring out the best in their husbands.[720] Tony, having experienced a little fear of death, stopped stealing and finally experienced joy. Although it took a bit longer, he eventually reconciled with his father-in-law when they named their twins Jean and Jeanne.

There were however Gordons with which Marco became involved who were not so good, namely Gordon, Ltd., headed by Mde. Gordon. They made a loan to a Craven descendant, Sir Melmoth Craven, for his campaign against John Orme. Although Enid Garth was actually behind the loan in attempt to avenge herself for how she thought he had mistreated her twenty years before, her daughter Margaret fell for him, dumping Orme. When Enid called in the loan, Craven responded by kidnapping Margaret, which was ultimately what ruined him, not Enid. Orme mercifully accepted the wiser Margaret back, won the election and they are married.[721] Enid, as often happens, found her happiness in her grandchildren.

During prohibition we found Marco again on the high seas as "Pietro Castilliano", first mate under "Capt. Joe", smuggling rum out of the Bahamas. When he discovered Secret Service agent Jerry Burke and "Capt. Joe" had fallen in love, he led a mutiny against her and left them both behind. They however were able to escape to a small island and send a radio message to her father, a cashiered naval officer. "Castilliano" however intercepted the message and returned for them before rescue came. Polly O'Day, now no longer "Capt. Joe", sent another message to a passing U. S. Warship, that captures "Castillo" and her former crew, though "Castilliano" blew up the boat and the contraband. Burke called in some favors to get Polly's father cleared of false charges and re-instated with his former rank. She gave evidence against "Castilliano" and was released into Burke's custody, until death did they part.[722] They named their sons Joe and Peter, and their daughter Jo. When his father was finally killed by the mob, Joe turned undercover vigilante.[723]

We found Marco in chaotic Vienna after World War I as "Scherenschleifer", a poor aristocrat. Like the Von Berg family, he was chastened by war, famine, and death. Fanny Von Berg chose Gustav Schmidt, a dealer in war supplies and owner of a gambling establishment, over her former fiancee Count Maxim Von Hurtig.[724] Schmidt gambled on the National Socialists and lost along with them. In an alternative timeline she became the Countess Von Hurtig and her sister Corinne married Pauli Birbach only to have their children, Gustav Birbach and Corinne Von Hurtig give up everything resisting the Nazis a generation later. Corinne survived with her daughter Fanny.

After the "Hellion" gang was broken up "Meggs" apparently joined another, robbing the patrons of Tom Stewart's ranch. Stewart confirmed his guide Lawrence's explanation of the incident as a staged stunt for their benefit like a Wild West Show, but wrote for help from his old gunfighter friend, Jeff Morgan. Morgan however sends his son, Junior, who although also a sharpshooter and good rider, was shy and awkward around Stewart's daughter Pauline. Junior proved himself by eventually capturing Lawrence, the leader of the gang, and his accomplice Laura Mayhew.[725] Marco and the rest of Lawrence gang scattered and apparently reformed. Junior and Pauline named their first son Jeff Morgan, II, their second Tom and their third Paul. Their daughter, Ann, became instantly world famous under her stage name, "Ann Darrow", when she was kidnapped by a gigantopithicus.[726]

On his own "Meggs" was thwarted by Jim Davis "The Vanishing Rider" every time that he tried to do away with Mary Allen,[727] but when he was on the run for killing a man was able to find sanctuary with the evil banker "Big Bill" Dawson of Juniper City. The man's son, cowboy Wally Fraser, soon arrived intending to avenge his father. After rescuing Mildred Crawford, Fraser get the job from her father of driving his cattle to the railroad. "Meggs" however sold the money. During the resulting shoot-out Fraser killed both "Meggs" and Dawson. It turned out that it was Dawson, not "Meggs", who had killed his father. Fraser settled down in Juniper City.[728]

Marco, of course, did not remain dead. He was re-born in a very close timeline as "Ramon Baxter". Hiding out from the law at "Robber's Roost", he encountered Cal Reynolds, "the Utah Kid". When local school marm Jennie Lee was kidnapped, Cal claimed she was his fiancée. Baxter and others did not believe the newcomer and get Parson Joe to tie the knot. Jennie, who was actually engaged to the town sheriff Jim Bentley. Cal, realizing that he is now really married, decided to reform, but when Bentley and a posse showed up the Roosters blamed the Kid. Cal was at first against Bentley and even wounding the sheriff, but later reconsiders and saves his life. Butch, the head Rooster, is killed by Cal in a duel and Jennie decides that Cal, rather than Jim, is the man for her.[729] Cal and Jennie named their sons Lee, Frank, Howard and Clark

"Baxter" escaped to join "The Phantom Bandit" gang. When another member, Bill Turner, was killed by Jim Breed, his look-alike Texas Ranger Jeff McCloud, pretended to be Bill Turner back from the dead and takes control of the gang from Breed, only to turn them all in, including "Baxter".[730] In trouble with the law again when he got out, "Baxter" got himself involved in the feud between Valdezes and Gordons who both claimed the same gold mine in New Mexico, when he tried the same masquerade as McCloud, assuming the identity of a cowboy, "Pug" Doran, killed in a stampede.[731]

In 1924 we found Marco as "Snipe[732] Collins", an drugaddict under the thumb of the despicable Senator Dornton. The senator tried and failed to thwart Adele Fenway from assuming the remainder of the governorship of her late husband. With henchman Snade, he stole the divorce papers for Governor Fenway's first marriage, to support the rumor that the governor was a bigamist. When Snade was knocked down the stairs by a punch by Adele's son Bob, "Collins" killed Snade, making it look like Bob killed him. Taking over for Snade, "Collins" helped Dornton also frame the new governor with impeachable charges.[733] All this turned out to be for nought however when the first wife produced her own divorce papers, the coroner's initial report was called into question and Dornton, not Fenway, was impeached. "Collins" served time for falsifying evidence, though not murder, and was able to overcome his addiction during his incarceration. Bob married Marian Lee and they had a son, Lee Fenway, who became a senator.

As lawyer "Dave Sinclair" Marco handled many complex cases, such as the case of John Rowan, that involved the theft of the deed to a gold mine, blackmail, and murder. All however eventually was resolved with the new owner Roland Deane and the daughter of the former owner, Ruth.[734] They named their oldest son John Rowan Deane.

As a struggling Eastern European immigrant, Marco tried to impress pretty nickel-a-dance girl Paddy at the Happy Hour Dancing Academy with his hard-earned ten dollar bill, only to have her give it away to a blind beggar once he gets her outside. He could not retrieve it because of the nearby cop who suspected him of trying to nick it. She held out for the even wealthier Jimmy Jessup and eventually they overcame her father's objections and were married.[735] They named their son Patrick.

In 1918 we found an Arabic time clone, when two escaped American POWs, a royal treasurer, Peter O'Gaffney and W. Daingerfield Phelps, III, appeared disguised as Arabs and kidnap Mirza.[736] When the War ended Phelps gave in and let O'Gaffney marry her. In 1919 we came across Owaza, a Native African time clone, who encountered the famous Lord Greystoke aka Tarzan.[737]

In Antebellum New Orleans we found Marco as "Fleming" involved in the sale of Antoinette Frombelle in a rivalry between Victor Jallot the barber and Capt. Remy, who had forged papers that she was a quadroon.[738] Jallot won the love of Antoinette and they named their daughter Victoria.

As Paspor,[739] Sudanese manservant to explorer Col. John Beetham, Marco had to deal with many problems, not the least of which was the infatuated Eve Mannering. Her father, Sir George, an old friend of Beetham's, hired detective Hillary Gatt to investigate her suitor Eric Durand. Gatt was murdered, wearing Chinese slippers, just like a London solicitor had been, implicating Beetham. Soon after Eve and Durand impulsively eloped. She very soon discovered that he was both an abusive drunk and cheating on her with the maid Nuna. She also found out that Alfred Pornick was trying to blackmail Durand for the murder. The newlyweds were followed through the Orient by Beetham thye following Durands and by Sir Frederick Bruce following both Beetham and the Durands, until Eve escaped into the desert. Bruce followed up missing women cases connected with Eric and with Chinese slippers for fifteen years until he and Eric caught up with Eve in San Francisco when Bruce was giving a lecture. There they also encounter the Hawaiian detective Charlie Chan. After Durand was killed outside the Cosmopolitan Club, Bruce himself was mysteriously found dead wearing Chinese slippers.[740] Although Eve professed her love for Beetham, he had only pursued them to try to prove his innocence and for the adventure.

"Scarface" Macklin, a member of Jack Drake's ivory poaching gang, kidnapped British secret agent Tom Trent. His brother Larry was joined by Diane Martin, searching for her missing father. All end up seeking the lost treasure of the ruined city of Nuhalla, guarded by a gigantopithicus and a dragon.[741] Drake escaped to become jewel thief "Crackerjack", who had to prove himself innocent of murder.[742]

As Turkish lawyer "Abdul Mohammed Bey", no relative of "Ardeth Bey", Marco came to Lord Montague's in murky London to read the will of an officer who died in India. Inspector Lewis also came, after "Monty" escaped being strangled, unlike four other vetrerans of Gallipoli. "Bey" reveals that his client left half his fortune to the surviving member of the unit. Things get even more murky by Lady Violet's Chinese medium, Sôjin, and Lady Efra Cavendar's strange tale.[743]

As a Corisan on Portuga Marco was a witness to another series of deaths supposedly by a giant devil fish or possibly at the hand of escapee from Devil's Island, John Dennis. Like the off-islanders, the Englishman and the Dutchman, he hopelessly longs for Nina. When her sponge diver brother Carl was killed, she offered herself as reward to whoever destroyed the beast, because her father Antone was incapable of protecting from would-be rapist Juan. As more and more men die, she puts her hope more and more on "Rev. Sims" aka John Dennis, forcing him more and more into the role of the minister and, as our Client undoubtedly had planned, more and more into the *Good Book*. He is saved from confronting the monster, and all the survivors disappointed, when Carl was proved not to be dead after all.[744] To protect his secret identity, however he had to marry Nina. They named their sons, John, Dennis and Carl Sims.

In another life he himself was a Devil's Island escapee who suffered for 20 years before finally being able to seek revenge against the evil Madame Louvere and the French Guinea seaman husband who had sent him there.[745] Another was Descius Heiss was a French expatriate, former Devil's Island prisoner, the proprietor of the Sly Corner Shop. He took care of his motherless, violinist daughter Margaret. His shop assistant Archie Fellowes however tried to blackmailing Heiss for taking in stolen goods.[746]

As "Ned Galloway" we found Marco in prison himself under the new warden Mark Brady, who had failed in his run for governor. The ex-DA seems to show favoritism to Robert Graham, who killed an unarmed man in the infamous Spelvins speakeasy, one of the many men he had sent to the 2500-man "Big House".[747] He even let him visit with his daughter Mary. When Jim Fales tried to break out and is shot down, when Runch exposes the plot to save himself, "Galloway" killed both Runch and head guard Gleason to avenge Fales. Brady however held Graham responsible for not telling what he saw.

After drugging Katie the housekeeper with a cuppa cha, that is tea, to insure his alibi, "Galloway" poured out the contents of the cup in the sink, but as criminals always do forgot and left the incriminating teapot. It would have gotten him the chair, even if he hadn't confessed.[748] Mary did not ask and Robert did not tell about his past and they worked together to make their future the best they could. They named their sons Mark and Edward. "Ned" settled on Bridwell Island.[749]

From there we tracked Marco as "Mustapha" working for big game hunter Harris. Their ship however catches fire and all the big cats escape. Blokes Ilgrey and "Bimi the Ape Man", fugitive Richard Grant disguised as an Arab, Otto Hoffmann disguised as "Mrs. Colby" and Muriel Armitage, searching for her missing brother Tom, all escape as well. Although Grant served time for Harris, he will not impersonate a raja for him. They find each others secrets, Tom, a diamond mine and much adventure.[750]

In 1931 we found Marco as "Boris Karloff"[571] trying to start a revolution in El Dorania after Zander Ulysses Parkhurst aka "Zup" won the crown in a crap game. Gen. Bogardus simply wanted to assassinate him just as he has the previous eleven monarchs and the widowed Queen Carlotta wanted to marry him. Meanwhile yet another contender millionaire Wendell Graham was trying to win over Minnie Van Varden so that he could marry Betty Harrington.[752] It took many timelines, but we finally stabilized one that saved Parkhurst, Carlotta, Graham, Van Varden, Harrington and El Dorania, but not Gen. Bogardus. "Karloff" fled.

After leaving El Dorania, "Karloff" replaced Luigi, butler to Areal Pacheco, the stepfather of Diane Forsythe. She was engaged to rich, old Clive Lattimer. Then the British ambassador Archie Lester introduced his friend Larry O'Brien to her and everything changed. "Luigi" as Pachecco called him kidnapped Diane, but O'Brien kidnaped her himself, getting Lattimer to pay the ransom.[753]

"Karloff" became an ecological revolutionary via shortwave as "the Voice",[754] leader of "the Vanishing Legion". His head field agent Marno however was not very protective of the environment. The Legionaires sabotage of "Happy" Cardigan's drilling for Milesburg Oil Company, not only would ruin Milesburg, and so heiress Caroline Hall, but Cardigan as well. In the meantime, Jimmie Williams's father, Jed, was framed for murder. It was actual Rex the Wonder Horse, not the Eye, that save the timeline this time.[755]

As "Joseph Williams", half-brother "William" tried to get young Midge Murray addicted, but was thwarted by Jim Donovan[756] and was associated with illegal gamblers like "Two-time Phil", "Back-to-back" Schultz and "Sleepy" Sam.[757]

"Karloff" acquired the nickname "the Professor" when he smartened up and teamed up with wealthy vigilante Pike Winslow, "the Reckoner", and Paul Hurst, "the Doc". The Eye helped them, Inspector Malcolm O'Neill and Detective Brady to clear Eugene Gerry of embezzlement. Winslow was then able to marry Gerry's daughter Barbara.[758] They named their sons Eugene, Gerry, Malcolm and Brady, who succeeded each other as "the Reckoner" in turn.

Because he was starving and "on a liquid diet", "Karloff" took a job as a stringer for The Gazette from Joseph W. Randall. Impersonating a minister he managed to get material for a new article on the old Voorhees case, upsetting ex-con Nancy and her new husband Michael Townsend and their daughter Jenny. Even publisher Hinchecliffe, who had pressed Randall for more sensationalism, regreted the unforeseen outcome. Jenny's fiancé, seeing her as hysterical as her mother, did not marry her, so that both their lives were saved. Randall resigned, married Miss Taylor and so both were saved. The Gazette providentially was not.[759]

"Mullins" was suspected of stealing a hundred grand by Dorothy Rogers and the detective she hired, Russell Thorne. They were trying to find and clear her father William, who mysteriously disappeared while reading The Fatal Warning, but also suspected, among others, bank president John Harmon, Norman Brooks, Marie Jordan, and even Roger's butler. Rogers guided the investigation from safety to lead to businessman Leonard Taylor.[760] To make amends for their false accusations, Dorothy and Russell Thorne named their children, John, Norman and Marie.

Oliver Hampton and Tavish McBride protect their discovery Marie Celeste from "Maurice Kent". They found her wandering in the Canadian woods, much like Marge O'Doone[690], after the apparent loss of her father Duncan and sweetheart Jules Barbier in a fire. They turned her into a popular Broadway musical comedy star, appearing in "The Ghost Breaker"[761], "Woman-Proof", "Old Home Week",[762] "Back Home and Broke"[763], "The Ne'er-Do-Well"[764], "The New Klondike",[765] "The Man in Hobbles",[766] "Just Married"[767], "Queen of the Night Clubs",[768] and "Honky Tonk",[769] until her carreer was cut short when she was innocently involved in a murder.[770]

In the Canandian Northwest Bob Donald searched for "Jules Gregg" who had been stealing his furs, while a local trader Pierre Blanc sought to take advantage of the situation. Instead Donald found a greater treasure, Doris, daughter of mounty Rayburn, aided by his dog Muro and horse Arab.[771]

In Marseilles "Gaston" got slightly involved in another complex romance between dancer Lita and sailor Jerry Flanagan, who killed one of her former lovers, Don Alvarado, in a fight. Judge St. Polis sentenced him to Devil's Island. Desperate to be near Flanagan, Lita rather foolishly married the meanest guard there. Flangan stopped a prison riot, but not before Lita husband was killed, but earned himself a pardon nevertheless, so that the couple moved to her native Britain.[772] Flanagan remained a short-tempered Irishman, so they then moved back to his native Ireland, and eventually on to America, where their descendant Patrick Flanagan became a lawyer for McKenzie Brackman in Los Angeles.[773]

Half-brother William as "Terry" killed D. A. Martin "Carter" Harrison just two days before the election for the local crime boss, M. H. Thomas. Moved up from the dusty archives by his editor E. T. Scudder, overeager cub reporter Dustin Hotchkiss tried to get the Scoop before the not-so-swift

"Speedy" Hanson. The Eye had a very difficult time helping "Dusty" as he couldn't remember the name of a key witness, was unable to describe a suspect's face, did not notice the fatal shots came from outside, falsely accused Constance, daughter of the reform candidate, Robert Hall, as murderer, letting "Terry" get away to "take care" of Scudder's ex, Pearl. Nevertheless we did finally manage to make it look like he had captured the crooks, so he could write the true story, win his job back, the election for Hall and Constance.[774] They named their sons, Robert, Martin and Carter.

During prohibition "Tony 'the Tiger' Ricca" was the patriarch of a crime family in New York. Even after they were force to relocate to Chicago "Tony" maintained the feud with their rivals the Palmeros. Young Marco Ricca however had taken the name "Smith" and pursued a career as an architect. When Mike Palermo killed the heir apparent, Benedicto Ricca, "Tony" retaliated by killing Mike's son Joe. Before he died however he was able to reveal to his father that his sister Maria's boyfriend "Marco Smith" was actually Marco Ricca. Grandma Nina Palmero helped Marco and Maria escape and get married, even to the point of killing her own son to protect them.[775] "Ricca" was sent to prison and involved in two failed escape attempts, with his cellmates, "Stan" and "Babe".[776] Because the warden's daughter's life was endangered by the prison fire, their sentence was increased.[777] "Ricca" mellowed over the years, primarily through contact maintained with his grandson, Tony. His comment upon seeing his great grandchildren, Tony, Jr., and Antoinette, for the first time in 1951, "They're great!", became an instant catchphrase. By the 1970's "Tony the Tiger, Jr.," himself was famous as a wreastling coach and referee.[778]

Also in Chicago during Prohibition was wild Irish "Tom Gaffney", one of O'Hara's men on the North side. When Johnny Lovo bought off the South side's Big Louis Castillo's bodyguard however he created a monster. This Tony, Tony "Scarface" Camonte, loved his new tommy gun and gleefully used it to wage war on all the competition, South and North, including "Gaffney". He proved however that he who lives by the gun, dies by the gun[779], but then too did nearly all of his victims.[780]

"Happy" MacDonald was not happy, knowing his wife Jill was cheating on him with Klauss, his dance manager, but then no one came to Happy's because they were happy. They came for the temporary illusion of happiness they created there. Both doorman Tim Washington and Tommy Gilman came to forget their own unhappy marriages.[781] We did manage to start a chain reaction by nudging Edith Blair to help Michael Rand to confront his mother. She had gotten away with shooting his father for his money. Ed Powell came to flirt with young, unhappy chorus girl Ruth Taylor, but was rebuffed. MacDonald also tried to push back when a bootlegger tried to pushed him into buying from the mob. Not unexpectedly the gangsters return to set an example, gunning down the MacDonalds and others. Rand and Taylor escaped.[782] They named their children Michelle and Taylor.

After prohibition "Jim Henderson" is unknowingly lured into another prison escape by "Quinn", actually federal agent Jack Holt. He led him, as Holt planned, to the drug smuggling ring headed by the mysterious "Mr. X". The smuggling is run through Dr. Steiner's Eastlake Hospitol where people getting in the way are "put out of the way for good" and their coffins stuffed with narcotics to be buried and dug up later. Holt was given the job of driver for Arnold and befriends Arnold's daughter Julie. After her father is killed and "Henderson" recaptured, she managed not only to overcome her captors by willing one to drop his gun, but also freed the otherwise helpless Holt. She is even a match for Steiner's henchwoman Nurse Edwards.

Mad Dr. August Steiner turned out, not too unexpectedly, to be "Mr. X.", but more surprizingly FBI Dr. Alec Munsell's evil half-brother.[783] The Hendersons named their oldest son Arnold, who inherited his mother psychokinetic power and also joined the FBI. Their son Ted and his wife Alice had a daughter, Elizabeth, who married Sean Sanders[784] George and his wife Nancy had a daughter, Sarah, and a son, Ernie.[785] Mike had a daughter, Tamara, and a son, Steve, before losing their mother.[786]

"Marcus LeFave" married Michele Bachmann, with whom he had five children, Lucas, Harrison,

Elisa, Caroline, and Sophia, and fostered twenty-three others. He supported her in 2000 when she was elected Minesota state senator, in 2007 when she was the first congresswoman from Minnesota and in 2012 when she was a nominee for president.[787]

In 1927 the feud between "Sheik Ali Ben Joseph" and rival sheik Hajj Ali was interrupted by rival razor blade company representatives, Earl Tinker and Madame Momora. Since Tinker was trying to disguise his industrial espionage as a pleasure trip his wife Jane and daughter, Olivia, and the daughter's suitor, Lawrence Ogle, further complicate matters. Madame only seems to threaten Earl and Jane's marriage and "too tall" Olivia finally lets Ogle catch her.[788] They named they son Earl and he became a Franciscan brother dedicated to Lady Poverty.

"Nikko", the owner of a Chinatown dive, made the clanger of turning down his usual kickback from John "Doc" Madison, by looking through the keyhole at Madison's girl, Helen. Madison reacts by throwing him over the bannister of their boarding house. The gang's fake healing of the contortionist "The Frog" however was exposed as fake when "The Patriarch" seemed to really heal.[789]

It seemed as if Marco might have fallen into the trap of being numbed to death, like poor time loopy Phillip Connors. Hopefully after enough death-and-rebirth loop de loops he might change for the better, but before that we had to reunion all the "Henries" and "Williams". Connors had young Rita praying for her future husband on the feast of the Presentation.[790] Marco seemed to be moving further and further from the Dr. Marco his wife Jane had known.

We found "Morgan Fenn", the love child black sheep of the Usher-like[791] Fenns in Wales in 1927. He was treated like a servant by both Horace and his deaf sister Rebecca, the mistress of the house. With the arrival of unexpected guests, especially Margaret Waverton, he finally could not endure the madness any longer and with an extra dose of "liquid courage" set free the imprisoned, pyromanic brother Saul. This drove out old "Sir Roderick" in the attic as well.[792] Holmes likened it to case of the Bates family where the son Norman impersonated his mother.[793] In this case it was Sir Roderick's psychotic daughter, Elspeth, the mother of "Morgan", impersonating her incestuous father. The inbreeding was obvious to me at once from all the family's congenetical defects.

Remembering his experiences in Egypt, ancient and modern, "Henry Morlant", which Holmes speculated was from the French "mort lente", slow death. He is dying from what appeared to me to be acromegaly. We encountered the classic case, Hal "the Hoxton Horror" Moffat, in the Borgia pearl theft[794], and in the F. Holmes Harmon[795] and Clifford Scott murders.[796] As an Egyptologist and Anubis-worshipper, "Morlant" bought a legendary jewel scarab talisman stolen by "Sheik" Aga Ben Dragore. He then ordered his clubfooted manservant Liang to bandage the jewel in his hand and warned him of dire consequences if his dying wishes were not carried out.

Of course, the warning was not heeded. "Morlant" revived with the full moon without the need of tana leaves, the jewel apparently transforming moonlight into vita-rays. This explains "Morlant's" superstrength when bending steel with his bare hands.

Rev. Nigel Hartley hiding in the statue in "Morlant's" crypt, a TARDIS like the statue of Melkar,[797] implied that he was actually a time lord, "the Reverend", attempting to recover the alien technology known as "the Eternal Light".

The hypothesis that this was a case of premature burial was not worth considering. Marco was however involved in a case of premature burial as "Dr. Thorne". He mistakenly declared his old friend Edward Stapleton dead when he was merely catatonic. He became suspicious when Stapleton married Victorine Lafourcade twenty-four years his junior. He however seemed happier than he had since his wife had died and understandably spent quite a bit of his fortune on preventing being buried alive again. He did not notice his wife's relationship with the painter Julian Boucher. "Thorne" finally managed to exposed Victorine's guilt with a little Holmesian theatrics,[798] reminiscent of Lady MacBeth.[799]

In 1917 we found "Valder" the French butler to Arthur Bennett was actually the German spy "Karl Schiller". Then we discovered that "Schiller" was actually a British double agent "Williams" like Helen von Lorbeer. She however finally exposed him as actually Franz Strendler working for the Jerries.[800]

In 1924 "George Miller" was framed for murder yet again. He was thought dead in 1934, but then finally freed in 1944 after his life sentence was commuted. Having become skilled at barbering while in prison, he pays a visit to "Ace", who had framed him for the murder he had committed, "unintentionally" frightening him for death with the dull edge of his razor.[801]

In 1936 on Riviera skint and sick "Dr. Sartorius" accepted a job from Lady Yvonne Clifford, that of killing her husband Sir Charles Clifford. She was interested in gigolo Capt. Arthur Holliday. Because of a change in the will she he could not however pay him the money for his research as she had promised. His nurse Eve Rowe discovered his poison-filled syringe, but he seemed to have second thoughts and does not kill her as he did Sir Charles. Rather he allowed her to escape and accuse him of also trying to poison the son Roger as he did his father. He, realizing he will never finish his research in the little time remaining, resorted to "doctor-assisted suicide", and injected himself, simultaneously leaving Lady Yvonne and Holliday charged with the murder of Sir Charles. Having saved his life, naturally Roger married Eve.[802] They named their son Charles.

In 1938 "Jevries", arrested years, nay yonks, ago for embezzlement, was suspected by Col. Rogers in murder at Powder Island Arsenal. At the same time Eddie and Sally Pratt tried to consummate their secret marriage, which Col Rogers did not suspect.[803] The murderer and the newlyweds were revealed. They named their son Jeffrey.

Brain surgeon "Dr. Ernest Sovac" tried to save his friend English Prof. George Kingsley's life by transplanting part of "Red" Cannon's brain, after both were shot down by rival gangster Eric Marnay. "Sovac" soon was made known of Kingsley/Cannon's resultant dual personality. Kingsley/Cannon returned to his moll "Sunny" Rogers and his half million dollars. In the end however "Sovac" makes the hard decision to kill his mosaic after both personalities seems to unite to avenge Marnay, even gloating at hearing him begging for mercy as he suffocates. Margaret Kingsley mourned the loss of her husband, while Jean Sovac mourned her father, electrocuted for Kingsley's murder.[804]

We found "Dr. John Garth", no relation to Edith, in a similar situation, on death row for mercy killing. The prison doctor, Dr. Ralph Howard, however believed that "Garth's" anti-aging serum shows promise and convinced Warden Thompson to continue the experiments together right up until the end, even to supplying prisoner's blood. "Garth" volunteered to be a Human guinea pig, knowing he would soon die and the serum worked. This time however he did not die, at least not yet, since his sentence was unexpectedly commuted to life. Containing as it did DNA from a murderer's blood, like Cannon's gray matter, the rejuvenating serum seemed to still be linked to a murderous evil spirit. He killed Dr. Howard and untrustworthy trustee Otto Krone, yet by blaming the doctor's death on Krone, he earned a pardon. His daughter Martha and his former assistant, Dr. Paul Ames, however both suspected something was wrong, even though "Garth" was now younger and free. Even the police began to suspect after "Garth's" old pianist friend, Victor Sondini, was found strangled.[805] Lest they forget the value of life at all ages, Paul and Martha named their sons and daughter after her father's victims, Ralph, Howard, Otto and Victoria. They all became policemen rather than doctors, except "Bobby" who ironically became "Dr. Rob".

"Dr. Paul Wade" had an old and superstitious patient, Stephen Denton, who needed new corneas. Although Chandler, the potential donor, dies without giving consent, "Wade" succumbs to the wiles of his former lover, Denton's wife, Valery.

"It's a matter of life and death," she said. "Not right and wrong!"

That simultaneously reminded both Holmes and I of Joshua's words, "See, I have set before thee this day life and good and death and evil."[806] Life cannot be separated from good, nor death from evil.

"Wade" however did take the corneas illegally. The superstitious Denton however overheard Holmes's complaint about my monopolizing the Eye as "Give me back my eyes!" and thought it was Chandler's ghost. Though he could see, he did not see that his imagination driving him to commit suicide. Valery's guilty conscience drove her to hysterical blindness.[807]

In the 1890s we found "Dr. Friedrich Hohner" was a regular at the Vienna Royal Theatre. He did more than just respond to the rare cry of "Is there a doctor in the house?" He had an unnatural influence over his mistress, the star soprano Marcellina, reminiscent of Tsarakov. The night before their marriage she suddenly vanished and it was thought that she had run off with another lover. "Hohner" returned faithfully every night for ten years as though waiting for her return, when he was the one who killed her out of jealousy. Even worse that watching her murder, we watched him preserve her body in a secret room like "Poelzig".

He finally heard another young singer, Angela Klatt, whose voice reminded him of Marcellina. His jealousy returned with a vengeance, but only old-timer Luice recognizes it. "Hohner" felt compelled to prevent her from singing for anyone but him, even if it means silencing her forever. We helped her fiancé and biggest fan, Franz Munzer, save her for his operetta's opening for Count Seebruck. "Hohner" died once again in flames with his lost Marcellina.[808]

"Elliot Starr", like "George Miller", was presumed dead and his "widow" Cora was just about to collect fifty grand in insurance money, so her new husband, Mark Devers, killed him, sending Cora into a coma, and him to the gallows.[809]

1947 David revived his dead and buried wife-assistant Ruth after an accident, but she remained brain damaged. Ed assisted but threatened to reveal the truth, saying "You can't stop science because of some kind of moral sense."[810]

"Lord Thomas Horfield" judged a complex murder case. The apparently happily married London barrister Anthony Keane however has fallen in love with the accused. He tried to frame the poor valet.[811]

In 1952 Carl Warner killed blackmailer Chester Poole from asylum, but his young wife Elaine killed Lt. Gregg and then Carl.[812]

Police psychiatrist "Dr. Francis Mason" got involve in a queer case that Col. March might have been baffled by. It started out rather ordinary. Edward Paige reported seeing a burglar in the apartment across from his strike a woman with his flashlight. When Lt. Davis and Sgt. Fenton searched the indicated apartment however they found nothing, no body, no evidence of a murder or burglary, no evidence even that anyone living in the empty apartment. "Mason" believed that Paige believed his story, but diagnosed it as a case of hallucination brought on by heat exhaustion.

The case became queer when the hoodlum Ralph Kerwin murdered his girlfriend Clara just as Paige had described in that very apartment after she moved in a few days later. Holmes, of course, did not believe it was precognition, and neither did Davis, but I and "Mason" were not so sure.[813] It was actually Kerwin who envisioned the murder ahead of time when he made the discovery that his wife was giving him up for a new and better boyfriend George.

In the alternative timeline in which neither she nor George were killed, she married George Appleby.[240] She did not stay out of trouble with him either. Then they encountered no less than three mad scientists, Drs. Charles Conway[814], Monroe[815] and Umlauf[816], neighbor Joan Williams' jealous husband[817] and perhaps the worse of all the Appleby reunion in Las Vegas.[818]

The case of "Clay Mace" was different. "Mace the Mentalist", a parody of "Swami Talpur", entertained audiences by pretending to read minds and the future with the help of his beautiful assistant Norine Burton. She was, of course, vital to his getting personal information about his audience, though his elaborate metaphysically spiel put them in the right mood. All that changed however when "Mace" had a vision of the future, of a boxer being killed in the ring.

Like Paige's "vision" this death happened just as described by "Mace". Norine's father, who acted upon "Mace's" prediction and won money on the boxing match, was also killed just as "Mace" envisioned. The police were beginning to get suspicious, even though they could not link the deaths to him. He does not want to lose Norine, but realized that he cannot continue the act if it means predicting deaths. He suspects it is because his own death lies ahead soon. Marco did not, at least not consciously, realize that he had become hypersensitive to the Angel of Death. Although Nadine had become like the daughter he never had, he lets her go off with her boyfriend Grant Dudley, with the blessing she'd never have gotten from her own father, though not without a warning not to take a certain dangerous route.

After they leave he had a last vision and realized that they will not be able to heed the warning he gave them. He desperately convinces his former manager Gus Kostopulos to intercept them. Gus and "Mace" manage to save the couple from going over the cliff to their deaths and "Mace", as he foresaw, died happy.[819] The Dudleys continue on to Grant's new job in Italy and they name their children Burton, Augustus and Argilla, Italian for clay.

We had thought "Prof. Konrad Markesan" dead in 1943, but we picked up his timetrail again in 1962 when his nephew Fred Bancroft, and his bride, Molly, visited him and found him not quite yet dead. They hoped to live with him until they can find jobs and rent a place of their own. He does let them stay, but made them promise not to leave their bedroom at night. They, naturally, become curious and find that he has locked them in. This triggered Fred's Markesan curiosity even more and he managed to secretly open the lock without letting his more cautious bride know. He discovered that his uncle is summoning his now dead colleagues who ousted him from the uni, Latimore, Holden, Charing, and Grant, trying to get them to acknowledge his power over the Angel of Death.

We could not convince poor Molly to submit to her new husband.[820] Fred found his zombi wife had been frightened to death upon seeing the undead corpses.[821] We managed to aid Fred in convincing the professors that they would never rest in peace until "Markesan" did and they changed their verdict against him. I used the vita-ray on Molly and restored her to better than she had been before. The Bancrofts had the mansion condemned, sold the property and never looked back. They named their sons Everett and Angus after Latimore and Holden and taught them to stifle their curiosity.

This however got me to finally open the history of psychic research Doyle had given me for Christmas. Breaking the dead silence of our sitting room, I said, "I say, Holmes, I may have found another timeprint of our quarry Dr. Marco."

Holmes put down the violin he had been fiddling with, took the book and read the passage I indicated.

"I do believe you have, my good man. This is only a vague reference to a theory of psychic phenomena by an anthropologist on the obscure Caribbean isle of Korbai back in 1883. This quote here though of 'no more war, no pestilence, no famine, perhaps no more death' however certainly sounds like a case of Marco megalomania. Considering what we've found him into before, I dare not form a conjecture on what bizarre things this "Dr. Carl van Molder" has discovered this time."

"I wouldn't either, Holmes, but I for one wouldn't mind a little vacation to the Caribbean just to warm these old bones, even if it is a virtual one."

"The game is afoot again then," he said as he shifted Gordon, to activate our makeshift "chronoscope", adding with a smirk, "… 'old' friend."

Focusing on Korbai 1883 we soon were observing the new arrivals, Andrew and Annabella Wilhelm. They had inherited the van plantation, when her uncle had only recently died a heroic death.

"Remember when we were on the island the first time?", she asked her new husband Andrew accepting his offer of rum, "to seek funds from my uncle for the International Anti-Saloon League against its rival the World's Women's Christian Temperance Union. Little did I know then that I was to learn for myself about the truly horrible evils in this world not caused by alcohol!"

"What you actually said then, my dear, and I still remember every word, was 'I come in a great cause, to make a better world.'"

"That's right, I did, and uncle so kindly asked, 'How will it be accomplished?'

"And you so naively answered, "By destroying the demon, drink."

"And that's just what we've been trying to do ever since here, destroying destroying demons."

"And drinking." he added clinking glasses.

As they emptied their glasses of banana-flavored drink, Andrew continued, "We certainly learned more than we wanted to of the real demon that needed destroying, Damballah."

I had come to know rather more than I had ever wanted to know about both deadly snakes and voodoo already from the Roylott[822] and Murillo cases[823], but Holmes as ever was eager to learn more about all things deadly.

We learnt that "van Nolder" had been working on a technique of using the banana snake venom to stimulate psychokinetic powers, three centuries before kironide would be identified.[824]

"Capt Labesch was trying to make the island better in his own way, but as the doctor warned him. 'He who lives by the sword …"

"Dies by the sword." I thought remembering Bible quote.[825]

But Andrew finished the captain's quote quite differently with '… must have a strong arm.'"

"In the end he sacrificed himself for me."

"For all of us, dear." he added, taking one of the twin boys in her arms. "Pierre alone recognized your uncle as possessed by Damballah. He came to finally believe in Daballah when he heard the devilishness for what it was. I didn't realize it at the time myself, but that must be why he shot uncle Carl, to break the demonic link, to break the curse of Korbai."

"Yes, it was only later after we had examined Santanon's place that we figured out that as uncle freed the dwarf from the demon, it had transferred itself to him."

"He had called Baron Samodi the messiah of darkness earlier. That's what must have stuck in the captain's mind. Even as he was being rapidly paralyzed by the snakebite, Labesch was strong enough to throw himself into the fire."

"Unfortunately though Kalea survived and seems to be regaining her lost followers, so our fight goes on."

That was our cue to refocus, I think," Holmes said. We would have to or rather already had returned to meld our minds with the doctor's and the captain's as we had with Craven against "Scarabus". That and the amplifying effect of the deposit of the kironide in the mountain had triggered an explosion.

When we returned to the moment we had left left, Andrew was saying, "Fortunately the combined will of the brave doctor and captain, unleashed a vast untapped psychic power that literally unbewitched the natives and broke the curse of Korbai." We had changed the timeline. Annabella proposed another toast, "To the heroes of Korbai, past and future..." and it was heartily returned with "… Carl and Pierre."

We continued to watch only enough to observe and make certain that the natives destroyed the every last banana snake egg. The Eye also helped the natives identify and exterminate the mind-altering devil's-foot[826] from which Kalea had concocted her devilish incense. Then our all too brief Caribbean respite was over; the Eye had once again made the world better, at least for a time.[827]

There were many timelines which we could not change for the better, for example, when Marco lived as "Gregori Rasputin"[828] and seemed unable to die. The Eye required the help of "Dr. John Smith",[829] so that "the Mad Monk" did not escape to America,[415] did not become undead[830] and have to be re-killed by Nicholas de Brabant,[831] nor sire the mutants, Ilyana "Magik" or Piotr "Colossus".[832] Others we managed to divert into the fifth dimension as mere legends, those of "King Arthur",[833] "Don Quixote",[834] "Fr. Knickerbocker"[835] and "Capt. Billy Bones".[836]

The Superboy helped by timelooped his superdog Krypto's preventing "Wart" from pulling out the sword Excaliber from the stone.[837] The Horwitz brothers with Shuyler Davis' time machine helped save Princess Elaine.[838] Trevor Stirling prevented "Arthur's" assassination by Brenna McEgan and Cedric "Lailokan" Banning from future.[839] The Eye on the other hand prevented Excaliber from being stolen,[840] helped Thomas "the Fly" Troy fight Sir Magred,[841] Oliver "the Green Arrow" Queen fight Sir Sagramor[842] and "the Shining Knight" fight Vandar "Vandal Savage" Adg's robots for "Arthur".[843] We also mercifully prevented his encounter with the Knights of Ni.[844]

In a timeline near "Rukh" and "Mandel", farmer Corbin Witley discovered a glowing green meteor whose radiation triggered gigantism in his plants. His son, "Nahum" experimented with the strange rock with tragic results for both him and his wife, Leticia. Their daughter Susan returned home and with the help of her fiancé Steven Reinhart, and the Eye, uncovered the family secrets and narrowly escaped the mutagenic effects of the rays. When the meteor freed "Nahum" from his wheelchair, apparently developing a will of its own like the living lava, he sacrificed himself to save Susan, Steven[845] and Leticia's nurse Helga, after whom they named their daughter. Like "Mace". "Nahum" proved that we were moving in the right direction, toward Love.[846]

Art dealer "Hiram Stokley" died without having lived a very good or happy life, but like Ebenezer Scrooge[847] found himself with one day to change his postmortem direction. He got the co-operation of his more experienced ghostly girlfriend, Cecily, whom Dr. Goldfoot had used as the model for his fembots.[172] Together they tried to stop his greedy lawyer, Reginald Ripper and his henchman J. Sinister Hulk from blagging, cheating and robbing, his rightful heirs. Chuck Phillips, Lili Morton, Hiram's cousin Myrtle Forbush, and her son brought along his beach party friends to the Stokley mansion for a pool party. Ripper's daughter Sinistra and her accomplices, "Chicken Feather" and Yolanda, literally crash the party, while Yolanda is pursued by Eric Von Zipper and his Malibu Rat Pack biker gang.[848] All hell nearly burst loose before "Stokely" could pass on, even with Holmes trying to mindswap with Ripper.

As "Dr. Pierre Vaugiroud" he nearly insured world peace, like Butt[410], but was killed by what we aptly called in my day an anarchist. Frank Rosenfeld of the CIA called in Bill Fenner, now a freelance journalist to recover the *Vaugiroud Report*, catch the bombers while protecting his ex-wife Sandra Fane.[849]

Rocket scientist "Don Ernesto Silvando", like "Vaugiroud" held anti-missile information vital to world peace. Although the memories of his life as "Alonso Quixano" seemed to have replaced the "Silvando" ones, though he imagined threats on every side. His bodyguards Kelly Robinson and Alexander Scott keep him alive while they and rival agents Kurt and Horst all try to find his twee, his precious "Rocinante".[850]

Wheelchair-bound "Prof. John Marsh" helped Robert Manning learn about his missing brother, Peter, who disappeared visiting the Morley mansion. "March" pursued witchcraft as historian and scholar, rather than the self-righteous, self-appointed judge he had been as "Bishop Pierre Cauchon".[851] He "happened" to arrive on the tricentennial of the village's main claim to fame, the burning of Lavinia Morley, the infamous Black Witch of Greymarsh. It reminded me of the uninhibited Festival on Beta III.[852]

While Squire Morley is outwardly welcoming and his niece, Eve, undeniably seductive, their servant Elder is just slightly sinister. Lavinia herself seemed to be still haunting the place, trying to force the remaining Mannings, Robert and Peter, to add their names to her grimoire. Robert saw a sacrificial goat and the Black Witch's minions. He is invited to a witch hunt through the forest, "a rather sophisticated kind of hide and seek", but doubts his own senses.[853] Robert was relieved to find that Eve was neither possessed nor a witch and was able to take her away from Greymarsh. They named their children John and Roberta.

"John Taylor" was cursed with a beautiful, young but party animal wife, Linda. After having everything put in her name she threatened to leave him. He cursed her and saw her begin to like a cat and to transform into a cat-like carnivore, a were-cat. Linda conveniently ate the corpses of Dr. Don who threatened to inform the police and the nosy neighbor that he shot. By the time Sgt. Gilligan investigated the complaints of public nuisance cat noises, all he found was the remains of a murder-suicide, but no cat.[854]

Even as an artist, a sculptor, "Franz Badulescu" still seemed to attract Death. He was unaware that the skeletons he has been using for armatures are the remains of the victims of his "helpful" wife, Tania. The Eye saved "models" Elga and Valerie from the cauldron of acid. "Badulescu's" last words to Tania, having just accused her of causing his blindness, was "Till death do we part I suppose."[855]

The respected neurosurgeon "Dr. Laurience" was labeled "Dr. Maniac" by Lord Haslewood's newspapers after he began to experiment with mindswapping. Against the advice of her boyfriend Dick Haslewood, Dr. Clare Wyatt bravely assisted "Laurience" in mindwapping between monkeys, rather like "Jekyll's" animal experiments.

Quadriplegic Clayton, like Ygor, wanted a new body, unlike Ygor, so "Laurience" wanted to upgrade to Human subject, even though he considered Clayton's mind as twisted as his body. Wyatt objected on ethical grounds to both using Clayton and Lord Haslewood's money for the exclusive story.[856] Clayton rather liked being mindswapped into Wyatt's body too well, so "Lawrience" swapped him with Dick. When both Wyatt and the Haselwoods demanded a halt to the experimentation, "Lawrience" swapped Wyatt and Clayton back and Clayton died happy. This however left Clare's mind in Dick's body and Dick's in Clare's body. They adjusted and had a remarkably happy marriage and I did not have to swap them back again.

Pioneer cryogenicist "Dr. Leon Kravaal" did not meet with the same fate as "Dr. Savaard". In 1930 he too had been accused of killing his patient with what he called "frozen therapy". He was saved by the preservation of both himself and his accusers with an "accidental" combination of poisonous gases, producing dilute liscom gas[857], the DA John Hawthorne, Dr. Henry Bassett, Sheriff Stanton and villagers. They were not discovered until ten years later by Dr. Tim Mason and his fiancée Judy in "Kravaal's" hidden Canadian lab. The cancer patient's greedy nephew, Tim Mason, destroyed the formula. "Kravaal" was compulsively determined to duplicate the process, by trial-and-error if necessary, but not unexpectedly found a lack of willing volunteers.[858] They all escaped leaving "Kravaal" with only himself to experiment on and he slept for a full hundred and fifty years, awaking in 2090. He was returned to 1940 by the timeloop created by rogue Temporal Corps agent Zeke S. Vettenmyer.[859]

By 1840 71-year-old "Dr. Thomas Bolton" had seen more than his share of suffering. In his attempt to find a suitable anesthetic however things got worse. He became addicted to narcotics and when one of his patients revived with a bad reaction he was barred from performing surgery. Making a shady deal for more experimental drugs with "Black Ben" and "Resurrection Joe", he signed bogus death certificates for the graverobbers.[860] Things went from better to worse to better though for "Dr. Charles Gaudet". For treating a wounded revolutionary, the respected French brain surgeon was sentenced to Devil's Island. There he rebelled himself against the inhuman conditions and incurred the wrath of the brutal commander, Col. Armand Lucien. When Lucien's daughter was injured in an accident however his attitude softened when only "Gaudet" could save her.[861]

"'Pop' Jenkins" became so familiar with death after forty years in the morgue, and after God only knows[862] how many death experiences, that he effortlessly communicated with the dead. Mostly they told him who had caused their deaths, but he kept it confidential. Harry Jervis and Tom Ellison however sought to take advantage of what they had overheard about the murder Prof. John MacFarland had gotten away with. "Jenkins" couldn't allow that. Appearing suddenly in from of Jervis's car he didn't stop an accident, as he had as "Mace", he indirectly caused it. Ellison was only injured in the accident, so he did not get back to the morgue until after Jervis, but in time to hear "Pop" explaining why he had to do what he did. Both Jervis and Ellison gave up their evil ways, one a bit sooner than the other.[863]

"Col. Jackson Beauregard Finchess" communicated with the dead over the telephone. It was a very special telephone, installed in his father's crypt after he was prematurely buried. It was also a tramatic experience not only for father Le Jean, but his daughter Emily also who from then was convinced that she could speak with the dead as she had with her "dead" father. When nephew Daniel Le Jean and his wife and partner in crime Nell were reported dead after a bank robbery shootout, the Finchesses were not surprised that they showed up at the old mansion. Neither were they surprised when Daniel, looking for the family treasure, called from inside the family crypt to tell them they were locked it. "Col. Finchess" was not quite as confident as his wife that their nephew and his wife were dead, but he knew that if they weren't they soon would be and the crypt is where the dead ought to be.[864] Emily herself lived to be a hundred and one, the last of the Le Jeans.

"Dr. Albert Farnham" witnessed to dwindling of the Sommervilles. When Aunt Sophia had her accident and died, that left only niece Ursula and Aunt Celia. Then a long-lost cousin Rutherford showed up. After a couple more mysterious "accidents" however" Dr. Farnham" began to get suspicious.[865]

"Dr. Thorne" helped prevent his friend and patient Edward Stapleton's premature burial. He had expected an early death for the cataleptic Stapleton ever since he married the beautiful Victoire Lafourcade, but did every thing he could to help him build a foolproof vault. His marriage seemed to invigorate his old friend. He never looked healthier, until he died far away from home on a hunting trip.

Through the Eye we encouraged "Thorne" in his thorough investigation. We could not get him to look for the missing medical alert medallion where Victoire had hidden it, but he did learn from locals that it had been missing. Stapleton may have had one of his seizures, not gotten treatment until it was too late. He could not be sure of the cause of death.

With his friend Dr. March he tested his theory. "Stapleton" come back from the grave exposed both the cowardice of Victoire's painter boyfriend and her own guilt.[866]

"Prof. Vladimir Karloff" also married trouble when he married his young wife Yelena. His brother-in-law Vanya and his former rival Dr. Astrov both coveted Yelena. Dr. Astrov however ignored his infatuated daughter Sonya from his first wife. All of which made for complicated dynamics in the Karloff household.[867] We managed to prevent the timelines in which Vanya or Dr. Astrov or Sonya or Yelena killed the professor or vice versa, so that "Vladimir" and Yelena had a son Boris[752] and Dr. Astrov and Sonya also had a son Boris who became a both a professor and a doctor.

The end of the life of "Dr. Carlo Marcabienti" proved to be a case worth of the Italian Department Queer Complaints. He had spent his life as the venerable, reliable country doctor, while his son Angelo had gone off to the big city. While Dr. Angelo was yet again trying to convince his father to move to the city with him, a local child needed an emergency tracheotomy but the father refused until the "real" doctor came, meaning "Dr. Carlo". He did come in time to save the boy's life, but then it was found that he had already died.[868]

"It was not anything supernatural or even paranormal. It was just Marco's natural rejecting a foreign body and his timemachine substituting into another living one. He just happened to do an unfinished sidejob along the way, like the Wandering Frenchman or 'Stokely'."

He had similar debunking remarks in the case of Santha Naidu. He was born in India in 1928, but seemed to have memories of Sita Vernoy who died the year before he was born. Rather than proof of reincarnation or postcognition, it was, he claimed, a case of metagnomy, mind-to-mind communication, like telepaths, common with aliens and rare in Humans.

"Or like Pre-Fall Adam and Eve or angels communicating between themselves", I thought.

Nevertheless Holmes made his point, "The only things that could be verified as memories of Sita Vernoy would be those things known by someone still living 'Armand' or Krishna Vernoy. Since our mad doctor 'Armand Vernoy' was, one might accurately say, 'not all there', it would be rather unlikely that his thoughts not resonate in a young, receptive mind like Santha's."[869]

A similar case was that of Ruth Cooper who seemed to acquire the memories of Peggy Perry, the daughter of Martha and "Ira Perry". That both of these cases involved Marco timeclones was queer, but rather to be expected. Dr. Gar Madison advised Ruth's mother Ellie to take her to the Perry's house. Peggy's dog seemed to recognize the Ruth as its mistress. When Ruth re-enacted the fall down the stairs that killed Peggy on her sixteenth birthday however, this time "Ira Perry" was able to catch her and she was no longer trouble by Peggy's memories.[870]

"Sgt. Chester Willmore" also had a queer case. It was not as queer as the visions of "Mace" or Paige. He did not even know there was awt queer about it at all since George Bosworth never told the sergeant that he had seen the murder of his brother while abroad.[871] This too Holmes explained away as merely fraternal telempathy, two minds so in sync that as one Bosworth left his body his brother saw it as well. As a doctor I rather saw all of these queer cases and even the not so queer as the handiwork of our Client. I dared not however share Hamlet's famous quote to Horatio to Holmes.[872] It was the greatness of the Great Detective that he could eliminate the less possible to find the most possible that made him sought out by lesser detectives throughout time and space. I sussed that "Dr. Phillip Nestri"[873] and the bobbins, that is expert witness, "Dr. Steven Johnson"[874] and many of the other doctors that our Dr. Marco had been or been associated with held a similar opinion.

Even such silly codswallop as the three "Bad Humor Men" as Kay Kyser called them was ultimately His doing. "Judge Mainwaring" was an old friend of Margo Bellacrest, who had looked out for her interests ever since he was a young lawyer. He, like the Alphonsus-like detective Fenniger, was suspicious of the so-called medium calling himself "Prince Saliano" that Margo had become enamored of. All three and the famous Kay Kyser of the College of Musical Knowledge were guests at the twenty-first birthday party of Margo's heir, Janis, arranged by her boyfriend-manager "Chuck" Deems.

Because this was the occasion of Janis's trust fund coming to maturity the tension was already higher than normal. It did not help that a storm washed out the only bridge to the estate stranding all the guests or that the mysterious things kept happening as "Prince Saliano" held his séance. "All's well that ends well", as "Shakespeare" quoted Mr. Peabody. The party ended well, contrary to Pudder.[875] The storm ended. To both "Judge Mainwaring's" and detective Fenninger's satisfaction "Saliano" was proved to be merely an entertainer like "Ish Kabibble" and Deems that he sincerely cared for Janis's best interests.[9876] They named their daughters Kay and Bella.

As "Charles Brandon"[877] he may or may not have retained memories of "Judge Mainwaring". The lives of rich, single women are always in danger from cold-blooded scoundrels.[878] "George Sims", the administrator of St. Mary's of Bethlehem Asylum, that gave us the word "bedlam", was one such fellow, a "William" clone. When Quaker Nell tried to get him to treat the patients like Dorothea and Wilkes with some Human dignity, he compared her delusional idea[66] to the impossible task given Hercules of cleaning out the Augean stables. When she called "Sims" "a sewer of ugliness and a gutter brimming with slop", even her guardian Lord Mortimer thought her mad. She became one of the asylum's permanent guests.[879]

Things did not end well for gentleman "Toff" nor his shipmates, Albert, Bill and Sniggers either. They were the victims of the curse of the ruby eye they had stolen from an Indian idol.[879] Things seemed good for Steve La Farge when her returned to his boyhood home after fifteen years and got re-acquainted with Ann Kimball, but the were bad for "Bennett Kimball", her still grieving father. Ann's mother had been murdered fifteen years before and he had never gotten over it. Then it got worse for

La Farge when he realized that he had been involved in Mrs. Kimball's death.[880] In the end the mystery is solved and Steve and Ann and "Mr. Kimball" can move on with their lives. They called their oldest son "Ben" for Bennett.

In the Eighteenth Century "Voltran", manservant to Alain de Maletroit, watched as his master also grieved for his beloved. It was not however, because she had died in childbirth, but because she had chosen to marry his brother, Edmond, rather than himself. Since her death he had kept Edmond locked up in his dungeon, rather like "the man in the iron mask"[881] without the mask. That was not punishment enough for the imagined offense. He sought out the most despicable suitor he could find to match with his niece Blanche, Denis de Beaulieu. By faking a murder "Voltan" was this time able to put an end to the madness[882] and Blanche was able to inspire Denis, like the former "Utah Kid",[729] to reform. They named their oldest son Edmond.

We continued to come across possibly supernatural cases which, though he dared not admit it, I could see that our Client was getting through to Holmes's mental barriers. "Peter Wade, Sr.", a pilot during World War II, insisted that his son, Junior, carry on in his aviation company. He did not want to, but did get his pilot's license. He nearly crashed however when a vision of another man's face appeared reflected before him on the plane's windshield. "Follow me!" it seemed to say. Although his co-pilot saved them from crashing and shook Junior from his trance-like state, the same experience happened again the next time he flew over the same spot on the same route. He saw a flash on the ground and investigated, finding an old wrecked plane.

It turned out that it was none other than the plane of MIA Wally Huffman, who had flown with "Wade, Sr." Holmes, of course, took it that the father's survivor guilt had triggered the message seemingly from the dead.[883] With the truth finally out, the father and son reconciled. Peter, Jr., named his oldest son, Peter III, but his second oldest son he named Wallace, "Wally".

As attorney "Jonas Atterbury" he took the case of another Junior who had a vision. Although he had stayed by his father until his death, while his brother James had disappeared years before, John, Jr. had been written out of the most recent will by his father who still hoped his long-lost son would return. He did, but only to find out if he had gotten an inheritance. That was when John, Jr., saw his vision of his death father and heard the message to look up Genesis 27.[884]

That was, of course, the story of the twin brothers Jacob and Esau, two brothers who coveted the same inheritance. The name "James", of course, is a variant of the name "Jacob". Like Rebecca, the boy's mother, Emma, lied and lead "Jonas" to believe that James was John and John was James. The will therefore gave the inheritance to the real James, fka "John, Jr." Holmes again chose to believe that Emma, who knew the truth, sent the message. I choose to believe it was our Client.

"Morgan Debs" was, like Potterville's Potter[885], the richest man in Debsville and the most feared. John Prescott discovered this when he picked up hitchhiker Lila Kirby and they encounter "Debs" when they stopped at a bar for a drink to calm her down. She seemed agitated when he had found her near Lookout Point, but panicked when she saw "Debs". Prescott knew there was a town scandal in all this when "Deb's" chauffeur clubbed him over the head. That however only made him investigate further. The queerness about this was that Kirby had died at Lookout Point trying to flee "Deb's" unwanted advances.[886] This was "Deb's" guilty conscience projecting a tulpa, which everyone in town had also seen, Holmes said. In an alternative timeline, which we managed to patch in, timelooping the old one, the Eye rather like a guardian angel, guided Prescott to Lookout Point to save Kirby from dying and she rode with him to his destination and far away from Debsville. They named their son Kirby.

Another well rich, but heart-sick old man, "Montgomery Royle" had been a professional musician, but went deaf. His bad mood turned decidedly stroppy when he discovered that his young wife had married him only out of a sense of duty, that she actually had been attracted to his nephew Bobby.

When he looked out of his window upon the people in the park, he was able to read their lips and discovered that he could still do much good with anonymous gifts of money. This Good Samaritan role improved his mood. What gave it an ever greater boost was seeing his wife rejecting Bobby and deciding to be faithful. To they vow she had made.[887]

"Judge Winthrope Gelsey" was a rather mad old man. Along with his old companions, a former prosecuting attorney and defense council they decided to reenact a mock murder trial with a hapless traveling salesman sought shelter during a blizzard. He looked like he would actually pronounce a death sentence against the stranger. That was not, of course, the end of it. The trio had great fun with many, many appeals.[888]

"Charles van Druten" was quite mad, but rather harmless. Sandra Carpenter answered his ad for a model as part of Inspector Harley Temple's investigation into the Baudelaire killer. Several women had gone missing iafter after answering personal ads in the London newspapers and with each disappearance came a cryptic and macabre Charles Baudelaire poem. One of the missing persons had been Carpenter's friend Lucy Barnard, so she volunteered as bait.

"Van Druten" had Carpenter model his dresses for a non-existent audience, since he hadn't had a proper, live fashion show in forty years. In the seat reserved for royalty there was an English billdog, but he wasn't very interested in the show.

When she answered an advert for a concert date, her date did not show, but she did meet Robert Fleming there and they saw more and more of each other. When she applied for the job of a maid for a banker, she discovered that it was part of a white slavery pipeline to South America.

She did finally discover the wild Jilian Wild was the one she was after, saved her friend Lucy and married Fleming.[889] They named their children Lucy and Bernard.

"Andre Giraud" tried to advise his nephew Edmond Valier against pursuing Marie Montcour, but he did nevertheless, like Edward Stapleton and Victorine. It relationship did not last last long, though Marie did give Edmond a parting gift, a crystal ball. In it see saw, though his uncle could not, the on-going infidelities of Marie with man after man after him.[890]

Both I and Holmes agreed on this one. It could only be Edmond seeing what he subconsciously expected to see in the crystal. When she gave other crystals to Charles Mar and Phillipe Jussard however I began to wonder.[891]

"Capt. John Elwood" did not take the advise given him not to marry Ruth and later regretted it. When she got bitten by a snake and he saved her life, but later regretted it. He kept comparing his wife to other women, younger, more beautiful, wealthy. More and more he regretted being married to Ruth. By 1830 he had come up with what he though was a foolproof plan to get rid of his wife so he could marry the rich widow Bessie. He pretended to invite Ruth on board ship with him the next time he sailed so she wouldn't be so lonely and to try to make up a bit for all the times they had been separated. Foolproof plans generally prove the planner a fool.

All went according to "Elwood's" evil plot until his first mate Calvin Logan refused to make the course change he had ordered. When he tried to poison Ruth's food the table cloth mysteriously pulled out from under it, like some unseen hand, perhaps Bessie's late husband's, had pulled it.[892] Holmes, as I had expected, had an explanation for this queer case too. It was, he said, a projection of "Elwood's" guilty conscience manifesting itself psychokinetically like the so-called poltergeist or "noisy ghost" that typically manifests with trouble adolescents. Eventually after spending the whole voyage with her, he gave up fighting his subconscious and began appreciating his wife again and remembering why he had married her, because no one else ever had wanted to.

Leslie Cronyn was attracted to an American nurse while in Paris, but he too was having doubts about her. She naively still believed the romantic notions about war that they had grown up with before "the war to end all wars". Having seen the ugly truth first hand and deserted, Cronyn was one of the

Lost Generation. He saw old "Mr. Guibert" and his wife and longed for what they had, but knew that he and so many others like him never would, never could.[893]

"Gen. Pollegar" too had seen a bit too much of war, so too had the maharajah of Bakore. Both were reluctant to take seriously the ravings of Gunga Ram that cultists had killed his sister Indria and her husband. It seemed much more likely that it was case of an accidental house fire. Ram had to take up the fight against the worshipers of the fire-god Sabaka single-handily. He confronted the high priest Maku Ponjoy and defeated him. He killed Ashok and whipped out this India offshoot of Zoroastrianists that "Pollegar" didn't think existed.[894]

"Sir Arthur Strangways" had dealings with an entirely different god via a strange man calling himself an Alchemist. Although he did not ask the Alchemist to conjured Eblis,[895] he did ask for a god of laughter. He got Hāhālālā. What Hāhālālā granted him for his wish was tomorrow's London *Times* a day ahead of time. "Sir Arthur" thought that a very shrewd request. Although the Alchemist advised him not to seek profit from a gift, "Sir Arthur" made stock purchases and placed bets according to the info, the gen gleaned from the paper. He calculated he would make millions overnight.

It wasn't until he looked at the newspaper the next morning that he notice the obituary page. He began to doubt that the paper he had read the night before was the one he read now. It had his own obituary in it. The shock was too much for poor, old "Sir Arthur" and his butler Snaggs saw him die on the spot.[896] Hāhālālā laughed.[897]

"Count Ledrantz" witnessed what happened to the Rothschilds.[898] In 1772 Mayer Arnschel Rothschild made a deal with the devil. The next year his first son Amschel Mayer Rothschild was born. The year after that Salomon Mayer Rothschild was born. In 1777 Nathan Mayer Rothschild was born, in 1788 Calmann Mayer Rothschild and in 1792 Jakob Mayer Rothschild, five sons in twenty years. By 1811 Nathan founded the Bank of England. In fifty years all five brothers became barons. By 1885 the Rothschilds controlled the finances of not only Germany, but Great Britain, Switzerland, Italy and France and so all of Europe.

Greed and envy are not the only evils that can destroy a family. Hugh Strickland's family was destroyed by accident when his wife Florence was killed in an airplane collision. His obsession with revenge on "Ward Allen" and Johnny Mark destroyed him eventually.[899] The worse case we ever came across was the Karloffs. "Gorca" was the patriarch and sought to rid his family of the threat of the infamous outlaw Ali Beg. He had been missing five days when Vladimir d'Urfe arrived and was immediately attracted to daughter Sdenka.

On his way to the Karloff household d'Urfe told them he had come across the body of a man stabbed in the back with a dagger, the same dagger that "Gorca" had taken with him. The dead man must have been Ali Beg, killed by him. It was rumored that Ali Beg was more than a mere bandit or even murderer, that he was a wurdalak, a vampire. "Gorca" had warmed the family not to let him into the house during the night, no matter how much he begged, to wait until daylight to be sure that he too had not become a vampire. If he lived beyond the dawn, his soul could yet be saved, if not, he would remain a creature of the darkness.[900]

They however did not heed his warning. One by one they too were bitten and infected. "Gorca's" son Giorgio was able to behead his brother Pietro, but wife would only allow him to bury their son Ivan. He could still rise from his grave, drink blood and contaminate others. Vladimir and Sdenka hid out in the abandoned abbey and Vladimir thought they were safe. When a bloodthirsty Sdenka approached him however he yielded to her.[901] We managed to timeloop this horrific timeline, like we did with Lila Kirby's, so that d'Urfe prevented Ali Beg from turning the any of the family into vampires. He became a hero to Sdenka for saving her father's life and they named their sons Gorca, Giorgio, Pietro and Ivan. Ivan Karloff's son named his son Vladimir who became a professor.[867]

This seemed to me the clearest case of the supernatural that we had ever encountered. Holmes however still resisted that conclusion.

"There are alternative possibilities." He pontificated, "If I am not mistake, and I rarely am, there very well might be some as yet unknown deficient in the blood of these bloodthirsty individuals that makes them crave other's blood and something else replacing it, like the secret ingredient of the tana leaves or 'Kravaal's' gas mixture, that inhibits cellular deterioration."

"What about the photophobia, the fear of light, or hagiophobia, the fear of sacred objects?" I countered.

"Light sensitivity, as you know already, doctor, can be caused by many things, including blood deficiencies. As for the other, it could be merely the power of suggestion again augmented by a mental deficiency."

To me it seemed as if what he was proving was Finangle's Third Law, "That which is most obviously correct, beyond all apparent need to check, is the mistake." In any case it was a miracle that neither I nor Mary nor Moriarty became infected when we were bitten in 1894. ("The Adventure of the Solitary Grave")

"Mr. Kurtz" on the other hand lead a moderately happy, though mundane, life although in wild British East Africa, unlike his visitor, the joyless jobsworth, Charles Marlow.[902] "George Redford" and his wife Dorothy also lead a rather dull life in the suburbs, until that is their daughter Elsie concocted a plan to enable her and her boyfriend to elope. She tipped off the feds that her father was a counterfeiter and their lives became anything but dull.[903]

"Amos Hinchley's" son-in-law, Waldo Trumbull, an Erasmus throwback, a came up with a creative way to get his way too. He was an undertaker who decided he could cut expenses and increase his profit but recycling his coffin. If he had his assistant Felix Gill, who "happened" to be an Alphonsus throwback, dig up the coffin after he'd buried it, they only needed one. This worked well until the number of people dying decreased. He soon owed rent money to the landlord John F. Black and decided to hasten the death toll by one.

What he didn't know was that the Eye intervened with Holmes mindswapping with Black. Since Black also had been a Shakespearean actor and was a cataleptic like Edward Stapleton, it was not too hard for him the thwart Trumball's evil plan. As a final resort Trumbull changed his plan to poisoning his father-in-law and then his wife Amaryllis and inheriting everything. Gill was not too keen on the idea. Trumbull's own attempts at poisoning "Hinchley" failed without the Eye's help, apparently with our Client's.

Finally "Hinchley" seeing his exhausted son-in-law gave him some of his "medicine".[904] With Black still alive and Trumbull now dead, Trumbull was the last to use the coffin. Amaryllis was free to marry Gill, who treated her a good deal better than first husband had. They named their sons Amos, John and Waldo.

We were getting close to a normal life for our missing Dr. Marco, but we had traveled very far from the timeline he had come from. We would never be able to reunite Jane Marco with the husband she knew. We had managed to reunite "Henry" and "William", not as "Henry William", but as "William Henry". This time clone was born to Eliza Sarah Milliard and Edward John Pratt, Jr. and became an actor. He took the name of the South American revolutionary he had dreamt of once, "Boris Karloff".[751] He gave life to all the roles he played, because to him they had been real.

Using the obvious alias "Mr. Sirob", he happened to cross paths with a couple of fellow actors all laying over at the same motel near the O'Hare airport on Halloween. They decided to see if their classic horror film roles could still get the same reactions as they once had. "Mr. Retep", yet another Alphonsus throwback, acted the part of a vampire, "awaking" in a coffin. "Mr. Nol" put on his wolfman make-up and "Sirob" played the part of a Frankenstein monster. The secretary trainees went along with the holiday fun, swooning on cue. Even the scab greeters Todd Stiles and Buzz Murdock got in on the act, though the girls were not so co-operative in playing their game.[905]

Still as he caught his flight to London he he ponder how much the world had changed, not just over his lifetime, but over the centuries of Human history portrayed in his many roles and how little mankind had changed. Holmes and I could not help but ponder as well. We watched as he died of emphysema and never got to play his final performance in the land of his birth for the Queen.

This too, I must confess, Holmes and I meddled with, making a timeloop to influence him to rather take the more mundane engagement of a showing of his classic films at a drive-in theater in Texas. He did not know, as we knew, that it would be his greatest role. Bobby Thompson, Jr., was at this drive-in, so "Boris Karloff" had to be there too.

Bobby had been forced to shoot a gun as a boy by his father. He had been forced to used a gun again as a sniper in the Vietnam War. The Post-traumatic Stress compounded by a brain tumor turned him into a madman. After shooting both his wife and mother he went out to shoot random drivers and passengers on the highway from a water tower.

Then there was "Karloff's" make-believe horror on the screen as Thompson invoked real horror from atop the screen overlooking a parking lot, he'd make his own private shooting gallery. He was playing god in "the gods", high above the commoners. Panic ensued as family member were shot randomly, fathers, mother, children, not knowing where death was showering down on them.

"Karloff" knew that he had to do something. Like the man who had tried to flee death only to encounter him in another town, "Karloff" knew that this was finally his time to die for the last time. He made his way up to Thompson's tower, despite two leg braces, and in the struggle both died, but "Karloff" gave his life to save his fans.[906] He had save directly or indirectly many, many more lives. He had accomplish his original objective, to save lives. Our Client had indeed taught us a lesson, "Greater love hath no man than this, that a man lay down his life for his friends."[907]

ENDNOTES

1 "The Street and the Detective" by A. L. Shern
2 (*Sherlock Holmes: The Time Machine Game*) 1920: Frederick Parmeriter, Alessandro Berardelli and "Dapper Joe" Elwell murders ("The Card Playing Cue Ball"), Ferdinando Sacco and Bartolomeo Vanzetti didn't kill Alesandro Beradelli and Frank Parmenter ("The Cobbler and the Fish Peddler"); 1922: Crabapple murder cases ("The Crabapple Killings") and William Desmond Taylor murder ("The Director's Demise"); 1923: the Dorothy "Dot" King murder case ("The Flapper's Last Bunny Hop"); 1928: Arnold "the Brain" Rothstein murder ("The Bullet for Mr. Big"); 1932: the Lindbergh kidnapping case ("The Ricketty Ladder"); 1934: the mysterious "death" of John Dillinger ("The Lady in Red", *War on Crime*); 1943: the Sir Harry Oakes murder case ("The 'Black Mack' Murder"); 1947: Elizabeth "Black Dahlia" Short murder case; 1955: the Serge Rubenstein murder case ("The Napoleon of Fifth Avenue"); 1963: the Lee Harvey Oswald murder case ("The Camelot Conspiracy"); 1966: Cheri Jo Bates murder case ("The Zodiac Crimes"); 1969: the Darlene Ferrin, Bryan Hartnell, Cecilia Shepherd and Paul Stine murder cases ("The Zodiac Crimes"); 1970: the Kathleen Johns murder case ("The Zodiac Crimes"); 1971: found "D. B. Cooper", but not $200,000 ("The Four Parachutes"); 1973: the Watergate break-in case ("The Unknown Informant"); 1975: the Jimmy Hoffa disappearance case ("The Vanished Teamster"); 1977: the mysterious "death" of Elvis Presley ("The King's Last Exit", "Men in Black II", *Mostly Harmless* by Douglas Adams), and the mysterious popularity of "Three's Company" ("Jack the Tripper")
3 1880: tried to substitute Dr. John Walker for Dr. John Watson" (*The Veiled Detective*), 1883: killed 36,000 in Krakatoa eruption ("His Greatest Case"), but not Holmes (*Erasing Holmes*), 1888: possessed by Redjak (*The Shadow of Reichenbach Falls*), 1893: escaped gallows ("Hands of a Murderer"), 1899: lead Thuggee cult (*The Siam Question*), 1896: allies with Dr. Omega and Zephyrin Xirdal, killing

28,000 in ("The Dynamics of an Asteroid"), stole cavorite from Fu Manchu (League of English Gentlemen, Vol. II), tried to use the *Nectronomicon* ("Nightmare in Wax"), 1908: killed 160,000 in Sicilian quake, 1909: killed Sir Clyde Horton as "Frank Ffellows" ("The Purloined Ruby"); 1868: had younger self kill Prof Harrington, 1911: Moriarty killed Pyotr Stolypin, 1940: Lev Davidovich "Leon Trotski" Bronstein, 1948: Mahatma Ghandi, 1951: King Abdallah, 1963: John Fitzgerald Kennedy, 1968: Martin Luther King, 1981: Anwar Sadat, 2001: Phitsanulok, 2014: Junior Rex, 2019: Johnny Wu, 2031: Sir John Morgenthaler, 2034: Hrachia Dashnakian, 2070: Philo Tremussen, (*Time for Sherlock Holmes* by David Dvorkin); 1913: killed Dilworthy ("The Remarkable Affair of the Pointless Robbery"), discovered hiding in Dreamland (*"The Adventure of the Dreaming Detective"*), 2249: threatened New Texas (BraveStarr: "Sherlock Holmes in the Twenty-third Century"). Besides the timetraveling Moriarty, there were also in 2203 the clone, Moriarty 2 ("Sherlock Holmes in the Twenty-second Century"), in 2268 the Moriartybot ("A Nostalgic Country of the Mind"), and in 2369 the holoMoriarty ("Elementary, My Dear Data").

4 "The Greatest Detective of All Time" by Ralph Roberts

5 *Sherlock Holmes and the Needle's Eye* by Len Bailey

6 King of Kings and Lord of Lords, ibid., "Trust in the Lord with all thine heart; and lean not unto thine own understanding." (Proverbs 3:5)

7 *The Eyes Sees* and *The Detective* Eye by Mark Schneider

8 John 21:25

9 Jacques Clouseau, 1963: vs. "the Phantom", Alexander Charles Lytton Fleming ("The Case of the Missing Ruby",michaelhalm.tripod.com/id158.htm, "The Pink Panther" by Maurice Richlin and Blake Edwards), 1964: the Gambrelli murder ("A Shot in the Dark" by Blake Edwards and William Peter Blatty), 1965: the Siamese triplet secret agent Welf/Wight/Wong ("The Great De Gualle Stone Operation" by John W. Dunn), 1966: Monsieur X ("Plastered in Paris" by John W. Dunn), mad bomber ("Napoleon 'Blown-apart'" by John W. Dunn), pearl smuggler Capt. Clamity ("Reaux, Reaux, Reaux Your Boat" by John W. Dunn), a Louvre burglar ("Cirrhosis of the Louvre" by John W. Dunn), Judy ("Ape Suzette" by John W. Dunn), Toulouse Le Moose ("Toulouse le Trick" by John W. Dunn), international secret agent ("Unsafe and Seine" by John W. Dunn), pickpocket Spider Pierre ("The Pique Poquette of Paris" by John W. Dunn), 1967: vs. the Pig-Al gang ("The Pig-Al Patrol" by Jim Ryan), Hassan the Assassin ("Sacré Bleu Cross" by John W. Dunn), 1975: "The Return of the Pink Panther" and (1976) "The Pink Panther Strikes Again" by Frank Waldman and Blake Edwards, 1978: "The Revenge of the Pink Panther" by Frank Waldman, Ron Clark and Blake Edwards, 1982: "Trail of the Pink Panther" by Frank and Tom Waldman, Blake and Geoffrey Edwards

10 cyborg detective Inspector Gadget, 1983: vs. "Dr. Claw" Zhao ("Gadget in Winterland" by Jean Chalopin and Andy Heyward), saved Prof. Frafkin ("Monster Lake" by Peter Sauder, etal.) and Prof. Von Slicksfein ("The Amazon"), vs. M. A. D. ("Gadget at the Circus"), found El Dorado ("All That Glitters"), Poot-Ta-Foot's treasure ("Curse of the Pharaoh"), vs. Rauruda ("Japanese Connection"), Prince Abar of Yetzanistan ("Arabian Nights"), Amster diamond ("Dutch Treat"), Dr. Focus's sneezooka ("Gone Went the Wind"), Labella stirs rebellion in Pianostan ("King Wrong"), found philosopher's stone ("Did You Myth Me?"), vs. "Nervous" Nick Defecto ("Quimby Exchange"), found the Star of Istanbul ("Birds of a Feather"), 1985: Eleanor Burian-Mohr, etal.'s vs. Great Wambini ("Magic Gadget"), found the diamond-spitting Alpacastani llama ("Wambini Predicts"), "Capeman" ("Crash Course in Crime", "Gadget's Gadgets"), 1988: ("Inspector Gadget's Last sic Case"), 1990: Inspector Gadget's Biggest Caper Ever: The Case of the Giant Flying Lizard")

11 Seward Willoughby, 1963: vs "Crash" McDash ("Coming Out Party"), vs Yeggs Benedict ("The Case of the Cold Storage Yegg"), vs "One-eyed Jack" Hook ("Hi-Seas Hi-Jacker"), 1964: vs Egg Foo Yung ("The Case of the Maltese Chicken"), 1965: ("The Case of the Elephant's Trunk")

12 aka "Agent 86" of CONTROL, 1965: saved Princess Ingrid from "the Claw" Chin. Zhao (Get Smart: "Diplomat's Daughter"), vs. Miguelito "Mr. Big" Loveless for Dante's inthermo ray ("Mr. Big"), Fred the robot and FLAG (*Get Smart!*), 1966: vs. "The Claw" Zhao again ("The Amazing Harry Hoo", "Hoo Done It"), vs. Gen. Pajarito in San Saludo ("Viva Smart"), saved Trinka of Marovia ("Maxwell Smart, Private Eye"), teamed with #4, #8, #11 at Spy City Retirement Home ("Dear Diary"), and Dr. Shortwire, Dr. Ratton and Mr. Natz and HYMIE ("Back to the Old Drawing Board"), Dr. X's invisibility formula (*Sorry Chief...*), vs. I. M. Noman (*Get Smart Once Again*), 1967: saved Tisha Heinschmidt Miss USA, though "Miss Formosa" killed Miss Transmania (Get Smart: "The Girls from KAOS"), destroyed dehydrator ("A Man Called Smart"), earthquake machine ("Supersonic Boom"), Lost Lake, Neb., jamming station ("Dr. Yes"), found X of Scorpion gang aka Cmd. Hathaway at Crashing Boar pub ("That Old Gang of Mine"), recruited 8th-grader Tyler "Dr. T" Tattledove who'd given inventions to Prof. Longnecker for "The Girl from GALAXY" series, including forcefield projector ("The Mysterious Dr. T"), worked with femme Charlie "Angelique" Watkins ("Pussycats Galore", "Smart Fit the Battle of Jericho") and femme Dr. Hans Svenson ("How to Succeed in the Spy Business without Really Trying"), worked with Your Espionage Network and Training Academy ("The Man from YENTA"), vs. magician Whitestone (*Missed It by That Much*), vs. Guru Optimo (*And Loving It!*), 1968: Charles of Caronia, son of Helena of Ruritania, vs. half-brother Basil, Rupert of Rathskeller, Princess Marta ("The King Lives?"), invisible Dr. Canyon ("One Nation Invisible"), Dr. Madre defects ("With Love and Twitches"), vs. Atrocities, Cruelties and Brutalities (ABC) led by Kubacek ("Die, Spy"), A. J. Pfister's nitrowhisperin ("Spy, Spy, Birdie"), Dr. Steele's lying pills vs. Sacred Cows ("Groovy Guru"), Wormer Von Boom (*The Spy Who Went Out to the Cold*), vs. Ways and Means (*Max Smart Loses CONTROL*), 1969: Princess Ingrid of Caronia ("To Sire with Love"), Simon the Likeable ("And Baby Makes Four"), manimal Mary "Jack" Armstrong ("The Apes of Rath"), aging via Dorian gray paint ("Age Before Duty"), drugged water ("Is This Trip Necessary?"), ("Ice Station Siegfried"), vs. assassin Arbuthnot (*Max Smart and the Ghastly Ghost Affair*), 1970: Duval's wax golem Ripper ("House of Max"), Balmanian rocket formula ("How Green Was My Valet"), Whip steals NARCO 5-12 ("I Am Curiously Yellow"), 1980: ("The Nude Bomb"), teamed with "Derek Flint", James "007" Bond, Avengers John Steed and Emma Peel, Illya Kuryakin, Napoleon Solo, and April Dancer of UNCLE (United Network Command for Law Enforcement), Mark Slate, John Drake, Matt Helm of ICE, Modesty Blaze of the Network, Alexander and Kelly Robinson vs. Shan Ming-Fu's Si Fan zombies (*Cold Men*), 1989: CONTROL vs. KAOS again ("Get Smart, Again" by Tom J. Astle, Steve Careel and Matt Ember)

13 Amanda "Mandy" Stevenson left UNCLE ("The Never-Never Affair" by Dean Hargrove) for CONTROL becoming agent "99" ("I Am Curiously Yellow" by Lloyd Turner and Gordon Mitchell), later aka Mrs. Maxwell Smart and "Diane 'Spy Girl' Caldwell" ("The Spy Girl Who Loved Me" by Paul Reisner), mother of son Zach ("Get Smart" by Tom J. Astle and Matt Ember), mother-in-law of Helen Renaldi, whose cousin was Mia of Genovia ("Princess Diaries" by Gina Wenkos, *Princess Diaries* by Meg Cabot) and grandmother of Mia Smart

14 Henry "Indiana" Jones, Jr., Holmes's half second cousin twice removed: 1899: Indy in Egypt ("My First Adventure"), 1908: Norman Rockwell, Pablo Picasso, Edgar Degas ("Passion for Life"), 1909: "Teddy" Roosevelt (Passion for Life: "British East Africa, Sept. 1909"), 1910: Tolstoy, Nikos Kazantzakis ("Travels with Father"), 1912: loses Cross of Coronado ("Indiana Jones and the Last Crusade" prologue), Indy and Shalimar diamond (*Indiana Jones and the Titanic Adventure*), 1913: traveled back to King Arthur (... *the Ghostly Riders*, "Keeping Up with the Jones"), (... *the Mountains of Superstition*), (... *the Plantation Treasure*), found the ring of Osiris (... *the Tomb of Terror*), Dentsen (... *the Child Lama*), Princess Tamar Rustava (... *the Princess of Peril*), a Stratavarius (... *the Violin of the Metropolitan*), (... *the Bermuda Triangle*), in Wales (... *the Ghostly Riders*), at Stonehenge (... *the*

Circle of Death), 1914: found the Pietroasa bowl (… *the Journey to the Underworld*), cross of Roger (… *the Curse of the Ruby*), Romany crown (… *the Gypsy Revenge*), knife of Cain (… *the Secret City*), (… *the Mountain of Fire*), (… *the Face of the Dragon*), ivory iskander and Kasim Khan (weretiger?) (… *the Eye of the Tiger*), 1916: Nancy Stratemeyer, Pancho Villa, Patton, Pershing ("Spring Break Adventure"), Sean O'Casey and Maggie Lemass and Easter Rebellion, Vicky Prentiss and Winston Churchill ("Love's Sweet Song"), as "Henri Defense"with Sigfried Sassoon, Robert Graves and Charles de Gaulle ("Trenches of Hell"), Mata Hari ("Demons of Deception"), 1917):Albert Schweitzer ("Oganga, The Giver and Taker of Life"), "Red Baron" (… *the Attack of the Hawkmen*), Karl of Austria and Vladimir Lenin (*Adventures in the Secret Service*), Franz Kafka ("Espionage Escapades"), T. E. Lawrence ("Daredevils of the Desert"), Ernest Hemingway, Edith Wharton, Lowell Thomas ("Tales of Innocence"), 1918: vampire Thomas "Latos" Caine and werewolf Andreas (*Masks of Evil*), Alexander's treasure (… *the Treasure of the Peacock's Eye*), 1919: Arnold Toynbee, Gertrude Bell and Robert Goddard ("Winds of Change"), roomie Elliot Ness, Ernest Hemingway, Al "Brown" (… *the Mystery of the Blues*), 1920: Peggy Peabody, Kate Rivers, Gloria Schuyler and George Gershwin (… *the Scandal of 1920*), Eric von Stroheim, John Ford, Wyatt Earp (… *the Hollywood Follies*), 1922: Magnus Völler found jade sphere (… *the Staff of Kings*), 1925: Diedre Campbell's gold scroll of Merlin vs. Adrian Powell (… *the Dance of the Giants*), 1926: Camozotz mask and shield, Deidre Cambell dies (… *the Seven Veils*), 1927: Vladimir Zobolotsky expedition (… *the Genesis Deluge*), 1929: moai (… *the Interior World*), 1930: (… *the Sky Pirates*), Caliburn (… *the White Witch*), berserker scroll (*Indiana Jones Adventures: Vol. 1*), Ramesses IX (… *the Curse of the Mummy's Crypt*), 1931: Wohat statues and Ali Bey ruby (…. *the Curse of the Invincible Ruby*), Henrik Mellberg finds Key to the Tomb of the Gods (… *the Tomb of the Gods*), 1932: amulet (… *the Feathered Serpent*), 1933: stolen Voynich manuscript, crystal skull of Cozán (… *the Philosopher's Stone*, "Voynich Manuscript"), ebony dove (… *the Curse of Horror Island*), yeti (… *the Giants of the Silver Tower, …the Mystery of the Yeti*), Mahatma Ghandi (… *the City of Fire*), Ghengis Khan knife, triceratops (… *the Dinosaur Eggs*), 1934: Ultima Thule (… *the Hollow Earth*), Aaron's staff, *Omega Book* (… *the Secret of the Sphinx*), (… *the Shrine of the Sea Devil*), Heart of the Dragon pearl, Dragon's Claw boomerang (… *and the Emperor's Tomb*), Thugs and Sankara stones (… *the Temple of Doom*), jewel of power (… *the Temple of Forbidden Eye*), cup of Djemsheed (… *the Cup of the Vampire*), 1936: the lost book of the Cabal (… *the Cursed Grimoire*), pendant of the Incas (… *the Legion of Doom*), Ark ("Raiders of the Lost Ark"), Mazatec Power Key (*Revenge of the Ancients*), (… *the Ikons of Ikammanen*), crystal cylinder of Stonehenge (*Gateway to Infinity*), Raven's Nest bombing (*Club Nightmare!*), 1937: ceremonial dagger (… *the Wrath of Hecate*), Eye of Shamash (*Double!*), Shiva statue, Chimu Taya arms (… *and the Arms of Gold*), shield of Perseus, eye of the Fates (… *and the Eye of the Fates*), 1938: vs. golden lotus for Ada ruby, fish head vessel of King Kataam (… *the Dragon of Vengeance*), staff of Genghis Khan (… *the Gold of Genghis Khan*), Covenant of Buddha (*Thunder in the Orient*), (… *the Lost Treasure of Sheba*), returns Grail ("… The Last Crusade"), 1939: Moses' staff (… *the Staff of Kings*), Skithblathnir (… *the Longship of the Gods*), Plato's *Hermocrates*, orichalcum bead (… *the Fate of Atlantis*), Lolongan I. (… *the Ape Slaves of Howling Island*), (… *the Sargasso Pirates*), Azudab's deathmask (*Facing Death!*), 1940: golden jaguar flute (*Skull!*), excalibur (… *the Legacy of Avalon*), 1943: (… *and the Gold of El Dorado*), Heart of Darkness black pearl of Haiti (… *the Army of the Dead*), Anasazi clay disc (… *and the Lost People*), 1944: (… *the Treasure of Monte Cassana*), (1945) spear of Longinus (… *the Spear of Destiny*), 1957: (… *the Iron Phoenix*), vs. Commies for Tool from Beyond that teleports to Shambala, Palawan I., Teotihuacan, Moroë and Babylon (… *the Infernal Machine*), found flying saucer, finally marries Marion Ravenwood, learns Mutt Williams is his son (… *the Crystal Skull*)

15 From the names and dates from several sources we have attempted to put together with some accuracy who lived when and their relationships. **Grandfather Lestrade** had two sons with the older one likely staying in England, while the younger son, **Jack**, went to America, settled in Oregon and married **Marta**. (Ernest Haycock and Ernest Pascal) The other son himself had four sons: (1) Inspector **Gerard** (Bernard J. Schaffer), (2) Inspector **Jules** with wife **Juliette** and daughter **Carrie** (Hilary Bailey), (3) Inspector **Sholto**, whose son Chief Inspector **Gordon** (J. Brooks Van Dyke) married **Fanny**, the daughter of Sholto's friend Harry Bandicoot and his wife Letitia, sister of twins Rupert and Ivo, who had a daughter Emma who was engaged to a Mr. Hood (M. J. Trow) and (4) Deputy Chief Inspector **Jackson** (Rob Rogers), who had a son Inspector **George** (Anthony Horowitz) with wife **Agnes** (Barry Grant) and two grandsons: (a) Chief Inspector **John** with wife **Maud** and a daughter (Mary Russell) and (b) Inspector **Jasper** (John A. Little), who being the one Lestrade without a daughter may have had the son who was the ancestor of Inspector **Beth** in the 22nd Century (Phil Harnage).

16 20th century WW I ("His Last Bow") and WW II (Robert E. "Papa Bear" (Hogan's Heroes: "The Missing Klink" by Bill Davenport), Pepper Flynt Busbee ("Little Boy" by Alejandro Monteverde and Pepe Portillo)), 21st Century WW III ("WW 3" by Toplitz), 24th Century WW VI ("Frostfire" by Marc Platt), 49th Century WW V ("Singularity" by James Swallow) and WW VI ("The Talons of Wang Chiang" by Robert Holmes)

17 John "Paul Finglemore" Clay(ton) ("The Redheaded League", "The African Millionaire" by Grant Allen), Scott "Dr. Evil" Luther and his clone Scott "Mini-Me" Luther 2 ("The Spy That Shagged Me" by Mike Myers and Michael McCullers), Alexander "Lex" Luther (Superman mythos), Lawrence Luther and his clone Lawrence "Kingpin" Luther 2, and David "Warbucks" Luther ("Little Orphan Annie" by Harold Gray) ("The Lethal Luthors: Or What Ever Happened to John Clay?" by Dennis Power)

18 "Action Man" aka "G. I. Joe" in U. S., able to sub for "Aquaman", "Batman", "Buck Rogers", "Capt. America", "Flash Gordon", "Green Hornet", "Lone Ranger", "Phantom", "Sgt. Fury", "Spider-Man", "Steve Canyon", "Superman", and "Action Boy" aka "Aqualad", "Robin the Boy Wonder", "Superboy", and "Action Girl" aka "Aqualass", "Robin the Girl Wonder", "Supergirl" ("What Ever Happened to the Man of Tomorrow" by Tim Crane)

19 from 29th Century ("Superwoman of Metropolis", "The Last Secret Identity", *Superman: Miracle Monday* by Elliot S! Maggin)

20 aka "Astro Man of Space", "Balloon Boy", "Baron Buzz-Saw", "Changeling", "Cometeer", "Giant Boy", "Human Icicle", "Hypnoman", "Jesse Quick", "King Kandy", "Lagoon Boy", "Master", "Mighty Moppet", Silver Age "Plastic Man", "Power Boy", "Protector", "Quakemaster", "Radar-Sonar Man", "Robby Robot", "Sphinx Man", "Super-Charge", Iron Age "Wizard", "Velocity Kid", "Whatsis", "Whirl-I-Gig", "Whoozis", "Yankee Doodle Kid", etc., etc. ("The Boy Who Could Change into a Thousand Superheroes" by Dave Wood)

21 "The Terrible Toymaster!"

22 "Dial V For Villain"

23 "Who Are the Heroes?"

24 Kal-El, Bruce Wayne, Henry Bartholomew Allen, Ray Palmer, Dinah Drake, Arthur Curry, Oliver Queen, J'onn J'onzz, Lex Luthor, David Clinton, Selina Kyle, Dr., Albert/Alvin Desmond, Oswald Copplepot, Felix Faust, Sinestro ("If I Kill Me, Will I Die?" by Mark Waid and Barry Kitson and Terry Dodson), Clark Kent and Clark Kent, Jr. mindswapped ("The First Superman Robot", "The Day That Lasted Forever", "The Day Superboy Became Superman"), Superboy and Krypto mindswap ("Krypto, the Human Superdog"), Superman and Batman mindswap ("Superman's Nightmare Dreams"), actor Gregory Reed mindswapped with Superman ("Superman vs. Superstar"), Troxx-55 "Demolisher" and Superman ("The Fantastic Foe Superman Could Never Meet"), Zenna Persik mindswapped with Diane "Black Canary" Drake ("Heritage"), then with Wonder Woman ("The Black Canary Is Dead",

Longbow Hunters), Jor-El and Kal-El ("Jor-El: Superman"), "Time Master" mindswapped with Clark "Superboy-Prime" Kent (DC Comics Presents #87), Vaalor and Superman ("The 'Monumental' Menace of Metropolis"), Lex Luthor and Superman mindswapped ("Bodyswap"), Superman and Madman mindswapped (*Superman/Madman Hullabaloo!*), using H-dial Kal-El becomes "Doc Fission", Bruce Wayne "Minuteman", Bartholomew Allen "Marionette", Ray Palmer "Mod-Man", Dinah "Miss Fortune" Drake, Arthur Curry "Terra-Firma", Oliver "Green Arrow" Queen "Poltergeist", J'onzz "Go-Go" vs. Lex Luthor mindswapped with "Superman", David "Cronos" Clinton with Ray "Atom" Palmer, David "Black Manta" with Arthur "Aquaman" Curry, Selina "Catwoman" Kyle with Dinah "Black Canary" Drake, Dr. Arthur Light with J'onn J'onzz, Albert/Alvin "Mr. Element" Desmond with Henry "Flash" Allen, Oswald "Penguin" Copplepot with Bruce "Batman" Wayne, Felix Faust with Oliver "Green Arrow" Queen, Sinestro with Hal "Green Lantern" Jordan (Silver Age 80-Page Giant #1)

25 "Year of the Comet", "The Origin of Superboy-Prime", and by extrapolation "The Origin of Supergirl-Prime"

26 superhero "Goldstar" (Goldstar #1) fka "Booster Gold" of the Linear Men and his son Ripley "Rip" Hunter (Booster Gold #1)

27 from 24th Century, aka "Time Trapper", Tibro, ("The Fun House of Time" and "The Crime Master of Time" by Robert Kanigher, "Trapped in Two Worlds" and "Manhunt in Time" by E. Nelson Bridwell, "Trapped in Time" by Michael Ryan, "Final Crisis: Legion of Three Worlds" by Geoff Johns, "Titan in a China Shop" by Mary and Tom Bierbaum, etal., "Future Shock!" by Keith Ian Giffen and Mindy Newell)

28 "The Greatest Detective of All Time" by Ralph Roberts

29 "The Adventure of the Hanoverian Vampires" by Marvin Kaye

30 "The Deadly Assassin" by Robert Holmes

31 *Relative Dementias* by Mark Michalowski

32 "Man of Molten Steel" by Elliot S. Maggin

33 I intentionally put in Mary's reference to our son James in "The Man with the Twisted Lip" aka "The Strange Tale of a Beggar"; our other children have been revealed by other Irregulars: Richard, Emma (*No Ordinary Terror* by J. Brooks Van Dyke), Joan (The Adventures of Shirley Holmes series by Basil Mitchell and Frederic Arnold Kummer), Patience Marie ("A Childlike Happiness" by poeticmaiden), Jady, Alexander ("Uncle Sherlock" by Christy Torland), Blair ("Ace" by IHKF). sister Jane ("Whither Thou Goest" by mf32), Janet, Nora, Donald and John Jr.

34 210-year-old Fr. Perrault in *Lost Horizon* by James Hilton. "The Journey to a Lost Horizon" by Robert S. Chambers, ""Hiatus in Paradise" by Dana Martin Batory; he did NOT marry an Abominable Snow-woman ("Sherlock and the Sherpas" by James Nelson), "wrinkled yeti of the club foot and his abominable life" (D. Martin Dakin)

35 Col. March of Scotland Yard series based on John Dickson Carr: ("The Abominable Snowman"), color-blind killer ("At Night All Cats Are Grey"), serial killer Pennacott ("The Invisible Knife"), ("The Headless Hat"), ("Death in Inner Space"), Barton's bust ("The Talking Head"), ("Murder Is Permanent"), ("Death and the Other Monkey"), ("The Silver Curtain"), ("Error at Daybreak"), ("Hot Money"), ("The Missing Link"), ("The Case of the Misguided Missal"), Mde. Richter ("The Case of the Lively Ghost"), ("The New Invisible Man"), ("Passage at Arms") by Leslie Slote; Dr. Patten murder ("The Sorcerer"), Rune "accident" ("The Strange Event at Roman Fall"), ("The Deadly Gift") by Paul Monash; spiritualism ("Present Tense"), ("The Second Mona Lisa"), ("The Silent Vow") by Paul Green; Fairway diamonds ("The Case of the Kidnapped Poodle"), Lord Telford death ("The Devil Sells His Soul") by Arthur Berstock;("The Stolen Crime" by Paul Tabori), ("Death in the Dressing Room" by Leo Davis)

36 "Passage at Arms" by John Dickson Carr

37 "The Twilight Zone" intro by Rod Serling

38 tvtropes.org explains that the Eyepatch of Power indicates fighting experience and coolness. The time Skip Eyepatch indicates that during the intervening time skip the character leveled up in fighting experience and coolness as, for example, the 93-year-old Henry Jones, Jr., did in "The Young Indiana Jones Chronicles" by George Lucas.

39 The Elgin Hour: "Sting of Death" by Alvin Shapinsley, Taste of Honey by Gerald Heard

40 "Mr. Wong, Detective" by Houston Branch, "The Mystery of Mr. Wong" and "Mr. Wong in China Town" and "The Fatal Hour" by Scott Darling, "Doomed to Die" by Michael Jacoby, *Murder By The Dozen* by Hugh Wiley

41 Tales of Tomorrow: "Past Tense" by Willie Gilbert

42 originally "emplosion" from 'mplosion with a truncated i- and a verbalized m-

43 "Sidewise in Time" by Murray Leinster, "Sliders" by Tracy Tormé and Robert K. Weiss

44 "Himself in Anachron" by Paul "Cordwainer Smith" Linebarger

45 "Notion of the Past and Can We Change It?" by Igor Dmitriyevich Krasnikov

46 *Many Dimensions* by Charles Williams, *Vanderdeken's Children* by Christopher Bulis

47 "Without father, without mother, without descent, having neither beginning of days, nor end of life." (Hebrews 7:3), Psalm 73:20

48 John 15:2

49 "You See But You Do Not Observe" by Robert J. Sawyer

50 "John Barr" by John Williams

51 Suspense: "Drury's Bones" by Harold Swanton

52 Eleventh Hour: "Agro" by Heather Mitchell

53 "The Two 'Failures' of Sherlock Holmes" and "The Case of Peter the Painter" by Donald Thomas

54 *Lestrade and the Leviathan* by M. J. Trow

55 "A Stop at Willoughby" by Rod Serling

56 *Time Travelers Never Die* by Jack McDevitt, powered by scriff (self-survival sliding energy) (Multiverser RPG)

57 *Wild Talents* by Charles Hoy Fort, Thomas Aquinas in his *Summa* described spirits as existing in eviternity, a state of everlastingness between time and eternity.

58 "Future Cop" aka "Tracers" by Danny Bilson and Paul De Meo

59 "Quantum Leap" by Donald P. Bellisario

60 "Spy Kids: All the Time in the World" by Robert Rodriguez

61 "The Greek Interpreter" by John H. Watson

62 "Back to the Future I & II" by Robert Zemeckis and Bob Gale, Matthew 26:24

63 originally the acronym "cetoht" from the phrase "close enough to our home timeline" and "aziz" which by folk etymology is from "as is", but actually was an allusion to case of Saudi Prince Abul Aziz ("The Secret Marriage of Sherlock Holmes" by Shariann Lewitt)

64 "The Whale Against the Wolf: The Anglo-American War of 1896" by Andrew Roberts

65 Michael Nostrand, ("Nostradamus" by Stephen P. Jarchow), Martin Padway (*Lest Darkness Fall* by L. Sprague de Camp)

66 "Theodoric of York, Medieval Barber", "Theodoric of York, Medieval Judge" by Steve Martin, "Exclusionism" (*New Lands* by Charles Hoy Fort), Fried's Law: "Ideas endure and prosper inversely to their soundness and validity.", as an acronym "ieapittsav".

67 deleted scenes of Saxon, Roman, Viking, Middle Ages, France from "The Mummy" by John L. Balderston

68 "The Dybbuk" by Sholom Ansky

69 Genesis 12:10-20
70 Genesis 14, King Bera of Sodom, King Birsha of Gomorrah, King Shinab of Adamah and King Shemember of the Zeboiim united against the three kings, King Amraphel of Shinar, King Arioch of Ellasar and King Tidal of the Goiim
71 Genesis 20
72 Genesis 26:1-14
73 Genesis 29-30, Acts 1:15-26
74 Revelation 21:12
75 "Hands Off" by Edward Everett Hale
76 Genesis 37:25-36, 41:45, Superbook: "A Dream Come True: Joseph"
77 Genesis 38
78 Numbers 26:20-21
79 *Histories* by Herodotus
80 "The Mummy's Ghost" by Griffin Jay, Henry Sucher and Brenda Weisberg
81 "The Mummy's Hand" by Griffin Jay and Maxwell Shane, "The Mummy's Tomb" by Griffin Jay and Henry Sucher
82 "The Mummy's Curse" by Bernard Schubert
83 1 Maccabees 2:3; 2 Maccabees 15:16
84 Alexander "Jonathan" Jannai's Salome Alexandria, Alexander's Alexandra, Herod's Mariamne, Aristabalus's Berenice, T. Flavius Sabinus's Mariamne Arria, Gaius Calpernius Piso's Mariamne Cæsina Arria, Arrius Calpernius Piso's Boionia Procilla Servilla, Trajan's Pompeia Plotina Claudia Phoebe Piso, Julius Calpernius Piso's Domitia Lucilla, Marcus Aurelius's Faustina, Crispus Commodus's Bruttia Crispina, Eutropius's Claudia Crispina, Constanius's St. Helena, Licinius's Constantina, Theodemir's Valentina Justina (370), Merovech's Verica, Childeric's Basina, Clovis's St. Clotilda (492), Murderic's Artemia, Arnoldus's Dode, St. Arnulf's Doda, Adagisel's St. Begga (650), Pepin's Chalpaida, Charles Martel's Rotrude de Bourgogne (713), Pepin III's Bertha de Laon (740), Charlemagne's Hildegard de Vinzgau (772), Louis's Irmengard of Hesbain (798), Louis's Judith Altdorf Welf von Bayern (819), Charles I's Ermentrude d'Orleans (842), Louis II's Adelheid Judith Liudolfing (875), Charles III's princess Eadgifu of Wessex (918), Louis IV's Gerberga of Saxony (939), Lothair's Irmengard de Tours, Lothar II of Lothuringia's Waldralda, Dagobert I's Ragetrud von Australasia, Clovis II's St. Balthildis, Thuderick III's Chrodechildis d'Austrasia, Lambert II of Haspengau's Chrotlinde d'Austrasie, Arnoul van Vlaanderen's Alix de Vermandois, Sigfreid the Dane's Elftrude van Vlaanderen, Ardolph de Guînes's Maud de Boulogne, Rudolph comte de Guînes's Rosella de Saint Pol
85 "What if Constantine Had Converted to Judaism Instead?" by Sam Harrelson
86 Shermer's Last Law: "Any sufficiently advanced alien intelligence is indistinguishable from god." (see 183, *The Mark of the Gods* by Rachel Tanner, Mithra aka Metatron (Satan), "one who occupies the throne next to the divine throne", transformed into spirit of fire with 36 wings and innumerable eyes (*The Gnostics and Their Remains* by King, *3 Enoch* ed. by Hugo Odeberg), metator, "guide, measurer" (Eleazer of Worms), "viceroy of Heaven" (*What is an Angel?* by R. P. Régamey) aka Metatton, Mittron, Merraton, Surya, Tatriel, Sasnigiel, Lad, Yofiel, Bizbul, Sam(m)ael "poisonous angel" (*The Ascension of Isaiah* ed. R. H. Charles), replaced by Michael (*Tanhuna Genesis, The War of the Sons of Light Against the Sons of Darkness*), tempter of Eve (*Sayings of Rabbi Eliezer*) and of David (1 Chronicles 21), equated with Typhon (*Three Books of Occult Philosophy* by Cornelius Agrippa), Angel of Death, that triggers dog howls (*The Golden Legend* by Henry Wadsworth Longfellow),
87 "Bread and Circuses" by Gene Roddenerry and Gene L. Coon
88 *The Wandering Christian* by Kim Newman and Eugene Byrne
89 "The Tomb" by Jack McDevitt, Matsch's Law, originally the acronym "ahebteh"

90 Genesis 24
91 *The Chronicle of Gregory of Tours*
92 *The Life of St. Bathildis*
93 2 Kings 9
94 *Les reines de France* by Paule Lejeune, *The Dark Ages, 476–918* by Charles Oman, *Sainted Women of the Dark Ages* by McNamara, Jo Ann; Whateley, John E.; Halborg, E. Gordon
95 "The Forfeited Birthright of the Abortive Far Western Christian Civilization" by Arnold J. Toynbee, Prestor John mythos
96 Other Holy Helpers included bishop Achatius or Acacius, who talked the Emperor Decius into pardoning him, bishop Blaise of Sebaste, patron of wild animals, Catherine of Alexandria, who advised Joan of Arc, Cyriacus, who cast a demon out of the princess of Persia, Dorothy, who sent apples and roses from Heaven, bishop Erasmus or Elmo, patron of sailors, Eustace, patron of hunters, Giles, patron of cripples, beggars and blacksmiths, Nicholas of Myra aka "Santa Claus", revert Pantaleon, and Vitus aka Guy, patron of dancers. *The Saints* ed. by John Coulson
97 Robert "the Admiral" Blount's Gundreda de Ferrers, Gilbert Blount's Alice de Colekirk, William Blount's Sarah de Munchensy (the peerage.com), Robert Grosvenor's Alice Blount (http://www.geni.com/surnames/grosvenor), not the alternatives, 4th Baron Robert's Baroness Alice Grosvenor
98 "Gil Braltar" by Jules Verne
99 "Bender's Big Score" by Ken Keeler
100 "The Mother Muffin Affair" by Joseph Calvelli, involving Napoleon Solo ("The Man from U. N. C. L. E.) and April Dancer ("The Girl from U. N. C. L. E.") keeping the nark daughter of a gangster alive
100 "Moriarty and the Diamond Jubilee" by John Stanley and Alfred Shirley
101 *The Raven League: Sherlock Holmes is Missing!* by Alex Simmons
102 *Sherlock Holmes and the Royal Flush* by Barrie Roberts
103 "The Adventure of the Seven Clocks" by Adrian Conan Doyle and John Dickson Carr
104 "The Adventure of the Amateur Mendicant Society" by John Gregory Betancourt
105 "The Case of the Amateur Mendicants" by Anthony Boucher and Denis Green
106 "The Case of the Amateur Mendicants" by June Thomson
107 "Death by Gaslight" by Michael Kurland
108 "Sherlock Holmes and the Loss of the British Barque *Sophy Anderson*" by Peter Cannon
109 "The Affair of the Politician, the Lighthouse, and the Trained Cormorant" by Howard Collins
110 "Sherlock Holmes, Dragon-Slayer (The Singular Adventures of the Grice-Patersons in the Island of Uffa)" by Darrell Schweitzer
111 "The Adventure of the Silver Buckle" by Dennis O. Smith; the Black Pig turned out to be a manifestation of As(h)toreh as Kalee (*Folk-Lore of the Holy Land* by J. E. Hanauer) or Kali the Black. (*Studies and Texts in Folklore* by M. Gaster)
112 "The Loss of the British Bark *Sophy Anderson*" by Gary Lovisi
113 "The Long Man" by Rafe McGregor
114 "The Case of the Vanishing Barque" by June Thomson
115 "The Sons of the Desert" by Byron Morgan
116 "A Chump at Oxford" by Charles Rogers, Felix Adler and Harry Langdon
117 "The Paradol Chamber" by Anthony Boucher and Denis Green; This was the wife I had searched for, Dr. Mary Morstan, from an alternative 1894. ("The Adventure of the Other Detective" by Bradley H. Sinor), after I had refused to trade Holmes's life for hers to Moriarty. ("The Hand-delivered Letter" by Simon Kurt Unsworth) She had her own adventures, ("Tea Time in Baker Street" by Russell

McLauchlin), being kidnapped by Vlad Tepes. (Sherlock Holmes vs. Dracula: "The Adventure of the Sanguinary Count" by Loren D. Estleman, *Sherlock Holmes and the Plague of Dracula* by Stephen Seitz)

118 Young Sherlock Holmes: *Death Cloud* by Andy Lane

119 "The Paradol Paradox" by Michael Kurland, named for the residence of French journalist Lucien-Anatole Paradol ("A Key to the Paradol Chamber" by Klas Lithner)

120 *The Difference Engine* by William Gibson and Bruce Sterling

121 "The Body Snatchers" by Philip MacDonald and Val "Carlos Keith" Lewton

122 *Dead, Mr. Mozart* by Bernard Bastable

123 *Too Many Notes, Mr. Mozart* by Bernard Bastable

124 "Fugue and Variations" by Stuart Falconer

125 Walt Disney's Tomorrowland's Visionanium

126 "Son of the Scarlet Pimpernel"

127 "Peeping Tom of Coventry and Lady Godiva" by W. Reader

128 "The Lure of the Bush" by Jack North

129 "King & Castle" by Ian Kennedy Martin

130 "Pirates of the Caribbean: Curse of the Black Pearl" by Ted Elliot and Terry Russio

131 Martina Cole's Lady Killers: "Mary Ann Cotton" by Sean Crotty

132 "Death and Diamonds" by Rolf Schulz and Christa Stern

133 "Hellraiser" by Clive Barker

134 "The Mutants" by Bob Baker and Dave Martin

135 "The Family Way" by Bill Naughton

136 "Words and Music" by Herman Ruby and Stanley Rauh

137 "The Shootist" by Miles Hood Swarthout and Scott Hale

138 *Chuck Norris: The Legend: 4,500 Hard Facts About The Man Who Counted To Infinity - Twice* by Braydon Batungbacal

139 The White Queen in *Alice in Wonderland* by Ludwidge "Lewis Carroll" Dodgeson, proving the Unnamed Law: "It happened, so it was not impossible.", as an acronym "ihsiwni"

140 Magnum, P. I.: "Smaller Than Life" by J. Rickley Dumm

141 "Runaway Bride" by Josann McGibbon and Sara Parriott

142 "Mars Attacks!" by Jonathan Gems

143 "Karate Cop" aka "Slaughter in San Francisco" by Lei "William Lowe" Lo, "Sidekicks" by Donald G. Thompson and Lou Illar, "Wind in the Wire" by Menahem Golan

144 *Prince Lost to time* by Ann Dukthas

145 "If Lafayette Had Held the French Reign of Terror in Check" by Joseph Edgar Chamberlain

146 "Empire" by William Sanders

147 *The Hand of Glory* by Sophie Masson

148 "Never Say If" by Arye Sivan

149 *Son of France* by Geoff Cush

150 *Operation Bonaparte* by Paul von Herck

151 "Gingerbread" by Jane Espenson, similiar to the 100-year hatchings of gargoyles (Special Unit 2: "The Brothers")

152 "National Treasure" by Jim Kouf, Cormac and Marianne Wibberley

153 Burn Notice: "Seek and Destroy" by Rashad Raisani, "Hot Spot" by Rashad Raisani and Michael Horwitz

154 "2001: A Space Odyssey" by Stanley Kubrick and Arthur C. Clarke

155 "Penny Dreadful" by John Logan

156 "Brisco County, Jr." by Jeffrey Boam and Carlton Cuse
157 "Sherlock Holmes v. Monsters" by Paul Bales
158 1938: Dr. Van Thorp's giant robot Bozo (Smash Comics #1), 1951: Gort ("The Day the Earth Stood Still" by Edmund H. North), 1957: (*The Iron Giant* by Ted Hughes), 1967: Plutonian robot Neutro (Neutro #1), 1973: sizeshifting Jet Jaguar robot ("Godzilla vs. Megalon" by Jun Fukuda), 1991: Dr. Bolivar Trask's Sentinels (X-Men #14 by Stan Lee), 2205: defeating Uagneiss (*Militar-Z, Giant Robot Detective*), 4002: (*Magnus, Robot Fighter* by Russ Manning)
159 Robert's Margery, Robert's Emma de Modburlegh, Ralph's Joan, Robert's Joan de Pulford, Thomas's Katherine Fesant, Ralph's Joan Eton, Robert's Johan Fitton, Robert's Catherine Norris, Richard's Catherine Cotton (1509), Thomas's Maud Poole (1529), Thomas's Anne Bradshaigh, Richard's Christian Brooke, Richard's Lettice Cholmondeley, Richard's Sydney Mostyn (1626), Roger's Christian Myddleton (1649), Thomas's Mary Davis (1677), Robert's Jane Warre (1730), Richard's Henrietta Vernon (1764), Robert's Eleanor Egerton (1794), Robert's Charlotte Wellesby (1831), Algernon's Catherine Simeon (1887), thepeerage.com), and Simeon, father of Helen.
160 "Sherlock Holmes and the Mummy's Curse" (1883), "MediEvil 2" (1886, 1386), "The Inheritance" (1954, 1032 BC), *Exploring the Titanic* (1912), Bart Simpson's Treehouse of Horror Spine-tingling Spooktacular: "Monty Kills a Mummy" (1939), The Thing: "The Inheritance" (1954, 1037 BC), Blue Beetle: "The Giant Mummy Who Was Not Dead" (1964), Melvin Monster #1 (1965), Santos: "Vengeance of the Mummy", "The Mummies of Guanajuato" (1970), Wonder Woman: "The Riddle of the Chinese Mummy Case" (1973, 28 BC), Nightstalker: "Legacy of Terror" (1974), Voyage to the Bottom of the Sea: "The Mummy" (1973, 1026), (Eerie, IN: "America's Scariest Home Video" (1991), "The United Monster Talent Agency" (2010), "Ninjas vs. Monsters" (2013), Perry Rhodan: "Use of the Kartanin" (4067); miracles (Ezekiel 37:1-14), the Marvin re-integration ray or other hightech "magic" can even restore the long dead to life.
161 "The Adventure of the Priory School"
162 "The Adventure of the Mazarin Stone"
163 Clarke's Law: "Any sufficiently advanced technology is indistinguishable from magic."
164 "The Woman in Green" by Bertram Millhauser
165 "The Raven" by David Boehm
166 "A Scandal in Bohemia" by John H. Watson
167 1. $Y+Y > Y$ (more minds of same consciousness level can overpower fewer) **2.** $YY > Y+...+Y$ (greater-ply minds can overpower lesser or fewer) **3.** $YY > Y...Y$ (higher-consciousness minds can overpower lower, lesser or fewer) (Lensman series by E. E. Smith)
168 There are at least $2x7x4 = 56$ extrapolated from Taco Magnon. ("Himself in Anachron" by Cordwainer Smith) sub and super refer to the metaphysical probability states, either moving toward (super) or away (sub) from Truth, Beauty, and Goodness (Godliness), back, central, down, front, left, right and up refer to the anachronic probability states, back meaning contrafactual, up or ana meaning futureward, right meaning moving conservatively or "sheepishly" slowly, left meaning moving liberally or "goatishly" fast, central meaning not moving at all or very little, down or kata meaning pastward, front meaning factual, formal, informal, resolved, unresolved refer to the meta probability states, formal meaning unchangeable (observed), informal meaning semi-changeable (partially observed), resolved means unobserved and unchangeable and unresolved means unobserved and unchangeable
169 The Star and the Story: "The Blue Landscape" by DeWitt Bodeen and Frank Burt
170 *Your Turn, Mr. Moto, Think Fast, Mr. Moto, Mr. Moto Is So Sorry, Mr. Moto Takes a Hand, Last Laugh, Mr. Moto, Thank You, Mr. Moto, The Return of Mr. Moto and Mr. Moto's Three Aces* by John P. Marquand, "Mr. Moto's Gamble" by Charles Belden, "Mr. Moto Take a Chance" by Lou Breslow,

"Mysterious Mr. Moto", "Mr. Moto Takes a Vacation" and "Mr. Moto's Last Warning" by Philip MacDonald, "Mr. Moto in Danger Island" by Peter Milne

171 Homer Bedlo ("Petticoat Junction" and "Beverly Hillbillies" by Paul Henning)

172 Adolphus throwbacks: Joel Cairo ("The Maltese Falcon" by John Huston), Gen. Pompellio Montezuma De La Vilia De Conde De La Rue ("Secret Agent" by Charles Bennett), Dr. Gogol ("Mad Love" by P. J. Wolfson and John L. Balderston), Montresor ("Tales of Terror: "The Black Cat" by Richard Matheson), Dr. Karl Rothe (*The Lost One* by Peter Lorre), Strangdour ("Muscle Beach Party" by Robert Dillion), Ugarte the Basque ("Casablanca" by Julius J. and Philip G. Epstein and Howard Koch), **Erasmus throwbacks**: Hans Bennett ("M" by Thea von Harbou and Fritz Lang), Dr. Richard Cross ("Shock" by Eugene Ling), John Carnby (Night Gallery: "The Return of the Sorcerer" by Halsted Welles), devil's advocate ("The Story of Mankind" by Irwin Allen and Charles Bennett), Dr. Goldfoot ("Dr. Goldfoot and the Bikini Machine", "The Wild Weird World of Dr. Goldfoot" by Robert Kaufman), Edgar "Egghead" Heed ("An Egg Grows in Gotham" by Stanley Ralph Ross), Edward Kendal Sheridan Lionheart ("Theater of Blood" by Anthony Greville-Bell), Frederick Loren ("House on Haunted Hill" by Robb White), Don Gallico ("The Mad Magician" by Crane Wilbur), Henry Jarrek ("House of Wax" by Crane Wilbur), Victor Marton ("The Foxes and Hounds Affair" by Peter Allan Fields), "Prof. Multiple" ("The Deadly Dolls" by Charles Bennett), Dr. Anton Phibbs ("The Abominable Dr. Phibbs" by James Whiton and William Goldstein), Dr. Jarvis Pym ("Is This Trip Necessary" by Dale McRaven), Geoffrey Radcliff ("The Invisible Man Returns" by Lester Cole and Curt Siodmak), Robur ("Master of the World" by Richard Matheson, *Master of the World* by Jules Verne), Paul "Dr. Death" Toombes ("Madhouse" by Ken Levison and Greg Morrison), Ernest Valdemar (Tales of Terror: "The Case of M. Valdemar" by Richard Matheson), Lord Edward Whitman ("Cry of the Banshee" by Christopher Wicking), **Estelle throwbacks**: Evie Bishop (Thriller: "The Closed Cabinet" by Jess Carneol and Kay Lenard), Fran Celane (Perry Mason: "The Case of the Sulky Girl" by Harold Swanton), Emily Doe (The Girl from U. N. C. L. E.: "The Little John Doe Affair" by Joseph Calvelli), Nancy Kettle ("The Kettles in the Ozarks" by Kay Lenard), Beth Pettit (Thriller: "The Watcher" by Donald S. Sanford), **Lenore throwbacks**: Anne "Gentleman Jack" Bonney (The Buccaneers: "Gentleman Jack and the Lady" by Zachery West), Elizabeth Carter (Wild Wild West: "The Night of the Returning Dead" by John Kneubuhl), Catherine Hagar (Mission Impossible: "Charity" by Barney Slater), Sally Meadows ("Model for Murder" by Terry Bishop and Robert Dunbar), Nurse Linda Parker ("Dr. Blood's Coffin" by Nathan "Jerry" Juran), Ellen Prestwick ("Devil Girl from Mars" by James Eastwood), Charlotte Scott (Twilight Zone: "The Fear" by Rod Serling), Leonie Vicek (Thriller: "Terror in Teakwood" by Alan Caillou), **Roxford throwbacks**: Frank Chambers ("The Postman Always Rings Twice" by David Mamet), Gino the Hitman ("The St. Valentine's Day Massacre" by Howard Brown), Randle Patrick McMurphy ("One Flew Over the Cuckoo's Nest" by Lawrence Hauben and Bo Goldman), Art Land ("Mars Attacks!" by Jonathan Gems), Jack "Joker" Napier ("Batman" by Sam Hamm and Warren Skaaren), Will Randall ("Wolf" by Jim Harrison and Wesley Strick), Jack Torrance ("The Shining" by Stanley Kubrick and Diane Johnson), Daryl Van Horne ("The Witches of Eastwick" by Michael Cristofer)

173 "Time Express" by Ivan Goff and Ben Roberts

174 *The Stepford Wives* by Ira Levin, "The Stepford Wives" by Paul Rudnick

175 "Avatar" by James Cameron

176 "The Sorcerers" by Michael Reeve

177 *Eye of the Crow* by Shane Peacock

178 "The Bells" by James Young, Le Juif Polonais by Emile Erckmann and Alexandre Chatrian, facilitated out-of-body experience (OOBE) (1898: "The Mesmerist"), Dolomar (1994: "The Mesmerist")

179 "The Adventure of Charles Augustus Milverton"
180 "Abbott and Costello Meet the Killer" by Hugh Wedlock, Jr., and Howard Snyder
181 originally the acronym "nais" ("Nothing's as it seems.")
182 Ecclesiastes 1:9, originally the abbreviated acronym "tinntuts"
183 "The Boogie Man Will Get You" by Erwin Blum
184 "Capt. America" by Joe Simon and Jack Kirby, no relation to the FLAG organization 12
185 aka "Billy Gilbert" and "Shemp" Howard, "Three of a Kind" by Earle Snell and Arthur Caesar, "Crazy Knights" by Tim Ryan, "Trouble Chasers" by George H. Plympton and Andre Lamb
186 The Spectre: "Introducing Percival Popp the Super-Cop"
187 *McSnurtle the Turtle, the Terrific Whatzit* by Martin Naydel
188 "Junior Army" by Paul Gangelin
189 extrapolation of "Forest of Time" by Michael Flynn
190 "Mr. Clay's War: A Metahistory" by Thaddeus Holt .
191 *Séance for a Vampire* by Fred Saberhagen
192 Vincent Leonard Price, Jr. "An Evening with Edgar Allen Poe"
193 "The Terror" by Leo Gordon and Jack Hill
194 *Nevermore* by William Hjortsberg, Erich Weiss is better know by his stage name "Houdini"., "Arthur Doyle" was an alias used by Robert Griffin, father by Phoebe Radcliffe of Irene Adler Norton and adoptive father of Paul Waller Doyle.
195 Telephone time: "The *Vestris*" by David A. Evans
196 *Only Yesterday* by Frederick Allen
197 "The Slocum Is Burning" by Christian Baudissin
198 aka the Piscatorians were founded during the Fire Deluge in the Third Millennium. (*Canticle for Leibowitz* by Walter M. Miller, Jr.) With John Fisher X, a survivor of the ill-fated Paradise VII colony, the Fishers in the Sixth Millennium added wealth and longevity to their hereditary telepathy. The Fishers allied with the underpeople's Holy Insurgency and helped end the religious embargo (Instrumentality series by Paul "Cordwainer Smith" Linebarger) under Pope Benedict CXXVII (*The Papacy: From Peter I to Peter III*). Through the Seventeenth Millennium they worked against the Islamistani empires, and their successors against the Abrahami and the Brahami, until Old Earth was finally reunited with New Canterbury under the Israeli empire. (*The High Crusade* by Poul Anderson). With the disappearance of Peter II in the Eighteenth Millennium, they became Tripetrists, those who believed in the prophesied Peter III, those persecuted as "Tripe". With the aid of some Fishers who were also chronoporting Tweens (Peter Holmes) or Brights, including Star Holmes ("Star Bright" by Mark Clifton), the Italian Alberighis, Spanish Xaviers, Chinese Liangs and Mings, the order's mission became to gather back the scattered Humankind of the Sheshak exile (*The Rise and Fall of the Sheshak Empire* by Michael Halm) after the fall of the Fourth Human (Dr. Who series) and New Federated Empires (*Federation* and *Empire* by Isaac Asimov) in the Fiftieth-fourth Millennium.
199 "Millennium" by John Varley, Rudin's Law: "In crises that force people to choose among alternate courses of action, nearly everyone chooses the worst alternative possible." ("nectwap") may apply here. We visited Rozher "Stane" Schtein in 461 with Manse Everard from 1954 and the Dannelans (*Time Patrol* by Poul Anderson, *Up the Line* by Robert Silverberg), helped Kenny Sharp and Moe "Capt. Galaxy" Stein (Quantum Leap: "Future Boy" by Tommy Thompson) Fortunately we did not often encounter the many rival timecops, except for Merlock Holmes of the Bureau of Time and Space ("Flint the Time Detective"), such as: the Guardians of Time ("The Tomorrow People" by Roger Price), the Time Corps (Future History series by Robert A. Heinlein), the Temporal Rectification Division (*Chrono Hustle* by Eric J. Barkman), GRIPE (Warlock of Gramarye by Christopher Stasheff), the Time Purists (The Missing series), the International Association of Time Travellers ("Wikihistory" by Dennis

Warzel), the Time Travel Overseeing Commission (*The Robot in the Closet* by Ron Goulart), the Time Variance Authority (Marvel Comics), Temps Aeteralis (The Umbrella Academy by Gerald Way), the Time Continuum Task Force ("Meet the Robinsons" by Jon Bernstein, Michelle Spitz, Don Hall, Nathan Greno, Aurian Redson, Joseph Maten and Stephen J. Anderson), the Chronoguard ("Thursday Next" by Jasper Fforde), the Temporal Police (*The Stainless Steel Rat* by Harry Harrison), the Time Commandos (Time Wars series by Simon Hawke), the Time Wardens (*Overtime* by Tom Holt), the Guardians of Forever (Genius the Transgression), the Bureau of Destiny (Exalted), the Time Repair Agency (Chrononauts), the Time Corps (Timemaster), the Menders of Ouroboros (City of Heroes), Sentinels of Hallifax (Lusternia), Sequel Police (Space Quest IV), Time Line Authority (TRU Life Adventures).

200 Both were at Ford's Theater when Lincoln was assassinated in 1865, at the crash of the Hindenburg in 1937, along the motorcade when JFK was assassinated in 1963, at the Mt. St. Helen's eruption in 1980, when Xol manifested as Mr. Stay Puff in New York in 1984 ("Ghostbusters" by Dan Akroyd and Harold Ramis), on a runaway bus in 1994 ("Speed" by Graham Yost), when a UFO zapped the White House in 1996 ("Independence Day" by Dean Devlin and Roland Emmerich), and at both the sinking of the *Cole* and the crash of the Concord in 2000.

(http://urbanlegends.about.com/od/mishapsdisasters/ig/Tourist-Guy/index.htm)

201 *Men In Black* by Lowell Cunningham, "Men in Black" by Ed Solomon

202 gigantopteranodon ("Rodan" by David Duncan), reptile ("Reptilicus" by Ib Melchior and Sidney W. Pink), blob ("Caltiki the Immortal Monster" by Filippo "Phillip Just" Sanjust), megalon ("Godzilla vs. Megalon" by Jun Fukuda), ("Godzilla, King of the Monsters" by Takeo Murata and Ishirô Honda), rhedosaur ("The Beast from 20,000 Fathoms" by Lou Morheim and Fred Freiberger), Baragon and Zigra ("Gamera vs. Baragon" and "Gamera vs. Zigra" by Joel Hodgson, etal.), the giant rat and cat of Faversham (All Star Comics #3), gigantopithici ("Mighty Joe Young" by Ruth Rose, "King Kong" by James Ashmore Creelman and Ruth Rose, M'Gana (Thrilling Comics #65), "Son of Kong" by Ruth Rose, "Konga" by"Aben Kandel and Herman Cohen), gi-ants ("Them!" by Ted Sherdeman, "Empire of the Ants" by Jack Turley), Gigantis and Angurus ("The Volcano Monsters" by Ib Melchior and Ed Watson), Claw Monster ("Panther Girl of the Kongo" by Ronald Davidson), Deemer tarantula ("Tarantula" by Robert M. Fresco and Martin Berkeley), ("The Deadly Mantis" by Martin Berkeley), locusts ("Beginning of the End" by Fred Freiberger and Lester Gorn), wasps ("Monster from Green Hell" by Endre Boehm and Louis Vittes), giant mollusks ("The Monster That Challenged the World" by Pat Fielder), spiders ("Earth vs. The Spider" by László Görög and George Washington Yates, "The Giant Spider Invasion" by Richard L. Huff and Robert Easton), gila monster and shrews ("The Giant Gila Monster" and "Killer Shrews" by Jay Simms), leeches ("Attack of the Giant Leeches" by Leo Gordon), ("The Giant Behemoth" by Eugène Lourié), moth and ghidra and shrimp ("Mothra" and "Ghidrah, the Three-Headed Monster", and "Godzilla vs. the Sea Monster" by Shin'ichi Sekizawa), griffi-saur ("Sea Devils"), Guiron ("Gamera vs. Guiron" by Fumi Takahashi), rabbits ("Night of the Lepus" by Don Holliday and Gene R. Kearney), dog ("Digby — The Biggest Dog in the World" by Michael Pertwee, "Clifford, the Big Red Dog"), Batragon or Yetriger (Marvel "Godzilla"), Firebird, Seaweed Monster, Sub-Zero Terror or Time Dragon ("The Godzilla Power Hour"), Gorath ("Gorath" by Takeshi Kimura), crabs ("Island Claws" aka "Night of the Claw" by Jack Cowden and Ricou Browning), rats ("Deadly Eyes" by Charles H. Eglee, "Food of the Gods II" by Richard Bennett and E. Kim Brewster), lobster (gargons) ("Teenagers from Outer Space" by Tom Graeff), cockroaches ("Mimic" by Matthew Robbins and Guillermo del Toro), mosquitoes ("Skeeter" by Joseph Luis Rubin), worms ("Squirm" by Jeff Lieberman), man-o-war ("No Escape from Death" by William Welch), white blood cells ("The TV Show That Menaced Metropolis"), jellyfish ("Graveyard of Fear" by Robert Vincent Wright), protoplasm ("Cradle of the Deep" by Robert Hamner), amoeba ("Once a Green

Lantern, Always a Green Lantern"), termite ("Squeak and the Terrible Termite"), octopus ("It Came from Beneath the Sea" by George Worthing Yates and Harold Jacob Smith), bees (Tomb of Terror #8: "The Hive"), eel (Scoop Comics #2), Hedorah and Suruga ("Godzilla vs. the Smog Monster" by Yoshimitsu Banno and Takeshi Kimura), ("Yongary, Monster from the Deep" by Ki-duk Kim and Yun-sung Seo)

203 Gargantua and of Pantagruel (*The Life of Gargantua and of Pantagruel* by François Rabelais), the Brobdignagians (*Gulliver's Travels* by Lemuel Gulliver), Glenn Manning ("The Amazing Colossal Man" by Mark Hanna and Bert I. Gordon), Ymir ("20 Million Miles to Earth" by Robert Creighton Williams and Christopher Knopf), Bruce Barton ("The Cyclops" by Bert I. Gordon), Nancy Fowler Archer ("Attack of the 50-foot Woman" by Mark Hanna), Cassie Stratford ("The Attack of the 50-foot Cheerleader" by Mike McLean), Leonard Freiburg (*The Attack of the Giant Baby* by Kit Reed), apish George, reptilian Lizzie and wolfish Ralph (Rampage game), William "Giant-Man" Foster (Marvel Two-in-One #55), Thark (Man from Atlantis: "Giant" by Michael I. Wagner), Ambrose Dinwoodie ("A Day in the Life of an Amazon" by Robert Kanigher), Kha-Ef-Ri ("The Giant Mummy Who Was Not Dead"), Harold Joseph "Freak" Hogan (Tales of Suspence #74 by Stan Lee and Don Heck), Vargas ("Giant from the Unknown" by Frank Hart Taussig and Ralph Brooke), Jimmy Olsen ("The Human Skyscraper" by Otto Binder), Nordac the Giant (Double Comics), "Giant Man" of Urganas (Zip Comics #1), Brentwood "Green Giant" (Green Giant #1), ("Giganta, the Gorilla Girl"), Susan "Ginormica" Murphy ("Monsters vs. Aliens" by Maya Forbes, etal.), ("Frankenstein Conquers the World" by Takeshi "Kaoru Mabuchi" Kimura)

204 *Godzilla, Past, Present, Future* by Arthur Adams, "Godzilla vs. the Devil" by Tomoyuki Tanaka, "Destroy All Monsters" by Ishirô Hondo and Takeshi "Kaoru Mabuchi" Kimura, *Giantkiller A to Z: A Field Guide to Big Monsters* by Dan Brereton, Johnathan William Duncan "Jack" Robinson ("Jack and the Beanstalk: The Real Story" by James V. Hart, Brian Henson and Bill Barretta), Jack Strong ("Jack and the Beanstalk" by Nathaniel Curtis), and Jack Fairfax ("Beanstalk")

205 "The Colossus of Ylourge" by Clark Ashton Smith

206 Jumbo Comics #68

207 "The Luckiest Man in the World" by Frank D. Gilroy

208 "Unbreakable" by M. Night Shyamalan

209 The Punishment of Sherlock Holmes: "Nautical Story" by John Sielke

210 Roanoke RPG

211 *Dare* by Phillip Jose Farmer

212 "Unconquered" by Charles Bennett

213 "The Tap Root" by James Street and Alan Le May

214 *The Legend of Zoey* by Candie Moonshower

215 maharani of Rampor, partner of both John Edward Marco, Sr., and Muhammad Yusef Ali Khan Bahadur

216 "The Night of the Golden Cobra" by Henry Sharp

217 "The Adventure of the Empty House" by John H. Watson

218 "Man from Downing Street" by Lottie Horner, Bradley J. Smollen, Clyde Westover and Florine Williams

219 *The Rise and Fall of Khan Noonien Singh* by Greg Cox

220 "Space Seed" by Gene L. Coon and Carey Wilber

221 "The Wrath of Khan" by Jack B. Sowards

222 "The Adventure of the Extraterrestrial" by Mack Reynolds

223 This aphorism originated with Holmes as "La route de l'enfer est plein de bonnes volontés et désirs." It however has been repeatedly misheard and misquoted without the initial "la route de" many times, firstly by St. Bernard of Clairvaux in 1150. It was then a reference to our case in 1992 in which we saved Charlie Sykes and Rachel Clark from the demonic guardian of the Nevada hellgate ("Highway to Hell" by Brian Helgeland) and so helped give the world the exorcist Fr. Clark "Demonbane" Sykes. Clark's vigilante uncle, Norbert Sykes, was "the Badger", who fought with the extraterrestrial Hammaglystwythkbrngxxaxolotl, better known as "Hamilton J. Thorndyke", against Lord "Slotman" Weterlackus (Badger #1). His cousin and sidekick was Lois "Badger Girl" Sykes, granddaughter of Treve N. "T. N. T." Thorndyke (Amazing Man Comics #21).

224 "Alien Terror" aka "The Incredible Invasion" by Juan Ibáñez, Karl Schanzer, Luis Enrique Vergara

225 "Jack Reed: The Badge of Honor" by Andrew Laskos

226 the common ore of the super-actinide Kryptonium, *Superman the Man of Steel Sourcebook* by Roger Stern, "Smallville" by Alfred Gough, Miles Millar and Carmine Infantino

227 Tobit 11

228 Since they include four men, two of them doctors, and two women, they are most likely those saints in the painting by Sandro Botticelli: Mary Magdalene, John the Baptist, Francis of Assisi, the Holy Helper Catherine of Alexandria, Cosmas and Damian.

229 "Canst thou by searching find out God? Canst thou find out the Almighty unto perfection? It is as high as heaven; what canst thou do? Deeper than hell; what canst thou know? The measure thereof is longer than the earth, and broader than the sea." (Job 11:7-9) "The Spirit scrutinizes all matters, even the deep things of God." (1 Corinthians 2:10). many things are hidden from the learned and clever but revealed to the merest children. (Luke 10:21)

230 Wilhelm Kühne discovered dirhodopsin could be "fixed" like a photographic negative, but expanding the fovea centralis, the actual focal point of the image on the retina, remained a problem. In 1880 he photographed Erhard Gustav Reif's retina. In 1924, Fritz Angerstein confessed after a similar test. In "At the End of the Passage" by Rudyard Kipling and "Claire Lenoir" by Villiers de l'Isle-Adam, optography is a paranormal power, like the supernatural eye images on the tilma of our Lady of Guadalupe.

231 "The Invisible Ray" by John Colton

232 "For what shall it profit a man, if he shall gain the whole world, and lose his own soul?" (Mark 8:36)

233 "The King and I" by Oscar Hammmerstein II

234 "The Fear Chamber" by Jack Hill and Luis Enrique Vergara

235 "The Monolith Monsters" by Norman Jolley and Robert M. Fresco

236 "The Return of the Monolith Monsters" not by Norman Jolley and Robert M. Fresco

237 "Arsenic and Old Lace" by Julius J. Epstein

238 The Ford Theater Hour: "Arsenic and Old Lace" by Joseph Kesselring

239 Dr. William Fall's from 2098 to 1970 (Night Gallery: "The Little Black Bag" by Jeannot Szarc), Dr. Roger Full's from 2160 to 1969 (Out of the Unknown: "The Little Black Bag" by Julian Bond), Dr. Arthur Fulbright's from 2450 to 1951 (Tales of Tomorrow: "The Little Black Bag" by Cyril M. Kornbluth and Mann Rubin)

Sheshaktech (http://michaelhalm.tripod.com/id102.htm) that we found most useful for using through the Eyehole has included: the Allen shrink ray (Ray "Atom" Allen, "Birth of the Atom" by Gardner Fox), **Atron ray** for neutralizing superpowers ("The Secret World of Alex Mack" by Ken Lipman and Tommy Lynch), the **Bradbury ray** (Ray Bradbury), the **Bryant energizing ray** (grir, gamma ray/infrared) (Andrew Bryant, "The Origin of Captain Future"), the **Cloyd scrooch ray** ("Jet Fuel Formula" by George Atkins, Chris Hatward, Chris Jenkins and Lloyd Turner), the **Cyclops reverse-nature ray** ("The Secret of the Seventh Super-Hero" by Jerry Siegel and Mort Weisinger), **Johnson honesty ray** ("The Rocket Man" by Lenny Bruce, George W. George, Jack Henley and George F.

Slavin), **Harryhausen animation ray** (Ray Harryhausen), the **Hundecoph transformation ray** that changes gender (Richard Hundecoph, "Umlaut House" by by Allan C. Ecker), the **Knight blackout ray** (Sandra "Phantom" Knight in "The Saga of Solomon Grundy" by Roy and Dann Thomas), **Kru-El ray** that mindswaps ("Jor-El: Superman" by E. Nelson Bridwell), the **Kyrri aqua-ray** that liquifies ("Menace of the Aqua-Ray Weapon" by John Broome), the **Marvin ray** for reintegrating the disintegrated ("Hare-Way to the Stars" by Michael Maltese), **Milland ray** that stimulates cryptaesthesia (Ray Milland, "The Man with X-Ray Eyes" by Robert Dillon and Ray Russell), the **Metchnikoff's g and e rays** for increasing life expectancy 200 years ("John Jones Dollar" by Harry Stephen Keeler), the **Minyan pacifier ray** ("Underworld" by Bob Baker and Dave Martin), the **Morgan astro-pyro ray** for empowering with fire control and flight (Ted "Red Blazer" Dawson, "Origin of the Red Blazer" by Al Avison), **Payton empowering ray** (Will Payton, "Starman" by Christopher Priest), the **Rachael ray** for making anything taste wonderful (Rachael Ray), the **Randall ray** that stimulates levitation and force field generation (Ray Randall, "Birdman and the Galaxy Trio" by Alex Toth), the **Robinson ray** (Robinson, Ray Charles), the **Sardath null-zeta** ray for boosting both ego and intelligence ("The Super-Brain of Adam Strange" by Gardner Fox), the **Slade vita-ray** that revives injured or dead to supernormal ("The Origin of Mystico"), the **Snart freeze-ray** (Leonard "Capt. Cold" Snart, "The Coldest Man on Earth!" by Robert Kaniger), the **Stanz spirit-stunning ray** (Ray Stanz, "Ghost Busters" by Dan Aykroyd and Harold Ramis), **Szalinski enlarging ray** ("Honey, I Blew Up the Kid" by Thom Eberhardt, Peter Elbling and Garry Goodrow), the **Weldon time-ray** for interdimensional time-swapping (Amos Weldon, "Superboy's Switch In Time" by Henry Boltinoff, Jack Schiff, Jerry Coleman and Otto Binder), the **Zak-Kul enlarging ray** ("The Shrinking Superman" by Otto Binder), the **Zinger ray-gun** that interferes with superspeed power ("Who Put the Zing in the Flash" by Cary Bates), **Zinj devolution beam** (Treks Not Taken: "Jurassic Trek" by Steven Boyett)

240 Clem Kadiddlehopper is a grandson of "Deadeye" Appleby, nephew of Mortimer and Elaine Brewster Cook and cousin of Theodore "Cookie" Cook, Richard "Cauliflower" McPlugg, George Appleby, Richard "San Fernando Red" Appleby, III, Frederick "Freeloader" Appleby, William Lump, Jr., Bolvar Shagnasty and Ludwig von Humperdoo ("The Red Skelton Show") and orphan Ambrose C. Park ("The Great Diamond Robbery") aka Rusty Morgan ("Public Pigeon No. 1" by László Vadnay and Martin Rackin), Buddy McCoy ("The Big Slide" by Edmund Beloin and Dean Reisner), Merton K. Kibble ("Ship Ahoy" by Harry Clork), Cornie Quinell ("Texas Carnival")

241 The Red Skelton Show: "He Who Steals My Robot, Steals Trash"

242 "Scream and Scream Again" by Christopher Wicking, *The Disorientated Man* by Peter Saxon

243 "Dick Tracy Meets Gruesome" by Robertson White and Eric Taylor,

244 The son of "Fearful" Fosdick (*Fearless Fosdick Battles Anyface* by Lester Gooch), 1950: Old Faithful Beans disaster ("The Case of the Poisoned Pickles"), 1951: Atom Bum (*Fearless Fosdick and the Case of the Red Feather*), 1952: vs. Ally Oom ("The Onion Ring"), vs. Mr. Ditto lookalike, robot Frank N. Stein, "Match Head", "Frog Man", Harris Tween "The Suit", "Evil-Eye" Fleegle, Noah Naps insomniac killer ("The Sleepwalker"), Batula, 1959: vs. headhunter Nelson Shrinkafeller ("The Hat"), 1961: EDS (Electronic Detective Substitute) replaces Fosdick, 1965: as "James Bumm" vs. Boldfinger

245 "The Black Room" by Arthur Strawn and Henry Myers

246 "The Good, the Bad and the Ugly" by Luciano Vincenzoni, Serio Leone, "The Good, the Bad and the Weird" by Jee-Woon Kim and Min-suk Kim; both Pudder's Law: "Anything that begins well ends badly. Anything that begins badly ends worse." ("atbweb atbbew") and the Unspeakable Law: "As soon as you mention something, if it's good, it goes away. if it's bad, it happens." ("iigiga", "iibih") often apply.

247 William T. and W. Thomas Riker, "Second Chances" by René Echevarria

248 *The Holmes Dracula File* by Fred Saberhagen, Journal of the Gypsy Lore Society: "The Vampire"

by Tatomir P. Vukanovič, reprinted in *Vampires of the Slavs* ed. by Jan Perkowski as "Dhampir as the Chief Magician for the Destruction of Vampires."

249 Cardula an anagram of Dracula series by Jack Ritchie, 1976: "Kid Cardula", 1977: "Cardula to the Rescue", "The Cardula Detective Agency", 1978: "Cardula and the Kleptomaniac", vs. Van Jelsing in "Cardula's Revenge", 1982: "Cardula and the Locked Rooms", "The Return of Cardula", 1983: "Cardula and the Briefcase"; similar to recovering vampire Angel's detective agency with Cordelia Chase, Wesley Wyndham-Pryce, Charles Gunn and Winifred "Fred" Burkle ("Angel" by David Greenwalt and Joss Whedon)

250 *Rasputin's Revenge* by John T. Lescroart, in which Holmes helped "Auguste Lupa" escape "Rasputin"

251 Nero Wolf series by Rex Stout

252 *Sherlock Holmes in New York* by D. R. Bensen

253 *The Language of Bees* by Laurie R. King

254 *Whitechapel: The Final Stand of Sherlock Holmes* by Bernard J. Schaffer

255 "Cabaret Aux Assassins" by Cara Black

256 *The Canary Trainer* by Nicholas Meyer and *Irene Good Night* by R. D. Benson

257 *Hellbirds* by Austin Mitchelson and Nicholas Utechin

258 *Sherlock Holmes and the Titanic Tragedy* by William Seil

259 ("A Scandal in Montreal" by Edward D. Hoch), father of Edward Norton, Sr. 67, grandfather of Edward Norton, Jr. ("The Honeymooners") That Irene was also the mother by "Baron von Kramm" of Wilhelm von Kramm aka "William Kramden", father of Ralph Kramden is more doubtful. ("Scandal in Bensonhurst" by Kenneth Lanza)

260 "The Adventure of the Second Generation" by Ken Greenwald

261 *Sherlock Holmes and the Railway Maniac* by Barrie Roberts

262 *Killer Finish* by Denny Martin Flinn

263 "Cannon" series by Quinn Martin and Edward Hume

264 "Jake and the Fatman" by Douglas Stefen Borghi, Dean Hargrove, Joe Steiger

265 "Knight Rider" by Glen A. Larson

266 "Sherlock Holmes, Jr." by Edwin S. Porter

267 "Holmeses of Baker Street" by Basil Mitchell, Baker Street Irregulars series by Terrance Dicks

268 *The Secret of Sherlock Holmes* by Gary F. Boothe

269 *The Lady in Red: The Son of Sherlock Holmes* by Byron Pries

270 *Sherlock Holmes and the Case of the Jersey Lily* by Katie Forgette

271 "The Musgrave Version" and "The Adventure of the Celestial Snows" by Reginald Musgrave, *The League of Dragons* by George Alec Effinger; This contradicts the theory of C. Arrnold Johnson in "An East Wind" that Moriarty followed Holmes to Tibet under the name "Fu Manchu". see 630, Holmes did identify him as the murderer, "Dr. Grimsby Defoe" in the Crosby murder case in 1895 (*The Vampire Serpent*)

272 "The Devil Dr.: The Early Years History of Fu Manchu" by Dennis E. Power

273 1926: *The House without a Key*, 1927: *The Chinese Parrot* and 1929: *Behind That Curtain*, 1931: *Charlie Chan Carries On* and *The Black Camel*, 1934: *Charlie Chan's Courage* by Earl Derr Biggers, "Charlie Chan in London" by Philip MacDonald, "... in Egypt" by Robert Ellis and Helen Logan, 1935: "... in Paris" by Edward T. Lowe and Stuart Anthony, "... in Shanghai" by Edward T. Lowe and Gerald Fairlie, 1936: "Charlie Chan's Secret", "Charlie Chan at the Circus", "...at the Olympics" by Robert Ellis and Helen Logan, "... in Shanghai" by Edward T. Lowe, Jr., and Gerald Fairlie, "... at the Opera" by Scott Darling and Charles Belden, 1937: "... on Broadway" and "... at Monte Carlo" by Charles Belden and Jerry Cady, "... in Honolulu" by Charles Belden, 1940: "... in Panama" by John Larkin and

Lester Ziffren, "... 's Murder Cruise" by Robertson White and Lester Ziffren, "... at the Wax Museum" by Jerry Larkin, "Murder Over New York" by Lester Ziffren, 1941: "Dead Men Tell" by Jerry Larkin, "... in Rio" by Samuel G. Engel and Lester Ziffen, 1942: "Castle in the Desert" by Jerry Larkin, 1944-46: "In the Secret Service", "The Chinese Cat", "Black Magic", "The Scarlet Club", "The Shanghai Cobra", "The Red Dragon", "The Dark Alibi" by George Callahan, 1946: "Shadows over Chinatown" by Raymond L. Schrock, "Dangerous Money" and "The Trap" by Miriam Kissinger, 1947: "The Chinese Ring" by Scott Darling, "Docks of New Orleans" by Samuel Newman and Scott Darling, 1948: "Shanghai Chest" by Samuel Newman and Scott Darling, "The Golden Eye" by Scott Darling, "The Feathered Serpent" by Oliver Drake, 1949: "The Sky Dragon" by Oliver Drake, 1957: "Your Money or Your Wife", "The Last Face", "The Counterfeiters", "Backfire" and "Dateline -- Execution" by Richard Grey, "The Secret of the Sea", "The Circle of Fire" by Tony Barrett, "Blind Man's Bluff" by Paul Conlan, "The Great Salvos", "The Death of a Don", "Charlie's Highland Fling", "The Sweater" by Jerry Sacheim, "The Patient in Room 21" by Robert Leslie Bellem and Paul Erickson, "The Punjab Ruby" and "The Noble Art of Murder" by John K. Butler, "The Final Curtain" by Gene Wang, "Death at High Tide" and "Patron of the Arts" by Lee Erwin, "An Exhibit in Wax" by Sam Newman, "A Hamlet in Flames" by Robert Leslie Bellem, "Three Men on a Raft" by Jan Leman and Ted Thomas, "No Holiday for Murder" and "The Airport Murder Case" by Peter Gilbert, 1958: "Kidnap" by Doreen Montgomery, "The Sweater", "Three for One", "The Man in the Wall", "The Man with a 100 Faces", "The Chippendale Racket", "Rhyme or Treason" by Jerry Sackheim, "The Hand of Hera Dass" and "A Bowl of Cellini" by Lee Erwin, "The Invalid" by Jan Leman, "No Future for Frederick" by Terrence Maples
274 "Charlie Chan at the Circus"
275 "Charlie Chan at the Olympics" by Robert Ellis and Helen Logan, "The Amazing Chan and the Chan Clan"
276 "Charlie Chan in Honolulu" by Charles Belden
277 The New Adventures of Charlie Chan series by Earl Derr Biggers, etal.
278 There is a generation gap of about forty years here, so obviously the Charlie Chan in The Amazing Chan and the Chan Clan series is Jr. rather than Sr., 1972: "The Crown Jewel Caper", "Will the Real Charlie Chan Please Stand Up", "To Catch a Pitcher", "The Phantom Sea Thief", "Eye of the Idol", "The Fat Lady Caper", "Capt. Kidd's Doubloons", "Double Trouble", "The Great Illusion Caper", "The Mardi Gras Caper", "The Greek Caper", "The White Elephant", "The Chan Clan at Scotland Yard"; "The Return of Charlie Chan" by Gene Kearney, 1981: "Charlie Chan and the Curse of the Dragon Queen" by Stan Burns and David Axelrod, 1989: "Charlie and the Yakuza" by Phillip Chan, 1993: "Lady Hunter", 1994: "You Are Not Chinese", 1997: "24-Hours Ghost Story"
279 "Charlie Chan and the Curse of the Dragon Queen" by Stan Burns and David Axlerod
280 The one Chan in this Chan clan that did not need our help since he seemed to have the paranormal ability to rewind time like the Omega 13 device "Galaxy Quest" by David Howard, Kong-sang "Jackie" Chan ("The Big Brawl") aka "Si To" ("Fist of Anger"), "Chen Yuen Lung" ("No End of Surprises"), "A Lung" ("New Fist of Fury"), "Wa 'Tiger' Wu-Bin" ("Killer Meteors"), "Cao Lei, Lung Cheng" ("To Kill with Intrigue"), "Yi-Lang" ("Spirited Kung Fu"), "Cao Lei, Lung Cheng" ("Snake in the Eagle's Shadow"), ("Magnificent Bodyguards"), "Tang How-Yuen" ("Dragon Fist"), "Shing Lung" ("The Fearless Hyena"), "Jiang" ("Half a Loaf of Kung Fu"), ("The Young Master"), "Hsiao Hu" ("Dragon", "Dragon Strike"), ("Winners and Sinners"), "Chan Lung" ("Fearless Hyena 2"), "Muscle" ("My Lucky Stars", "Twinkle, Twinkle, Lucky Stars"), "Tat 'Ted' Fung" ("Heart of a Dragon"), "Asian Hawk" ("Armor of God", "Chinese Zodiac"), ("Police Story", "Police Story 2"), ("Operation Condor"), ("Supercop", "Supercop 2", "Crime Story"), "Keung" ("Rumble in the Bronx"), "Chan Ka Kui" ("First Strike"), "Hu Amei" ("Who Am I"), ("The Dark Hand"), ("The Tiger and the Pussycat"),

"Tagert McStone" ("Agent Tag"), ("The King and Jade"), "Eddie Yang" ("The Medallion"), "Chan Kwok-Wing" ("New Police Story"), ("Steelhead", "Shinjuku Incident")

281 1902: "Lair of the Star-Spawn" by August Derleth and Mark Schorer

282 1904: "The Suicide Room" by Harry Ashton-Wolf, "Enter the Death Room" by Max Haines, or transliterated as "Xan" in 1984, "Buckaroo Banzai Against The World Crime League" by Earl Mac Rauch

283 1913: "The Riddle of the Golden Monkeys" by Loren D. Estleman

284 "The Lost Lady" and "Satan's Stepson" by Seabury Quinn

285 "The Eye of Oran" by Win Eckert

286 "The Counter-clock Incident" by John Culver

287 "Flash Gordon Conquers the Universe" by George H. Plympton, Basil Dickey and Barry Shipman

288 "Zatara the Magician" by Fred Guardineer

289 "From Eternity" by Jim Mortimore

290 most notably in the Black Mass

291 *The Chronicles of Narnia* by C. S. Lewis

292 "The Flash" by Gardner Fox

293 "Wink of an Eye" by Arthur Heinemann, Genesis 3:20

294 "The Deadly Years" by David P. Harmon

295 "Return to Tomorrow" by Gene Roddenberry

296 "The Wizard of Oz" by Noel Langley, Florence Ryerson and Edgar Allan Woolf

297 The Hands of Shang-Chi, Master of Kung Fu series

298 "Daughter of the Dragon" by Lloyd Corrigan and Monte M. Katterjohn

299 "The Face of Fu Manchu", "The Brides of Fu Manchu", "The Vengeance of Fu Manchu", "The Blood of Fu Manchu", "The Castle of Fu Manchu" by Harry Alan "Peter Welbeck" Towers

300 "The Mask of Fu Manchu" by Irene Kuhn, Edgar Allan Woolf and John Willard

301 "A-Team" by Frank Lupo and Stephen J. Cannell

302 "The Black Lotus" by James "Brett Halliday" Reasoner

303 *Dr. Jekyll and Mr. Holmes* by Loren D. Estleman

304 "The Strange Case of Dr. Jekyll and Mr. Holmes" by Steven Philip Jones and Seppo Makinen

305 "The Two Faces of Dr. Jekyll" by Wolf Mankowitz

306 originally acronym "welithom", from the oft-repeated phrase by Holmes's cousin Kent Allard Rassendyll, aka "the Shadow".

307 a mutagenic drug with unpredictable effects much abused in *The Rise and Fall of the Sheshak Empire* by Michael Halm **198**

308 "Abbott and Costello Meet Dr. Jekyll and Mr. Hyde" by Lee Loeb and John Grant

309 Rodenthropy is a form of bimorphism, similar to lycanthropy in which the person transforms into a wolf or wolf-person, in which they become a humanoid rodent, a mouse or rat. Mammal metamorphosis seems to be the most common with sufferers called "furries". Some of most well documented cases are Walter Elias "Mickey Mouse" Disney (http://www.imdb.com/find?ref_=nv_sr_fn&q=mickey+mouse&s=all) and George Clarence "Bugs" Moran. *(Bugs Bunny: 50 Years and Only One Grey Hare* by Henry Holt*)*

310 *New Werewoman Handbook* (http://bigclosetr.us/topshelf/fiction/31012/new-werewoman-handbook)

311 Carol Burnett and Friends: "Dr. Jekyll and Ms. Hyde"

312 "Jekyll and Hyde" by David Wickes

313 daughter of Sir George Carewe, "Dr. Jekyll and Mr. Hyde" by Thomas Russell Sullivan

314 daughter of Sir Danvers Carew, "Dr. Jekyll and Mr. Hyde" by Samuel Hoffenstein and Percy Heath

315 "The Strange Case of Dr. Jekyll and Miss Osborne: The Bloodbath of Dr. Jekyll" by Walerian Bororwczyk
316 *The League of Extraordinary Gentlemen, Volume II* by Alan Moore and Kevin O'Neill
317 "Dr. Jekyll and Sister Hyde" by Brian Clemen
318 "I, Monster" by Milton Subotski
319 "Son of Dr. Jekyll" by Mortimer Braus and Jack Pollexfen
320 *The Hyena* by Robert E. Howard
321 "The Two Faces of Dr. Jekyll" by Wolf Mankowitz
322 The Grimm "Thing", ("The Fantastic Four" by Stan Lee, "Hydden Time: A timeline of the Jekyll Family" by Dennis E. Power)
323 cousins, son of Brian and Rebecca Walters Banner, Robert Bruce Banner ("The Hulk" by Stan Lee) and son of Frank "Jolly Green Giant" and Nanette Sherwood Banner, David Bruce Banner ("The Incredible Hulk" by Kenneth Johnson)
324 "She-Hulk" by Stan Lee
325 Apprentice Adept series by Piers Anthony
326 "Daughter of Dr. Jekyll" by Jack Pollexfen
327 "A Letter to Marty" by Jasmin Ayala and Joey Sinko
328 "Call of Duty: Black Ops II" by Dave Anthony, David S. Goyer, Craig Houston and Micah Wright
329 "The Ugly Duckling" by Sid Colin and Jack Davies
330 "Jekyll and Hyde ... Together Again" by Monica Johnson, Harvey Miller, Jerry Belson and Michael Leeson
331 "Here Come the Munsters" by Bill Prady, Jim Fisher and Jim Staahl
332 "Hyde and Sneak" by Bill Danch
333 Woody Woodpecker in "Prehistoric Super Salesman", "A Lad in Bagdad", "Robin Hoody Woody", "Buckaneer Woodpecker", "Roamin' Roman" by Walter Lantz
334 "Where in Time Is Carmen Sandiego?" aka "Carmen Sandiego's Great Chase Through Time"
335 Superbook: "The Miracle Rod: Moses" by Akiyoshi Sakai
336 "To the Promised Land" by Robert Silverberg
337 *The Saga of Erik the Red*
338 "The Shakespeare Code" by Gareth Roberts
339 "Christopher Columbus Popnecker"
340 *The Edison Mystery* by Dan Gutman
341 "Worlds Apart" by Jill Sherman and James D. Parriott
342 "Soy la Libertad!" by Robert Coulson
343 Warehouse 13: "What Matter's Most" by Diego Gutierrez
344 "Perchance" by Micahel Kurland
345 "Requiem for Methuselah" by Jerome Bixby
346 "The Ninth Symphony of Ludwig van Beethoven and Other Lost Songs" by Carter Scholtz
347 "Symphony in a Minor Key" by H. G. Stratmann
348 "Peabody's Improbable History" by Ted Key
349 "Bill and Ted's Excellent Adventure" by Chris Matheson and Ed Solomon
350 Mentors: "A Ninth of Beethoven" by David Wiechorek
351 *Natural History* by Pliny
352 *Metamorphoses* by Ovid
353 Warehouse 13: "Reset" by Jack Kenny and Nell Scovell
354 Atlantis: "The Gorgon's Gaze" by Julia Jones
355 "The Price of Hope" by Howard Overman

356 Hercules Zero to Hero: "Hercules and the Green-Eyed Monster" by Madellaine Paxson
357 Adventures in the Book of Virtues: "Responsibility" by Glenn Leopold
358 Ecclesiastes 6:1-6
359 1 Chronicles 3:5, 2 Samuel 12:25
360 *Exile* by Nihon Telenet
361 Acts 4:12, Jesus the only Name by which one may be saved
362 "Slaves of Babylon" by DeVallon Scott
363 "higher" criticism's J(oshua, "The Lord saves."), E(zra, "Help"), D(euel, "knowledge of God") and P(altiel, "deliverence of God")
364 *Christ Legends*: "In the Temple" by Selma Lagerlöf
365 "Capt. Marvel" by Bill Parker and C. C. Beck; "And the Spirit of the Lord shall rest upon him, the Spirit of Wisdom and understanding, the Spirit of counsel and might, the Spirit of knowledge and of the fear of the Lord." (Isa 11:2)
366 Perry Rhodan
367 Green Lantern: "Time and Time Again"
368 "The Real-Great Adventures of Terr'ble Thompson!, Hero of History" by Gene Deitch
369 "The Day That Dropped Out of Time" by John Broome
370 *Wraiths of time* by Andre Norton
371 "Queen of Asia" by Judith Tarr
372 "Conquest Denied: The Premature Death of Alexander the Great" by Josiah Ober
373 *Conquistador* by S. M Stirling
374 Daniel 11:3-4
375 Luke 36:19-31
376 John 12:1-11
377 Dr. Lazarus of "Galaxy Quest" by Howard Gordon (David Howard and Robert Gordon) and Howard "Lazarus Long" Howard of *Time Enough for Love* by "Robert A. Heinlein" (Howard Howard), James Cathcart ("The Lazarus Man" by Dick Beebe)
378 *The Holy Blood and the Holy Grail* by Michael Baigent, Richard Leigh and Henry Leigh, *The DaVinci Code* by Dan Brown, "Time Machine: Beyond the DaVinci Code" by Thomas Quinn and Rob Blumenstein; Dan Brown was aka "Jean XXVIII", a nautonnier of Priory of Sion, successor to Pierre Plantard de Saint-Clair (Jean XXVII), Jean Cocteau (Jean XXVI), Claude Debussy (Jean XXV), Victor Hugo (Jean XXIV), Charles Nodier (Jean XXIII), Maximilian de Lorraine (Jean XXII), Charle de Lorraine (Jean XXI), Charles Radcliffe (Jean XX), "Isaac Newton" (Jean XIX), Robert Boyle (Jean XVIII), Johann Valentin Andrea (Jean XVII), Robert Fludd (Jean XVI), Louis de Nîvers (Jean XV), Ferdinand de Gonzaga (Jean XIV), Connétable de Bourbon (Jean XIII), Leonardo da Vinci and "Leonardo da Vinci" (Jean XII), Sandro Filipepi (Jean XI), Iodande de Bar (Jean X), René d'Anjou (Jean IX), Nicholas Flamel (Jean VIII), Blanche d'Évreux (Jeanne VII), Jean de Saint-Clair (Jean VI), Jeanne de Bar (Jeanne V), Edouard de Bar (Jean IV), Guillaume de Gisors (Jean III), Marie de Saint-Clair (Jeanne II), and Jean de Gisors (Jean I)
379 "The Son of Jesus" by Jefferson Airplane
380 *The Legend of Mary Magdalene* by Philo of Alexandria
381 *History of the Kings of Britain* by Geoffrey de Monmouth
382 *Once and Future King*: "The Sword in the Stone" by T. H. White and "The Sword in the Stone" by Bill Peet
383 "The Origin of the Demon" by Jack Kirby
384 Time Tunnel: "Merlin the Magician" by William Welch
385 "The Revenge of Lana Lang" by Henry Boltinoff

386 "The Aerial Burglar" by Percival Leigh, "Sherlock Holmes vs. the Monsters" by Paul Bales, *Century Shock* prequel to *Millennium Shock* by Justin Richards
387 *Morlock Night* by K. W. Jeter
388 *Excalibur* by Chris Claremont and Alan Davis
389 Dr. Who: "Battlefield" by Ben Aaronovitch
390 *Annales Cambriae*
391 *The Time Travel Trap* by Dan Jolley
392 "Mr. Peabody and Sherman" by Craig Wright
393 Futurama: "Bender's Big Score" by Ken Keeler
394 "City of Death" by David Agnew
395 *Who Stole the Mona Lisa?* by Geronimo Stilton and Demetrio Bargellini
396 *The Revenge of Moriarty* by John Gardner
397 *The Strange Doings of J. Leslie Ryder* by Daniel Gracely
398 Prof. Augustus St. Francis Xavier Van Dusen, "The Thinking Machine" (*The Chase of the Golden Plate*, etc. by Jacques Futrelle)
399 "L'Arrestation d'Arsène Lupin", etc. by Maurice Leblanc
400 ornithrope **Jacques "The Rooster" Clouseau**, grandson of **Tabaret**, "Père Tireauclair" (*L'Affaire Lerouge*, etc. by Émile Gaboriau), ancestor of "miserable bunglers": **Jacques Clouseau**, and 9 his son by Maria Gambrelli, **Jacques Gambrelli** ("The Son of the Pink Panther" by Blake Edwards and Madeline and Steven Sunshine), Inspector **Gadget** through Chimeney and charlady Charlotte "Char" Clouseau Gadget fka Gâchette 11 ("Gadget's Clean Sweep") and **Maxwell Smart** 12 through secret agents "Smart **Alec**" and **Diane Clouseau Smart**
401 "Murders in the Rue Morgue" by Edgar Allen Poe
402 *The Achievements of Luther Trant* by Edwin Balmer and William B. MacHarg
403 "The Ides of March" by E. W. Hornung
404 fallaciously called by Hutchinson Hatch "the Society of Infallible Detectives" ("The Adventure of the Mona Lisa" by Carolyn Wells)
405 *The Lost Mona Lisa* by R. A. Scotti
406 "Voyagers on the *Titanic*" by Jill Sherman and James D. Parriott
407 wereduck Benjamin Smyth "Scrooge" McDuck ("The Status Seeker" by Carl Barks), "Buck" McDuck vs. James gang ("The Cattle King"), 1884: sold rights to Anaconda copper mine ("Raider of the Copper Hill"), 1895: vs. Daltons in Pizen Bluff, AR (*The Life and timesof Scrooge McDuck*), 1896: as "Great Platypus" rescued Jabiru Kapirigi, found and returned giant opal of Bindagbindag ("Dreamtime Duck of the Never Never"), 1897: found Goose Egg nugget at White Agony Creek ("King of the Golden River", "North of the Yukon", "Back to the Klondick"), 1904: sold music ("The City of Gold Roofs"), 1913: hunted sunken treasure ("Only a Poor Old Man"), 1930: ("Birdman of Wall St.") becoming richer than maharajah of Howduyustan ("How Green Is My Lettuce"), 1955: ("The Secret of Atlantis", "Trala La", "The Fabulous Philosopher's Stone"), 1956: ("Land Beneath the Ground", "Lost Crown of Genghis Khan"), 1961: ("Uncle Scrooge's Rocket to the Moon"), 1963: ("Crown of the Mayas", "Rocket Digger"), 1965: ("McDuck of Arabia"), 1987: on Ronguay I. ("Treasure of the Golden Sun"), 1990: died at 123 ("Scrooge's Last Adventure")
He was a descendant of Petronius "Duckman" Paperonius, cursed with ornithropy by the witch of Vesuvius, founder of the MacDuich clan, fka Pah-Peh-Rheo, uncle of Cleopatra. ("Petronius Paperonius and the Invasion of the Barbarians" by Alberto Savini, "Daisy Duck and Papyrus of the Pah-Peh-Rheo" and "Petronius Paperonius and the Gold of Pippus Augustus" by Guido Martina)
408 *Sherlock Holmes and the Titanic Tragedy* by William Seil
409 "The Adventure of the Dying Ship" by Edward D. Hoch

410 *From Time to Time* by Jack Finney
411 "Two Roads, No Choices" by Dean Wesley Smith
412 Supernatural: "My Heart Will Go On" by Eric Charmelo and Nicole Snyder
413 *Chrononauts* by Andrew Looney, *The Company of the Dead* by David Kowalski
414 "The Resonance of Light" by Geoffrey Landis
415 "100 Years: The World Changes!!!"
http://www.alternatehistory.com/discussion/showthread.php?t=155066
416 "Way of the Wicked" by Matthew Robert Kelly
417 The Chrononauts: "Milk Run" by Andrew Fudge
418 *The Second War of the Worlds*
419 *The World Set Free* by H. G. Wells
420 *Terra Two Sequence* by Stephen Ames Barry, *Reich Star* by Ken Richardson, *Hitler: The Victory That Nearly Was* by Bruce Quarrie
421 "Hitler's Bomb: Target: London and Moscow" by Forrest Lindsey, 1945 — Psychobilly Retropocalypse RPG
422 "If I had been ... Hideki Tojo in 1941" by Louis Allen
423 "The Old Man and the C." by Sheila Finch
424 "The Amazing Colossal Man" by Mark Hannah and Bert I. Gordon
425 The Incredible Hulk #1 by Stan Lee
426 "Capt. America" by Don Ingalis
427 *Future Wars* by Paul Chusset
428 Exodus 20:6, Psalm 105:8, Isaiah 65:20, Revelation 16:16
429 *The Island of Dr. Moreau* by H. G. Wells
430 *The Underpeople* by Cordwainer Smith
431 "The Time Bandits" by Michel Palin and Terry Gilliam
432 *Tonight on the Titanic* by Mary Pope Osborn
433 *Exploring Titanic* by Agnieszka Anderson, Bill Kelleher and Michael Biskup)
434 "Rendezvous with Yesterday" by Harold Jack Bloom and Shimon Wincelberg
435 The Highlander: Raven: "The Devil You Know" by Durnford King
436 "The Unsinkable Molly Brown" by Richard Morris
437 Sanctuary: "Next Tuesday" by Damien Kindler
438 "Martin Meets His Match" by Gene Thompson and Bill Kelsay
439 "The Innocents" by Marc Platt
440 *Time Cat* by Lloyd Alexander
441 JumpStart Adventures 3rd Grade: Mystery Mt.
442 "Uh-oh, Leonardo" by Robert Sabuda
443 *DaWild, DaCrazy, DaVinci* by Jon Scieszka
444 *Lady with an Alien* by Mike Resnick
445 http://www.voyagersguidebook.net/theomni.htm

Originally the mark that a timeline had been restored by "Daedalos" or his son Ikaros, who he'd gone back and saved, contrary to Greek legend, or any of their fellow chrononauts who became known as Voyagers, was a simple Omega, Ω, for "Óla kanoniki." ("All normal."), Omega Kappa, OK, okey. Over the millennia it elaborated into the Chad ideogram and became linked with the ubiquitous Voyager George Kilroy from the Thirtieth Century. ("The Message" by Isaac Asimov) This lead Hitler in the Twentieth to believe that Kilroy was the codename of a high-level Allied spy. During WW I the mysterious graffitist was identified as Foo and mistakenly believed to be a gremlin. Other notable Voyagers have been Isaac "Wildman" Wolfstein, "Clem", "Flywheel", Heffinger, "Herbie", Józef

Tkaczuk, Julito, Luke "the Spook", Overby, Robert Motherwell, Sapo, Smoe, Pvt. Snoops, Vasya (https://en.wikipedia.org/wiki/Kilroy_was_here) and last and least the Machiavellian Drake. The motto on the Omnis, "Time waits for NoMan.", refers to the voyage of Ulysses aka NoMan (*Odyssey* by Homer) and/or Capt. Ulysses of the starship *Odyssey* ("Ulysses 31"), both aliases of the timetraveling Akharin.
446 "Ever After: A Cinderella Story" by Susannah Grant, Andy Tennant and Rick Parks
447 Discovering da Vinci: "Hidden Door found at Machu Piccu", Isabel Soto Adventures: "Investigating Maccu Pichu" by Emily Sohn
448 "About Seven Brothers" by Ere Kokkonen, Spede Pasanen and Jukka Vitanen
449 discovered by Baird and Hernandez on the secret moonship *Benjamin Franklin* in 1968 and covered up ("The Light")
450 "Silent Leonardo" by Kage Baker
451 "DaVinci Rising" and *The Memory Cathedral: A Secret History of Leonardo da Vinci* by Jack Dann
452 *Pasquale's Angel* and "The Temptation of Dr. Stein" by Paul J. McAuley
453 "Age of Miracles" by Richard Mueller
454 *The Royalty Project* by Carl Amery
455 *The Hidden Family* by Charles Stross
456 *Heartfire* by Orson Scott Card
457 *Nick of Time* by Ted Bell
458 *One with Darkness* by Susan Squires
459 *Time for Eternity* by Susan Squires
460 *A Twist in Time* by Susan Squires
461 *The Mists of Time* by Susan Squires
462 the devil Eng., diabolos Grk. (1 Jn 3:8, Mt 13:39, 1 Pt 5:8-9), Satan Heb. (Numbers 22:22, Job, 1 Chronicles, Psalms, Zechariah, Mark 1:13, *Dante's Infernal*), Arretian Natas, prince of this world (John 16:11), prince of the power of the air (Ephesians 2:2), ugly one (*The Legends of the Jews* by Louis Ginzberg), whose consort Barbelo, was both daughter (*Gospel of Mary, Apocryphon of John*) and mother of the jinn Pistis Sophia (*Texts of the Savior*); fka Metatron until replaced by Enoch, aka Beelzebub "god of flies" aka Belzebud, Belzaboul, Beelzeboul, Baalsebul, etc., worshiped by Philistians (2 Kings 1:3), prince of demons (Matthew 10:25, 12:24, Mark 3:22, Luke 40:15), lord of chaos (Valentius), identified with Rahab "violence", Heb. *sar shel yam* "prince of the primordial sea", Job 26:12, Psalm 37:4, demon of insolence and pride (Isaiah 51:9) and with Leviathan, Behemoth (*Midrash Genesis Rabba, Talmud Sanhedrin*), tried to hinder crossing of Red Sea
463 "evil mind" (*Essays* by Haug), John 8:44, Angra-Mainyu evil spirit "mighty serpent" (*Vendidad, Non-classical Mythology, The Flesh Transfigured* by R. J. Campbell)
464 Shem-yaza "strong" begot demonspawn by "Methuselah's" foster sister, Naamah (*Semitic Magic* by R. Campbell Thompson)
465 *Egypt, Heaven and Hell* by E. A. Wallis Budge
466 aka Nehaha "negation" (*Legend of the Winged Sun-disk*), who consorted with Nephythys aka Nebkhat "lady of the body" (*Gods of the Egyptians* by E. A. Wallis Budge), Nebthet, both begotten from Kronos (Seb) (*Isis and Osiris* by Plutarch), enemy of brother Oriris, aka Suti, enemy of Horus (*Book of the Dead* by E. A. Wallis Budge), identified with Typho(n) Grk., Sephon Heb. "dark" (*Three Books of Occult Philosophy* by Cornelius Agrippa), aka Bebon, Syn, concubine Taurt aka Thueris (*Isis and Osiris* by Plutarch)
467 Isis: "The Wrath of Set" by Steve Skeates
468 Henry Jones, Sr., found Mjölnir, the hammer of Thor, gave up his umbrella and became a

superhero (Superhero City: "Starship Command: Battle for Earth")
469 Perry Rhodan: "Imperator of Akron", "Moons of Secrets", and "Jewels of the Stars"
470 Corinthians 6:15, *Das Buch Beliel* by Jacobus de Teramo, ambassador to Turkey, identified with Mastema (*The Toilers of the Sea* by Victor Hugo), aka Mansemat *Acts of Phillip, The Apocryphal New Testament* ed. by M. R. James, Matanbuchus "worthless gift", *mithdabek* "one who attaches himself", Mechembechus, Meterbuchus, "father of evil" (*The Zadokite Fragments and the Dead Sea Scrolls*), tried to kill Moses (Exodus 4:24ff), demon of hostility (*Discovery in the Judean Desert* by Geza Vermes), identified with Beliar, demon of lawlessness or Mastema (*The Ascension of Isaiah* introduction), aka Mansemat (*Acts of Phillip, The Apocryphal New Testament* by James)
471 2 Kings 23:13, aka Astaroth, equated with Diabolos (*Pseudo-Monarchia* by Johannes Wier), equated with Astoreth (*Paradise Lost* by John Milton), resides in America (Grimorium *Verum*), visited Faust (Collin De Plancy)
472 aka Astarte Syrian, Ashtoreth, Is(h)tar, Aphrodite Greek "foam-sprung" (*Smith's Classical Dictionary*), Venus Roman (*Gods: A Dictionary of the Deities of All Lands* ed. by B. G. Redfield), Asherah Can. aka Anat "lady of the mountain" who slew 7-headed Lotan, mother of Ba'al, aka Qadesh Phoen. "holy", Lilith *ardat lili* femme demons aka Abeko, Abito, Amizo, Batna, Eilo, Ita, Izorpo, Kali, Kea, Kokos, Odam, Partasah, Patrota, Podo, Satrina, Talto (*Studies and Texts in Folklore* by M. Gaster), Abro, Amiz(u), Avitu, Bituah, 'Ik, 'Ils, Kalee, Kakash, Kema, Partashah, Petrota, Pods, Raphi, Satrina(h), (*Folk-lore of the Holy Land* by J. E. Hanauer), Abyzu, Ailo, Alu, Ardad Lili, Gallu, Gelou, Gilou, Lamassu, Thiltho, Zahriel, Zefonith (*A Dictionary of Angels* by Gustav Davidson), enemy of infants, manifests as screech owl (Isaiah 34:14), or woman with serpent's tail (*Alphabet of Ben Sira*), consort sic of Sammael (*Mada'e ha Yahadut* article by Scholem), aka Kali "the black" (*Studies and Texts in Folklore* by M. Gaster), Chandi "fierce", Bhairavi "terrible", manifests with skull necklace and armgirdle, killed husband Shiva
473 Nick Bogey aka Nicholas the Ancient, from Iniquity or *nickar* "destroying principle" (*Pleasant Notes upon Don Quixote* by Edmund Gayton), aka Ol' Scratch from Angel of Death's scythe ("The Story of Jack Spriggins and the Enchanted Bean"), Old Serpent (Revelation 12:19)
474 "The Devil and Tom Walker" by Washington Irving
475 *The Devil and Daniel Webster* by Stephen Vincent Benét
476 as "C. W. Saturn" (*Miracle Monday* by Elliot S. Maggin)
477 "End of Days" by Andrew W. Marlow, "The Book of Life" by Hal Hartley
478 "The Seventh Seal" by Ingmar Bergman
479 "What If Catherine Ballou Had Married Lawrence van Helsing's Son and Had a Werecat Daughter?" ("Cat Ballou" by Walter Newman and Frank Pierson, *The Ballad of Cat Ballou* by Roy Chanslor, "Horror of Dracula" by Jimmy Sangster, "Cat People" and "The Curse of the Cat People" by DeWitt Bodeen)
480 "Twilight" by Melissa Rosenberg, *Twilight* by Stephanie Meyer, "Immortal"; rarely Romeo-Juliet couples like werewolf Lucian and vampire princess Sonja revolted against vampire king Viktor in 1206. ("Underworld: Rise of the Lycans") In 1462 Vlad "Dracula" Tepes vanquished the First Vampire Varnae of Atlantis, cursed by Darkhold cult in 9704 BC. In 1472 he vanquished Nimrod-Lothos and in 1933 werewolf John Talbot, Jr., became doubly cursed as the vampire Grodinn (Children of the Night)
481 "The Black Cat" by Peter Ruric, aka "The House of Doom" in England, where a black cat is good luck, in Hungarian *végzet* means not only "doom", but also "destiny, fate, nemesis, fatality", Luke 4:18
482 *King Lear* by Shakespeare, *History of the Kings of Britain* by Geoffrey of Monmouth **381**
483 "If It Had Been Discovered in 1930 that Bacon Really Did Write Shakespeare" aka "Professor Gubbin's Revolution" by J. C. Squire
484 considered forgeries by William Henry Ireland in 1790s

485 for occupier King Philip in an alternative 1598 (*Ruled Britannia* by Harry Turtledove)
486 "Duck Soup" by Bert Kalmar and Harry Ruby
487 "The Shakespeare Code" by Gareth Roberts
488 *The Empire of Glass* by Andy Lane
489 "Mario's Time Machine" by Wes Jenkins, Jim Pearson, Valerie Singer and Andrew Iverson; Mario and Luigi Mario ("Super Mario Bros." by Parker Bennett, Terry Runte and Ed Solomon)
490 Mentors: "Such Stuff As Dreams Are Made Of"
491 *Newton's Cannon* by Gregory Keyes
492 *The Calculus of Angels* by Gregory Keyes
493 *The Story of My Life* by Helen Keller, "The Miracle Worker" by William Gibson, "The Miracle Worker" by Monte Merrick
494 aka "The H. M. S. *Pinafore*"
495 aka "The Pirates of Pinzance"
496 aka "The Mikado"
497 "Our Man Flint" by Hal Fimberg and Ben Starr
498 *That Man Flint* by Gary Phillips
499 *Danger A Go-Go* by Gary Phillips
500 *Day of the Destroyers* ed. by Gary Phillips
501 "Our Man Flint: Dead on Target" by Norman Klenman
502 "Compound Interest" by Larry Warner
503 Star Fleet Command
504 *Cry of the Onlies* by Judy Klass
505 Holmes categorized Lal as a *yang-tul*, the subcreation of a subcreation, the "offspring" of Data, an android subcreated by the Human creature Noonian Soong created by The Creator. ("The Offspring" by René Echevarria) So too was the holographic simulacrum Regina Barthalomew Moriarty, wife of the holographic Prof. Moriary subcreated by Geordi LaForge for Sherlockian Data ("Ship in a Bottle" also by René Echevarria) If the Creator's relationship to His creature is Reality, that of the creature's subcreation, these AIs, for example, are *tulpas*. That of the subcreation's subcreation is called a *yang-tul* and that of the creature's subcreation's subcreation a *nying-tul*. The nested realities of Twentieth Century has a similar relationship. The Iron Age (1980-2000) were the *tulpa* of the Bronze Age (1970-79), the *yang-tul* of the Silver Age (1956-69) and the *nying-tul* of the Golden Age (1939-1955). These metallic designations were, of course, based on the four empires of Daniel's prophesy. (Daniel 2:38-40)
506 "The Dead Lady of Clown Town" by Paul "Cordwainer Smith" Linebarger
507 *Bibliotheke* by Pseudo-Apollodorus, *Fabula* by Hyginus
508 "Flash Gordon" by Alex Raymond
509 "The Tower of London" by Robert N. Lee
510 *Richard III* ed. by William Shakespeare
511 *Sometime Never...* by Justin Richards
512 William Preston and Theodore Logan in the bogus "Bill and Ted's Bogus Journey" by Chris Matheson and Ed Solomon, with their wives formed the group "The Wyld Stallyns". Ted married Elizabeth and had children named William and Joanna and William married Joanna and had children named Theodore and Elizabeth. The children got together as "The New Wyld Stallyons" and changed their future. Edward and Richard and Elizabeth and Joanna and their children became the famous folksinging Fleetwood family and also changed their future for the better.
513 PPOs (Permanently Paranormal Objects) based on the linkage between body and soul, even when temporarily disembodied, the basis for the power relics, as opposed to TPOs (temporarily paranormal objects), charms and talismans, whose paranormal power can be removed by disenchantment

514 1 Samuel 28

515 "The Devil Commands" by Robert D. Andrews and Milton Gunzburg, *Edge of Running Water* by William Sloane; We encountered many causes for zombism, alien parasites, mutations, various mindcontrols. Whatever the cause it usually turned out to be ooby, having to do with an out-of-body experience, where the Spirit keeps the body alive, while neither the person's soul nor a dybbuk is in control. The body is on "automatic pilot", in the worse, ghoolish cases in flesh-eating or brain-eating mode. Severing the "silver cord" and allowing the victim to die is the preferable alternative as it is with other kinds of undead. The problem usually is find the way to do this, without abusing the corpse.

516 "Web Therapy" by Dan Bucatinsky, Lisa Kudrow and Don Roos

517 Alex Rider: Operation Stormbreaker by Anthony Horowitz

518 "The Strain" by Guillermo del Toro and Chuck Hogan

519 "The Haunted Strangler" by Jan Read

520 Shanghai 1932, Kiev 1974, Mars 2105, Alchernar II 2156, Deneb II, Rigel IV, Argelius II 2267 ("Wolf in the Fold" by Robert Block), 1928 (*The Ripper Returns*), Milwaukee 1974 ("The Ripper"), Lake Havasu, AZ, 1985 ("Bridge Across Time"), 1986 ("Way of the Wicked"), 1988 ("Jack's Back"), 1999 ("Ripper"), 2014 ("Way of the Wicked"), 2285 (*Wolf on the Prowl* by Tony Isabelle), 2370 (*Enter the Wolf* by A. C. Crispin and Howard Weinstein), 2,001,979 (*An East Wind Coming*), (Voyagers!: "Jack's Back" by James D. Pariott)

521 "The Crime and the Glory of Commander Suzdal" by Paul "Cordwainer Smith" Linebarger

522 The intergalactic war between the Virgin (Virgo supercluster) and the Dragon (Draco supercluster) (Genesis 3:15, Revelation 12)

523 Davros of Skaro's time traveling mutants attempted to devolve all sentients other than themselves into subhuman mutants like themselves. ("The Daleks" fka "The Mutants", not to be confused with "The Mutants" by Bob Baker and Dave Martin 134 and "The Genesis of the Daleks" by Terry Nation) The devolution of the humanoid Kaleds into subhuman Daleks was indicated by a Davrosism or amagran, an anagram in which the initial and final consonants are swapped. A devolved Human would therefore be called a numah, as prophesied in Psalm 22:6, "I am a worm, and no man; a reproach of men, and despised of the people." Conversely in general any sentient devolved into an animal would be called by the amagran for animal, "Aliman, the exact opposite of an animal artificially evolved into sentience, like manimals **429** or underpeople **430**. Both the Time War and the Virdra War will hopefully be featured in *The Rise and Fall of the Sheshak Empire*. **198** For alien names from A'hwetk to Zusyi see the alien animals at xoology. (http://michaelhalm.tripod.com/id60.htm)

524 "The Ape" by Kurt Siodmak

525 Frances Clifford became Mrs. McCarthy ("The Saxon Charm"), had a son Bernard, then became Mrs. Sloane ("Unwanted" by Terence Maples), had a son Adrian and then became Mrs. Robinson ("Millionaire Ellen Curry" by Lawrence L. Goldman) whose husband adopted them both, making them Frances Clifford McCarthy Sloane Robinson ("The Beat"), Bernard McCarthy Robinson and Adrian Sloane Robinson.

526 "The Walking Dead" by Ewart Adamson, Peter Milne, Robert Hardy Andrews and Lillie Hayward

527 If Napoleon had Won the Battle of Waterloo: "What if Constant Rebecque Had Obeyed Wellington's Order of 7 pm, 15 June 1815, and Abandoned Quatre Bras?"

528 *Operation Bonaparte* by Paul Van Herck 150, *Caroline, Oh! Caroline* by Michel Védéwé

529 *The Napoleonic Wars* by Felix C. Gotschalk, "The Other Adventure of the Six Napoleons"

530 "Old Hickory and the Pirate" by Robert Janes

531 Mother Saint Michel Gensoul and Our Lady of Prompt Succor,
http://www.neworleanschurches.com/promptsuc/promptsuc.htm

532 *Frankenstein, or the Modern Prometheus* by Mary Shelly, "Gothic" by Steven Volk, "Haunted

Summer" by Lewis John Carlino
533 *Vampyr* by John William Polidari
534 Time Travel Trio: *Nightmare on Joe's Street* by Jon Scieszka, Peter Hirsch and Zachary Rau, this interdimensional shifting is similar to that of the Thermian's *Historical Record Guide* found on Desing's world in 2409 in which the *Minnow* survivors weren't rescued, while the *Protector* was launched ("Those Poor People, or The Island on the Edge of Forever" by G. L. Peabody) and the alternative timeline in which they were and it wasn't. ("Rescue from Gilligan's Island" by Sherwood, Elroy and Al Schwartz and David P. Harmon)
535 originally the acronym "ymmir"
536 Drazen's Law, originally the acronym "tuafvithlittfu".
537 "Frankenstein 1970" by Richard Landau and George Worthington Yates
538 The Frankenstein-Dracula War: "Triumph and Tragedy" by Jean-Marc Lofficier
539 "The Evil of Frankenstein" by Anthony "John Elder" Hinds
540 "The Curse of Frankenstein" by Jimmy Sangster
541 originally the acronym "tanats"
542 "Frankenstein Created Woman" by Anthony "John Elder" Hinds
543 "Frankenstein Must Be Destroyed" by Bert Batt
544 "Frankenstein and the Monster from Hell" by Anthony "John Elder" Hinds
545 "The Revenge of Frankenstein" by Jimmy Sangster
546 "Black as the Pit, From Pole to Pole" by Utley and Waldrop, there are wildly differing accounts of this Inner World by other visitors, Niels Klim's *Underground Travels*, Adam Seaborn's *Symzonia*, *The Narrative of Arthur Gordon Pym of Nantucket*, Otto Lidenbrock's *Journey to the Center of the Earth*, and David Innes's *At the Earth's Core*, William R. Bradshaw's "The Goddess of Atvatabar"
547 *The Cross of Frankenstein* by Robert J. Myers
548 "I, Frankenstein" by Stuart Beattie and Kevin Grevioux, gargoyles are stone statues or idols animated by demons or alien technology like the Harryhausen ray, or aliens (Special Unit 2: "Brothers", "Gargoyles", "The Girl with the See-Through Mind"), closely related to the larger, hairier, clawed trolls, trolds or trollds from Scandinavia, the smaller more humanoid Danish trolls, the Gudmanstrup trolls, the humpbacked Ebletoft trolls, the beautiful, red-haired Norwegian she-trolls, one-eyed, giant Icelandic trolls; the trows or drows of the Shetland and Orkney Islands include cave or mound-dwelling land trows, the small fairy-like peerie trows and merfolk-like sea trows. All trolls abduct Humans, particularly young women, children and poets. (*Spirits, Fairies, Leprechauns and Goblins* by Carol Rose) They polymerize upon exposure to light. ("Under the Bed" by Lawrence Meyer)
549 "Abraham Lincoln: Vampire Hunter Sequels" by Nick Corirossi and David Fergusson
550 "Victor/Victoria" by Reinhold Schünzel
551 "The Adventure of the Frankenstein Monster" by Don W. Baranowski
552 "The Slave of Frankenstein" by Robert J. Myers
553 *A Rebel in Time* by Harry Harrison
554 *Fire on the Mountain* by Terry Bisson
555 "Children of the Night" by Charles Loridans
556 *Frankenstein Lives Again* by Donald Glut
557 "Munsters, Go Home!" by Joe Connelly, Bob Mosher and George Tibbles
558 "The Munsters" by Ed Haas and Norm Liebmann, "Children of the Night" by Charles Loridans **555**; Vladimir "Sam" Copplepot aka "Grimpot the Vampire", was bitten by Vlad Tepes, but not "Dracula" himself as sometimes claimed, related to Gertrude Kabelput and her son, Oswald Chesterfield Cobblepot. aka "the Penguin" **24** and tried to cure Norman Hyde/Brent Jekyll **331**;

Edmund Wolfgang Glendon Munster was the biological son of Dr. Wilfred and Lisa Lee Glendon ("Werewolf of London" by John Colton) and husband to Wednesday Friday Addams. ("Addams Family" by Charles Addams) Marilyn Krogh Munster was the niece of both Inspector Krogh ("Son of Frankenstein" by Willis Cooper) **595** and of "Lily" Copplepot Munster and so cousin to Ruth Parrish Krogh van Helsing (*Vampirella*). After they were falsely accused of bank robbery ("The Munster's Revenge" by Arthur Alsberg and Don Nelson), "Grandpa" put all into suspended animation between 1966 and 1988. ("The Munsters Today") There was also a werewolf son of "Sam" (no relation to "Son of Sam", Richard David Falco aka "David Richard Berkowitz") named Leslie ("Mockingbird Lane" by Bryan Fuller).

559 "House of Frankenstein" by Edward T. Lowe, Jr.
560 Superboy: "Young Dracula" by Cary Bates and Ilya Salkind
561 World Of Darkness games by White Wolf, Genesis 4:15
562 (Son of) Svengoolie's "Werewolf of London" by Rich Koz
563 "Frankenstein" by Garrett Fort and Francis Edward Faragoh
564 "The Bride of Frankenstein" by William Hurlbut
565 "Lust for Frankenstein" by Jesús Franco and Kevin Collins
566 "Jesse James Meets Frankenstein's Daughter" by Carl Hittleman
567 the archenemy of James West and Artemus "Craig Kennedy" Gordon (Wild, Wild West: "The Night the Wizard Shook The Earth" by John Kneubuhl and Michael Garrison, "The Case of Helen Bond" by Arthur B. Reeve
568 "Frankenstein's Castle of Freaks" aka "Terror! Il Castello delle donne maledette" by Mark Smith, William Rose and Roberto Spano, This was caused by As(h)toreth as Beelzebub, the lord of chaos.
569 "Santo and the Blue Demon vs. Dr. Frankenstein" by Alfredo Salazar
570 "Casanova Frankenstein" by Massimo Franciosa and Luisa Montagnana, possessed by Ol' Nick as Māra "tempter", "destroyer" entering body through eyes or ears. (*Buddhism* by Williams), aka Dipaka "enflamer", not to be confused with Capt. Amazing's archenemy. ("Mystery Men" by Neil Cuthbert and Bob Burden)
571 "The Specter of Tullyfane Abbey" by June Thompson
572 "The Adventure of the Forgotten Umbrella" by Mel Gilden
573 "The Adventure of the Highgate Miracle" by Adrian Conan Doyle and John Dickson Carr
574 Sherlock: "A Study in Pink" by by Steven Moffat
575 *The Disappearance of Mr James Phillimore* by Dan Andriacco
576 "The Remarkable Disappearance of James Phillimore" by Edith Meiser
577 "The Adventure of the Extraterrestrial" by Mack Reynolds
578 "The Singular Adventure of the Eccentric Gentleman" by Alan Stockwell
579 "The Problem of the Sore Bridge -- Among Others" by Philip José Farmer
580 "The Case of the Vanishing Head-Waiter" by June Thomson
581 "There's a Time and a Place for Everything" by Marvin Aronson
582 originally the near-acronym "cubi"; Sherlock Holmes admittedly did often assume false identities, so often that of actors who had impersonated him that the distinction tended to became blurred. 1905: Gilbert "Broncho Billy" Anderson; 1908 Viggo Larsen; 1910 Otto Lagoni; 1911 Mack Sennett, Einar Zangenberg, Alwin Neuß, Lauritz Olsen; 1912 George Tréville; 1913 Harry Benham; 1915 Hector Dion, Eugen Burg; 1916 H. A. Saintsbury, William Gillette; 1917 Hugo Flink; 1918 Ferdinand Bonn; 1920 Willy Kaiser-Heyl; 1921 Eille Norwood; 1923 Eman Fiala; 1929 Carlyle Blackwell, Clive Brook; 1931 Raymond Massey, Arthur Wonter; 1932 Robert Rendel; 1933 Martin Fric, Reginald Owen; 1937 Bruno Güttner, Siegfried Schürenberg, Louis Hector; 1939 Basil Rathbone; 1949 Alan Napier; 1951 Alan Wheatley, Andrew Osborn, John Longden; 1954 Ernst Fritz Fürbinger; 1955 Ronald Howard,

Wolf Ackva; 1957 Jalmari Rinne; 1959 Peter Cushing; 1962 Christopher Lee; 1964 Douglas Wilmer; 1965 Jerome Raphael, John Neville, Paul Frees; 1967 Eric Schellow, Jacque François; 1968 Peter Cushing, Nando Gazzolo; 1969 Peter Jeffrey; 1970 Robert Stephans; 1971 Radovan Lukavský; 1972 John Rutland, Stewart Granger; 1973 Henri Verlojeux, John Cleese; 1974 Raymond Gérôme, Rolf Becker; 1976 Nicol Williamson, Roger Moore; 1977 Christopher Plummer, Peter Cook; 1978 Jeremy Clyde; 1979 Vasil Livianov; 1980 Geoffrey Whitehead, Keith McConnell; 1981 Frank Ganella; 1982 Guy Henry, Tom Baker, Paul Guers, Peter Lawford; 1983 Roger Ostime, Peter Toole, Ian Richardson; 1984 Taichirô Hirokawa, Fat Chung, Peter Evans, Guy Rolfe; 1985 Nicholas Rowe, Jeremy Brent, Ian Richardson; 1986 James Downey; 1987 Michael Pennington; 1988 Brent Spiner, Rodney Litchfield, Michael Caine; 1989 Maurice LaMarche, Brian Bedford; 1990 Edward Woodward, Reece Dinsdale; 1991 Charlton Heston, Rupert Frazier, Jeremy Irons, Juan Manuel Montesino; 1992 Richard E. Grant; 1993 Jim Cummins, Anthony Higgins, Radoslav Brzobohatý; 1994 Patrick Macnee, Fan Ai Li; 1995 Jeff Benett; 1996 Bill Barretta, Francesco J. Basilio; 1997 Rhéal Guévremont; 1999 Jason Gray-Stanford; 2000 Matt Fewer; 2001 Joaquim de Almeida, Eric Legrand, Hervé Ganim; 2002 Richard Roxburgh, James D'Arcy; 2004 Rupert Everett; 2005 Eugenio Monclava, Ted Rooney; 2007 Jonathan Pryce; 2008 Christopher Bevins; 2009 Ian Buchanan, Louis Macleod; 2010 Benedict Cumberbach, Vincent Aubert, Ben Syder; 2011 Robert Downy, Jr. (See *The Curse of Sherlock Holmes*, the sequel to *Sherlock Holmes and the Mad Doctor*)

583 "The Sorcerer" by Ahkarin aka "William Schwenck Gilbert"

584 *All-Consuming Fire* by Andy Lane

585 Call of Cthulhu: "The Yorkshire Horrors"

586 The curiously femme name of Isadora, rather than Isadore, was a clue to Persano's ambiguous gender, rather more than just a feminym like Benjamin Franklin's "Mrs. Silence Dogoody" or Sir Walter Scott's "Crystal Croftangley". In "The Problem of Thor Bridge" I rightly described him/her as a journalist and duelist, but also mad. S/he was married to Marina, from whom we learnt of his/her enemies, Carlos Vicente Gasca in Mexico ("The Case of the Remarkable Worm" by Brian M. Thomsen) and the family of Francisco de Cassales in Guahanna. ("The Mystery of the Mumbling Duelist" by Paul D. Gilbert) S/he posed as a medium in Florence, likely for grist for one of his/her notorious exposés. Holmes exposed one for Cesare Lombroso, Oliver Lodge, B. K. Mallik, Winifred Lewis, Arthur Conan Doyle and Madame Blavatsky. They were however not impressed. ("The Case of Isadora Persano" by Ted Riccardi). They had just the opposite epistemolgy as Joe "Just the Facts" Friday. ("Dragnet" by Jack Webb) Persano's connection with Phillimore was confirmed by Raffles and Bunny who found him/her unconscious in Phillimore's garden with an unhatched sapphire-like worm egg. **580**

587 *Aladdin and the Enchanted Lamp and Other Stories* by John Payne

588 *Flatland: A Romance of Many Dimensions* by Edwin A. Abbott

589 *The Incredible Umbrella* by Marvin Kaye

590 "The Executioner" by Lawrence C. Connolly

591 originally "into a dorthy gale" from Dorothy Gale the heroine in *The Wonderful Wizard of Oz* by L. Frank Baum

592 "The Enigma of the Warwickshire Vortex" by F. Gwynplaine MacIntyre, "A Long Step" by Bruce Dettman

593 "The Modern Prometheus" by Lovern Kindziersky

594 "The Bedevil'd Brood" by David Jacobs

595 "Son of Frankenstein" by Willis Cooper

596 "Angel vs. Frankenstein", Simon's Law: "Everything put together comes apart." ("eptca") applied here.

597 "The Ghost of Frankenstein" by Scott Darling

598 "Frankenstein Conquers the World" aka "Frankenstein vs. Baragon" by Kaoru Mabuchi

599 "War of the Gargantuas" aka "The Frankenstein Monsters" by Ishirô Hondo and Kaoru Mabuchi,

600 Frankenstein Conquers the World serial: "Frankenstein vs. Odako", "Frankenstein vs. Gamera", "Frankenstein vs. Godzilla", "Frankenstein vs. Rhodan", "Frankenstein vs. Motha", "Frankenstein vs. Megalon", "Frankenstein vs. Gorath", "Frankenstin vs. Atragon", "Frankenstein vs. Dogora", "Frankenstein vs. Gappa", "Frankenstein vs. Negadon", "Frankenstein vs. Viras", "Frankenstein vs. Ghidora"

601 "Gamera vs Baragon" by Niisan Takahashi

602 "Destroy All Monsters" by Ishirô Honda and Kaoru Mabuchi

603 a shaggy dog story that never ended because "The Monster that Ate Battle Creek" was a cereal (serial)

604 "Frankenstein vs. the Spacemonster" by George Garrett

604 "The Pajama Party" aka "The Maid and the Martian" by Louis M. Heyward, The pet name "George" was also popular with Hugo the Abominable Snowman, ("The Abominable Snow Rabbit" by Tedd Pierce)

605 "Mars Needs Women" by Larry Buchanan

606 Frankenstein #18-33

607 Prize Comics #24

608 Creatures of the Unknown #1 by Jeff Lemire, Prize Comics #34: "Frankenstein vs. the Nazis"

609 "The Horror of Hyborea" by Schildiner

610 "Frankenstein's Army" by Chris W. Michell and Miguel Tejada-Flores

611 "Frankenstein Meets the Wolfman" by Curt Siodmak

612 "Bud Abbott and Lou Costello Meet Frankenstein" by Robert Lees, Frederick I. Rinaldo and John Grant, Seay's Law: "Nothing ever comes out as planned." ("necoap") applied here.

613 "The Invisible Man Returns" by Lester Cole and Curt Siodmak, he may however have also have time traveled like his relative Milton Radcliffe (*Lorien Lost* by Michael King) or Migelito Loveless via paintings

614 "Young Frankenstein" by Gene Wilder and Mel Brooks

615 The Brooklyn Paper: "Wolff & Byrd, Counselors of the Macabre"

616 *Argonautica* by Apollonius of Rhodes, *Odysseus* by Homer

617 "Frankenstein Island" by Jaques Lecouter

618 "Mad Monster Party?" by Len Korobkin and Harvey Kurtzman

619 "Dracula vs. Frankenstein" aka "The Revenge of Dracula" by William Pugsley and Samuel M. Sherman,

620 This Strange family was especially strange because it was, as far as we could determine, completely unrelated to the evil Golden Age Dr. **Hugo** Strange (Detective Comics #36) the Silver Age mystical Dr. **Steven** Vincent Strange ("Dr. Strange" by Steve Ditko), the ex-priest **John** Strange ("Strange" by Andrew Marshall), **Erica** Strange's family: **Barb**, **Gary**, **Leo**, **Samantha** or **Zayde** ("Being Erica" by Jana Sinyor), **Walter** ("The Day of the Triffids" by Richard Mewis), **Jonathan** ("Jonathan Strange and Mr. Norrell"), **Kay** or **Nevile** (*Towards Zero* by Agatha Christe, "Towards Zero" by Kevin Elyot), Sir **Bartholomew** (Agatha Christe's Poirot: "Three Act Tragedy" by Nick Dear, "Murder in Three Acts" by Scott Swanton), **Nicholas** ("The Mail Van Murder" by James Eastwood), **Allen** ("The Journey of Allen Strange" by Tommy Lynch), **Adam** ("Strange Report") or **Ken** ("Death Goes North" by Edward R. Austin).

621 "Santo vs. the Daughter of Frankenstein" by Fernando Osés; Samson de la Llata seems to share the same paranormal power as "Indestructible Girl" Claire Bennet ("Heroes" by Tim Kring)

622 "The Night of the Bloody Apes" by René Cardona, Sr. and Jr.

623 "Santos vs. the Grave Robbers" by José Diaz Morales and Rafael Garcia Travesi, "Santos vs. the Riders of Terror" by Jesus Velazquez Quintero, "Santos in the Wax Museum" by Alfonso Corona Blake

624 "Santo and Blue Devil vs. Dr. Frankenstein" by Francisco Cavazos

625 "Lady Frankenstein" by Edward di Lorenzo

626 "Flesh for Frankenstein" by Paul Morissey

627 *Descent into Hell* by Charles Williams

628 *The Great Divorce* by C. S. Lewis

629 The comte de St. Germaine was not a vampire, though made immortal by his brother Phillipus Areolus Theophrastus Bombastus von Hohenheim aka "Paracelsus" by an elixir along with his wife Charlotte and son Nicholas von Hohenheim in 1541 (Warehouse 13: "Lost and Found") Holmes, Watson and Irene Norton were still alive in 1945 (The New Adventures of Sherlock Holmes: "The Purloined Ruby" by Anthony Boucher and Denis Green) because of Holmes's elixir.

630 "Red Reign" by Kim Newman

631 The Tomorrow People: "Castle of Fear: Ghosts and Monsters" by Roger Damon Price

632 "Frankenstein and Me" by Richard Goudreau and David Sherman

633 "The Monsters Among Us!" by Paul Levitz and Len Wein

634 "Frankenstein '80" by Ferdinando de Leone and Mario Mancini

635 "What Was He Doing, Young Dr. Frankenstein, in May 1981 and May 1968?" by Jean-Pierre Andrevon

636 "Silent Rage" by Joseph Fraley

637 *Dracula* by Abraham "Bram" Stoker

638 "The Monster Squad" by Sahne Black and Fred Dekker

639 Henry "Blue Raja" Azaria, Janeane "the Bowler" Carmine, Paul "Spleen" Reubenfeld, William "Shoveler" Macy, Jr., Kel "Invisible Boy" Mitchell, Wesley "Sphinx" Studie and Benjamin "Mr. Furious" Stiller (Flaming Carrot series by Bob Burdens, "Mystery Men" by Neil Cuthbert and Bob Burdens)

640 "Frankenstein: The College Years" by Bryan Christ and John Trevor Wolff

641 Superman: Man of Steel #6

642 "Return of the Werewolf"

643 "Alvin and the Chipmunks Meet Frankenstein" by John Loy

644 "Universal Kombat"

645 *Frankenstein Factory* by Edward D. Hoch

646 "Frankenstein Meets Dracula"

647 "Mistress Frankenstein" by John Bacchus, John Paul "Clancy Fitzsimmons" Fedele, Joe Ned and Michael "Beckerman" Raso

648 "Frankenstein" by John Shiban, *Prodigal Son* by Dean Koontz and Kevin J. Anderson, *City of Night* by Dean Koontz and Ed Gorman, *Dead and Alive* and *Lost Souls* and *Dead Town* by Dean Koontz

649 "Frankenstein vs. the Creature from Blood Cove" by William Winckler

650 "Frankenstein Reborn" by Leigh Scott

651 "Movie Monster Insurance" by Paula Haifley

652 The Telling: "Sorority Sisters" by Joe Lessard, "Fear Lives Here" by Ben Bray and Tina Sen, "Demons in Daylight" by Lillard Anthony and Eric Marks

653 "Monster's Comedy Roast of Satan" by Jim Bruce, Tom "Bernie Drac" Griffin, Brian McNett and John Patrick Nelson

654 "Little Nicky" by Tim Herlihy, Adam Sandler and Staev Brill

655 *Carrie* by Steven King

656 "MID: Murder Investigation Unit" by Dirk Voetberg

657 Frankenstein #9 Gary Freidrich and John Buscema

658 Frankenstein #11 by Gary Freidich and Bob Brown

659 Silver Surfer #7 by Stan Lee and John Buscema

660 Frankenstein #18 by Bill Mantlo and Val Meyerik

661 Frankenstein #16 by Doug Muench and Val Meyerik

662 Al Fiene ("Harry Putter and the Chamber Pot of Secrets" and "Harry Putter and the Sorcerer's Phone" by Jeremy Gustafson and Benjamin Latz)

663 "Tales of the Dead" by Tim Rassmussen, Jr.

664 Ari Lehman ("The Wicked One" by Tory Jones)

665 "Night on Has Been Mt." by Tim Rassmussen, Jr.

666 "The Frankenstein Theory" by Vlady Pilysh and Andrew Weiner

667 "Bikini Frankenstein" by Fred Olen Ray

668 son of Béla Ferenc Dezső "Aldelbert" Blaskó, scientist in "Glen or Glenda", alien invader in "Plan 9 from Outer Space" and Glen's father in "Glen or the Bride of the Night of the Plan 9 from Outer Space" by Ed Woods

669 "Monster Brawl" by Jesse Thomas Cook

670 "Ninjas vs. Monsters" by Justin Timpane

671 "Ninjas vs. Vampires" by Justin Timpane

672 "Ninjas vs. Zombies" by Justin Timpane

673 *I, Frankenstein* by Kevin Grevioux, "I, Frankenstein" by Stuart Beattie

674 "Frankenstein vs. The Mummy" by Damien Leone

675 "Monster Force"

676 *Frankenstein Unbound* by Brian Aldiss, "Roger Corman's Frankenstein Unbound" by Roger Corman and F. X. Feeney

677 "Sabrina and the Grovie Goolies" by Bill Danch, Len Janson, Jack Mendelsohn, Chuck Menville, Jim Mullian, Bob Ogle, and Jim Ryan

678 "The Black Castle" by Jerry Sackheim

679 "Joe vs. the Volcano" by John Patrick Shanley

680 "Brain Shrinkage May Predict Altzheimer's" by Denise Mann

681 "House of Evil" aka "Dance of Death"

682 "The Man They Could Not Hang" by Carl Brown

683 "The Case of the Laughing Mummy" by Charles Early

684 Stingers: "Hit Me" by Mac Gudgeon

685 The Inner Sanctum: "The Wailing Wall"

686 "The Mad Genius" by J. Grubb Alexander and Harvey Thew, "The Idol" by Martin Brown

687 "Peter Pan or the Boy Who Wouldn't Grow Up" by J. M. Barrie, "Hook" by James V. Hart and Malia Scotch Marmo, "The Secret World of Eddie Hodges" by Norman Jewison

688 *Capt. Hook: The Adventures of a Notorious Youth* by J. V. Hart and Brett Helquist, *Capt. Sazarac* by Charles Tenney Jackson, "The Eagle of the Sea" by Julien Josephson, "Peril of the Wild" by Isadore Bernstein and William Lord Wright, *The Swiss Family Robinson* by Johann David Wyss

689 "The Deadlier Sex" by Fred Myton and Bayard Veiller

690 "The Courage of Marge O'Doone" by Robert North Bradbury, *The Courage of Marge O'Doone* by James Oliver Curwood

691 *The Scarlet Pimpernel* by Emmuska Orczy

692 curse #3 in "Countdown: Real or Not? 6 Famous Historical Curses" by Marc Lallanilla

693 "Mystery of the Hope Diamond Curse" by Benjamin Radford
694 from Hindi for "belching"
695 "The Hope Diamond Mystery" aka "The Romance of the Hope Diamond" by John B. Clymer, Charles W. Goddard and May Yohe, *The Mystery of the Hope Diamond* by Lady Frances Hope
696 "The Man with the Twisted Lip"
697 "The Entertainers", "Chim Chim Cher-ee" by Robert B. and Richard M. Sherman from "Mary Poppins" by Bill Walsh and Don Da Gradi based on Mary Poppins by Helen Lyndon Goff aka "Pamela Lyndon Travers"
698 Jack Benny Show: "I Stand Condemned"
699 "The Yellow Hand": "If it should ever strike you that I am getting a little over-confident in my powers, or giving less pains to a case than it deserves, kindly whisper 'Norbury' in my ear, and I shall be infinitely obliged to you."
700 reference to vampire Lucy Westerna (*Dracula* by Abraham "Bram" Stoker) 646 and to the gorgon Medusa (*Fabulae* by Hyginus)
701 "Charlie Chan at the Opera" by Scott Darling and Charles Belden
702 "His Majesty, the American" aka "Sa Majesté Douglas" by Joseph Henabery and Douglas "Elton Banks" Fairbanks
703 *The Prince and the Betty* by P. G. Wodehouse, "The Prince and the Betty" by Fred Myton
704 "The Prisoner" by Edward T. Lowe, Castle Craneycrow by George Barr McCutcheon
705 "Without Benefit of Clergy" by Rudyard Kipling
706 "The Infidel" by Charles Logue and James Young
707 "The Fight at Grizzly Gulch"
708 "The Big Horn Massacre"
709 "The Fighting Cowboy" by Louis V. Jefferson
710 William Berke as William Lester, Aileen Allan Goodwin as Aline Goodwin in "The Hellion" by Bruce M. Mitchell
711 "Prairie Wife" by Hugo Ballin, *Prairie Wife, Prairie Mother, Prairie Child* and *Open Water* by Arthur Stringer
712 "The Cave Girl" by Guy Bolton and George Middleton
713 "The Woman Conquers" by Violet Clark
714 Emily Gerdes as "Tootles" in "Dynamite Dan" by Bruce Mitchell, "Aunt Betty" in "The Rip Snorter" by Mark Goldaine, and a Brockton family member in "Heir-Loons" by Grover Jones
715 "Cheated Hearts" by Wallace Clifton, Barry Gordon by William Faquahar Payson
716 "Omar the Tent Maker" by Richard Walton Tully
717 *Biography of Omar Khayyam* by Edward J. Fitzgerald
718 Matthew 7:18
719 *The Altar Stairs* by G. B. Lancaster, "The Altar Stars" by George Hively and Doris Schroeder
720 "For how do you know, wife, whether you will bring your husband to salvation?" (1 Corinthians 7:16)
721 "Without Mercy" by Monte Katterjohn, Without Mercy by John Goodwin
722 "Forbidden Cargo" by Fred Myton
723 "The Subhuman" by Daryll R. Hall
724 Germ. "scissors grinder" ("The Greater Glory" by June Mathis, *Viennese Medley* by Edith O'Shaughnessy)
725 "The Man in the Saddle" by Charles Logue
726 "King Kong" by James Crelman and Ruth Rose
727 "The Vanishing Rider" by Val Cleveland, George H. Plympton and William Lord Wright

728 "Meddlin' Stranger" by Christopher B. Booth

729 "The Utah Kid" by Frank Howard Clark

730 "The Phantom Buster" by Betty Burbridge and Walter J Coburn

731 "Burning the Wind" by Gardner Bradford and George H. Plympton, *Daughter of the Dons* by William MacLeod Raine

732 The nickname "Snipe" may seem to refer to his ability as a sharpshooter, a sniper, which he may have lost at about the same time as he became addicted. It may however be, as it is in Shakespeare, a term of abuse (*Othello* I. iii. 377), or a reference to his other addiction of smoking discarded cigarette stubs (*Tramping with the Tramps* by J. Flynt), or his previous job in the "black gang" as a navy fireman (*Navy Explained* by L. E. Ruggles) or all of the above. (*Oxford English Dictionary*)

733 "Her Honor, the Governor" by Doris Anderson

734 "The Golden Web" by James Bell Smith, The Golden Web by E. Phillips Oppenheimer

735 "The Nickel-Hopper" by Frank Butle, Stan Laurel and Hal Roach

736 "Two Arabian Knights" by Wallace Smith and Cyril Gardner

737 "Tarzan and the Golden Lion" by William E. Wing, *Tarzan and the Golden Lion* by Edgar Rice Burroughs

738 "The Love Mart" by Benjamin Glazer, *The Code of Victor Jallot* by Edward Childs Carpenter

739 Sudanese for French Passeport, manservant to Philias Fogg (*Around the World in Eighty Days* by Jules Verne)

740 "Behind the Curtain" by Sonya Levien, George Middleton and Clarke Silvernail, Behind the Curtain by Earl Derr Biggers

741 "The King of the Kongo" aka "Urskovens Søn" ("Jungle Son") by Harry Sinclair Drago and Wyndham Gittens

742 "The Man with a 100 Faces" by Basil Mason, A. R. Rawlinson and Michael Pertwee, *The Man with a 100 Faces* by William Blair Morton Ferguson

743 "The Unholy Night" by Edwin Justus Mayer and Dorothy Farnum

744 "The Sea Bat" by Dorothy Yost, Bess Meredyth and John Howard Lawson

745 The Boris Karloff Mystery Playhouse: "Mad Illusion"

746 The Boris Karloff Mystery Playhouse: "The Shop at Sly Corner"

747 "The Big House" by Francis Marion

748 "The Criminal Code" by Martin Flavin

749 "Clifford the Big Red Dog" by Brooks Wachtel

750 "King of the Wild" by Wyndham Gittens and Ford Beebe

751 "The Devil's Chaplain" by Arthur Hoerl, http://www.kinomania.ru/people/472/

752 "Cracked Nuts" by Al Boasberg

753 "I Like Your Nerve" by Roland Pertwee and Houston Branch

754 "The Voice" also voiced "How the Grinch Stole Christmas" by Irv Spector and Bob Ogle, based on *How the Grinch Stole Christmas* by Theodore "Dr. Seuss" Giesel, "The Emperor's Nightingale", "The Ugly Duckling", "The Little Match Girl" by Hans Christian Anderson, "The Juggler of Our Lady" by R. O. Blechman, "The Pickwick Papers" by Charles Dickens, "The Pied Piper of Hamlin", "The Pony Engine and Other Stories for Children", "tHE Three ittl Pigs and Other Stories for Children", "Just So Stories and Other Tales" by Rudyard Kipling, "Hunting of the Snark" by Charles "Lewis Carrol" Lugwidge; the Voice also sang: "Those Were the Good Old Days" and "The Girl Friend of the Whirling Dervish" (The Gisele MacKenzie Show), "You Do Something to Me" and "I Get So Frightened" (The Lux Show), "You'd Be Surprized" and "Children Have Quizzical Ways" (The Rosemary Clooney Show), "The Peppermint Twist" (Shindig!), "We're Horrible, Horrible Men" (Lagosi: Hollywood's Dracula), "Poor Daft Jamie" (The Body Snatcher), "Horror Boys of Hollywood" (One in a Million),

755 "The Vanishing Legion" by Wyndham Gittens, Ford Beebe and Helmer Bergman

756 "Cokey" Joe in "Young Donovan's Kid" by J. Walter Rubin, "Big Brother" by Rex Beach

757 "Sport" Williams in "Smart Money" by Kubec Glasmon, John Bright, Lucien Hubbard and Joseph Jackson

758 "The Public Defender" by George Goodchild and Bernard Schubert

759 "Five Star Final" by Louis Weitzenkorn, adapted by Byron Morgan and Robert Lord

760 "Fatal Warning" by Wyndham Gittens

761 by Paul Dickey and Charles W. Goddard

762 both by George Ade

763 by George Ade and J. Clarkson Miller

764 by Rex Beach

765 by Ring Larder

766 by Peter B. Kyne and Jack Natteford

767 by Adelaide Matthews and Anne Nichols

768 by Addison Burkhard and Murray Roth

769 by Leslie S. Barrows

770 "Little Wild Girl" by Cecil Burtis Hill

771 "The Phantom of the North" by George C. Hull and Carl Krusada

772 "The Bad One" by John Farrow, adapted by Howard Ennett Rogers and Carey Wilson

773 "L. A. Law" by Steven Bochco and Terry Louise Fisher

774 "Graft" by Barry Barringer

775 "The Windy City" by Jo Milward and J. Kirby Hawks, "The Guilty Generation" by Jack Cunningham

776 "Sous les verros" ("Under the Lock") and "Pardon Us" by Stan Laurel

777 "De Bote en Bote" ("From Cell to Cell") by Stan Laurel

778 Tony the Tiger, mascot for Kellogg's Sugar Frosted Flakes "Frosties" cereal; Antonio Ricca, Jr., was a coach for the Monster Wrestlers in My Pocket and a referee for the Monster Sports Stars in My Pocket (https://en.wikipedia.org/wiki/Tony_the_Tiger)

779 Matthew 26:52

780 "Scarface" by Ben Hecht, *Scarface* by Armitage Trail

781 "Behind the Mask" from "In the Secret Service" by Jo Swerling

782 "Bob & Carol & Ted & Alice"

783 "Harry and the Hendersons" by William Dear, Bill Martin and Ezra D. Rappaport

784 "The Henderson Kids"

785 The Flying Dutchman's answer to "What ever happened to Boris Karloff's character?": "He went into a time machine and ended up being a supporter of Michelle Bachmann."

786 "Business and Pleasure" by William M. Conselman, based on "The Plutocrat" by Arthur F. Goodrich, based on *The Plutocrat* by Booth Parkinton

787 *The Miracle Man* by Robert H. Davis and Frank L. Parkard, "The Miracle Man" by George M. Cohan, adapted by Waldemar Young

788 "Groundhog Day" by Danny Rubin and Harold Ramis

789 "Impatient Maiden" by Richard Schayer and Winifred Dunn, The Impatient Virgin by Donald Henderson Clarke, "Bride and Gloomy" by John Kirkpatrick, "Rafter Romance" by H. W. Hanemann and Sam Mintz

790 "Night World" by Richard Schayer

791 "The Fall of the House of Usher" by Edgar Allen Poe

792 "Old Dark House" by Benn W. Levy, Benighted by J.B. Priestley

793 "Psycho" by Joseph Stephano, *Psycho* by Robert Bloch
794 "The Pearl of Death" by Bertram Millhauser
795 "The House of Horrors" by George Bricker
796 "The Brute Man" by Dwight V. Babcock, George Bricker and M. Coates Webster
797 "The Keeper of Traken" by Johnny Byrne
798 Thriller: "The Premature Burial" by Edgar Allen Poe, adapted by William D. Gordon and Douglas Heyes
799 "MacBeth" by William Shakespeare, Gruoch ingen Boite, wife of MacBethad MacFindlaich, *Holinshed's Chronicles*
800 "British Intelligence" by Anthony Paul Kelly, adapted by Lee Katz
801 "Creeps by Night: Final Reckoning"
802 "Juggernaut" by Alice Campbell, adapted by Cyril Campion
803 "The Invisible Menace"
804 "Black Friday" by Curt Siodmak and Eric Taylor
805 "Before I Hang" by Robert Hardy Andrews and Karl Brown
806 Deuteronomy 30:15
807 Mystery Playhouse: "Those Who Walk in Darkness"
808 Broadway Television Theatre: "The Climax" by Curt Siodmak and Lynn Starling, from play by Edward Locke
809 Inner Sanctum: "Death for Sale"
810 "Death Robbery"
811 Theater '62: "The Paradine Case"
812 "Birdsongs for a Murderer"
813 The Veil: "Summer Heat"
814 The Red Skeleton Show: "Appleby and the Ape", "The Unearthly" by John D. F. Black aka "Geoffrey Dennis" and Jane Mann
815 The Red Skelton Show: "Appleby and the Ape", "The Black Sleep" by John C Higgins
816 The Red Skelton Show: "Appleby and the Ape II"
817 The Red Skelton Show: "George Appleby's Neighbor"
818 The Red Skelton Show: "The Many Skeltons in Las Vegas", see 240
819 Thriller: "Premonition" by Donald S. Sanford
820 "Wives submit yourselves unto your own husbands as unto the Lord." (Ephesians 5:22)
821 Thriller: "The Incredible Doktor Markesan" by August Derleth, adapted by Donald S. Sanford
822 "The Adventure of the Speckled Band"
823 "The Adventure of Wisteria Lodge"
824 "Plato's Stepchildren" by Meyer Dolinsky
825 Matthew 26:52.
826 "The Adventure of the Devil's Foot", mind-controlled aka adjective "trilby" from Trilby O'Ferrell, mind-slave of Svengali (*Trilby* by George du Maurier)
827 "Isle of the Snake People" by Jack Hill
828 Suspense: "The Black Prophet" by Michael Dyne, see 250
829 *The Wages of Sin* by David A. MacIntee
830 "Anastasia" by Susan Gauthier, Bruce Graham, Bob Tzadiker and Noni White
831 *Forever Knight:* "Strings"
832 X-Men: "Day of Future Past" by Simon Kinberg
833 Studio One in Hollywood: "A Connecticut Yankee in King Arthur's Court" by Samuel "Mark Twain" Clemens, adapted by Alvin Sapinsley

834 Alonso Quixano, CBS TV Workshop: "Don Quixote", *Don Quixote* by Miguel Cervantes from *The Annals of la Mancha*
835 Shirley Temple's Story Book Theater: "The Legend of Sleepy Hollow" by Washington Irving, adapted by Norman Lessing
836 The DuPont Show of the Month: "Treasure Island" by John Lee Mahin, *Treasure Island* by Robert Louis Stevenson
837 "How Krypto Made History"
838 "The Three Stooges Meet Hercules", "Squareheads of the Round Table", "Knutzy Knights"
839 *For King and Country*
840 "Quest for Camelot"
841 "Sir Fly"
842 "Green Arrow in King Arthur's Court"
843 "Yesterday Begins Today"
844 "Monty Python and the Holy Grail" by Graham Chapman, John Cleese, Eric Idle, Terry Gilliam, Terry Jones and Michael Palin
845 "Die, Monster, Die", adapted from *The Colour Out of Space* by H. P. Lovecraft
846 "Beloved, let us love one another for love is of God and everyone that loveth is born of God and knoweth God." (1 John 4:7), "There is no fear in love, but perfect love casteth out fear, because fear hath torment. He that feareth is not made perfect in love." (1 John 4:18), "Greater love hath no man than this, that a man lay down his life for his friends." (John 15:13)
847 "A Christmas Carol" by Charles Dickens
848 "Bikini Beach" by William Asher and Leo Townsend, "The Ghost in the Invisible Bikini" by Louis M. Heyward and Elwood Ullman
849 The Man from U. N. C. L. E.: "The Venetian Affair" based on Helen MacInnes' novel
850 I Spy: "Mainly on the Plains" by Morton S. Fine and David Friedkin
851 He got the Burgundians to give St. Joan of Arc over to the English and then presided over her "trial". (The Hallmark Hall of Fame: "The Lark" by Jean Anoulh, adapted by James Costigan)
852 aka the Red Hour in "The Return of the Archons" by Boris Sobelman
853 "(The Curse of) the Crimson Altar" aka "The Crimson Cult" by Mervyn Halsman and Henry Lincoln, "The Dreams in the Witch House" by H. P. Lovecraft
854 Lights Out: "Cat Wife" by Arch Obler
855 "Cauldron of Blood" aka "Blind Man's Bluff"
856 "The Man Who Changed His Mind" aka "The Man Who Lived Again" by John L. Balderston, Sidney Gilliat and L. du Garde Peach
857 6.7% concentration of liscom gas from Desigma (Delta Sigma) IV (*A Time to Love*)
858 "The Man with Nine Lives" aka "Behind the Door" by Karl Brown
859 *Timequest* game
860 "Corridors of Blood" aka "The Doctor from Seven Dials" by Jean Scott Rogers
861 "Devil's Island" by Kenneth Garnet and Don Ryan, adapted by Anthony Coldeway and Raymond L. Schrock
862 originally the acronym "gok"
863 Thriller: Dialogues with Death: "Friend of the Death" by Robert Arthur
864 Thriller: Dialogues with Death: "Welcome Home" by Robert Arthur
865 Thriller: "The Last of the Sommervilles" by Ida and Richard Lupino
866 Thriller: "Premature Burial" by Edgar Allen Poe, adapted by William D. Gordon and Douglas Hayes
867 Masterpiece Playhouse: "Uncle Vanya" by Anton Chekhov adapted by H Philip Minis

868 The Veil: "The Doctors" by David Evans

869 The Veil: "The Return of Madame Vernoy"

870 The Veil: "Whatever Happened to Peggy" by Stanley H. Silverman

871 The Veil: "Vision of Crime" aka "The Murder That Never Happened" by Fred Schiller

872 "There more things in Heaven and Earth, Horatio, than are dreamt of in your philosophy."

873 Climax: "The White Carnation" by Raymond Chandler

874 The Chevrolet Tele-Theatre: "Expert Opinion" by Robert Middlemoss

875 Pudder's Law: "Anything that begins well will end badly; anything that begins badly ends worse." The counter-intuitive corollary would be "Anything that begins worse will get better and end well."

876 "You'll Find Out" by James V. Kern

877 Schlitz Playhouse of the Stars: "The House of Death" by Vincent McConnor

878 "A Case of Identity": "That fellow James Windibank will rise from crime to crime until he does something very bad, and ends on a gallows." like murdering Mary Sutherland (Howard Brody)

879 Suspense: "A Night at an Inn" by Lord Dunsany, adapted by Halsted Welles

880 Robert Montgomery Presents: "The Kimballs" by Mitchell Wilson, adapted by Agnes "Agnes Eckhardt" Nixon

881 *The Man in the Iron Mask* by Alexandre Dumas

882 "The Strange Door" by Robert Louis Stevenson, adapted by Jerry Sackheim

883 The Veil: "Destination Nightmare" by Ellis Marcus

884 The Veil: "Genesis" aka "Where There's a Will" aka "Two Sons" by Sidney Morse

885 "It's a Wonderful Life"

886 The Veil: "Girl on the Road" aka "Lookout Point" by George Waggner

887 Lux Video Theatre: "The Man Who Played God" by Maude T Howell and Julien Josephson, based on Gouveneur Morris

888 "Suspicion: "The Deadly Game" by Friedrich Dürrenmatt, adapted by James Yaffe

889 "Lured" aka "Personal Column" by Jacques Companéez, Simon Gantillion, Ernst Neubach and Leo Rosten

891 The Crystal Ball" by Robert Joseph

892 The Veil: "Food on the Table" by Jack Jacobs

893 "To the Sound of Trumpets" by John Gay

894 "Sabaka" by Frank Ferrin

895 Arabic, Persian aka Iblis, Haris ("despair"), fka as Azazel the heavenly treasurer (*Vathek* by Beckford, *Koran* sura 18, *Legends of the Jews* by Ginsberg), turned into a jinn (*Enchiridion* 28 by Augustine), an intermediate spirit between the good angels and the evil demons

896 Lux Video Theatre: "The Jest of Hāhālālā" by Lord Edward John Moreton Plunkett Dunsany, adapted by David Shaw

897 "The Lord shall laugh at him for He seeth that his day is coming." (Ps 37:13)

898 "The House of Rothschilds" by Nunnally from play by George Hembert Wesley

899 Playhouse 90: "Rendezvous in Black" by Cornell Woolrich, adapted by James P. Cavanagh

900 According to demonology, demons or IDIs (infradimensional intelligences) categorized by their focus against goodness: terrestrial (animals, men), aerial (wind, sound), aqueous (unholy water), heliophobic (darkness, shadows), igneous (fire); sub-terrestrial or super-terrestrial.

901 "The Black Sabbath: "The Wurdalak" from "(Semýa vurdalak" by Alexei Konstantinovich Tolsoy, "Night of the Devils" by Eduardo Manzanas Brochero, Romano Migliorini Gianbattista Mussetto, "The Vampire Family" by German Klimov, Igor Shavlak and Marina Sobe-Panek;

The psi power (ESPK, extrasensory perception/psychokinesis) manipulation levels as interpolated from Christina Larner's are: **a1**: limited manipulation of simple psi powers (incantation, hypnotic suggestion), **a2**: dangerous but limited use of simple psi powers (fetishism, transvestism, masturbation, vouyerism), **A1**: simple manipulation of psi powers (love charms, talismans) , **A2**: dangerous manipulation of simple psi powers (voodoo, porn), **b1**: limited ritualized individual manipulation of psi powers (positive thinking), **b2**: dangerous, but limited, ritualized individual manipulation of psi powers (cursing), **B1**: ritualized individual manipulation of psi powers (auto-suggestion), **B2**: dangerous ritualized individual manipulation of psi powers (conjuring), **B3**: fully ritualized individual manipulation of psi powers (chod, channeling), **c1**: limited ritualized individual manipulation of psi powers (positive thinking), **c2**: dangerous, but limited, ritualized individual manipulation of psi powers (cursing), **C1**: limited ritualized group manipulation of psi powers (tarot, ouija, seance, orgy, animal sacrifice), **C2**: dangerous ritualized group manipulation of psi powers (CE2K) (demonophany, sabbat, blood-drinking), **C3**: fully ritualized group manipulation of psi powers (CE3K-CE7K) (Black Mass, sabat, Human sacrifice, cannibalism, robonomization, zombiism, vampirism), They can also be categorized by the closeness of the encounter of between sender and receiver, CE1K 5-7 extrapolated by Jim McKeever: CE0K imagining (possibly telepathic or crosstime contact, 5D), CE1K: sighting (eye contact or line-of-sight), CE2K: physical evidence (proximity), CE3K: touching (hand/body) contact, CE4K: communication (mind/ear contact, within hiershot), CE5K: commitment (heart contact), CE6K: transformation (heart-changing), CE7K: union (one-heartedness), CE8K: Communion (One-heartedness), CE9K: hierogamy (two-as-one-heartedness), CE10K: Triunity (Three-as-One-heartedness), NOTE: not-so-close encounters can be once, twice, or more times removed (1R, 2R, 3R) as in 3rd or lower class relics, relay telepathy as in foafs.

902 "Heart of Darkness" by Stewart Stern, adapted from *Heart of Darkness* by Józef Teodor Konrad "Joseph Conrad" Korzeniowski

903 The U. S. Steel Hour: "Counterfeit" by Ellen M. Villett, based on "Laburnum Grove" by J. B. Priestley

904 "The Comedy of Terrors" by Richard Matheson

905 Route 66: "Lizard's Leg and Owlet's Wing"

906 "Targets" aka "Before I Die" by Peter Bogdanovich and Polly Platt

907 John 15:13

Also available from Hierogamous Enterprises at Amazon:

> ➤ *Psalms, Hymns and Inspired Songs: self-hate to Love through Scriptures* by Michael Joseph Halm

This autobiography includes many Bible-inspired songs that have guided me from a hatred of my own sexuality to a relationship with God Who is Love.

> ➤ *Reignbeau's Riddles and Rhymes* by Reignbeau the Clown

This is a collection of riddles and songs suitable suitable for children of all ages.

> ➤ *Proverbials* by Michal Joseph Halm

This is, like Psalms, Hymns and Inspired Songs, a sample of making Scripture more meaningful by versification, this time focusing on Wisdom literature, including Jesus' proverbs.

> ➤ *Basilian Tales* ed. By Michael Joseph Halm

This is a book of fairy tales about the kingdom of Basilia, base on the Sunday Gospel readings.

> ➤ Crosswords with Jesus by Michael Joseph Halm

This book contains a hundred crossword puzzles collected from those published in *My People* newspaper, that do not exclude Jesus.

From hierogamous AT netzero.net

> ➤ *Hierogamous Hymns* by Michael Halm and Razilee Purdue

This is a booklet, a sampler of selections of songs from *Psalms, Hymns and Inspired Songs*.

> ➤ *The Luminous Mysteries of the Rosary: A play for 8-10 Year Olds* by Kathy McCarthy

This is a booklet describing how to put on a play illustrating the Luminous Mysteries of the rosary.

www.ingramcontent.com/pod-product-compliance
Lightning Source LLC
Chambersburg PA
CBHW070758120626
46557CB00002B/658